RISING

A BLOOD OF MIDITHRIAS NOVEL

AMBER YVE

ISBN 978-0-6455068-0-8

Revised Edition

Created with the incredible assistance of:

Cover Art Design by Jessa Harmon

Editing by B. D. Quinn

For the people who taught me to dream,
and the friends who supported me incessantly.
I am forever grateful to each one of you.

BEFORE WE BEGIN...

To help keep your reading a safe space please ensure you read through the following content concepts, that could be triggering for some readers, to ensure this book is still for you:

- Physical Violence

- Kidnapping

- Reference to Torture and Abuse

- Sexual Content

- Murder/Death

Pronunciation Guide

Character Names

Seraphine – Serah-Feen

Creston – Crest-un

Niko – Knee-co

Hyatt – High-At

Samil – Sam-eel

Veneficus – Van-if-ick-us

Places/Magic

Ithriax - If-three-ax

Keinteris – Ken-Tear-Us

Midithrias – Mid-e-three-ass

Elliphir – Elle-i-Fear

Elliphae – Elle-i-Fay

Your
Introduction
to Keinteris

We were always so confident that we knew everything about the world in which we existed, even if we didn't know where to begin. We stood where generations before us had, holding the tools they passed down, steady on the foundations we needed to understand the world around us.

What we so often forgot is that what we were given was not always the truth. Rarely was history passed down free of hate or prejudice. But how were we to know that, when we knew nothing else?

I'd always felt sure that I knew my world, a world of magic, in that all encompassing way one claims to understand any reality.

My world was carefully isolated from the mortal world, buried deeper and deeper throughout the centuries, for both our safety and theirs.

In all worlds, truths are hidden, so deeply and so desperately, that it often takes the free flow of innocent blood to release them.

In Keinteris, all that mattered is whether or not you have control of who you are, control of the Blessing in your blood.

Almost every child born in Keinteris was Blessed with the power over an element. As we grew into adulthood our specialisations varied, but we all began with a single elemental blessing.

By our Blessings we were Earth, Water, Air or Fire.

Our magic helped us find our place in our world, based on how those gifts grew within and shaped us. Some were trackers, others oracles, healers or warriors, in addition to their Blessed magic.

We found our magic in our blood, passed down through the bloodlines that stretch back to the Faerie ancestors who gave life to our kind. The Fae that started our race were, by all accounts, glamorous beings.

They visited the mortal realms long ago, enchanting mortals with their ethereal beauty. They were mistakenly worshipped by the humans as gods made flesh, since before history could find the word for what they were.

Whenever they chose to leave their realm for the mortal one, they attracted people with great talents. Artists, musicians, psychics and geniuses, were all drawn towards them.

In return, they also ignited the curiosity of those from the Faerie Realm, as the fleeting lives of mortals seemed so filled with passion.

Over time they sought out those they deemed extraordinary, to share the secrets of the worlds they had seen, to show them real magic and, eventually, to spark the creation of half-Fae children with mortals outside Faerie. Children that, regardless of their generation, were always born with a perfect balance of magic and mortality in their veins.

As these children grew and spread, it was discovered that Fae blood could never be diluted by more than half its natural power. Even without a full Fae parent for generations the half-Fae always share immortality with their Faerie inheritance.

Through magic linked to that inheritance, all the way back to Faerie.

Our histories called these Faerie ancestors The Seventeen. It was not truly known whether there were only seventeen of them, as Fae are free spirited creatures, but we passed down the words.

The Seventeen gave us our magic, and we owed our inherited elements to them, as we were marked by that magic from birth and throughout our lives. It was not born from nothing, as magic begets magic. If it was not within your blood, you did not inherit it. However, there were anomalies, darkness and magic that was born from the twisting of elements.

Over the centuries generations of us had all been born the same way, with parents prepared to raise a child with gifts they inherited from their blood. We found our name over the centuries too.

Elliphae.

Keinteris was my home, an island hidden within the vast, unexplored, oceans of the mortal world, pulled from the sea and raised above it by our magic for three centuries.

As Elliphae we used a combination of all our gifts to hide the island and keep us safe. Any ships or boats that wandered through our storms, or made it too close, are brought in. Those who remain, mortals who truly assimilate, were allowed to join our armies, or become healers, teachers and much more, often marrying and having children here. They led full lives and used whatever skills they possess to improve life for all.

It was not just humans drawn there, it was the Lost Ones too. Half-Fae born far from the island, growing without knowledge of their abilities, called by the concentration of our magic that once existed all over the world. These groups of Half-Fae had been exposed to something other than humans throughout history, our kind murdered or persecuted until we were forced deeper and deeper into hiding, as we are now.

Lost Ones arrived far less as the decades passed, but we didn't know why.

We were abandoned by The Seventeen, centuries ago. With them, our names and races began but as they watched us grow, something changed.

The birth of the first with a darkened blessing was a nightmare that chased children in their sleep. He was named Samil, and he was seen by The Seventeen as a great omen as he grew into his powers, as he became the first Elliphir child.

A sign that the creation of our race had gone against nature. That a race with magical ability, human empathy and immortal lifespans was to be cursed.

The tales passed down tell us that on the day Samil revealed to his people his twisted mind, and his tainted magic, The Seventeen took him and vanished from our Realm, returning to Faerie permanently.

They never returned, and as a result, had faded into the enigmas that dominate our histories, whispers and legends.

The Elliphir were the story that haunted us, their curse our greatest threat while growing, as they became a race of vengeful and vicious creatures. They were a force made almost entirely of Elliphae who could not control their magic, as well as mortals who were not found by our Rangers.

When an Elliphae was unable to harness their Blessed Magic, we were told they were slowly driven insane, as that magic overwhelmed them. Madness became their existence.

Generations had tried for a cure, but none could be found.

The Elliphir sent their best into our settlements, stealing children before their twisted magic showed, taking them to be with their own. The Elders told tales of them having a hive mind, aware of new beings of their kind. They slipped across the Divide in order to retrieve them, taking the children from their beds.

We once fought to stop them, but now there is nothing that can be done.

We had few alternative choices, as children allowed to remain here would face death or a lifetime of incarceration.

The woods had become dangerous as the generations of the Elliphir made it theirs. Only our Guardiens and Rangers were allowed beyond the living wall called the Divide, where it towers over our settlement on one side, cutting Keinteris in half.

We no longer knew how many of the Elliphir exist beyond that wall, the Rangers sent never returned with numbers, so we no longer sent them.

The Oracles began to whisper of unrest, a time where their darkness flooded the land.

It seemed inevitable for such a conflict to begin, but who and what is behind it we did not know.

And so, we waited, without truly being sure what it is we were waiting for.

PROLOGUE

I knew I would wake on fire before I'd let sleep take me.

It was coming.

The darkness that consumed me was faceless but not voiceless, the air around me filled with torments, fears and screams that weren't mine. Whatever it was wanted what I had, craved what was within me.

I ran from it, pushing through the blackness, pleading for light as I ran blind. I tripped and scrambled to my feet over and over, but no light came to clear the way, not even as hands reached for me in the darkness, clawing at my clothes, slowing me and drawing me backwards. Clarity overwhelmed me as a fresh scream crept its way up my throat. I did not need to find light. I was light.

With the thought, my fire erupted from within, destroying the hands that touched me, cutting through the darkness that threatened to consume me.

I was so bathed in light that I no longer feared the dark. I consumed it instead. *A beacon without fear, engulfed by flames.*

CHAPTER I

I woke up on fire. *Literally.*

Thudding to the floor with a curse, I snuffed the flames back out of existence, but the damage was done. My bed and blankets were ashes before the flames disappeared, and my clothes had fared no better, leaving me naked on the cold floor of my bedroom.

I huffed in frustration and climbed from what was left of the bed, tugging fresh clothes from a set of stone shelves in the corner.

My bedroom sat seperate to the much more delicate natural home that my brothers shared with my parents, so I didn't have to worry about all of them getting caught in my flames or barging in on me unexpectedly.

I didn't bother passing by the mirror to check myself for any harm before I dressed. I knew my body would merely be covered in ash and show no other signs I had been on fire. Additionally, I didn't need to stare at myself after a nightmare. I didn't need to see the darkness that lingered in my grey-mottled emerald stare, or to see the way my thrashing had undoubtedly turned my crimson curls into a knotted mess atop my head.

I'd already memorised both sights, so I instead focused on cleaning away the ash and redressing myself. My body had always filled both my frame and my clothes generously, forcing me to jump a little on the spot as I squeezed my thighs and the other curves of my body into my pants, using the motion to help them fit better. I tugged at the tunic shirt I slipped over my body, loosening the strings around my chest to give myself more room to breathe. Addressing my hair last, I attempted to free the knots with my brush, but it was beyond salvation without water and a lot more effort than I felt like expending first thing in the morning. I settled for a twisted braid, hiding away the worst of the frizzing curls.

When I felt more like myself I turned to examine the final damages left over from the nightmare, just as my younger brother hurtled himself through the door and into the room.

His jade eyes wide with excitement, words running together until they were almost indecipherable. "Phi! You're awake! Good. They're bringing in a boat! A mortal boat. We have to..." He drifted off as his eyes flickered towards my bed, seeing the mess that lay there he sobered slightly, voice taking on the odd tone that had started to possess him lately, features paling as he spoke. "The dark came again," he said, almost to himself. "It's okay, the red is coming too. Things will be better then, everything will be brighter." Niko looked back to me with more understanding glimmering in the depth of his eyes than should have been possible in an, almost, eight-year-old. "You have no bed now though." He frowned, shaking off the strange clarity as he glanced at the mess once more, warmth returning to his light brown complexion, tanned even darker than usual from spending so much time in the sun. He and our older brother took after our father, inheriting his warm brown complexion while I seemed to be take on our by our mother's paler white.

I moved closer to him, ruffling the halo of copper brown curls atop his head. "It's fine, Niko, I'll get Trae to make me a new one. You know how fast he works, maybe he can even teach you this time."

His expression immediately melted back into one of excitement, at the promise of a chance to expand his magic.

Trae, like Niko and the rest of my family, was Earth-Blessed, born with the ability to wield nature however they desired. Trae himself was adept in using the magic to create furniture and build homes with nothing but what the earth could offer. He had been tasked with the replacement of more than a few of my beds in recent months, making me wonder if I should give up on the earthen beds I was accustomed to and opt for one with a stone base, adorned with a mattress and blankets preferred by the other Fire-Blessed.

I had always fought against it, not wanting another thing to seperate me from my family, the way my magic had since it first presented in me as a child. I should never have been born to Flame, not when both my parents were Earth-Blessed, with all my siblings having magic to mirror them, as was the magical order to our kind.

"Do you really think he would teach me?" Niko asked, making me turn my mind back to him, practically vibrating with excitement.

I grinned down at him. "Of course. What are friends for if not to help out each other's crazy little brothers?"

He frowned. "I'm not crazy!" he exclaimed with a serious expression on his small face. "Now hurry up or we'll miss the whole arrival." He turned and ran from the room, disappearing outside in the direction of the main house.

I could understand his excitement. A new boat was a big deal for multiple reasons. The first being the mortals themselves, with these arrivals becoming fewer with each passing year, and the second was the ship they would arrive on.

The Reaper was the only vessel allowed to leave the safety of the storm cell that endlessly surrounded Keinteris, our island home. The ship often returned with supplies other than what we could create for ourselves. Being Fire-Blessed there was little I could create for myself without relying on others, so as I had grown older I had learnt to take advantage of the mortal amenities wherever I could.

I looked towards the ashes of my bed once more. "Bed twenty-seven," I muttered to myself as I snatched a jacket from my closet, adding this bed to the list of things destroyed by nightmares in recent months. I left my room, mind spinning.

The nightmares were almost always the same.

I was surrounded by darkness and had to use my fire to get away, somehow meaning that I had to also be surrounded by flames when I woke too. Both my closest friends had been with me the first night it happened, and Trae had explained what it was like to witness it; my whole body ignited with flames so hot they turned pale blue, and I seemed to pulse with the flames, before everything I touched turned to ashes.

I'd had no idea how I had done it, and that first time had terrified us all.

I stepped out of my room and closed the door behind myself, taking a moment to breathe before heading towards the main house.

My room was made of stone and had been separated from the rest of my family after my sixteenth birthday, a gift from my father. Eight years later I was even more grateful for the separation. It meant that while I feared my nightmares, I never feared hurting those I loved during one of them.

Slipping into the house, I headed for the kitchen, following the sound of Niko's voice to find him and our mother by the bench, our mother making him breakfast.

"Morning," I greeted as I sat beside Niko and picked up an apple from the perpetually full bowl that always sat on the kitchen bench, largely so that I did not always have to ask when I wanted something to eat. Another quiet reminder that I was the magical outlier in my family.

"Morning, honey, how did you sleep?" My mother's expression was open, but her tone conveyed the wariness I was beginning to expect from her each morning.

I shook my head as I took a bite of the apple, not wanting to admit that I'd had another nightmare.

Her expression tightened in understanding. "Do you need me to fix your bed? Or your father?"

I shook my head again quickly, gulping down the bite of fruit so I could speak. "Please don't. I'll ask Trae. He can show Niko some tricks while he's at it." I stood up from the stool, turning to my brother. "We should go, before we miss the boat."

Niko's eyes widened and he hastily jammed the last bites of his breakfast into his mouth, leaping off his stool. "Race you!" he attempted to shout, the words muffled by the food as he shot towards the door, throwing a goodbye to our mother before he disappeared outside.

I rolled my eyes, tossing the half eaten fruit into the compost that my mother kept for me, before hurrying after him. I knew that given half a chance, and too much of a head start, he'd beat me to the docks before I had a hope of catching him. He was short, but he was fast.

I managed to fall in step with him halfway there, my longer legs proving beneficial against his speed. I ran faster, moving past him with a taunt, nearly missing the root that sprung from the ground in my path. I leapt and stumbled past it as Niko pulled ahead of me once more. "Hey!" I huffed as I strained to catch him once again. "No magical obstacles! That's cheating!"

When we finally stopped, my breathing harsher than I cared to address, Niko sighed and looked up at me. "No one ever lets me have fun with my magic."

"Well, you should know better than to use it to cheat in games." I ruffled his hair gently. "You can always use it to create things, that's the best way to play with it, you know that."

He watched me for a moment before sighing, the sound marked my victory against his momentary annoyance. My baby brother never stayed upset for long, but he was still very young, and I understood the need he had to use his magic. Unlike me, he would be able to toy with his freely, with none of the fears I had carried at his age.

He crossed his arms. "I just want to have fun with my magic, Phi, it's hardly fair. Zavier is the only one who ever lets me do fun things with it."

I cringed at the mention of our older brother, one prone to a rebellious streak in the oddest of moments, and who enjoyed using his magic in all the ways Niko wanted to as a child. "You know Zav gets into lots of trouble for skulking around with his magic. Remember what he did to the town hall last year? He was in trouble for months. Uncle Broderick had to pull a lot of strings to get him a warning." I rubbed his shoulder and made him start walking again. "We can find ways for you to use your magic for fun, but later, okay? Right now we have to get going or we really will miss everything."

Niko needed no more prodding than that to peel away from my side and hurry towards the docks that had come into view ahead of us.

I slowed and took a breath of cool salty air as he made use of his magic, creating a small ladder at the side of one of the smaller docks. The vines wove into place before Niko launched himself upwards, scaling the ladder with ease.

Once we were both up, we had a clear view of the Reaper ship as it turned into the port.

It was a sight that always stunned me. The ship was huge, made entirely of living material, vines and branches woven together by Earth-Blessed to form it. The vines shifted slightly every so often, as if to prove they were living, under the watchful eye of the Earth-Blessed that lined the sides of the ships deck.

The magic that created the ship was an extension of each El-liphae on board, easily controlled, managed and monitored as it moved through the oceans. The sea rose around the base of the ship as it sliced through the waters. There was no need for sails of any kind. Wa-ter-Blessed could move the ship far faster by using the sea itself, rather than relying on Air-Blessed to source sail materials strong enough to withstand the degree of winds they created.

Instead, Air-Blessed Elliphae were merely onboard to protect the ship from any storms that threatened the vessel, keeping their journeys smooth and safe. It was also how they were able to navigate through the ever present storm cell that protected our island against the rest of the mortal world.

Magic and illusion protected the vessel beyond our waters, magic as old as our race. Glamour magic that came from Faerie. A rare talent for our kind.

CHAPTER 2

I stood beside my brother as we watched the Reaper slow to a gentle stop beside the much larger dock further down the coast from us. Vines wove their way down from the ship, creating a large staircase that reached from the ship's upper deck to the edge of the dock.

I glanced around, keeping my hand on Niko's shoulder to stop him from getting carried away in the crowd around us. Like us, everyone was eager to see if there were new arrivals to our community.

There were other Elliphae gathered along the waters, watching the ship with a prideful awe. It was, after all, a masterpiece created by our blooded magic alone. I smiled as a familiar face appeared at the top of the staircase.

The Reaper's Captain, Quint Levati or Captain Q, as he was usually known, was the first off the ship, followed closely by his second Zion Jeslin, Trae's uncle. After them followed three males I had never seen before.

Two of them had the same almost raven black shade of hair, while the third male had paler russet hair, and all their skin held dark tans, the type you would expect from white skin after days in the sun aboard a ship's deck. I wasn't close enough to see all their features, but they seemed healthy enough from this distance, so I had hope they hadn't been stranded on their boat before being found.

They were the sole reason the ship had been dispatched yesterday. Their boat had been spotted within the storm, having passed through the veil of magic that kept us so well hidden from the rest of the world. It was rare that it failed, but it happened, and they were the proof.

They weren't brought in to be returned to their world, not with their memories intact at least. It was a tricky task, removing all memory of us, dangerous enough that very few of our healers and telepaths had ever performed it, but we couldn't risk them returned with the knowledge of our home.

Most mortals couldn't take it, with the magic driving them to insanity instead, but those who made the choice to try always did so with the full list of the risks. Even then, when it went wrong, it was a sadness that haunted the Elliphae and Enlightened, the mortals who existed among us with full knowledge of everything we were.

I looked back towards the others who watched, searching for any people I knew in the crowds. I found more than enough familiar faces, but none were the one I was looking for.

Trae wasn't there, and it struck me as odd. This wasn't something he ever missed, but movement at the other end of the docks drew my attention once more.

A new group had appeared, a form of officials for our island. At their head was the Leader of the Enlightened, Elijah Tanner. Behind him trailed other Enlightened members who would be involved in the rehabilitation and education of the three men that had arrived on the ship. The oldest known Elliphae on Keinteris followed behind the Enlightened, Ladrius Vaelle. The grandfather of another of my friends.

I watched as the two younger mortals, and another male I guessed was their captain, walked across the deck towards their awaiting welcoming party. If I looked closely I could see their emptied boat tied behind the Reaper, but it was an afterthought now. Unless they chose to leave, the boat would be stripped.

The two younger males were similar enough that I had to assume they were related, by the way they walked together as if they could offer the other their strength by mere proximity. I concluded that they were brothers, either by blood or simply by a bonding of time. They didn't seem afraid, not that they had a reason to be, they would be offered a new life here, but they gazed at the gathered members of my community with wariness.

There was a moment of pause as they reached the group at the dock. Words were spoken too softly to carry to even my sharpened hearing, and then they were moving again, quickly led inside a large building that dominated the end of the dock. It was usually reserved for markets, but today it became an official housing for the formal beginning of their new lives in Keinteris. If they chose to remain anyway, after the risks of their other choice were explained.

I often wondered what it was like to find our world, what those who arrive first thought of us. We looked human enough to make them comfortable, but we also inherited enough features from our Faerie ancestors to set us apart. The pointed tips to our ears were the biggest tell, as well as our angular features, and most importantly the magic we were capable of.

"Do you think we'll get to meet them soon?" Niko whispered beside me, despite the fact we were too far away to be heard, dragging me from my thoughts. "Those guys look your age, Phi, you'll help them learn." There was an excitement in his bright jade eyes and a surety in his tone as I looked down at him before glancing back towards the doors the males had disappeared through.

I was both curious and fearful at the thought. "Perhaps you're right, Niko, but we'll just have to wait and see, won't we?" I turned and nudged his shoulder gently. "Let's go, you have classes today and I need to go find Trae before he starts teaching with the Enlightened." Deciding not to bother with Niko's ladder, I jumped from the edge of the dock, landing in the soft sand, waiting and watching as he climbed down after me, using his magic to return the ladder to the earth before we set off for home, walking pensively this time.

We were almost home when he spoke again. "Phi, do you think they're scared when they come here?" he asked, continuing before I could answer. "It's just an accident that they ended up too close, they weren't trying to find us, but they did and then we keep them here. I would be scared if it was me." He spoke softly, still deep in thought.

I laid my hand on his shoulder and pulled him closer to my side as we walked. "I think they're probably a little scared at first, anyone would be, but we don't hurt them, Niko."

They were all give a chance to choose, sometimes they left, not many did, but some always would. What happened after they left wasn't something I knew or could tell him.

"You've spoken to Elijah before, you know how it works, but when they're free to roam around you can make sure they're okay yourself. How does that sound?" I ran my hand over his curls as I looked down at him.

A small grin lit up his face at the thought. "I'd really like that." He half hugged me before running away as our home came into view. He vanished inside without another word.

I stopped walking as I watched him disappear, able to hear his excited shouts to our parents from here. I smiled to myself. My little brother was full of so much boundless excitement, and I adored him for it. It helped chase away the shadows that seem to cling to the edges of me.

"Have fun watching them arrive?"

I jumped as a voice spoke from the brush beside me, my hands rising in my defence as flames flared around me, my mind taking a moment to register the voice.

My elder brother Zavier appeared from within the foliage beside me, using his gift with a flourish I came to expect from him. My older brother was tall and lean, and he had the same light brown skin and copper curls as Niko, but he did his best to hide them by keeping his hair cut short and close to his scalp, perhaps to make him look more menacing. His jade eyes also matched our youngest brother and mother, though his were often cooler as he evaluated the world around himself.

I dropped my hands back to my sides and drew away the flames. "Zavier, fuck," I said, blowing out a breath. "I could have hurt you. You're such an idiot. You know you're not supposed to do that near me."

He held up his hands in a false surrender. "I'm not the one with the itchy power trigger. Better watch those flames, Phi, can't have them shipping you off to join the Elliphir this late in the game." He smirked at me, his eyes glimmering with his own joke. My brother made it his goal in life to torment me about my control every chance he got, softening the blows that came from others whenever he did.

At least that was what I hoped was his intent. Maybe I was wrong and he truly did hate me for the way my magic was, but I couldn't find a truth depth of hatred in him, no matter how hard I tried. He could be an ass, but he was my brother first, and I knew when the line was drawn he was on my side.

"Hiding in bushes and jumping out at any Elliphae is a bad idea, we're taught to jump at shadows. Maybe I should have singed you, just to teach you a lesson." I crossed my arms as I glared at him.

His grin only grew. "Maybe I like the risk."

I rolled my eyes and glanced towards the house once more, before I looked back to my brother. "Do me a favour? Tell Mum and Dad that I'll be home later, I need to go see Trae. He wasn't at the welcoming, and that's unusual for him."

"Yeah, okay. I'm sure your Lord of Libraries is just doing what he does best, getting lost in books." Chuckling, he flashed me a grin. He enjoyed tormenting Trae just as much as he enjoyed jumping out to scare me.

"Maybe you could put those powers to good use for once and grow yourself a new sense of humour while I'm gone." I shook my head and turned away, waving a hand over my shoulder in dismissal as I headed off.

My brother and I had been born nearly thirty years apart, not an unusual gap for our kind, but still quite a gap when it came with a whole other life for him.

Our parents had raised him with the help of Nicola, a mortal female they had loved as deeply as they continued to love each other, but age had caught her before my third birthday. Zavier had lost a parent before I could form full sentences, and it had always put a strain on our relationship, until I had grown older, and could truly understand what my family had lost, who Niko was named after, and who the smiling face in my earliest memories was.

Now I often forgot that he neared sixty years of age when he looked barely a few months older than my twenty four years.

The hardest part of our relationship was my magic, something that had become more obvious as I grew. I had no idea how to right the fact that I had been born differently, that for some reason I never inherited the Earth magic my entire family shared. I knew he felt burdened by it, either by my difference, the way I was treated because of it, or because it hadn't been his curse to bear. And perhaps some part of him was terrified to lose someone else.

I glanced back as I walked away from him.

He still stood in the natural archway that led to our home, watching me silently. Something about the way he watched me sent a chill down my spine. There was a weight in his gaze, words he would never tell me, ones I probably didn't want to hear.

I shook off the sensation, turning away and hurrying towards Trae's, trying to centre myself.

Chapter 3

Trae was one of the people in my life who had become a safe haven, someone I trusted with everything, even my nightmares. After all, he had been there the very first time I'd experienced one.

We had been camping in the woods by the Divide as part of a stupid dare from other kids, one that we should never have accepted. We knew how much trouble we would get into if anyone knew where we were, but we went anyway.

I could only blame the naïvety of being a teenager who felt invincible, I suppose. Trae had set us up with blankets and hammocks made of woven vines, strung between trees he coaxed from the earth. My attempts to help had been limited to building us a fire, a task as easy as breathing for me. I had wrapped a blanket around myself, more for the comfort than against any weather, as being Fire-Blessed gifted me with an immunity to the cold.

Cleo had been with us too, and as an Air-Blessed she hadn't had much to do either, except organising what we ate.

With all the set up done, we had sat and spoken for hours, about everything. The three of us had always been like that, always been together. For as far back as I could remember they had been by my side. Back then we'd laid out the plans for our lives. Trae was obsessed with knowledge, of all things, even so young, and wanted to be a teacher or an Elder one day. Cleo's desires were similar, she wanted to help Veneficus with early magic training in those approaching their testings. I talked about following my father, and becoming a Guardien like he always had been.

Eventually exhaustion had taken over and we had each settled into our hammocks to sleep. I was swiftly swallowed by a nightmare, the very first one I'd ever had about the darkness. I'd screamed, fighting against forms that didn't exist, before my dream was filled with blinding light.

I'd woken as I'd thudded to the dirt, my hammock gone and my body naked as the flames disappeared. I had looked up as I curled into a ball, hiding myself, finding two sets of eyes watching me.

Trae and Cleo were both awake, torn from their slumbers by my screams, staring at me with wide, horrified gazes. I still couldn't say which of us was more terrified.

"Please don't tell anyone," I'd whispered to them in the night, sure that I was losing control of my powers.

They'd never told another soul, and when the nightmares continued but my magic remained, we knew it had nothing to do with me losing control. I had full control, while awake, but as I used my fire to fight the darkness in my dreams, my body did the same in reality.

I shook myself from my memories, looking down at the path that lead me towards Trae's home. He'd built it for himself after his father had grown frustrated with his constant clutter and building, designing his home similar to a rabbit's warren, filled with shelves and offshoots to house his ever-growing collection of books.

Trae was a genius, an Earth-Blessed with strengths in mechanics, architecture and design as well as healing. He spent any spare time he had honing his gifts and finding new ways to control them, as well as reading whatever he could get his hands on. Some days I just sat by and watched, because it was truly enthralling to witness him work with his magic.

I hurried up to his door and knocked four times. That was our rule, four knocks, so we knew. Some days it was a flawed plan, but most days it worked out for us just fine. Given that the rule had been made by the three of us at the tender age of nine, it was bound to have its flaws. We still carried it through, fifteen years on.

Listening closely, I waited, hearing him moving around inside before the door swung open.

I was welcomed by the sight my friend's broad smile, his greenish-blue eyes glimmering, the sun lighting his features as he took me in.

Trae was tall and lean, puberty having gifted him far more height than it allowed me. His dark hair was cropped short again after years of being grown out, but it freed the angles of his face, and somewhere in the past few years he'd grown into the cut of his jaw. Silver rings glittered against his dark brown skin where they curved along his left ear, an addition one of his older brothers had masterminded during his last birthday.

"Phi! Great timing, come in." He stepped back with the door, sweeping his hand in a welcoming gesture, inviting me in.

I cocked an eyebrow, surprised at the grin on his face. "Not the mood I exactly expected to find you in. It's still early and you're already smiling," I teased as I moved inside, greeted by the familiar scent of flowers and earth, his entire home spotted with small flowers blossoming within the vines. As I stepped in further, I could feel that something was different. There was an unfamiliar energy coming from Trae. I turned and pinned him was a suspicious glare. "What's going on? You never miss an arrival."

"Honestly? I stumbled into something in some new books, I've been lost in them for days." He flashed me a shy grin. "I just put one down to take a break, then here you are, perfect timing." He closed the front door and I led the way down the hall.

"So, is this the kind of 'lost in a book' where I have to force you to shower? Or the type where you have taught yourself nine languages, just because you're bored?"

He laughed behind me as he followed me deeper into the house. "I promise I've been showering. But that's another reason to keep you around, to make sure I'm reminded to be alive sometimes." He nudged passed me into the living room.

I shook my head as we both sat down. "You know I'm not actually your mother, right? She lives about five minutes from here."

"Oh, don't worry, I know. Though, you do play the role well." He ran his hand over his short dark curls as he relaxed, looking me over lazily. His dark features made the pale colour of his blueish-green eyes even more piercing. "So, anyway, you came here first. Was there something you needed?"

I crossed my arms loosely over my chest, studying him for a moment before shrugging. "I guess I was just checking up on you. You weren't at the docks when the Reaper arrived, it worried me. You're usually as excited as Niko over that kind of stuff. Clearly other things required all your attention." I flashed him a smile, but it was too tight, as I tentatively forced out the rest of what I needed to say. "But...maybe you could swing by home later too? I need a new bed."

His expression dropped, a frown curving between his brow. "Again? Phi, you're having those nightmares almost every night now? Maybe you need to see someone about it all, maybe you could ask other Fire-Blessed for guidance? You know I'll make you a new bed either way, but I worry about you."

"You know that the bursts don't hurt me," I said, waving away his concern. "And you know why I can't see anyone about it. My dad gets upset enough when he knows I've had them, and that he can't help stop them. If it got out, people would mutter about madness, and we know I'm in control." I sank deeper into one of the chaises Trae had crafted, nestling against the soft furs and silks that covered it.

It was my second favourite seat here, the first being the silk cushioned couch that Trae currently occupied, watching me with an evaluating gaze. Its intensity was odd, even for him.

"I'm fine," I said, only a little annoyed at his concern.

"And you're still haven't been burned by it?" He leaned forward on the couch, resting his elbows on his knees, watching me.

"Is there a point you're getting to?"

"You know as well as I do, that it's not possible, or it shouldn't be possible. It messes with the balances."

Which is why you've worked so hard to hide yourself from anyone who might get too close. The words went unspoken between us, but I could hear them nonetheless.

I huffed. "We established my freak status a very long time ago, Trae, why does it suddenly matter now? Planning on ratting me out to the Elders? Because, somehow, I don't think they care about exiling me."

He jerked upright, eyes wide. "What? No! I would never do that." He shook his head. "I just think...I don't know. Maybe this isn't something we should keep ignoring, maybe we should research it more, see if we can find anyone else like you in the histories."

"You must really need an excuse for a deep dive," I said, rubbing my temple against a sudden headache. "We already know there hasn't been anyone else, my parents looked for others when they realised I wasn't expressing any Earth magic. They said they couldn't find anything, and that they stopped looking. When I grew up in control of the Fire, they decided it no longer mattered."

"It's *possible* that's true, or maybe that's just what they told you," he said, his face taking on that faraway expression that told me I was about to lose him to his books. "Maybe they did find others, and just kept it from you." He stood, turning away he sauntered over to look out the window, his mood shifting suddenly. "People do that, especially here."

"You say that like you know something I don't." I stood slowly, but before I could move towards him the window in front of him closed, vines sliding across the open space at his will.

"I know lots of things you don't," he murmured, and what would have normally been a lighthearted jest, felt like a weapon.

"Trae?" I asked, frowning, knowing that there was more he wasn't saying.

"You need to leave. I'm going to look into things." He skirted around me, refusing to meet my gaze as he slipped from the living room, still talking. "Something I read doesn't sit right anymore. If I find more, I'll come to you."

I followed, finding him with the front door held wide open for me.

He swept his hand outwards, urging me through the door with the gesture.

"My bed?" I asked numbly as I stepped through the door, the sudden change in his demeanour making my head spin as I turned to look at him in the doorway.

"I'll fix it before dark," he promised with a nod. "Go home, Phi."

With the simple dismissal he closed the door in my face. I didn't move, watching as vines slithered back over the doorway, devouring the space in the same way they had taken the window inside, until there was no evidence a door had ever existed on this side of the house.

I walked away slowly, still too puzzled to challenge the change in my friend. Never in our years of friendship had he turned me out of his house in such a way, nor had he ever dismissed me so oddly.

I forced myself to follow the path back towards my own home, trying to catch whatever I had missed in our exchange to explain what was wrong with Trae.

I stopped halfway home, standing in the middle of the main road, feeling an all too familiar need tugging at my mind.

It was quiet. I could hear others going about their days, see some of them further along the road. The Elliphae were rarely thrown off course by the arrivals after so many. We were, almost, used to the fuss and the return to our quiet normalcy.

Trae kicking me out had derailed my day. Going home felt too much like walking into a cage. I glanced at the path that would take me home, staring at it for a long moment, before I turned away, the tether inside that kept tugging me in another direction winning out over the prospect of being trapped at home.

I walked quickly in the opposite direction, careful to stay out of sight as I got further from Keinteris' centre and closer to the deserted stretches of open woods and field. Closer to the Divide.

Getting caught out here would cause more trouble than it was worth, but I had done it enough to know I could hide if anyone came too close. I could form an easy lie if they caught me on this side of the Divide.

I wove my way through the thickening woods, the path mapped so deeply inside me that I could probably walk it blindfolded.

The giant trees that made up the Divide suddenly towered over me. There was no way to define just one tree in the wall, all of the branches, vines and leaves so intertwined that I couldn't tell where one ended and another began. It was like a wave of earth suspended above me, and as a child I had often feared it would collapse and devour us all in its grip. It was made of magic as old as Keinteris itself and needed little maintenance. The Divide was a symbol more than anything else. The line between the Elliphae and the Elliphir, one that was only crossed by the latter when they came for one of their own.

I slipped out of the tree line and burnt away at part of the wall, close to the campsite I had shared with Trae and Cleo the night of my first nightmare. I ducked through the small doorway I had created, pausing for a moment to take stock of my surroundings.

Everything on the other side of the Divide seemed the same. The trees were still green, far more overgrown and crowded, but they were living.

As children we were told that beyond the Divide was darkness and terrors, tall tales that claimed all the trees had died long ago and nothing would grow over here. They were lies. Lies that haunted the nightmares of little Elliphae children well into adulthood. The fear ran deeply enough that few strayed anywhere near the Divide

Yet for me it was different. Here I felt no fear, instead I felt at peace, like some part of me could only be calmed here.

CHAPTER 4

I walked further from the wall and deeper into the trees on the other side of the Divide, taking a deep breath of air that felt cleaner, as it unwound the tension I never seemed to be free of anywhere else.

I'd found myself here more and more often. Once a month had become once a week, until I was drawn out almost every day. The quiet helped me centre myself, keeping me in control of my magic and my temper. I was cautious as I moved through the trees, careful to avoid making any more noise than was totally necessary. The last thing I needed was to be caught, though I wasn't sure whether the Elliphae or Elliphir would be worse.

Making my way to my usual spot, a fallen tree that created a perfect seat, I ducked beneath a low hanging branch that rustled softly and loosed a gentle rain of white petals from the small flowers that bloomed along its branches. I shook my head to rid my scarlet frizz of the small petals, watching as they scattered around my face and drifted to the ground.

I smiled at the simple beauty in their descent to the densely covered forest floor around my feet.

The ground was still thick with evidence of our previous fall, creating a mosaic of browns, reds and yellows beneath the fresher colours of new life growing above.

After a moment, I sank down onto the thick log wedged between two larger trees, the trunk above me creating cover from the elements. I had sat in this exact spot and watched it rain around me more than once, like the trees had grown on either side of the log to keep it safe from the ravages of the weather. I closed my eyes and took a breath of the fresh cool air, listening to the sounds of the woods.

My woods, my mind whispered to me. I opened my eyes to look around again, watching the world around me, listening to the birds chirping and moving above, as small butterflies and bees flitted through the undergrowth in search of fresh flowers to feed on. I often lost track of time as I sat and watched, at peace with myself and the quiet nature of what felt like a secret world around me.

As a child I had found similar peace by the coast, watching the waves crash against the shore. But over time the violent nature the waves could take on had somehow become unsettling to me, and I didn't truly know why. The need for my own space had eventually led me here.

Too late, I heard the soft crack of a branch beneath the deep leaves behind me. The cool edge of a blade appeared against my throat a breath later.

I froze, eyes wide as I was pinned between the blade and the sudden heat of a hard chest against my back, a second arm slung across my shoulders and collarbone, holding me firmly in place.

"You're on the wrong side of that wall."

My eyes closed involuntarily at the nauseatingly familiar growl that broke the silence in the woods around me. My breath burned from my lungs as I slumped ever so slightly against my captor. "Creston," I choked out softly, cautious not to move to far while the blade still remained against my throat, knowing that he had the skill to keep me uninjured so long as I didn't thrash in his grip.

Just as swiftly as he had grabbed me, I was released.

I leapt to my feet, lifting a hand to rub at my neck, reassuring myself that he hadn't actually cut me. I whirled to face him, my angry response readying in my throat, until the instant I saw the fury that burned in the set of midnight blue eyes that watched me. My words died before I could even open my mouth as I dropped my gaze from his to assess him properly.

Creston stood behind the log, his natural height meaning that even at a distance he loomed over me. His tall form was draped in black, the clothes tightly framing his broad shoulders and the lean roll of muscles through his body as he moved. The dark colours matched the same darkness in his hair. His body had widened since I had last seen him so close, and there was a faint tan to his skin that warmed his features. His time as a Guardien had added more muscle to his frame with each passing year, or perhaps it was his Settling, his coming of age, that had allowed his body to broaden.

As I met his eyes again, I could see the fire there, his anger at me as clear as it could be.

Of all the people to catch me here, he threatened to be the worst, because disappointment would surely follow that anger.

I clenched my jaw, straightening my own shoulders as I held his gaze, waiting.

Creston Vaelle was one of Keinteris' most renowned Guardiens, a natural warrior, and on days like today? My own personal pain in the ass.

He sighed deeply as he watched me, moving to slip the blade back within the sheath strapped beside its twin on his chest, the blade making a satisfying sound as it sank into place.

I dropped my hand from my throat, swallowing against my suddenly dry mouth as I found my voice once more. "Cre—"

"Don't bother," he cut me off before I could finish his name, vaulting himself forward over the log, suddenly in front of me as his coat fell around his muscular form.

The scent of him was overwhelming. Oak and vanilla. I refused to let my desire to be covered in that scent distract me now.

"You cannot be out here, Seraphine, you know that. You know how dangerous it is beyond that wall." His eyes flared with his anger once more as he hovered over me, his voice a growl.

"I am not useless, Creston, and last I checked you were not my keeper." I crossed my arms over my chest, my own anger rising to the surface as he glowered down at me, his jaw tight. "I can take care of myself."

His lips pulled into a vicious smirk. "Oh, Phi," he muttered, shaking his head. There was something in the way he spoke it, some weight that was only right when it passed across his lips. He made it sound warm, full of promises. "I am aware that a Fire Blessing is no weak magic, but I was following you from the road."

"So you're stalking me now?"

"You never once thought to look around you," he continued, ignoring my interruption. "I could have killed you twenty times over in the time that you sat there and stared at the world." He shrugged and stepped back, giving me some air as he crossed his arms to mirror my defensive stance. "You have a violent magic, and keen senses, but you are untrained. And that makes you weak. Yours is an arrogant weakness, Seraphine, the type that could get you killed. Fancy flames will only get you so far."

I sighed, turning away from him as my mind churned over his words. He had a point, I knew that. If he had been anyone else, I could be dead right now. I looked around me, letting silence fall between us for a few moments, pondering my choices. "I can't stop coming here. I won't." I turned to face him again slowly. "It's the only place I feel calm."

"That is like saying you feel calm on the crumbling precipice of a cliff," he said, almost sounding incredulous. "You can't ensure your safety out here, and I can't be your personal guard each time you need to escape." He stepped towards me, closing all the distance I had created in three long strides. "I am sorry, Phi. I know what it means to you, to be out here. I have seen it. But I cannot ignore the risks. You could get hurt, or killed. I cannot, and will not, risk either one, even if you hate me for it."

I stared up at him, a new resolve growing within me, a grin pulling at the edges of my lips. "You say that like you'd tell me no if I asked you to come here with me."

He cocked a dark brow. "If my memory serves, which I know it does, I've told you no plenty of times in our lives."

"Have you?" I asked, blinking up at him innocently.

"Yes, I have," he said, an edge of caution slipping into his tone. "Every time you get *that* reckless look in your eyes, the one I only see in you and one other person, when something I don't like is about to happen."

I almost grinned, but I held it back, not wanting him to know that he was reading me right, a plan beginning to form in my head.

Creston had lingered on the edges of my life since we were children, always appearing when I least expected him to, but usually when I needed him the most. His skills in appearing at the right time had only increased with age, as he had been trained as a true Guardien, and not just as a boy with a protective streak and well hidden rage.

His eyes narrowed as he noticed the change in me as I looked him over slowly. He knew me well enough to worry over the look that had settled into my expression.

I straightened as the resolve became purpose. The plan turning into direction. "Then train me."

CHAPTER 5

Creston's dark brows shot high on his forehead, the request definitely not the argument he had expected from me. "Run that by me again." He tilted his head in astonishment.

"They won't let me become a Guardien, even just so I can use the training, I couldn't pass the damned exam. But *you* can still train me," I said, not above fluttering my lashes at him. "You could give me the skills I need, teach me the tools I lack to protect myself properly, so I can keep coming here. Please, Cres." I leaned into the familiar shortening of his name, watching his expression twitch.

I had started using it when he had first partnered himself with me as a child, after he found a group of children beating me with their magic, punishing me for not having the right magic, for being a tarnish to my family. Their parents had whispered about me, but the children? They were far crueler in their ignorance.

After that day, Creston had made it his job to ensure that I was safe, offering me his strength from then on. He was a born Guardien even at nine, watching over the scraggly six-year-old with too many bruises and the wrong kind of magic.

I grabbed his hands, ignoring the current of electricity that zinged through my body. "Come on. It would work for both of us. You wouldn't have to worry about whether or not I'm safe here, and I get to keep my little slice of peace. Please, Cres." I looked up at him through my lashes, working what charm I had as best I could.

He let out a frustrated sound. "You, Seraphine Nantir, are the most infuriating female in existence." He broke away from my grasp, turning away to pace, deep in thought for a few minutes.

Biting my lip, I kept silent, hoping he would see my side of things.

"Fine," he sighed, turning to face me once more. "I'll train you. In secret. No one else is to know, not if you want to keep training. I can't have my ass handed to me by the Elders, or by any of the other Guardiens. That means that Trae is not to be told, and neither is Cleo. Are we clear?" He stared down at me with a fierce look in his eyes, a look I rarely saw in him.

It was more of an order than a question, but I didn't care. Unable to contain the smile, I launched myself at him, hugging him tightly. "Thank you, Creston."

He wrapped his arms around me loosely, drawing me against him briefly before sighing once more and stepping back, putting some distance between us. "We do this on my terms. I decide if it becomes too risky, and if we have to, we stop and find you somewhere else to sit while you stare into the void. Got it?" He paused and waited for me to nod. "Alright. There's a clearing that we can use, not too far from here, on this side of the wall. I'll show you where it is, we'll train there and *only* there. It will mean that I am pulling you out of bed before sunrise, you sure you're prepared for that?"

"Yes," I lied. Few things sounded worse than getting up at dawn, but I needed this. "With the new arrivals here, things will be quiet, at least until they're dropped in with the rest of us to educate, so I have plenty of free time."

Creston tugged his fingers through the waves of his dark hair, nodding. "Perfect. That will give us time to get started, so no one will notice your exhaustion and bruises." He smirked at me at the mention of bruises. "Don't worry, I'll go easy on you. At first." He dropped his hands from his hair and turned away, heading towards the wall. When I didn't immediately follow he paused, looking at me over his shoulder. "Come on."

I hurried after him, watching as he stopped just short of the Divide and changed directions, walking alongside the wall rather than trying to pass through it. We walked without speaking until we reached a slightly worn path, hidden well enough that you wouldn't have noticed it unless you were looking for it.

"I found this place a few years ago with Hyatt. Some of the older Guardiens used to use it for sparing practice, before they built the training centre," he explained.

Hyatt's name was familiar, as was his reputation with his lovers, although I had never been introduced to the male. I had seen Hyatt at Creston's side on more than one occasion, and he seemed to be Creston's fair haired shadow in the same way Creston was mine. It made sense that this was something they would have found together.

As he led me along the path he ducked beneath branches, holding troublesome ones back out of my way, until we stepped out into a wide opening in the trees.

The clearing was an almost perfect circle, with only a few trees starting to grow within it. As though the woods were threatening to take the space back.

I wandered into the centre of the clearing. "What do you use it for?" When silence met my question, I turned towards Creston, finding him watching me, a small smile playing on his lips. I smiled back, perplexed. "What?"

He chuckled. "Nothing. You're just more perceptive than most, except when it comes to your safety it seems." He moved towards me. "I come out here to be alone, to think, the same way you do when you sit on that log of yours. Except of course for the fact that I am armed and can properly defend myself, unlike you." He winked as he stopped beside me, jerking his chin upwards. "It's also great after dark, you can see the sky really clearly here." There was something in his tone that stirred a fluttering feeling in my stomach.

We both looked upwards, as if somehow doing so would turn the day to night and reveal the sky he talked about.

I clapped my hands together after the silence stretched out too long, anxious not to give him the chance to change his mind. "Okay, so where do we start? Basics? Keep the thumb outside the fist?" I teased as I looked up at him.

As his attention returned to me, I was rewarded with a grin and punished with an eye roll. "Uh-ah. No way, we're not starting yet. I have a job I'm going to be late for, and you need to get back home before someone realises you're missing. I only wanted to show you where this was, so you can meet me here if I need you too." He held his arm out, gesturing back the way we'd come. "After you."

"Killjoy," I huffed as I headed back towards the pathway.

"I prefer 'Ass Saver'," he drawled. "Now move yours, I have things to do and I would rather not get caught out here by someone far worse than me." He poked my lower back with his fingertips, spurring me forwards faster.

I did as he wanted, hurrying while still careful to keep my footfalls quiet. Even with Creston at my back I wasn't stupid. I knew that crashing through the undergrowth could still attract unwanted attention out here.

Before long, we reached the still healing part of the wall that I had burnt through earlier and I slowed to a stop, looking back at him. "So, are you going first, or am I?"

"I'll go first, just in case someone else has decided today is the day they wander this far out. Last thing we need is for you to get your ass hauled to the Elders over this." He slipped past me and eased through the wall with an easy liquid grace that was part of what made him so very lethal as a Guardien.

I waited, listening to him on the other side, to be sure he, or I, weren't spotted. Ruin to my sanctuary on this side of the wall was an ever present fear I carried.

"Okay. Your turn," he called to me after a long moment of silence, using his magic to open my poor excuse of a doorway further for me to move through.

Tucking a few stray strands of hair behind my ear to keep them from getting caught in the branches, I moved through. I attempted to be as graceful as he had been, and it worked. Right until my foot slipped on a root and I found myself sprawled on the the ground at his feet. I groaned and rolled onto my back. "If you laugh at me, I will set your jacket on fire," I warned as I got up.

He choked on the laughter he had been about to unleash, coughing to cover it.

I shot him a glare as I brushed the dirt off myself.

Creston's eyes glimmered with his swallowed laughter as he watched me compose myself.

I pointed an accusatory finger at him. "That never happened, got it?"

He smirked down at me, chuckling despite my threats. "Get home. Before you break something important." He turned away swiftly, heading towards the road, to wherever he was supposed to be.

I watched until he disappeared from sight. When he was gone I had little else to do but follow the paths towards my own home. I had no idea what would await me with my family, whether my mother would keep my nightmare to herself or if Niko would have said something in one of his too excited rants.

The idea of facing my father with another conversation about my nightmares and the destruction they caused turned my stomach. There were only so many places I could go to keep myself from that conversation without drawing attention to where I truly spent most of my time.

I dug my hands into my pockets, passing the path to my home and continuing towards the more populated part of our settlement, seeking out Cleo's home instead. I let my mind wander as I walked, considering what might be involved in Creston's training, and how much pain I was going to be in after a week of it.

My body held more curves than muscle, and I knew that whatever he was planning to put me through would push fitness levels I didn't yet possess. I had missed out on the tall and slender aspects of my Faerie ancestry, something that wasn't completely unusual, but it would just mean I had to push myself harder to keep what I wanted. But if whatever I had to go through earned me Creston's respect and trust that I was safe alone when I needed to be, then it was well worth it, to keep that thing inside me quiet. That tug that forced me back beyond that wall over and over for a few moments where I felt truly calm.

I took one last look back at the Divide, where it loomed above the edge of the horizon. I couldn't give up the feeling I got from being over there. I knew I should, I knew it was dangerous, but I refused to compromise on something that made me feel whole in a world where I only felt half welcome.

CHAPTER 6

I rapped on the front door of Cleo's house. As Air-Blessed, her family hadn't built their house, so it was built in a more standard style, made with a combination of stone walls, vine-woven doors and windows as well as an entirely waterproof wooden roofing.

These were the kinds of homes that were built by Earth-Blessed for those of other magics, usually in exchange for some other favour, or as an inheritance from a family member that had moved on. It was also built far closer to the other homes than my family's was, meaning she had grown up deeper inside our community than I had, proximity she had used to gather knowledge and friends all our lives. She knew who everyone was, who their families were, and who all their exes might be. It came in handy at times.

Most of the time the houses were pretty similar, but Cleo's house had one wall entirely covered in a violet-coloured flowering vine that I had been told, by her mother Sandrina, was called Bougainvillea. It was beautiful and gave off the most amazing scent, something I now associated with Cleo and her family.

As children, Cleo and I had picked the flowers from it, trying to make perfumes from it. Admittedly, adding water to a crushed flower didn't quite do the trick.

I rocked on my heels as I waited for someone to answer to the door, thinking about life as a six-year-old, when everything was far simpler.

"Phi!" A cheerful voice tore me from my reveries and back to reality.

I turned and met the light blue gaze waiting on me. It occurred to me, as she lunged forward and crushed me in a tight hug, that I seemed surrounded by a sea of various blue eyes lately.

"I haven't seen you in days! I was starting to think I would have to hunt you down." She grinned as she released me, stepping back.

Cleo was delicate and elegant where I was rough and wild, her Air-Blessing shining in her features and her presence, as was common for second and third generations of any Blessing. Her platinum hair and bright eyes made her look as though the sky itself had brought her into this world. Her features were soft and welcoming, her skin holding a warm tan that I could never manage from long days in the sun. Her angular eyes were sharp and too often all knowing, an icy blue colour that could read a whole room and all its inhabitants in seconds, and she had those eyes narrowed on me.

I shot her a guilty smile. "Sorry, I've been distracted. Niko's testing is really soon."

Her smile melted into concern, and suddenly she was frowning at me, her eyes distant as something scratched at my mind. "You're still having nightmares, all the time. And you're passing that wall." She shook her head, refocusing on me. "Phi, I told you that you were going to get yourself caught out there, and by Creston Vaelle no less." His name was drenched in disapproval and I knew what she was doing.

"You promised you wouldn't!" I took another step away from her, glaring. "My memories and thoughts aren't yours to judge." I worked on imagining a wall of fire around my mind, blocking her out.

When frustration flickered over her features I knew I had succeeded. She was cut out, hopefully before she reached the part where Creston offered to train me.

Cleo was Air-Blessed, but that wasn't her only gift. She was a telepath, able to press into the minds of those around her, to hear thoughts and access memories, replaying them in her own mind as though they were hers. It was an incredible talent, but it could also be invasive.

"I'm sorry, but I couldn't help it." She moved around me to open her front door. "No one is home today, let's eat and talk properly. I know you haven't eaten again." She tossed her satchel on the floor as she stepped into the hallway, looking back at me when I didn't immediately follow. "Come in, Phi, I swear I won't try your mind again." She jerked her chin towards the hall before heading further inside.

I followed her in after a few moments of hesitation. I knew she meant well, but I preferred sharing things with her my way. Where I could control what was left out and ensure I didn't break promises to others simply because she could read me. And she was right, I had forgotten to eat anything substantial. I often did, too distracted by things around me to remember to involve food.

"It's just becoming easier to do now, even without meaning to. I reach out as soon as I start speaking to someone," Cleo said as she led us into the kitchen, pulling steel cups from the cupboards for us. "I'm working on controlling it with Veneficus. He says he can help me get it under totally control, so I'm not invading anyone's minds accidentally like I do now. I hate it as much as you do." She looked at me apologetically from across the bench as she poured juice into each cup for us, carrying them to the table and sitting down.

I sat opposite from her and we stayed there in silence for a while, each sipping at our drinks. The juice was cool and sweet, with the tang of a fruit I couldn't identify no matter how many sips I took. My mind wandered, and I could tell by the blank look in her eyes, she was doing the same thing, likely taking advantage of the quiet without her mothers being home.

I looked around, taking in the space, the hand carved tables and chairs made by Cleo's other mother when she was born. The home was filled with warmth and love. Pale colours covered the space, matching the flowers in various vases throughout. Most of the furnishings were made by Dirra, Cleo's more creative mother, while her other mother Sandrina had been pregnant with their only daughter, but there were also a lot of pieces in the house that came from the mainlands. Cleo was born in the way many were here, when there was desire for a child without a third in the relationship, the Healer's Hall serving up exchanges, with females willing to carry children for the male couples and other males willing to assist in the conception for the female couples. There were records of all biological links, but as far as I knew Cleo had never asked for details on who her blooded father was, as her mothers had always been more than enough.

I had always been more comfortable here than in my own home, surrounded by furnishings that weren't made of magic but instead from hard work and craftsmanship. It made me feel less out of place, the way I often felt at home, where I watched my family create new pieces as practice or simply on a whim. I feared destroying their things far more than I feared ruining these.

"Okay enough, Seraphine," Cleo said suddenly, breaking my reverie.

I jumped as she broke the silence.

"No more of this. I saw you jump the Divide, freak when Creston grabbed you, and that was it. You cut me out before I could see what else happened. I'm sorry I dug, but don't give me the silent treatment

now. Talk to me, about whatever it was that made you come to me."
She tipped back her cup, swallowing the last of her juice, reaching up
to sweep her platinum hair into a ponytail before crossing her arms
over her chest when she was done. Her eyes never strayed from mine.

I finished my drink, rolling the sweet liquid over my tongue slowly
to stall, but it didn't last and I sighed softly. "Alright, I'm still crossing
through the Divide, but you know how I feel there. You've felt it
through me."

She nodded in understanding. "I know, you feel at peace there.
Personally?" she asked, and waited for me to nod. "The whole damn
place gives me the creeps, just being near the Divide I always feel like
I'm being watched. I don't know how you do it." A small smirk pulled
at the corner of her lips. "Then again, you are the crazy one."

I huffed a laugh. "Me? Crazy? Pfft." She cocked an eyebrow at me
and I flashed her a grin. "Alright, fine. I'll admit I am a little crazy, or
maybe I'm after the adrenaline." I shrugged, getting up to toss our
cups into her sink.

"Maybe you are, but there's a difference between looking for trouble and putting yourself at risk." Cleo rose from the table, following
me and leaning against the other side of the bench, her icy blue eyes
clouded with concern as she watched me. "I worry about you."

"Too many people worry about me. I'm fine." I brushed her off and
moved back to the table, watching as she turned and lifted herself onto
the bench, swinging her legs as she sat on the edge. "And I'll stay fine."
Creston will train me well enough to ensure that, I added to myself.

Her eyes narrowed as she watched me, realisation dawning on her
face. "That's it isn't it? He didn't drag you home. He gave you an out."

CHAPTER 7

I hesitated as I stared at her, mind churning over the promise I had made to Creston. Not to tell what he had offered. But this was Cleo, and she had guessed all on her own. "It was the only way he'd let me keep going out there without losing his mind about it. Plus, having some self-defence skills outside of my magic can't be the worst idea I've ever had. But you cannot tell a soul."

She sighed and shook her head at me. "I don't like it, Phi, you're going to get yourself into trouble. Someone is eventually going to notice that you go missing over there. Or worse, you could be attacked by the Elliphir for being on their side of the island."

"That's why I've got Creston, to help me. It's not like Fire is a weak magic to begin with, but with a little work, if I need it, I can use my fists too." Creston's words about my arrogance about my magic being a weakness rang through my mind, but I pushed them aside.

She stared at me for a long moment, assessing exactly how serious I was. "Fine. I know I can't talk you out of it, but if you get hurt, I'll have Creston teach me how to fight, just so I can kick your ass for being stupid. Deal?"

I breathed out a half laugh, smiling at her. "Okay, I can live with that. Deal."

She smiled back. "Okay. Now that we've caught up with your stupid, what else is going on that I didn't see?"

"Eat and talk?" I suggested, my stomach suddenly perilously empty.

Cleo nodded and got up again to get us something to eat. I set the table while she worked on the food.

"I have one topic we can start with." She grinned at me from the kitchen, cheeks reddening with a sudden flush. "I have a date, kinda."

I smiled back at her instantly. If she was blushing at just the thought it had to be a good sign.

Her moods were notoriously contagious. When she was happy she lit up a space, almost like the sun shone a little brighter wherever she was at that moment. It made people gravitate towards her, drawn in by her glowing charms, balancing out the darkness that seemed to radiate from me.

Her shine was never something I had envied, in fact I had more often been grateful for it, proud of her and her abilities as we grew side by side.

"Alright, spill your guts, you're clearly dying to tell me who the lucky person is. Male or female this time?"

She giggled softly. "No way, I'm not spilling anything until I know if it's something worth telling. Especially not after last time." She still beamed at me, despite the reference to her past.

Her last relationship had been with one of the Enlightened males, and he had been cruel to her. She'd never told him she could read his thoughts, and knew he was only using her for notoriety, but she had been adamant that she loved him and that he loved her too, deep down. Eventually she listened to the arguments that Trae and I had put forth and stopped seeing him. She was heartbroken for weeks, but slowly, she grew back into herself again.

"I'm happy for you, Cleo, and I hope I hear all about it, but before you explode with all that giddy joy, can we eat? I'm starving." As if supporting my cause, my stomach growled loudly. I grinned and pointed at it. "See? Starving,"

She rolled her eyes and wandered over to the table with what she had found in the pantry; some fruits and nuts for us to eat. They were fairly common staples for us, as we could not stomach the meat of any animals. She set it up at the table and we settled in to eat, exchanging more relaxed topics as we ate.

It was easy for us. We knew each other well enough that even silence could be more relaxing than an entire day with anyone else. We eventually migrated to the living room, with Cleo stretched out on the couch and me on the floor. As we sat there, I filled her in on the weirdness I had experienced while visiting Trae earlier on.

"So what do you think he's actually up to?" Cleo asked when I was finished explaining. "It must be something intense, if he's sealed himself in. I knew it was something he was capable of, but I've never actually seen him do it."

I rolled onto my stomach, toying with the strands in the rug beneath me as I swung my legs in the air. "I don't know what he's onto, but he's gone all out obsessive, so it must be something good." I shrugged as I glanced up at her. "When he has what he's looking for, he'll resurface. Until then, we just have to wait. If I wasn't used to him getting obsessed with things so suddenly, I'd be much angrier at him for closing the door in my face."

Cleo nodded, a thoughtful expression on her face. "I guess. I could go around, see what I can read from his mind from outside," she offered. "Make sure we don't need to be really worried." As I opened my mouth to protest she held up her hand. "He wouldn't have to know. I would only be checking on his welfare, nothing else. It wouldn't be weird if he caught me anyway, he would understand our concern."

I shook my head at her. "No, Cleo, it hasn't even been a day. We give him time, and only resort to spying if we have no other choice." I go to my feet. "I should go, I haven't been home all day, and even though they're focused on Niko and his testing, I don't want to attract any questioning from my family right now."

"They wouldn't be wrong to worry. The Elders could throw you in a cell for violating the treaty by crossing the Divide. We both know your dad wouldn't take it well either, not with how your family is."

I winched at the mention of my familial obligations as both high ranking Guardiens and Elders. "I won't get caught." When she cocked an eyebrow at me I rolled my eyes. "Okay, I won't get caught *again*."

She shook her head again. "I suppose not everyone watches you as carefully as Creston does."

I shrugged, heading for the door. "I'll see you later. Come find me if you hear anything from Trae? I'll do the same."

CHAPTER 8

I made it home and slipped into my room without anyone noticing. A perk of my bedroom being external to the house, for all they knew I had been home for hours and they just hadn't seen me, unless they had specifically sought me out. Which I doubted. I only really needed the main house for meal times, my room was equipped with an attached bathroom and enough space to keep me busy inside. It gave me the freedoms I needed.

Despite being twenty-four years of age, I was still considered young in Elliphae years, as the true beginning of my adulthood would come after my Settling, nine months from now when I turned twenty-five. Having the separation from my family, even only by a small distance, was a relief. Especially with a younger brother frequently tearing through the house.

Inside my room I found a brand new bed, vines intricately woven together to create the frame and hold the hammock-like centre up above the floor. It was different to the usual style Trae grew for me, but with the hammock I no longer needed to go in search of new mattress materials. Instead, all I'd need would be blankets.

I was thankful for the effort but knew it was likely wasted as the bed probably wouldn't last the night. I needed to invest in a greater long-term idea, but until I stumbled across an idea that wasn't horrifically uncomfortable, I'd take what I could get.

Tugging off my jacket, I tossed it on the chair in the corner of my room before turning to the mirror. I let my hair down, gently picking out the remaining petals from my curls. When they were all gone, I pulled my hair back from my face once more. Feeling calm and clean, I headed into the main house.

"Mum? Niko?" I called as I kicked off my shoes and padded through the house, heading towards the kitchen. It was our central hub and usually the best place to find my family.

"Living room, Seraphine." My mother's voice echoed down the hallway.

I followed the sound of her voice and found her on one of the chaises, reading a well-worn novel, something from the small library near the school. The books there came from mortal collections, a common item that were brought back during the Reaping trips. My mother loved to read, which was exactly why she had been the first to volunteer to run the library when it was built. I'd never seen her happier.

I smiled as I sat across from her. "What did you do with the boys?" I teased as I leaned back against the pillows. The house was far too quiet for my brothers to be anywhere close by.

She laughed softly as she folded the corner of her page and sat the book in her lap, focusing on me instead. "Your father took them out to practice with their blessings for an hour or two. Niko wants to learn more about what he can do with vines, other than tripping people over." She shook her head. "Your little brother is a troublemaker for sure."

"You're not wrong there. I almost ate dirt this morning because of that trick."

My mother shifted in her seat. As she sat up, her hair brushed over her shoulder, a shade of honeyed brown more beautiful than my red. My mother was a breathtaking creature, tall and curved with the same bright jade eyes shared by both Zavier and Niko. She barely appeared a decade older than I was, despite the fact she was nearing her five-hundred and fifth birthday, according to her calculations. "How was the arrival this morning? Niko was too filled with excitement to explain properly beyond the basics of the mortals being taken away."

"I'd assumed you wouldn't be able to shut him up, I'd just expected all the details to rush from him." I shrugged. "It was a small boat, a fishing vessel perhaps. Three people, an older male and two closer to my own age. I think. It is still too soon to know all that much about them." As we spoke, they would be learning all about us.

"I'm sure Elijah will have them circled among us before too long, provided they choose to remain with us and don't prefer to return to the mortal realm," she said, waving a hand dismissively. "Though that world seems to be filled with never ending changes for the worst, I can see why they may choose their families over the magic here." She frowned, her expression suddenly troubled and her gaze distant.

"Mum?" I asked, the sudden drop to her mood startling. "What is it?"

She blinked, looking back at me, smiling tightly. "It's nothing, Seraphine. It has just been some time since I heard from the rest of your older siblings. Leaving them in the mortal lands to live their lives has never been easy."

I understood then. My mother and father had been together for an astonishing four and a half centuries, and out there in the world I had siblings that had not been born on this island, siblings I had never met. I knew them only from the stories that my parents had told us of them, and the small painted portraits that my mother stored in their room.

My mother sighed softly and pushed herself to her feet. "I'm tired, I think I'll rest for awhile," she said, ending the brief conversation about her other children. "Will you set dinner for the others? Everything you need is already there, your father prepared most of it before they left."

"Sure can. You go rest." I nodded.

"Thank you. Wake me in an hour if I fall asleep." She leaned down to kiss my forehead softly before she slipped away to her bedroom, her shoulders hunched against the deep sadness I knew lingered in her heart.

I relaxed as I listened to her door close, grateful that my day hadn't come into question.

With my father and brothers out practicing with their magic I knew my whereabouts for the day would not be questioned, and it was a relief not to have to fumble through excuses to my former soldier father. I hated lying to my family, but in this situation it was necessary.

I got up and wandered into the kitchen, finding the vegetables my father had grown to be used. I sliced and cooked what was needed, falling into a rhythm that soothed me almost as well as the Divide did, setting it all on the table as dusk fell outside. By the time I was done I could hear the boys heading towards the house, with Niko's excited tone carrying far ahead of them before falling silent as they entered the house.

"Sonia?" my father called as he came inside, kicking off his shoes by the door.

I poked my head into the hallway. "Hey Dad, she's having a nap."

He nodded. "Okay, we'll leave her there then." My father smiled and kissed my forehead as he reached me, before glancing back to my brothers. "Go clean up for dinner."

Zavier grumbled, but dutifully led Niko down the hall towards the bathroom. Niko adored our older brother, even when Zavier didn't want him hanging around.

I had a tendency to send Niko to annoy Zavier if he had been bothering me during the day. It was the best payback, because no matter how much Niko got on his nerves, he was never cruel to him. No one was.

There was simply something about my baby brother that rendered us incapable of doing anything but loving him. Perhaps it was his age, or the way the world excited him. Whatever it was, I found myself hoping it would never change.

CHAPTER 9

When they were gone, my father returned his attentions to me. "Was it Trae or Cleopatra today?" He smiled and tapped my chin before moving past me into the kitchen, looking over what I had prepared.

"Actually, it was both," I said. "Trae was a little busy, doing another deep dive, and I'm not sure if he's going to end up building things, or disappear for the next few weeks with minimal contact. You know how he is." I shrugged it off, not having to stretch any truths about my friends. "And Cleo was hyper as per usual, working more on her telepathic abilities in her training now."

"Cleo is a promising young user, I'm glad she is expanding her abilities before her Settling," he mused. "I also wouldn't worry too much about Trae, we both know he'll return to normal in a few days time, perhaps all the better for it." He winked at me as he poured himself a drink of water from the jug on the bench. "Dinner looks great, Phi, thank you for letting your mother rest."

I nodded in response, letting him have a few moments of silence. My brothers, whilst goodnatured and fun, could leave in the best of us exhausted at the end of the day.

He took a sip of the water, staring at the table as he swallowed and rubbed his face, scratching at his uncharacteristically bearded jaw. "She hasn't been well in the past few days. It's unlike her to need so much sleep."

"She spends so much of her time taking care of us, and the library, she deserves the rest. I'm sure she'll be back to herself in no time." I wandered over and sat on one of the stools beside the kitchen bench.

Like the majority of the furniture in the house, it was made using earth magic, created with intricately woven vines. In the past, I hadn't understood how they remained to strong, and alive, for such lengths of time. Until I noticed that my family members would run a hand over a surface absentmindedly and it would suddenly be brighter, stronger. They fed the magic constantly without even realising it.

I would never understand life the way they did, but they would also never understand fire the way that I did. All they could see was heat and destruction. I saw, and felt more, but it wasn't something I had ever been able to put into words they could understand. Not that I expected them to try, it was part of my very being to understand it, not theirs.

My father ran his fingers through his rich brown hair. "We shall see. If she doesn't improve before too long we'll see the Healers, ensure there is not more to it."

I nodded as my brothers came into the room. "Should we eat?"

"I'll go see if your mother is awake, start without us, we'll join you." My father wandered past the table, setting his glass in his place before disappearing to his bedroom.

Zavier shot me a frown, but I shrugged and looked to Niko. "Hungry?"

Niko grinned up at me. "Starved!"

"Well, that we can fix." I laughed and helped him fill his plate before settling in with my own to eat.

None of us spoke as we ate. Zavier was brooding over something and Niko was more than content trying to get as much food as possible into his mouth. Keeping up with his growing appetite was a task for all of us lately. I found myself pushing my food around on my plate, eating very little of it as our parents returned and sat at the table with us.

"Niko, please do slow down and chew your food first. You're a child not an animal," my mother chastised him as he continued to shovel food into his mouth.

He flushed and nodded, slowing his eating like she asked, grinning mischievously.

She rolled her bright jade eyes with a smile, before digging into her own meal, no evidence of that bone deep weariness I'd seen on her face earlier.

The table was quiet, with only the clinking of cutlery against plates and soft sounds of everyone eating to fill the space.

I narrowed my eyes, looking between them all, trying to figure out why I felt uneasy. Something was off. My family was never so silent, especially at the dinner table. There were usually jokes or arguments of some description being thrown across the table, but tonight there was nothing.

It seemed that everyone had something to themselves that was bothering them, things that weren't going to be shared tonight.

I excused myself to my bedroom as soon as I was finished, closing my eyes as I sealed myself in, leaning against the closed door for support.

There was something going on with my family, but I couldn't afford to raise questions about it. I feared they would begin to question me in return, and my training would be over before it had even begun.

I opened my eyes, the lanterns around my room flaring to life in the same instant. I started towards my closet, pulling out a fresh nightgown and some underwear, bundling them under my arm, before slipping through the adjoined door into my bathroom.

I didn't bother lighting the fire beneath the water tank outside to warm it before I got in, knowing my body temperature would automatically rise against the cold as the icy water touched me. We'd discovered it when as a child I'd sprinted full pelt into the winter ocean, shrieking with joy while my mother had waded in after me, shivering, to drag me out. She'd nearly become hypothermic, but I'd been fine.

I tossed my dirty clothes on the floor and got in, scrubbing away the strange day and relaxing under the cool spray of water. I let my mind drift as I washed my hair, wondering what Creston might have planned for me in the morning and how early he had truly meant. The thought of the training made me feel more solid than I had in a long time. It was training I may never have to use, but I valued it nonetheless.

I stepped out of the shower and reached for my magic, drawing a wave of flames over my wet skin, watching as the droplets of water sizzled out of existence. It left only my hair wet, ready for it to be pulled into a ponytail to keep it from frizzing during the night. I pulled on my fresh clothes and climbed into my new bed. The hammock swayed a little while I settled in, the lanterns still bright as I laid a blanket over myself.

I stared up at the ceiling, dimming the flames in the lanterns. It was still early, but I wanted to sleep, to leave behind this day and start my next. I hoped that I would still have a bed when I woke, that I could be spared from Creston seeing the wrath of my nightmares first hand. The nightmares had an effect on me that I just couldn't control.

I closed my eyes, relaxing into sleep. My last thoughts before darkness took me, were a plea.

Don't let me dream...

Chapter 10

I wasn't being chased. Yet darkness surrounded me. There were no whis-
pers, no screams and no hands tearing at my body. There was just me
and the dark. Endlessly.

I turned where I stood, searching for more in the nothingness. There
was a flicker, a flash of red all around me. But as quickly as it came, it
was gone.

"Where are you?" The voice seemed to echo around me, bouncing in
the endless darkness that should absorb it. Like a shout in a cavernous
space.

"Lost." The word passed over my lips without thought. Was I lost? Is
that what was wrong? I didn't know.

The red flashed again, before it all slipped away.

I woke with a start, yanked from my sleep with my mouth dry
and my heart racing. My eyes flew open at the soft scraping sound
of something over the floor beside my still intact bed. I had woken
before the nightmare could fully take hold. I sat up and frowned into
the darkness of my room, reaching out with my magic to reignite the
lanterns, swearing as light flared in the room.

"Trae, what the fuck?" I hissed, staring at my best friend as he sank
down onto a stool beside my bed, one he must have created when he

arrived, explaining the sounds that had woken me. "Don't you know how to knock?" I ran a hand over my restrained hair, feeling the pieces that had broken free and frizzed while I slept. I held back a sigh.

I frowned at Trae when he sat unresponsive, staring at me as though he were the one waiting for me. He studied me until I squirmed, anxiety knotting my stomach against his scrutiny.

"You're freaking me out. Say something."

His gaze remained steady as I spoke, but he never reacted, as though I wasn't really there.

I shivered, getting up from my bed I stepped towards him, slapping him. "Stop it!" I snapped, heart racing from the almost nightmare and his weird intrusion.

His expression melted as he flinched against the slap, reaching up to rub his cheek as he finally focused on me properly. "That hurt."

Refusing to feel guilty about it, I tugged a blanket off the hammock to wrap over my shoulders. "Good, it was supposed to. Now spill your guts." I crossed my arms over my chest as I looked down at him.

He dropped his hand from his face. "I think I found something. I've been at it all night and all day yesterday, since you left my place, mostly." Something flickered on his face, too quickly to decipher, as he looked at me again. "But I've learned a lot, things I'm not totally sure of some things yet. I need you to do something for me. Can you touch fire?"

I cocked an eyebrow at the request. "Have you gone mad? I made the Fire, of course I can touch it."

"No, I don't mean the fire you create. I mean other fire. Like you did years ago, I have to make sure it was real." He stood and pulled out a candle from his pocket, matches appearing from another. Striking one he held it to the wick until it held the fire on its own. He let it burn a moment before shaking the match to extinguish it. The matches disappeared back into his pocket, but the candle remained, a small flame flickering as he held it towards me. When I did nothing, he stepped closer.

"Touch it, Seraphine." His tone was quiet but demanding, something I'd never heard from him before.

After a moment of hesitation, I ran my fingers through the flames slowly, watching his reactions rather than the way the flames danced at my fingertips. I could feel it, the urge to take control of the flame. To make it my own, but he hadn't asked that of me, so I left it.

His own gaze remained intently on my fingers as they brushed through the flames over and over, unharmed and barely warmed by the candle's small flame. Suddenly he blew the candle out and shoved it back into his pants, leaving a lip of wax on the edge of his pocket.

He gave nothing away, his stool receding back into the floor, vines slithering out of sight before he took his first step away from me. "That's all I needed. I will be back later; I need to check a few things. Don't come looking for me. I'll come to you." He held up his hands as I opened my mouth. "No, later." He turned sharply and disappeared out my door and into the darkness outside.

I wanted to throw something at his retreating figure but by the time the thought had formed, he was already gone.

I cursed, and with nothing else to do I went back to my bed, laying down and trying to go through what had just happened. I was still too close to sleep to make much sense of things. I extinguished the lanterns in my room and laid there, awake in the darkness.

I didn't know how long I laid there, but sleep never returned to me. I watched out my small window as the night turned to dim grey in the moments before dawn broke through. I decided then, that I had to get up, to ensure that I would be ready when Creston arrived to for my first day of training.

Tugging on a pair of comfortable black pants, I did a few jumps and bends to make sure I would be able to move easily in them. I pulled on an tunic shirt and slipped a jacket over the top. I studied myself in the mirror, my hair gathered back tightly and curled into a bun to keep it out of the way as best as possible. It was as good as it was going to get.

I looked around my room, deciding suddenly that I didn't want Creston to see the scorch marks on the stone wall by my bed or the remaining ashes beneath it that I hadn't yet cleaned. I didn't need him to know about my little late night fire shows.

I jammed on my shoes and slipped outside, standing against the wall of my room out of sight of the house but with a clear view of the tree line and the pathway to the house. I waited there for Creston.

The sun started to turn the sky orange as it rose between the trees, and I closed my eyes as it danced across my face, basking in its gentle warmth. It was a cool morning, but the warmth of the sun held the promise of a heated day. The air was filled with the scent of morning dew and opening flowers. When I opened my eyes, I was met with the sight of Creston's midnight blue gaze.

He flashed me a crooked grin from only a few feet away.

I flushed, not having heard him approach. He was right, I really did need to work on paying more attention to the sounds of the world around me, so he didn't keep sneaking up so easily.

"Good morning." He grinned as he wandered the last few feet towards me. "Ready to have your ass handed to you on a silver platter?"

I laughed. "No, definitely not. But let's go anyway." I brushed past him and headed towards the trees, trying to stay out of sight of the windows in the house, just in case someone in my family was awake and spotted us.

Creston chuckled before he fell in step beside me. "Well, someone has their brave girl pants on this morning, let's see how you feel after an hour of hand to hand," he taunted, matching my pace easily, walking beside me so I could see the smug look on his face.

He was going to enjoy this much more than he should. I scowled at him.

As if guessing what I was thinking he winked at me. "I have a lot of memories of you being a stubborn pain in my ass to get even for, it's going to be so very fun, for me at least." He ran his fingers through his hair and grinned at me sideways. "Starting now. Get running, Firefly, warm-ups start on the way to the Divide." He nudged me before breaking into a jog himself. "See if you can keep up."

I faltered a little at how easily his childhood endearment for me weaved itself into his orders, a flush creeping up my neck. I allowed myself a moment to smile before breaking into a speedy jog to catch up to him.

CHAPTER II

I matched Creston's pace, but not without some effort. By the time we reached the wall I was stifling my need to gasp for lost breath.

Creston wasn't fooled. He shook his head at me as he *finally* stopped by the Divide. "Breathe properly or you'll pass out. I'm not going to judge you for panting. Just get through there and jog the rest of the way to the clearing we were in yesterday." He stood beside a doorway he had opened up within the Divide and waited for me, hands on his hips, breathing *normally*.

I took a few seconds to inhale slowly, trying not to vomit, then passed through the wall, forcing myself to jog to the clearing without stopping to catch my breath again. I didn't want Creston to think I was weak, but my lungs were burning and my legs were shaking by the time I got there. It was only a couple of minutes, but it only touched the edges of how hard this was going to get. I was healthy, but I wasn't fit.

I leaned over and clutched my thighs, closing my eyes and focusing on getting my breathing right. I could feel Creston behind me somewhere, waiting. When I was ready, I straightened and looked over at him, regretting it instantly.

He hadn't broken a sweat, nor was his breathing piqued.

I sighed and shook my head at myself.

He made no comment on the wait.

"Ready to get started?" he asked, scanning me from head to toe. "Your heart rate is up, and your muscles are warm, at least a little. I don't want you tearing any of those weak little muscles you got going, Firefly. So first..." Like the soldier he was, he rattled off lists of stretches and demonstrated them as he went.

After what seemed like an eternity of my muscles screaming in protest against each position he put me through, he finally seemed satisfied with what we had done.

I wiped the sweat off my face and tried to smooth the hair that was sticking to the back of my neck from the tangle of my ponytail.

"Okay, I think you're ready. You're still going to be in pain tomorrow regardless, but that should help." He shot me a wicked grin at the mention of pain. "I'm going to start with the basics. No weapons, just fighting. When you can handle yourself without weapons, I'll let you pick one up." He walked over to me and adjusted my stance, kicking my legs a little further apart. "That's better." He stepped back he studied me for a moment, eyes narrowed as his expression became thoughtful.

I remained silent and waited once again, ignoring the goosebumps that rose on my skin wherever his eyes landed.

His eyebrows shot up, before he snapped his fingers and turned away, disarming himself and throwing his jacket over the top of his carefully discarded weapons. It left him dressed in loose grey pants and a tight black shirt that dipped down his chest in a slight V, giving a glimpse at the tattoos that marked his lightly tanned flesh in various places.

I cleared my throat as he turned back and looked me over again, shifting my weight from foot to foot until I couldn't stand it any longer. "I'm dying over here, Cres, can we move this along?" I groaned after a few more seconds of watching him stare at me, silent and unmoving.

His expression morphed into a calculating smirk. "Patience really isn't your strongest trait, is it?"

I made a face at him as he stepped towards me before backing up at the expression he wore.

With a predatory stride, he circled me, taunting me with that smirk as I moved to keep him in sight the whole time. I blinked and he was on me, the ground no longer beneath my feet.

I gasped as my back hit the ground. His hand followed me down, fingers wrapping around my throat, not enough to choke me but more than enough to hold me down.

"Dead." He shook his head as he looked down at me smugly.

Using the brief distraction of his arrogance, I brought my knees up and kicked out, my feet landing against the hard wall of his abdomen, earning a grunt from him as his hand was torn from my throat. I rolled from beneath him and scrambled to my feet, turning to try to put distance between us.

He got up quicker than I ever expected someone of his size could move and caught me around the waist, hooking his arm round my throat. "Dead," he repeated in growl just below my ear. "Never turn your back on your enemy." He dropped his grip, and pushed me away. "You keep your eyes on them at all times. Never let your guard down, never fall for it when they go down. You stay on them until they stop faking it or stop moving. Got it?" His arms crossed over his chest as he looked down at me, his intense midnight gaze sending piercing shivers down my spine.

I nodded and moved to face him properly.

He nodded in return. "Good, now attack me." He held up both

hands curving his fingers towards his palms to give me a 'come get it' gesture.

I took a breath and focused. He was no novice and if I wanted to stand a chance against him, I needed to make my moves carefully. I took a step towards him, then hesitated. That was a mistake.

Once again, I found myself on the ground, my legs pinned down as he knelt over me, his knees on the ground either side of my thighs and his ankles hooked across my shins.

Creston wrapped his fingers around my wrists, and pinned them above my head. "Dead again. You hesitated, it could have cost you your life in a real fight. If you're going to attack, follow through." He stared down at me inches from my face.

I cleared my throat, trying to shift beneath him. "Okay, I get it. I screwed up, will you get up off me so I can stand again?"

My struggles only earned me a smirk from my trainer, accompanied by two words. "Make me."

My eyes narrowed at the challenge. I smirked back at him, closing my eyes and focusing on my magic, like flexing a muscle. Taking a deep breath and letting it out slowly as my body temperature rose, I heard him hiss in air softly when I grew hotter and hotter, flames appearing in my hands. I opened my eyes as his weight left me suddenly. I pulled the heat back and got to my feet, and taking advantage of his distraction, I moved behind him. I grabbed his ankles, yanking them out from underneath him.

Creston cursed as he lost his balance, crashing down onto his chest, unable to catch himself fast enough. He cursed again as I leapt on his back, digging my knees in and leaning my weight onto his elbows, forcing his arms down.

"You got distracted and now *you're* dead," I growled as I pressed down as hard as I could.

His body shook beneath me. He was laughing. "Well, well. You fight dirty." His voice was warm with his sudden humour. "Good work, but..." He sat up suddenly and flipped us so once again he was holding me down, fingers pressing into my throat as he gripped it. "Gloating too soon is a dangerous thing as well. Dead." He smirked down at me as I groaned.

"Damn it, Creston. I can't help it if you're a fully trained soldier and I am not." I looked up at him, frustrated by my inability to win against him, even if it was asking too much to be as good as he was on the very first day.

Creston tapped my nose gently. "Relax, I've been training for years, you've had an hour. Tops. And this is just skirmishing, I wanted to see what you had, and what you reverted to in order to protect yourself. Nice trick with your Fire, it stung." He got up and pulled me up with him, keeping hold of my hands as he looked down at me. "We'll start with basic moves for today. That's enough full-on hand to hand, but if all else fails and your attacker is unarmed, set the fucker on fire. It's your greatest advantage."

I flushed and nodded, stepping back to put some more distance between us. He affected me more than I would like him to know, especially while he was training me. "I'll remember that for future reference." I pushed a few stray curls back away from my face. Being tossed on the ground multiple times wasn't encouraging my hairdo to stay in place. "What exactly do you have in mind for us next?"

Creston brushed some of the dirt and leaves off his clothes as he looked me over. "Now that I know what you revert to without any experience, I know where to start training you properly." His lips once again twisted up into a knowing smirk. "You're going to hurt tomorrow, Firefly, I promise you that."

I groaned softly, knowing he wasn't lying.

Chapter 12

True to his promises, for not just the day, but the next week I woke with aching muscles, climbing gingerly out of bed and spending more and more time in the shower in an attempt to soothe them.

Every morning I trained with Creston and every afternoon he ordered me to run, to help my stamina increase gradually. The greatest positive to my constant exhaustion was when I collapsed into bed each night, I did not dream. No nightmares had found me since the first day of my training.

It was a great relief not to have the time to fear the sleep I needed, and to have my bed remain intact for as long as they stayed away. And with Trae's current state of self-induced solitude, it would have been very difficult to have a new bed made, without having to involve my brothers or father, especially as they were preoccupied with training Niko in every spare moment.

I attempted to visit Trae on one of my runs, a few days after I last saw him.

Once again his home was totally sealed, and short of burning the place down around him, I had no way of getting in.

Cleo hadn't been around either, so I could only assume he'd either dragged her into his obsession or she was deep diving into her abilities with Veneficus.

A few days later, as the dark outside my window turned grey, I dragged my sorry ass out of bed and got dressed for a fresh morning of training with Creston. He'd been starting us even earlier every day, particularly this one. We had to be present in The Square before midday for the introduction of the mortals as part of the Enlightened, it was a mandatory event. He'd offered to skip today's lessons, but I'd brushed it aside, wanting to keep going, keep improving.

As I slipped out of my door, I found Creston leaning lazily against the wall beside it. He turned to me, beaming.

There was no other smile in existence capable of making the concept of waking before sunrise seem so fantastic.

I rolled my eyes at him and but couldn't help it as I smiled back. "Good morning, Cres," I said, closing my door and stepping onto the path.

"Morning, Firefly. Shall we get going?" He continued before I could answer, "I want to start extending your running distance, so, this morning we'll run to the old watch tower then back to our usual crossing." He nodded towards me as he pushed away from the wall, sliding his fingers though his dark hair.

I studied him for a moment before letting out an acquiescing sound and starting to stretch my legs for the run. "Don't you also need to stretch, *boss*?" I put extra emphasis on the one word to taunt him. I had discovered that he despised the word during our training sessions, but with the pain he was putting my body through I couldn't resist the digs.

He snorted and shook his head at me. "I stretched before I came here. By the time I get to your home, I've already run over half of what I make you do."

And yet he never seems to have broken a sweat, I sneered internally as I worked through my stretches. By the end of my relatively short run, I was almost guaranteed to be gasping for air, and sweating like a pig. As the days went by it has seemed to lessen, but I was still far from Creston's soldier stamina.

"Hey, that reminds me, where is your place?" I asked, glancing at him as I sat to lean forward and grasp my toes through my shoes.

Creston regarded me with surprise at my sudden curiosity before his expression melted into another of his smiles, one that made me suspicious. "I think I'll keep that to myself for now, Firefly. If you don't already know then I must be doing quite well with hiding my home away. Can't have just anybody dropping in on me, now can I?"

"What could you possibly have to hide, Creston Vaelle?" I got to my feet and cocked an eyebrow at him.

Something in his expression dipped, just for a moment, as though for a moment he considered what he might have to tell me, but he recovered quickly.

"If I told you, it would ruin the mystery." He winked. "Now, come along, we have work to do." With that he took off in a run, his movements smooth and practiced. Grace in all things came to him as easily as breathing; it was so much part of who he was.

I followed him as quickly as I could, knowing that if he got too far away, he wouldn't wait. He would only run faster, mainly to goad me. I pushed myself faster, trying to match his pace. By the time we reached the road I had gained enough ground to run with him, without having to force it. The small surge of pride in myself was enough of a boost to maintain the pace.

"I'll make you a trade," I told him as we ran, almost side by side. "I'll tell you something, and you can share whatever it is that made you pause just before."

He gave me a sideways glance. "Are you not running hard enough?"

I rolled my eyes. "Come on, what could it hurt?"

He went quiet for a little while as we ran, and I was sure he was going to ignore me, until he cleared his throat. "Someone I care about has volunteered to do something stupid."

"Is it stupider than what I'm making you do?"

He laughed dryly. "Almost equally."

"Well, I can promise to listen, if you want to talk about it." My breathing was growing harsher as I spoke and ran, but I was determined not to stop him if he was going to open up.

"Hyatt has decided to try his time as a Ranger."

"And you don't trust that he can do it?"

"It's not that. It's..." He trailed off, and I tripped trying to look at him better. His hand snapped out, catching me and righting me without faltering in his own steps. "That's enough talking, focus on where your feet are," he grunted, and I knew whatever door he had opened was thoroughly sealed again.

We ran side by side in silence after that, with only the sounds of the dirt crunching beneath our feet and my heavy breathing filling the space. In the distance birds started their morning song, warning us that the sun was growing closer. Our day had started long before theirs, another tribute to the early hour of my training.

Creston glanced at me every so often, presumably to reassure himself that I wasn't going to collapse quite yet. I pretended not to notice as I focused on keeping my feet planted one after another without tripping on the uneven surface of the road. The last thing I needed was to face plant in the dirt and prove my incompetence to Creston.

So that was where my focus stayed, rather than imagining what he would be seeing as I ran beside him. My face was heated and I was beginning to sweat, but I refused to slow my pace. I could tell that his pace was already restrained to prevent me from hurting myself, knowing I couldn't compete with his years of built-up training and stamina. The proof was in his ease at this pace, his breathing barely accelerated, and not a single bead of sweat had formed as far as I could tell. Though I could only spare the briefest of glances as I tried to manoeuvre the ground in front of me without incident, but it didn't even look as if a single hair on his head was out of place.

I let out a frustrated sound, inciting a throaty chuckle from the male at my side.

"Don't stress so much. You're doing well for someone new to all this running, eventually your stamina and endurance will increase," he told me, his voice warm with the humour he found in my frustration.

Breathlessly, I sighed, and tried to keep my concentration on the path in front of me. "Doesn't make it any easier for me now. You look like you're going for a stroll, and I feel like I'm going to die." Okay, perhaps a slight exaggeration, but the way the muscles were beginning to burn in my legs was a discomfort I wasn't yet accustomed to.

"Well, we could stop all this now, you'd just have to stop going over the wall," he coaxed sweetly, as though I would consider the bait in my current state.

I snorted derisively. "Yeah, right. I already told you, I'm not stopping. Aren't you supposed to be encouraging me towards success or some shit like that?" I was starting to huff now, my words broken to accommodate the breaths needed between them as we finally reached the half-way point, turning and heading towards the hole in the Divide that we now used daily.

My comments earned me another deep chuckle from Creston. "Right you are, sorry Firefly, but I'm just trying to keep you from risking your pretty neck for a little peace and quiet." He let out a soft laugh. "Then again, life would be pretty boring for me if you weren't always finding some kind of trouble to get into."

As I tried to concentrate on pulling air into my straining lungs, I managed to stick my finger up at him, only causing his laugh to deepen.

CHAPTER 13

By the time we reached the Divide, I was gasping for breath, bracing myself with my hands on my knees. My lungs burned with each gulp of air, my body demanding more. Gradually though, my breathing slowed, until once again, I could speak.

I glared up at Creston, as he stood patiently against the Divide, hardly showing any side effects of the run that had left me breathless. "Such a show-off," I muttered as I slid through the small doorway he had opened. "You could at least pretend that the run was hard." I brushed my hand absently along the foliage on this side of the wall, staying close by it on the way to the clearing we used for our actual training.

It was too small to be good for much running, unless I wanted to make myself outrageously dizzy, which I had discovered early on in our training, much to Creston's amusement. To his credit he had warned me, I just hadn't listened.

"You're leaving burn marks," he said, ignoring my previous comment, chastising me as he followed me towards the clearing.

I frowned, dragging myself from my thoughts and looked down at my hands. Sure enough, where my fingers had slipped through the leaves I had left behind black marks, some of the leaves still smoking. I pulled my hand away and clutched it to my chest.

"I wasn't...I wasn't even trying to..." I stuttered, confused. I hadn't been reaching for my powers, so my hands shouldn't have been hot enough to cause those marks. I stepped away from the wall and felt a hand on my shoulder, keeping me steady.

"It's okay, you were just distracted, you didn't set it on fire." His tone softened as he turned me, putting a finger beneath my chin gently, tilting my head back so I would meet his sharp gaze. "Don't freak out, okay? Everyone has lapses, you were just mad at me for being so superior." He grinned and stroked my cheek with his thumb lightly.

I pushed him away, unable to help the giggle that escape me.

His grin grew. "That's more like it. Now get moving, we're *burning* daylight."

With a small smile, I rolled my eyes and shoved him again, before turning away and continuing to walk towards the clearing, keeping my hands to myself. "There isn't enough daylight to burn yet. Give it an hour and you can use that line."

He followed without another word, walking through the brush just loud enough for me to hear, as though he were reminding me he was there if I needed him.

I found the small path through the trees and followed it down into the clearing. Once there, I pulled off my jacket and laid it over a log, keeping it from the damp ground. There was still a chill to the air, but after the run it was no longer enough to cut through me, though even if it had, I would have taken it off anyway. Keeping my jacket on would only result in excess sweating, something I'd rather not have Creston witness. I turned back and found him doing the same, laying his jacket over mine, his weapons following. I waited for him to walk over to me before I spoke again.

He stopped a few steps from me, watching me with an evaluating expression on his face, waiting for me to make a move.

"So, what are we doing today, boss?" I crossed my arms over my chest as he shot me a glare.

"Don't call me that," he sighed, as though saying it was exhausting, and with the number of times he'd said it I guess it probably was.

But it was one of the few things I could torment him with, while still preventing rougher beatings during our training sessions. It seemed to exhaust rather than enrage him, giving me very mild advantages. Sometimes.

"I want to work on your defences, you need to be faster with your reactions to blows. Right now your best chance in a hand to hand is to hit first, hit hard and make it count. That isn't overly reliable as a defence for your life." He uncrossed his arms and rolled his shoulders, raising his fists in front of him, his tall muscular frame falling into it as though his body defaulted to the position.

Meanwhile, moving my own body into a similar stance felt forced and flawed. It was the effort that counted, apparently. I rubbed my hands together as I prepared myself, watching him carefully. "Okay, bring it."

One side of his lip twisted up and then he was on me. I ducked the first blow directed toward my head, following through with a hit of my own, striking his abdomen, causing him to hunch over and clutch at it briefly.

Grinning, I swept at his legs, missing the arm that caught me in the side of the head and had me in a heap on the ground in the next second, I coughed as the air rushed from my lungs, and recovering quickly, I scrambled away and got to my feet.

"Always kick them when they're down and don't—" He swung at my midsection but missed as I blocked it, moving away again as we circled each other and trading blow after blow until he, once again, had me pinned down. "—ever believe they're hurt," he finished in a huff.

I grunted in response, trying to ignore the burn where his body pressed against mine. I was there to learn, not rub myself against him like a cat to see how far I could push that sensation through me.

He smiled at me suddenly, and it was like sunlight washed over me. Blushing furiously, I looked away, clearing my throat.

"I think that's a new record for you, and without using your fire. You're getting so much better." His voice was full of unexpected pride as he let go of my arms but remained in a half push up above me.

I looked back into his dark eyes and smiled back. "Thanks, I've had a pretty okay teacher," I teased with a soft laugh.

He chuckled, dropping his head and looked up from beneath his dark lashes. "Maybe one day soon you'll actually manage to win against me. But I'm comfortable in the knowledge that if someone attacked you now, then you would be able to defend yourself, enough to run away and not collapse after a few minutes." Creston's eyes glimmered with humour as he remained above me.

I felt my cheeks heat as I flushed again. "Thank you, Creston, I mean it. You training me lets me keep my freedom over here. You're risking termination by training me over here, if anyone found out..." I frowned and shook my head. In the beginning I hadn't even thought about it, but the more we'd come here, the more I'd realised how much he was risking helping me. I'd get a slap on the wrist and perhaps a permanent escort, but Creston would lose so much more.

He lifted his head and levelled his gaze to mine. "I chose to do this. If I get caught, then I have to deal with that. I'm a big boy, I can handle the consequences of my actions." There was no wavering in his tone. He had obviously made peace with his decisions here. He moved off me, standing and holding out his hand for me.

I took it and let him pull me to my feet, trying not to consider exactly why he would take such a huge risk for me.

"Personally, I think the Elders should be running defence training for everyone instead of just having it for the novice Guardiens and Rangers," he continued. "They keep pretending the Elliphir are an absent threat. I think they're wrong." He dropped my hand once I was on my feet, wandering over to the water bottle he kept stored by our things.

I pondered what he had said, while I watched him unscrew it and take a deep drink, before holding it in my direction. I shook my head and let my hair down as he screwed the lid back on the bottle and dropped it to the ground. He met my gaze expectantly, knowing, somehow, that my silence was a thoughtful one.

"You're right," I said slowly, realising in that moment how much I didn't know. "This *is* your choice, and I am glad you're training me." I shrugged. "I'm not the soldier you are, but you're right. We're taught so much that is worthless to us if we were ever truly in danger, maybe it would be safer, but the Elliphir haven't attacked for us as long as I've lived, they've only come to take the children. Why provoke them?"

"Has your father ever told you the stories? Or your mother?"

I shook my head.

"Well, mine did. My father told me some as a child, Raphael always wanted to know more." His gaze darkened at mention of his brother, but he continued. "On the mainlands, when the Elliphir and Elliphae lived freely in their settlements all over the world, the Elliphir created havoc, but the Elliphae fought back. Once we were stronger, once *we* were a greater force to reckon with in battle, we were able to escape to places like Keinteris, and they still followed. They are our balance, our opposition, our fears, everything we aren't, and the Elders are all too content to hide behind a wall that doesn't keep them out while we grow weaker, and they do not. Do you know what I hear by being observant, Seraphine?" he asked fiercely, a wildness to his stare.

Again, I shook my head. I'd never heard the stories that clearly haunted him.

"The Oracles whisper now, darker and darker things, they know something has changed. What, I do not know, but soon the Prophecies won't be carried on whispers, they'll come out as screams." His expression darkened as he spoke, eyes that were usually so inviting became pools of something vicious, as though he knew much more of the darkness than he spoke aloud.

I swallowed beneath the force of that gaze. The edge in him, hidden save for small moments like this, was something I knew he showed to very few in his life. It was not the first time I'd witnessed it.

That had been after he'd watched the first of my Earth-Blessed classmates use their powers against me.

I stepped towards him slowly, and as suddenly as the darkness had come, it disappeared. I wanted to do something to ease the tension that dominated his body, the pulsing anger that had appeared out of somewhere deep inside him, but I didn't know what to say, what to do.

His gaze and expression softened as he watched me move closer, and face flushing, combed his fingers through his hair.

I came to a halt a few steps from him as he caught himself and relaxed once again.

"I'm sorry, I shouldn't...let myself get like that, not around you," he said, looking anywhere but at me. "That's not who I want to be, at least not for you to see." He scrubbed his hands over his face, recovering hastily. "Come on, we're done for the day. I'll walk you into The Square and get you something for breakfast. I know you never eat before I come to you in the mornings." He stepped forward and brushed the loose curls back from my face gently, flashing me a grin that left my heart skittering in my chest and my cheeks flushed.

I shrugged. "I don't feel like eating that early. I eat afterwards. I'm obviously not starving."

He chuckled and looked me over, slowly and purposefully. "Nor should you be trying to starve. You're perfect as you are." He winked at me, sending my heart into another stutter, before moving away again to grab our things, handing me my jacket first before he grabbed for his own, shrugging it on and waiting with his bottle in hand as I did the same. "But I'm still going to make sure you eat, just in case you forget later, you can't push your body without feeding it too."

I took a breath to centre myself again. My reactions to Creston's flirtations were becoming more obvious, I was sure of it. Each day we trained I felt more and more drawn to him, like an invisible string tugged me towards him. Some days pulling away almost hurt.

Whether he felt it too I had no way to know, but I was not going to willingly discuss it unless he was the one who broached it first. Until then, it was another secret I kept to myself.

With both of us refitted in our jackets, we headed out of the clearing. Taking the overgrown dirt pathway back to the wall, we walked in comfortable silence, both lost somewhere deep in our minds as we followed the wall cautiously to the section that was our doorway to this forbidden side.

Without a word, Creston slid lithely through the wall using his magic to part the way, making sure that there was no one around to catch him, or me, upon our return.

While I waited, my attention shifted to the sound of a stick or branch snapping. My eyes narrowed as I turned my gaze towards the dense trees.

There were no paths directly across from the doorway. *Was this it?*

Had somebody finally seen us, finally realised we were crossing this line?

I frowned when everything seemed to still, the shadows seeming to grow darker as I took a step towards the sound, recalling the ways Creston had taught me to fight if I needed to. I froze, feeling the first of the shadows.

They stroked at me, like the hands in my nightmares, seeking me out, their icy touch bringing all the hairs on my body to their ends.

Flames appeared like gloves over my hands and I stared towards the shadows in the trees. I held my breath, barely able to move, waiting for something to change. I could feel eyes watching me from within that darkness, but couldn't find their source.

"Phi!" Creston grabbed my arm, only to snatch his hand back with a snarl that died in his mouth when I turned my gaze to him.

The feel of the hands had disappeared as soon as he touched me.

He paled as he looked at me. "Fuck. Your eyes," he breathed in astonishment.

CHAPTER 14

I frowned, drawing back my fire after a final glance at the trees.

The darkness was gone, as though it had never been there in the first place. I stumbled backwards until my back hit the cool leaves and tightly knit branches of the wall. I closed my eyes and took a deep breath.

It's happening. I'm going insane.

I resisted the urge to cry at the thought, I would not let myself crumble. When I opened my eyes again, Creston was standing not far from me, still cradling his hand. I pushed away from the wall. "I burnt you." I took his hand gently to make sure it wasn't severe.

He pulled it away gently. "I'll live, Seraphine. Tell me what just happened." There was nothing light in his tone. He was confused and concerned but there was also a ferocity in his gaze. He reached out with his unburnt hand to touch beneath my eyes gently.

"Nothing happened," I muttered, turning my face away so he would stop stroking my skin.

He snorted derisively. "I was calling you from the other side of the wall, but you didn't respond, and when I grabbed your arm, it was like touching hot iron. Your hands were the only thing on fire, but you were conducting it, and your eyes." He paused to look at me with a mix of surprise and fear. "Phi, your eyes were like pits of flames. No green left." He dropped his hand from my face and shook his head.

That was new, but it wasn't something I wanted to discuss with him. I was unnerved by that lingering feeling of being watched, that something had been *reaching* for me, and I wanted to leave.

"What happened?" Creston pleaded as his blue eyes bored into mine.

I crossed my arms over my chest as I looked away. "I don't know what happened. There was....I don't know. There was something wrong, that is all I know." I met his gaze again, and this time it was my turn to plead. "Don't tell anyone, I need to find some things out first. I promise I'll tell you everything when I can. Okay?"

He stared at me for a long moment, his eyes narrowing as if he were going to press for the information now, but when he sighed softly and nodded, I released a breath.

I stepped forward and hugged him gently. *Trae, I needed to see Trae.* "Thank you, Cres," I murmured as his arms wrapped around me in return.

He pressed his lips to the top of my head, easy to do with his height above me. "If you're in danger, or if something is wrong, I need to know, Firefly. I need to be able to help. And I will, whatever it is that you're dealing with, I'll stand with you to fight it," he breathed against my hair.

I let myself relax in his arms. I felt safe there, with his strength like a wall around me. But it was short lived. We had to go before someone missed us.

We both stepped away reluctantly and I flashed him half a smile before moving through the wall. I waited on the other side as he followed me, mostly closing our doorway so that only a sliver remained to mark it.

I spared no glances back through the Divide for the darkness that had touched me. If it remained, I didn't want to see it.

As I walked away from the wall and towards the road, Creston fell into step beside me without a word. I shoved my hands deep into my jacket pockets as I tried to decipher what had happened.

Creston didn't try to draw me from the silence, and a glance at him proved he was also deep in thought, a small crease between his dark brows as he clenched his bottle with whitening knuckles.

The closer we got to The Square at the centre of our settlement, the more we both were each forced from our thoughts. We paused as one on the edge of The Square and looked around. It was empty. We shared a confused look.

"The Square is never empty, especially at this time on the morning of an introduction," Creston said, his eyes scanning the rooftops, the tree lines, anywhere danger might lurk. "Unless..."

My eyebrows rose as we spoke as one. "The Oracles."

We no longer hesitated, falling into a run as we headed towards the home of Keinteris' High Oracles.

A small castle-like domain by the beach, it was aptly called the House of Prophecy, by the Elders and Elliphae for centuries before my birth. It had alway felt like a cage to me, and every time I saw the Oracles paraded, like I was watching little birds flit past the bars trying to find their escape, if only I could get the doors opened.

We slowed as we approached the crowd surrounding the Oracles' home. Smoke billowed from the chimney, a sign that they had news for the Elliphae of our island, summoning them for the announcement. The Elders would already be inside taking the prophecies first before they let the rest of us know what was happening.

"Red smoke means that more than one of the Oracle had the vision," Creston breathed from beside me as he pushed his tousled onyx hair back from his face. At least until it slipped back near his eyes again, as it did constantly.

I clenched my hands into fists against the sudden urge to push it out of the way for him. Forcing myself to ignore the nagging desire to touch him, I turned to gaze at the chimney. "I didn't know that," I admitted.

"The Elders will be assessing how this news is going to affect us and the Enlightened." He looked around at the murmuring crowd as he spoke.

I tore my gaze from the smoke to scan our surroundings.

At least a hundred of the Elliphae were here already, standing in small groups as they, like us, awaited the news.

I looked up at the smooth stone that made the walls of the Oracles' castle home.

It, like many other buildings, had been made using Earth magic. The dark stone walls held carvings, runes of the elements, the same symbols used as tattoos by those among the us who chose to wear their magic openly. Other runes were for other particulars of magic that many Elliphae held, such as that of the Oracles.

Each oracle that lived inside had the rune of Prophecy tattooed on their cheeks, marking them as the High Order of Prophets. My gaze rested on the rune for Fire, following the curves of the symbol with my eyes over and over. I craved to have the image on my skin but had resisted it on the day of my eighteenth birthday. With my twenty fifth birthday closing in with the spring, I was growing more resolved to have it. My Settling was cause enough to celebrate with one.

Creston nudged my side gently, pointing to the top of the Castle, drawing my attention away from the castle walls to the sky above it. Crimson smokes no longer billowed from the House of Prophecy. "It won't be long now." He rubbed his hands together slowly as the crowd gradually fell silent as the others noticed the absent smokes as well.

We waited like that, silent and anxious, for the inevitable announcement. It had been a long time since there had been a prophecy of this level, longer than my life had lasted so far. My mother had told me stories about it, the prophecy of a flame that hadn't made sense to most of Keinteris' inhabitants at the time. Even now I wasn't sure it did.

I looked to the intricate wooden doors and expected them to open, as would have many others, until a voice drew my gaze and the eyes of all waiting upwards, to the castle roof.

Teetering on the ledge stood one of the few male Oracles, dressed in a white ceremonial robe that shifted with the breeze. He looked down at us as his voice carried. He shouldn't have been there.

I gasped, pressing a hand to my mouth. Was he going to jump?

Creston tensed beside me, ready to leap into action, obviously thinking the same thing I was. I noticed other Guardiens around The Square started to move towards the base of the house, eyes fixed on the Oracle.

"With the sunrise this morning, the House of Prophecy was struck with a communal Vision, a vision of days to come, and a warning not to be suppressed," he shouted, eyes wide. "It is as follows. '*When the darkness descends only the flame that does not burn can cure the lands ravished by shadows*'."

Something akin to lightning shot down my spine at his words, and a nagging voice inside me tugged on a memory I couldn't fully recall.

Other Oracles appeared on the roof, suddenly and quickly guiding the speaker out of sight. But they were too late to stop him.

I went very still as the world seemed to slow.

Shadows. Like those that had sought me out beside the wall? Perhaps it hadn't been my imagination.

I turned my head slightly towards the crowd and met the dark gaze of Veneficus Pedriff.

He stared at me with an expression far too intense to be a mistake, and I took a small step closer to Creston. But his stare never wavered. Only when a body appeared in my line of sight, was I spared. I blinked up in surprise.

Standing in front of me was my absent best friend.

"Trae, where have you been? I've been trying—"

He held up a hand to cut me off. "This isn't the time or the place. You need to go home right now." He turned his gaze on Creston who had moved closer, cautious of the edge in Trae's tone, frowning at my best friend. "You can come with me, you need to see what I have to show." Trae's attention returned to me. "Go, Phi, now. Don't stop for anyone. We'll meet you there soon, but stay out of sight. I know it doesn't make any sense now, but it will, I promise. *Go*." He was more forceful now, it wasn't a question or a request. It was an order.

I backed away from them both. Creston turned to watch me, his brows still pinched together, and I shot him a pleading look, hoping he'd argue for me to stay with them. He only nodded in the direction of my home, whatever he understood from Trae enough for him to believe I should be leaving, whether I wanted to or not.

I crossed my arms over my chest. "I don't take well to being ganged up on. If you two haven't arrived in the next half hour, I'll come find you and force the answers out of you."

The statement drew a grimace from Creston, and rightly so. He was the one teaching me how to hurt others without actually breaking anything. It was already proving a useful skill, even as only a threat. Or perhaps it was his burnt hand and thoughts of my fire that made him unwilling to test me.

I turned away from them then, heading back towards The Square, and when I was no longer in their sights, I ran.

CHAPTER 15

By the time I reached home a satisfying burn had developed in my legs, my breathing a little harsh as I slowed.

As was quickly becoming my habit, I paused before coming into sight of my home, allowing myself some time on the road to catch my breath and fix my hair, pulling it back tightly before I started through the trees and onto the stone pathway.

I'd only taken my first step on the stone when my brother appeared from within a dense section of the underbrush, the branches and leaves brushing over him as though he were rising from a liquid pool of nature rather than dense trees.

Zavier was in total control of it all as it settled behind him.

I scowled at him, my hands still raised from the panicked moment before I realised it was him and not a shadow moving towards me. "I asked you not to do that anymore. I nearly lit you on fire last time," I chastised as I stood in front of him, crossing my arms over my chest.

His jade eyes were cool and calculating as he assessed me silently.

I shifted uneasily as I stared into them. I wasn't afraid of my brother, but something about the way he looked at people made me feel like he saw through to the very bone, like nothing was hidden from him. "What the hell are you doing lurking out here in the damn trees anyway?"

"I was waiting for you. I went to your room, and you weren't there. Where did you go so early?" He brushed his hand over his trimmed hair as he looked down at me curiously. When I offered no answers, he shook his head. "Whatever. What I wanted to tell you, to show you, was your new bed. One you won't be able to destroy," he said, turning and walking back to the house without waiting for an answer.

I paused, staring after him for a moment before hurrying to catch up. "You know that it's the nightmares that do it," I grumbled. "How did you find a bed that won't burn?" I demanded as I tried to catch him, grabbing his arm and making him stop again. This was a conversation I didn't want to have in front of our mother.

"I asked Corielius," he said, looking surprised that I'd initiated contact. "He's Fire-Blessed but he's also a creator. He made the bed out of a formation of steel, woven together like vines. I've covered it in greenery, so it looks like its living. So long as Dad doesn't touch it or try to make it grow, you're safe." He looked back at me tentatively.

I frowned at him. Never before had he been protective of me and my little defect. "You covered for me?" I couldn't keep the shock from my voice.

He tossed me a pained smile. "I'm not always an asshole, Phi, and I don't want Dad to start thinking you're losing control of your powers. You don't remember what it was like when that started, but I do."

I started in surprise, not having expected the conversation to take this turn.

"And I do feel brotherly urges for you every so often," he continued, looking away from me. "They're uncomfortable for both of us, trust me, but they do exist." He shrugged and shoved his hands deep in his pockets.

"What's going on with you? You're never like this. What's

changed?" I asked, squinting at him in suspicion.

My brother had never been cruel to me but I'd never describe him as warm and cuddly. He had always been strong and stoic, rarely showing affections in any way unless absolutely necessary, so his sudden need to protect me struck me as out of character.

He sighed, expression transforming into one of frustration as he glared down at me. "Can't you just say thank you and get over it?"

"Thank you for fixing my bed, Zav. I appreciate the help, and I know Dad worries about me." He nodded and just like that, it was my turn to sigh. "I would never have thought of doing what you've done. You're a good brother when you want to be," I said quietly, unsure if I should hug him or not. He wasn't really the hugging type. "You should keep that in mind around Niko, he worships you. Don't abuse that."

Fixing me with a withering look, he muttered, "I'll keep that in mind," before he started walking towards the house again.

This time I let him go, staring after him, still surprised by his thoughtfulness, before I continued towards my room, slipping inside. The lanterns around my room came to life with my arrival and an errant thought for need of more light. The bed was perfect, and as promised, it looked as though it was made only of vines and other living matter. I smiled at my brother's kindness.

Sitting down on my new bed as I awaited the arrival of my best friend and his answers.

Whatever part Creston had to play, I didn't know. Just calling him another of my friends felt like more of a betrayal to myself than it should have, but calling him anything else didn't feel right either.

After what felt like an age, I was just about ready to keep my word, and go in search of them when my door opened and they strode inside.

Trae entered first, arms full of leather-bound books, far older than any of us. I frowned as Creston appeared carrying more still. In seconds, Trae had created a large desk in the centre of the room and deposited the books there. Slipping a satchel from his shoulder, he took out a notebook of his own while Creston placed the rest of the books on the table. Neither of them said anything as they moved around each other.

As I stood up from the bed, Creston glanced at me and looked almost apologetic, but there was something guarded in his gaze. His silence spoke more than Trae's. *He knows and he's afraid.* Whatever was happening, he knew what it had to do with me now.

"Alright, I've had enough of this bullshit," I said finally, after several more moments of Trae arranging and rearranging the books in silence. "Tell me what is going on and tell me now before I start using those—" I pointed to the books. "As kindling for a very nice fire." I turned my gaze on Trae.

He shook his head. "Don't do that, we need them. I promised I'd explain, and I will. But it's easier for me to explain with the evidence I have to support what I know, okay?" His eyebrows rose, sharpening his dark features, as he waited for me to push him again.

I didn't. Instead, I walked over to the desk he'd set up and ran my hand over one of the books.

The cover was worn but the title was still burned into it. History Of Faerie; Gifts, Prophecies and Curses.

"These aren't light reading, nor are they easy to get your hands on." I looked up at him again.

He shrugged one shoulder as he started opening the books to specific pages, pages holding pieces of paper scrawled with notes in his hand.

Scanning quickly through the rest of the books, my brow furrowed. The paragraphs and notes made no sense to me. Nor should they have, they weren't written in any language that the Elliphae were fluent in.

Noticing my confusion, Trae smirked. "It's the Old Language. Few know it now, so I taught myself. It seemed safer that way." He said it so simply, as though learning the Old Language was something he did over his breakfast. He continued to open up book after book, laying out his notes with them.

I turned my attention away as I became aware of Creston's absence at the table.

He was moving around the room silently, taking note of my books and items on the shelves that lined the walls. As he reached out and righted a leaning book on my shelf, I realised that this was the first time he'd ever set foot inside my room. He had been inside the main house many times, but never in here, as I had made a point of waiting outside for him every morning we trained. He'd never questioned it or asked to be let in.

Now he was here, and I felt exposed, self-conscious of the items out for him to see. Like the clothes strewn over a chair beside my closet, the closet they should be hanging in, where I wished I had thought to put them before they had arrived.

He paused to look curiously up at the tapestry hanging on the wall.

It was one my mother had made for me, a tree made of flames with a girl sitting at its base, a shimmering gown made of the same ashes that pooled around her, smouldering still. Her hair, too, seemed to be on fire in the darkness of the image. The night sky around the trees was not filled with glimmering stars but instead held a repetition of the fire rune beside another odd rune I had never seen anywhere else.

I went to Creston's side as he looked up at the familiar imagine that I had memorised in my childhood and kept with me always. "My mother said it came to her in a dream, when she was pregnant with me.

She spent the last four months of her pregnancy creating it," I told him softly, keeping my gaze on the tapestry, even as his attention shifted to me. "She claims it was me telling her to be prepared for who I was. She never imagined I would be born of Fire rather than Earth. The day she found out was the day she gave me this." I looked at him then.

His dark eyes were filled with an indiscernible emotion. Pity, perhaps, but there was something else too, something that said he understood.

It made me turn back to the tapestry. "Being different from who everyone else thought I should be hasn't been easy. But my family have always loved me, even if they do worry too much."

Creston turned to me fully, taking my chin in his hand gently and turning my gaze back to him. "They made you magnificent, Firefly. Even if they didn't always understand you, they were still by your side. That's important," he said softly.

I flushed beneath his gaze and his tender touch. "You helped too. You were there when I was being tormented, you've been my Guardien for as long as I can remember, my friend as well. Whatever you're keeping from me, whatever Trae is about to tell me, I can handle it."

He smiled, and something about it made me feel flushed. "Oh, I know you can. You're stronger than most will ever believe." He tucked stray hair back from my face and his fingers lingered against my cheek as his dark eyes bored deeply into my green ones, as though he were searching for something in them. Some rejection of his closeness, his gaze or his touch. He found none.

He opened his mouth as if to say something more but was interrupted by the clattering of the door. He stepped back immediately, dropping his hand to his side, whatever moment between us now over.

I tore my gaze from him, and frowned at the new arrival.

CHAPTER 16

"I'm here! I'm here!" Cleo huffed as she dropped one last thick leather book onto Trae's desk. "Damn, Trae, seriously, you could have asked me to get a lighter book."

"They don't exactly have these things in a lighter edition, Cleo. You obviously managed." He rolled his eyes as he opened the new book, sweeping though it for whatever he needed.

She shrugged. "Yeah, whatever, but next time I'm not being the muscle." She turned her gaze to where I stood, still close enough to Creston to make her eyebrow quirk, but she said nothing.

Carefully I ensured the walls I'd learned to build around my thoughts were securely in place. Her eyes narrowed when I grinned at her, and I knew she'd been trying to find out what was happening.

I wasn't angry, it was just part of who she was, but I didn't like not having privacy in my own head. I couldn't guarantee that either of the males in the room knew to do the same, but that was their problem, though it occurred to me that I should warn Creston about Cleo at some point.

I walked back to the desk covered in old books and fresh notes. "I'm the only one in this room who doesn't know what the hell is going on, and I want answers."

"Technically," Cleo said, walking around the table and over to my bed, testing it out before she sat down. "I just knew I needed to bring that book, so that makes two of us in the dark."

I groaned. "Stop stalling." I switched my attention to Trae, who seemed to be surveying the table with glee, as though the mess of books and papers was some form of artwork. "You. Talk now. Before I lose my mind." I jabbed a finger into his chest.

"Okay, okay. Relax." Trae held his hands up in mock defeat. "Sit down, and I'll go through what I've figured out so far."

I crossed my arms, taking a similar pose to the one Creston still held as he leaned against the wall across the room. "I'll stand. Just tell me why you're all being so weird, what the hell it has to do with me, and why you showed up in my room that night." I frowned at the three of them.

Cleo avoided my gaze.

Creston jerked his chin towards Trae as my gaze landed on him. "Let your friend speak," he said in a quiet, firm, tone.

When he spoke like that, and looked at me like that, it was hard *not* to forget that he was almost three years older than me. Sometimes I did, when he was taunting me, being childish and annoying, but when he shifted back into the Guardien he was renowned for being, it was impossible to forget. I nodded and once again looked to Trae, silent now, as I awaited his answers.

He cleared his throat as all eyes went to him. "Okay, we are all very aware that you, Phi, are different, you're unique and it's always made me curious, but about a month ago I found this." He pointed to one of the books. "It talks about Halflings of Fire, ones that could control any fire, and never be harmed by it. This was back before we were named Elliphae in any written text. I kept digging, and these books…" He paused, gazing down at them reverently. "They all hold some information. It took time and very little sleep, as well as some sneaking and thievery on Cleo's part, but this last book has the last piece. The name for what you are—"

"And it was damn hard to steal that thing from V," Cleo interjected from where she remained on my bed.

"You stole from Veneficus?" I demanded. "Are you crazy?" I shot them both horrified looks.

Trae flicked his hand dismissively. "That's beside the point, I needed the book, he wouldn't give it up, so we took it. That's why Cleo is involved, she's been training with him and has the open access we needed." He shrugged and picked up one of his various sheets of notes.

I exchanged a glance with Creston, who looked just as concerned as I felt.

"Phi, as a Fire-Blessed, we all know you should be able to create and control your own fire," Trae continued, sounding annoyed at the interruption. "Which you do, but here's the issue. You shouldn't be able to touch, control or extinguish fires that aren't your own, and yet, you can." He grinned at me. "You're not just unique because you weren't supposed to be born with Fire. I found vague records, of others who were like you. Still half Fae and half Mortal but apparently you're misbalanced towards Fae. The histories and lore I could find say that Fire-Fae are born in times when the Elliphir and Elliphae are closest to each other." Trae's eyes glimmered with his excitement, as though he could barely contain himself and the knowledge he had gained. "You're powerful Phi."

Creston took advantage of the pause. "It explains what happened earlier. When I touched your arm, Phi, well, if I had held on much longer, I'd have serious damage to my hand. And your eyes...they were all fire."

I bit my lip and stared down at the books laid out on the table in front of me. They were right, it did make sense. I'd always felt more capable than what the other Fire-Blessed seemed to display, and there were things I'd never told anyone I could do because of it.

I felt the tingle of power as Cleo reached out to brush against my mind, trying to see it I was okay.

Ignoring her, I asked, "Does it say anything about being able to sense other fires? Like...muscles in my body can feel them, and I know I could control them all at once if I knew how to reach them all at once. Or about..." I glanced at Creston, and not wanting to see the fear on his face, looked back at Trae, clearing my throat. "Or about the dreams, the ones where I wake on fire." I rubbed my arms, shivering, not from cold but the memory of the shadow hands on my skin.

"That's all in here," Trae replied gently. "Whatever you're seeing in your dreams, that's the reason you are the way you are. Whatever haunts your nightmares is the very thing that caused your creation, for lack of a better term." He smiled at me apologetically. "I wrote down some things I thought you'd need to know." He gestured to the many pieces of paper. "I'll translate them first of course. Or go through them with you, either way."

I nodded. "Okay, sounds manageable." Pausing, I tried to absorb all the new information I was being bombarded with. "But what does it mean? Besides the fact that I'm more of a freak than any of us thought already."

"You're not a freak," Creston growled from where he remained in the corner, and with a glance I saw the frustration in his gaze and tension in his jaw as he gritted his teeth.

I flushed and looked away again.

"Anyway," Trae said, drawing out the word, attempting to alleviate some of the new tension in the room. He tapped on the final book, the one stolen from Veneficus. "This book gives your kind a name. They called you a Phoenix."

"Like the creature?" Creston asked, still not moving closer despite his interest in the subject.

Trae shook his head. "Not quite, she's not going to turn into a giant fire bird, not from anything I've found at least, it's more of a symbolic title. Like the bird, she is of fire, it cannot burn her. And if it did so, it would only cause her rebirth, or something to such an effect. I don't know. There are still hazy details." He frowned down at the stolen book then returned his attention to us. "What I do know is that there's more to the prophecy the Oracle proclaimed today. It's close to the other variations I've found in the history texts. It has a purpose; it is a warning of war and a confirmation that a Phoenix walks among the Elliphae. And the fact that Veneficus had this of all books, makes me wary, there is no way he hasn't read them. He spends as much time learning as I do."

"He was staring at me," I muttered. "After the proclamation of the Oracle, I looked down and found him staring at me. It creeped me out." I frowned.

It made no sense to me. I'd hardly had anything to do with Veneficus, beyond lessons on controlling my magic as I grew. He was weird and intense, but aside from that we'd not interacted.

Something clicked inside my mind and I stared at Trae, eyes wide. "What if he does know? I mean, he trained me as a child. He helped all of us, what if he tested me then, but I don't remember?"

Trae ran his hand over his hair. "It's possible, I guess, but wouldn't he use that information to make sure you knew? Or that you were properly trained? I can't imagine you're an asset in any war without training. The Phoenixes of the past were trained from childhood, but there hasn't been one that I can find recorded in over four hundred years. I doubt even the Ancient Elders would have much memory of them."

Frustrated by the amount of questions we didn't have answers to, I shook my head. "Perhaps he wasn't sure, not until the prophecy was read. I don't know, Trae, you're supposed to be the one with answers." I stepped away from the table as I felt my control over my emotions begin to falter.

Confusion, frustration, anger and fear all threatened to overwhelm me. My fire flared in response, the lanterns growing as I took another step from the table. I had never felt so out of control. I closed my eyes and tried to breathe through it.

"Okay, that's enough for today," Creston said, his voice cutting through the drowning feeling. "You're overwhelming her, Trae, without all the facts. Take Cleo and find more in that book. I'm sure she will be of aid."

I felt rather than saw him move to my side, keeping my eyes closed, trying to keep control of my emotions so my magic didn't break free.

Was this what happened while I slept? My emotions taking control of my fire and letting it burn the shadows I dreamt were touching me?

The shadows had touched me today and my fear had brought my fire.

Creston didn't touch me now, cautious of the heat my skin could carry, of the damage it could cause him.

"Phi?" There was a cautious lilt to Cleo's voice, as though she'd just realised I was losing it.

"Leave her," Creston said, a little harshly, "Just pack up and leave. I have this."

"What gives you the right?"

"She does, Cleopatra, so help Trae collect those books and trust her judgement." His voice was cool and commanding, all Guardien.

I shuddered, still fighting for control. "Please, stop."

She sighed, and I could hear her moving away.

Creston was so close now that I could feel the heat of his body, sure I could reach out and touch him without opening my eyes. The hairs on my arms stood up with his proximity, the air between us crackling with something intangible. I took another deep breath and felt the tension inside my head easing.

I opened my eyes, to watch as Cleo and Trae started closing the books and stacking his notes into them.

She turned suddenly, pinning Creston with an exasperated look. "We *are* hurrying," she grumbled as she closed up the last heavy book.

He recoiled, surprised by her answering whatever was spinning in his mind as he'd watched them. He pressed his lips together into a thin line as she laughed, the other half of the conversation lost to the rest of us, as she again answered him.

"Yes, yes, I do."

"*Fuck,*" he muttered.

CHAPTER 17

I realised as Creston swore that I had completely forgotten, again, to warn him about Cleo's abilities. My eyes narrowed as I looked at her, wondering what she could be reading from him that would make him so wary.

"I can keep things to myself, Guardien, but don't push it," Cleo said finishing their obvious silent conversation aloud, while she and Trae started heaving the books on to a small cart Trae had created, vines still attached to the floor beneath it to hold it steady.

Recovering from his surprise, Creston crossed his arms again, as his attention suddenly caught by something else. A glance proved that he was scowling at Trae as they packed up the books, but as I opened my mouth to ask what was wrong, he spoke. "You couldn't have made one of those on the way over here? Instead, you made me carry those ancient bricks like a pack mule."

Trae flushed and turned away. "I didn't think of it then, obviously." His back straightened and he turned to look at Creston again. "Why? Were they too much for you to carry, Guardien? I thought you guys were supposed to be strong, or is that just a show to help you get girls?" There was a challenge in his tone and an open invitation for aggression in his smirk.

"You were the one who refused to carry more than two books," Creston replied in a low voice before stepping back and lowering himself to sit in Cleo's vacated spot on my bed.

I frowned, glancing between the two of them, unsure where the new tension between them came from.

Cleo sighed dramatically and dropped the last book into the cart with a thud. "Can we go now? I'm getting tired of whatever the hell you two think you're fighting over. We have things to do, and I estimate we only have the rest of the day before V realises that book is missing. I have to get it back before I work with him in the morning." She opened up the door and shot me a look that promised I'd be seeing her later.

Trae shot an annoyed look at her, but relented. The desk he had created disappeared, the vines slithered back into the earth where they belonged. He stepped towards the door, looking at me over his shoulder. "If you need me, I'll be at home."

I nodded and watched as he left, the cart moving behind him without needing to be pulled, following his will.

Cleo rolled her eyes and blew me a kiss. "I'll see you later, Phi. Don't worry, I still love you even if you're a weird fire bird." She shifted and pointed a warning finger at Creston before she slipped outside. "Watch it." As the door closed behind her I could hear her shouts as she ran from the house. "Hey, Trae! Wait up."

I sighed, still a little overwhelmed at all the new information, and glanced at Creston, his expression dark.

He picked up a pillow, rising to his feet and holding it up against his chest. "Hit it."

I blinked at him. "I don't need you confusing me right now too, Cres."

"I'm not. You're losing it, you need an outlet." He folded the pillow and held it firmly against his chest. "Show me you pay some attention when I'm teaching you."

I considered refusing him and boxing all my feelings away, but I didn't want that, I wanted to feel better. I moved over to him, lashing out at the pillow with furious hits that surprised even me.

Creston didn't move or flinch, taking on the impact of every hit through the pillow, blow after blow, until I was panting and starting to sweat. I stopped, running a hand over my brow to get rid of some of the sweat.

It wasn't as calming as truly unleashing my fire would be, but I had never been able to do that and wasn't sure I ever could, so this would do.

The darkness in his expression had faded when I looked up at him, as the ghost of a grin crossed his lips. "Better?"

I nodded. "Yes."

He tossed the pillow back where it belonged, sitting down on the edge of the bed. "So..."

I raised an eyebrow at him. "What?"

He sat up straighter, slipping his fingers though his dark hair, and I couldn't help but notice that the lanterns gave the black strands a red tinge. "Your friend doesn't like me all that much."

He was changing the topic, drawing me away from the things likely to keep me on edge, and I wasn't sure if it was a good idea or a bad one. "Trae has never been quiet with his thoughts."

"And Cleo is a telepath? Would have appreciated a warning on that front." He looked exasperated, pink appearing on his cheekbones.

I was unable to keep a smile from appearing, and was desperately curious to find out what Cleo had heard in his mind. "Firstly, he doesn't have to like you, I guess, but he's probably overtired and lashing out because of it. He doesn't know you the way I do. You've always been around me, but never around them." I shrugged and sat down at the head of the bed, pulling my knees up to my chest and leaning back against the vine covered metal of the headboard. "Secondly, I'm sorry. I should have warned you."

Creston watched me wordlessly as I got comfortable. "Whose idea was the steel?" he asked after a few long moments of silence, running his hand over the blanket on the bed. "I can feel it beneath the vines and leaves."

"My older brother Zavier, he put it in here today. I keep burning my beds in my sleep." I squirmed awkwardly against the bed.

"Because you're having nightmares, right? You never told me about that. Trae did," he said in what sounded suspiciously like a hurt tone, frowning.

I shrugged. "I didn't want you to think I was weirder than you already knew, or that I wasn't in control of my powers."

He shook his head and moved closer. "I wouldn't have thought that, I would only have been worried about you hurting yourself." He touched my leg gently, offering support I didn't know I needed.

Staring at him, I realised he was someone I should have trusted with the knowledge sooner. He was my friend, always there when I needed him, no matter the circumstances. Looking down at my pants and fiddling with a loose thread, I explained, "They started years ago, and they've grown more frequent lately, but I haven't had one since we started training. I think because I'm too exhausted when I go to bed, so I go straight to a deep sleep. It's been relaxing, not having to wake up on the floor and worry that someone was too close." I pulled at the fabric of my pants as I met his gaze again.

His expression melted into something close to pity. "I'm sorry you had to deal with it alone, but at least Trae might be offering answers now," he said, his voice softer now. "And if he's right, then the Oracles will send for you sooner or later. They, of all Elliphae, would have to know the identity of someone who is something important." He took my hand and tugged me towards him.

I moved so I sat beside him, as he wrapped his arm around me, and I laid my head on his shoulder, my treacherous heart pounding in my chest at the physical contact.

"I understand if you're unsure, but whatever happens I'll be here, like always." He squeezed me gently before moving back so he could look at me again. "It's still early, why don't we go inside and get you something to eat, then we can go for a walk or go swimming. The water is still warm enough in the cove." He tucked a curl behind my ear gently and smiled at me. "Whatever you want to do you keep you busy today, while we wait on more answers."

I smiled back and nodded. "I'd like that." Distraction was something I could handle. More distractions provided by Creston? That was another challenge entirely. He was a distraction simply by being so close, in a way I'd never quite seen before.

"It's settled." He got to his feet and pulled me up with him. "Food first. Then fun." He headed for the door, pulling it open, only to chuckle suddenly as he found Niko standing on the other side, his hand raised and ready to knock on the door.

Niko's eyes widened and a grin spread across his face. "Creston! What are you doing here? Did you come to go with us to the testing ceremony?"

I groaned and clapped my hands over my face.

With everything happening I had forgotten that today was Niko's eighth birthday, the day he would have his powers tested to officially define his elemental gifts, and reveal any other gifts he may have.

I let my hands drop from my face and looked back at the two of them standing by the door, frustrated at myself for being so forgetful about something so important in Niko's life.

Creston glanced at me and shrugged, looking back down at my brother. "I am now, buddy, but your sister needs some breakfast first. We'll meet you inside, okay?" He roughed up my grinning brother's hair.

"Sure! I'll go tell Mum and Dad." He scurried out of sight, his face flushed with excitement.

Creston chuckled again. "He's very energetic." He looked to me again, smiling. "Looks like our plans are on hold. For now," he said, his eyes darkening. "Come on." He nodded towards the still open doorway.

I ran my fingers over my poorly bound my hair, pushing myself to my feet to step outside with him. "I can't believe I forgot."

"You've got a lot on your mind, I doubt Niko will even know you forgot. And we're going now, so there's nothing to worry about." He led me towards the house, opening the front door open for me before following me in.

I headed into the kitchen, where my family waited.

CHAPTER 18

I paused in the doorway at the end of the hall, half a smile tugging at my lips as I watched Niko trying to climb onto a stool and take hasty bites of an apple at the same time. It was constantly surprising that while my little brother never seemed to stop while he ate, he never seemed to choke either.

My parents sat side by side at the table, finishing up their breakfast. Both of them looked up as Creston and I entered the room.

My father's smile faltered slightly as he took in Creston behind me. "Vaelle, what brings you to our home at this hour? If it's to pass word of the Oracles, we have already been told, and will address it at a later time," he said firmly, face hard as he stood, wandering over to rest a hand on Niko's shoulder. "Today is Nikolias' day." The warning was clear in his tone.

"I was here to see Seraphine, but Niko has asked me to come to his testing, I accepted the offer. Provided that it is okay with you, Commander?" He stood by my side and smiled stiffly, his posture rigid while his tone remained relaxed but respectful.

I glanced at the two males, unease crawling along my spine standing between them. I'd never really paid much attention to the way Creston's demeanour changed around my father, as though he were always on edge, always waiting for an order to obey. It struck me as odd, even if my father had trained him to be the Guardien he was today.

My father nodded, his eyes never leaving the male beside me. "You are more than welcome to join us, and Varis is acceptable while I am with my family."

"Thank you." Creston ran his hand over his hair before he looked to me, raising an eyebrow, then nudged his chin towards the kitchen as he leaned against the doorframe.

I rolled my eyes but headed into the kitchen, grabbing a ripe peach from the fruit bowl. I glared at him pointedly as I bit into it.

My mother laughed, watching the two of us. I flushed, realising we were far from alone, and leaned against the bench as she spoke. "So Phi, are Trae and Cleo coming with us as well?"

I looked at my mother and shook my head. "Uh, no, they're busy today, but they wish him luck of course." I took another bite of the fruit in my hand.

"Doesn't seem like all that long ago that the three of you were facing these tests yourselves," my father said, a small smile ghosting his lips.

"Time does seem to escape even us, my love," my mother laughed softly.

My father rolled his eyes in response, rubbing at the back of his neck. "What else do we need to organise for after the testing?"

"Phi, were you nervous when you went for your testing?" Niko asked, catching my attention as he finished his apple, wiping juice from his chin and dropping the core to the ground, where vines appeared and pulled it back into the earth.

Where it went, truly I didn't know, but it was gone. What came from the earth went back to the earth and all that.

I smiled and nodded. "I was. But it was all okay."

Creston pushed off the doorframe and came to crouch in front of my brother. "We're all nervous when we go for our test, Niko, it's a normal reaction, but you'll be fine, I promise. You have great control over your powers." He rubbed Niko's shoulder and smiled down at him.

Niko beamed up at him. "Thank you, Creston." He slid down off the stool. "It's nearly time! I have to go get changed." He ran out of the kitchen and disappeared down the hall.

Creston watched him with a strange look, shaking his head before turning to me again. "So much energy."

I laughed softly. "It gets old at around sunrise, trust me. I do love him though."

He flashed me a smile. "Of course you do, he's your brother." His smile faltered at the word, his expression becoming guarded, as though it would stop me from noticing the change in him, the sudden pain. But I knew where he had gone. The pain he hid.

He'd told me once what'd happened, when Niko was just a toddler and Creston had caught me crying, worried that my little brother's powers would be wrong like mine, or that he would become twisted and be taken away.

Creston had held me and told me that it would be okay. That he had been frightened too....but it had been his older brother who was taken and not him, even though his brother had been eight at the time, weeks from the very testing Niko was so excited to be part of. Creston had been six when it happened, and despite how young he had been I knew he remembered it clearly.

Our memories were perfect almost from the moment we turned three. Whether it was a Faerie characteristic or not, I wasn't sure, but it was our reality. Creston had only spoken of it that one time, but it weighed on him still.

In little moments I noticed it, the way his jaw set, his fingers twitched. The way his eyes glassed over as he relived something no one else could.

I sidled over to him and touched his arm, drawing him back from whatever space his mind had gone. "Don't do it to yourself, Cres. It's not on you," I assured him quietly as he turned to stare blankly at my hand on his arm, as though it were alien to him.

He didn't speak or move, still trapped in his memories.

"Cres? Hey." I squeezed his arm. "Look at me Creston."

Slowly, so slowly, he lifted his gaze and let it lock onto mine.

I could see the pain in the midnight blue depth of them. "It happens, you were just a kid, and it isn't your fault that it wasn't you."

He watched me for a long moment, weighing my words, before he nodded once. He closed his eyes and took a shaky breath. "I'm good," he muttered, voice rough, and opened his eyes. The pain was still raw on his face, but he no longer looked haunted. He cleared his throat and tried again. "I'm really okay, Phi, I just...ah....had a moment." He tried to smile but it didn't reach his eyes.

I scanned his face, knowing that he was lying, but also knowing him well enough that I knew forcing the issue would only make him shut down further. "It's fine, Cres, I got you." I rubbed his arm before letting my hand drop.

He caught my hand in his as it fell. "Thank you, Firefly, I mean it." He squeezed my hand gently then let it drop back to my side, running his now free hand though his hair.

"Let's go wait outside for Niko, okay?" I offered, trying to give him an out. Most Earth-Blessed felt calmer when surrounded by nature. "I'm sure he won't take much longer, and he'll want to get there first. My parents can catch up later." I took one last bite of my peach as I turned away. Unlike Niko, I couldn't make it disappear into the ground. Instead, I placed it into a bowl my mother had for such scraps.

Scraps that my family only added to so I wasn't the only one. Mother claimed that she added them to the garden, but we both knew she could nurture any plant without the need of the compost the Enlightened used on their own small gardens. Regardless, I was thankful for their desire to make me feel less out of place among my own blood.

I licked my fingers clean as I turned back to Creston and headed towards the door. We barely made it into the hall before Niko came barrelling towards us. Creston stepped back to allow my little brother to slip between us. My friend looked away from the grin on my brother's face, a pained expression flitting across his features.

"We're going now?" he asked me excitedly, tugging on my arm.

Giving Creston the illusion of privacy and pretending I hadn't noticed, I smiled down at my brother. "Yes, we're going to leave first, Mum and Dad will follow. How does that sound?"

Niko beamed ear to ear, his eyes alive with excitement. "Great! Let's go, I want to get there before everyone else does." He darted around me, heading out the door, looking back at us expectantly when we weren't right on his heels.

I looked over my shoulder at Creston. "Looks like we're going to end up on our second run for the day, trying to keep up with him."

Shaking himself from his long-held grief, Creston winked at me. "I'm sure I can keep up."

CHAPTER 19

We didn't truly leave until Niko was sure he had everything, returning to the house three times before we left.

He and Creston spent the entire run to the Ceremonial Temple competing, taunting each other and using their Blessings to slow the other down.

I ran close by, but let them have their fun. I knew that Creston was holding back to allow Niko small victories on the way. It made me smile to see them laughing and calling out torment to the losing member of the pair. Their happiness was welcome, but hardly a distraction from the other events of the day that gnawed at my insides.

I couldn't shake the sensation that Trae had tugged at a thread that would unravel more than we could handle, my previously simple life tumbling towards something I didn't recognise, and I wasn't sure whether to be afraid or excited.

All three of us came to a stop as we reached the edge of the testing grounds, settled outside the looming stone hall that was the Ceremonial Temple. Others had already arrived and lingered around the space, much to Niko's disappointment.

The Elders stood by the side of the field, including my father's older brother, my pensive uncle, Broderick Nantir. He nodded towards us when he noticed our arrival before turning away and joining in conversation with other Elders and prominent Elliphae from each element. Those who had undoubtedly set up each of the tests that Niko would have to pass or fail to define his powers.

The tests wouldn't be harmful for him. They were controlled environments where he would be asked to complete tasks that are simple, if one held the correct elemental power in their veins. Each station resembled a small circular bench, and each bench was covered for the moment, but I knew what they held.

For Water, one must bring the water into the first dish before moving it to a second dish, then lift it all above both dishes. They would return it to the dishes before moving it back and forth at varying levels, to show total control of the element in it's raw form.

The test was similar for each element.

For Air, you must be able to move an object around the circle. Earth was the creation of a plant and the moulding of that life into something else, an object of the child's choice, usually a bowl or a chair, nothing that was too large. Fire would be a plain bench, no bowls or any other items on the stone. A Fire-Blessed would create a fire on that surface, to prove they didn't need it to be burning anything for the flames to exist. From there it was a light show, creating images within the flames, showing one's ability to mould what can't be touched.

Niko was bouncing on the balls of his feet, a grin brightening his flushed face. "They have everything set up already." He wandered a little closer, as if he were drawn to the testing stage.

Creston rested a hand on his shoulder and held him back from going too far before he was formally allowed to do so. "Relax little one, you'll be set free on those things soon enough. We have to wait for both your parents to be here, remember?" His hand flexed on Niko's shoulder in a move that was half support and half a massage.

I stepped forward and knelt by his side. "Cres is right, Niko, we have to wait for Mum. You're not going to miss out on anything, this is all for you. Your big birthday. The one we've all been waiting for."

Niko nodded but kept his gaze fixed away from us, on the Elders and other Elliphae who were arriving to witness his testing. I looked at Creston over the top of him and smiled, rolling my eyes at my little brother as I stood.

He winked at me. "You were probably just as excited for your testing. Everyone usually is, a chance to flaunt what you've got."

I felt as my smile faltered as I thought about it, turning my focus to the circle again, looking at the Fire bench. I didn't remember ever having been excited to perform for the audience that had gathered to watch me, just as they now gathered for Niko.

No, I hadn't felt anything other than fear. My testing was a confirmation to many that my mother was disloyal, and I had borne that weight, until the moment the first flames had filled the space I needed them to. From there I had felt nothing but peace. I was happy as I used my Blessing. As a child it was my first true chance to work my magic, in an environment built to determine my powers.

I remembered giggling as I created a bird in the flames. A bird that I had sent soaring around the circle and into the sky before it swept down, crashing back onto the bench, returning to resemble a small camp fire.

The animal I'd chosen had felt unimportant then, but with Trae's new claims about my powers I wondered if it had been as spontaneous as I'd felt it had been at the time. I shook my head to free myself from the thoughts of a day long gone, looking back at Creston and my brother.

Creston gave me a questioning look, and I knew then that he had been watching me the whole time.

I flushed but offered no explanation to him. Niko was watching everyone moving in and around the circle intently, taking it all in.

My mother arrived and stopped by us briefly before my father joined her, before taking Niko over to the Elders to wait for the ceremony to begin.

I scanned the settling crowd. There were at least a hundred people there by that point, Elliphae and Enlightened alike. I was surprised when my gaze fell on Elijah, the leader of the Enlightened.

My surprise was not so much for Elijah, but the male beside him. It took me a moment but I recognised him, as one of the mortals who had arrived weeks ago on the Reaping Ship. He was watching the Elliphae, who were making the final preparations to the testings, arms crossed over a broad chest.

He was tall, as tall as Creston if not taller, his body lean muscle. He was attractive too, with cropped dark hair and a chiselled jaw darkened by the shadow of a beard. His skin was tanned a warm brown colour, one I suspected came from many hours on the deck of the ship he had arrived on.

As I examined him, his gaze shifted suddenly, my gaze locking with the striking storm blue of his eyes, clear even from where I stood.

My spine straightened as his eyes swept over me slowly, surveying me with that odd dark gaze, that was somehow similar to the blue I enjoyed so much in Creston, but with one great difference.

Where Creston's gaze was comforting, warm and enticing, this male's was something else entirely. Cold, calculating, menacing.

He eventually met my eyes again. I clenched my jaw and stared back, even as I felt the hairs on my neck raise to attention under the cool scrutiny of that gaze. *Who the hell is he?* some part of my mind whispered. I nearly yelped as a hand stroked my arm.

"Phi? They're starting." Creston's gentle tone drew me back, bring-

ing my attention to the ring as Niko stepped forward and was presented.

I heard the words that were spoken but paid no attention to them as
I glanced again at the male who stood by Elijah, only to find he was no
longer watching me. Instead, his gaze burned as he watched another.

Creston.

I frowned and turned my gaze to him as well.

Creston was paying the stranger no mind, watching Niko intently,
his eyebrows drawn with concern as he was left to begin. His hand slid
down my arm and his fingers laced with mine as Niko started his tests.
He squeezed my hand, mistaking my anxious state as concern for my
brother.

I looked across the circle again and found...nothing. Whoever he
was, he had disappeared. I studied the crowd in search of him but it
was a futile search. He had left without Elijah and before Niko had
even cleared the first test.

I turned my attention back to my brother, but my mind was elsewhere. Questions cluttered my thoughts and the whole ceremony
passed in a blur. Did Trae have answers? Who was that male? What was
I supposed to do with so many unanswerable questions about myself?
Round and round my mind spun. Only the sound of others clapping
broke my trance, making me realise I'd zoned out the whole thing.

It was over already and Niko had proven himself as an
Earth-Blessed. I looked to my little brother.

He practically glowed with pride as he ran to our parents, throwing
himself into their waiting arms.

Beside me Creston smiled proudly at Niko's display of happiness.
"He did really well," he murmured as he turned to look down at me,
still holding my hand.

I smiled, nodding. "Of course. Niko has always known how to

use Earth properly, the rest of the family were always helping him." I looked back to my family.

Zavier had appeared and was standing by them as Niko talked animatedly. I couldn't hear his words but I knew he would be talking about each part of his test in detail.

I felt my smile fade as I looked at them, a pang in my chest forming. They were all so similar and I was such a stark contrast within them.

I'd never looked like I really belonged with them, not that I hadn't been loved or given my love in return. But I was an oddity against their shared darker colouring, with my paler complexion and vivid red hair. Both of my brothers shared our father's warm brown complexion and our mother's bronzed hair. They had pieces of our parents that shone in them so brightly, and while I was told I had my mothers smile, it didn't show the same way as everything else did in them. They matched, they fit.

All blessed with Earth, not a drop of Fire within them. While I drowned in it.

CHAPTER 20

A pit opened up in my stomach, despair suddenly overwhelming me. I turned away from the sight of them quickly, dropping Creston's hand as I stepped away from him too. I couldn't breathe. I needed to leave, to get away from the way I was feeling.

"I've got to go," I muttered before I took off, aware of Creston calling my name before my speedy walk broke into a full on run. I tore down the road and kept going, stopping only once I hit the wall that was the Divide. I paused, my muscles and lungs burning as I gasped for air. I laid my hands against my thighs and leaned there for a few moments as my breathing started to slow.

When I could breathe again without serious effort I stood up straighter, resting my hands on my hips. I looked towards the stretch of the wall I usually passed through, deciding whether or not to go through to the other side now, to seek more peace where few would think to look for me.

"Want to tell me what the fuck that was all about?"

I jerked around at the familiar tenor of Creston's voice, almost horrified that he'd caught me unawares in a very similar situation to the first time.

He stood a few feet from me with his arms crossed over his chest, his face barely flushed from the run he'd obviously taken to have caught me so quickly.

I looked away, unable to level myself under his concerned gaze. I kicked at the ground gently. "I needed space, I couldn't breathe."

"Uh huh. Firefly, how about we try that again, and this time you tell me what's really going on." Creston took a step towards me.

I backed up against the wall as I looked at him again, the branches rigid against my back. "I just...I couldn't." The words seemed to spill out, and as much as I wanted to bite them back, they would not stay. "I was looking at my family and all of a sudden I was just overwhelmed. By all of it, but mostly by how little I seem to belong with them. They just look like a whole family without me, and even when I'm standing with them, I know I just look out of place. Like a dead tree in a lush forest, I am a part of the life around me, I just don't belong to it."

Creston sighed sympathetically and stepped closer to me, putting a hand on the wall on either side of my face, pinning me in place as he leaned forward. "Seraphine, your family loves you. You're so lucky to have that. I wish I had that," he almost whispered, resting his forehead against mine for just a moment, before pulling back again to look down at me.

That buzz returned to my skin where he touched me, and I was painfully aware of how close he was, surrounded by the scent and heat of his body, making my heart pound.

"All my family is gone, you know that. I only really had my grandfather, and even he wasn't sure how to be what I lost." He frowned down at me. "After my brother was taken...my father seemed to slowly wither away, especially after my mother disappeared. Your family doesn't care that your magic is different from theirs, or that you have such a glorious mane of red hair." He ran his fingers over my bound curls, his gaze focused on the hair, as though he were somehow mesmerised by it.

My cheeks burned with new warmth as his gaze returned to mine, heat stirring in the depth of his eyes as his hand slid from my hair to cup my cheek in his palm gently. "There is absolutely nothing about you that means you don't belong in a family that only loves. Fuck whoever made you believe that you don't belong there, they're wrong."

Distantly, part of me was reminded that I had, in fact, slept with one of my childhood bullies as an adult, but I pushed the thought away as quickly as it came, eyes only on the male in front of me.

My heart thundered in my chest as he leaned even closer, barely inches between us. Suddenly, all my anxiety and panic was gone, swallowed up by the feeling of being so close to Creston. I looked up at him as I attempted to keep my breathing slow enough not to be embarrassingly obvious.

There was no one in my life that affected me the way that he did. I had somehow missed when he'd started to effect me this way, but I couldn't remember a time where his touch, and closeness, hadn't ignited a burn inside me I was sure only he could soothe.

He stared down at me, gauging my response to his proximity, his lips curving into a small grin as he leaned in, pressing his lips against my forehead softly.

I closed my eyes for a moment, enjoying the intimacy and gentleness in the action, before he pulled away, tucking nonexistent stray stands of my hair back behind my ear, almost as if he simply sought a reason to keep touching me.

Does he feel it too? I wondered.

"Better?" he asked, watching me almost shyly.

I sighed and nodded, clearing my throat before attempting to speak again. "Yeah, I am. Thank you. I don't know what's wrong with me, I haven't lost it like that since..." I frowned, trailing off at the unhappy memory.

"Since those kids had you cornered the week after your testing," he finished for me in a gentle tone. "I helped you then too."

I met his gaze and smiled slightly. "You did. Maybe it has something to do with you being a Guardien." *But you make me feel safe,* I added the last to myself as I rested my hands on his chest gently.

His jaw clenched at the contact. "You're stronger than you give yourself credit for, Firefly. Being upset and afraid, or even just overwhelmed, doesn't diminish your strength. It just gives it a chance to be used." He drew me in closer and kissed my forehead again.

The gesture was comforting and more familiar than I expected it to be. I wanted more but didn't know how, or what, to say to get it. So I said nothing, flushing and looking to my hands as they rested on his chest. I could feel the warmth of him beneath his clothes, as well as the lines of the leather sheaths on his chest. I knew if I slid my hands down I would find the blades he kept there, but I didn't.

"Why don't you date?" I asked suddenly, turning my gaze back up to meet his midnight blue stare.

He looked shocked by my question for a moment, then embarrassed. He took a step back away from me, breaking the intimacy we had shared.

My hands drifted along his chest before they dropped to my sides.

"I used to," he said, looking away from me. "I've dated a few who were in my Earth magic development classes, among others, but I haven't dated since I became a Guardien." He shrugged and once again ran his fingers though his thick dark locks. "I'm also not in the habit of having my relationships on display for everyone."

Three years? Even with my poor attempts, *I* had still seen people in that time. "Can I ask why it's been so long?"

"Nope. Definitely not," He shook his head and gestured for me to move around him back in the direction I'd run from. "Come on, we need to get back. Niko will wonder where you've gone." He waited with his arm outstretched until I walked past him.

"I don't want him worried about me, he's just a kid, and he already worries too much," I said as we walked slowly back along the dirt pathway that led from the wall, trying to ignore the sting of disappointment I felt without him close.

As though he didn't want distance between us either, Creston walked close enough to my side for our hands to brush with each step, keeping the crackle of tension alive between us. "He's probably still too wrapped up in all the excitement to truly notice that you're gone, so long as we're back soon it will be fine. I'd be more worried about a stern look from Elijah for the unexplained exit. You might even earn one of his famous glares." He turned to me and did his best to copy the look Elijah had perfected over the years, when he was suspicious of a person. And he always seemed to be that way.

I laughed and shook my head. "You've spent far too much of your life receiving that look if you can mimic it that well, Cres."

He threw me a crooked grin. "I have a secret bad streak. And you don't know everything about me, Firefly." He winked.

A bolt of heat tore through me, my mouth suddenly dry. "I'm not even going to touch that topic today."

We laughed together as we continued back towards the testing grounds.

CHAPTER 21

By the time we returned the crowd had thinned out noticeably, only close friends left around my family, with the exception of Elijah, who was waiting with the male I had noticed during Niko's tests.

They stood together to the side of the testing circle. Elijah was speaking softly to the male as we headed towards the group with my family. Elijah noticed our return and quickly headed towards us, cutting us off before we could get too far.

He smiled at me, but it was too tight. I knew then that whatever he needed was likely going to be unpleasant. The last time I'd been on the receiving end of this same smile was when he had persuaded me to help him move boxes of records from his home to the Enlightened housings. The records turned out to be hundreds of thick leather-bound books. I wasn't sure my back had ever recovered.

"Seraphine, is everything okay? You left in quite a hurry before." As if on queue his face morphed into the very look Creston had mimicked on our return. I heard Creston stifle a laugh behind me and glared at him as he turned away to further hide his laughter.

I smiled at Elijah as convincingly as I could manage. "Oh, everything is just fine. Not to worry. Was there something you needed? I'd like to join my family."

"Yes actually," he said, apparently *not* convinced. "As you know, we recently had an arrival of three men of oblivious origin. This is Kylan." He gestured to the male beside him. "He is the youngest of the arrivals."

"Hi." He gave me a small smile and wave, obviously uncomfortable with the attention, at odds with the focus I'd seen while he had watched Creston and I from across the testing field.

"Hey, I'm Phi." I smiled at him as warmly as I could, but I couldn't ignore the cold knot forming in my stomach in his presence. It wasn't a feeling I could place but one I knew I had felt before.

"Seraphine, I would like you to act as a sort of transitional escort for Kylan, if he has any questions about anything you will make yourself available to answer them. He will be assimilating on his own first."

My eyebrows shot up as I felt Creston shift a little closer to my side. "What? I know nothing about helping a transition into our world. Don't you have someone more experienced to help him? No offence to Kylan, of course." I spared a glance at him.

He just smiled at me. I think it was supposed to be warm, but it never reached his eyes, which up close, were a mix of grey, blue and green, like a storm over a sea. His gaze was appraising but not welcoming, and it made me anxious.

"I apologise if my phrasing was not clear enough for you, Seraphine, but this is not a question," Elijah said firmly. "The plans are already in place. We all commit to taking on this responsibility, and you were recommended, as you have not taken on the task with any of the arrivals before, it's your turn. I understand that today is an important day for your family, so I will apologise for the timing." Elijah nailed me with censuring stare, "But I will expect you to take this seriously." He turned to Creston. "That goes for you as well, Guardien Vaelle."

Creston hesitated for a moment, looking to me before nodding. "Of course, Elijah. Wouldn't dream of being a detriment to another's ability in living among us."

Elijah's eyes narrowed but he nodded and clasp his hands together, letting them hang down in front of him. "Then it is settled. I look forward to hearing how you help. Come along, Kylan."

Kylan nodded. "I am very eager to learn about this place and your people." He smiled again, but this time his gaze shifted to Creston. "It was a pleasure meeting you too, Creston."

He nodded in response, placing his hand on my lower back as he took a step closer to me, away from the male.

Elijah walked away first, heading towards The Square, the opposite direction to the mortal housings. Where they were headed was the least of my problems. Why Kylan made me so anxious? That was closer to the top ten.

"Let's go rejoin your family, Phi, looks like everyone is leaving now and they've already seen us standing here," Creston said, using the hand still on my lower back to guide me over to my family, dropping his hand only as we neared them.

"There you two are, we thought you'd disappeared on us." My mother smiled brightly at our reappearance. "Creston, would you like to join us back at the house for lunch? We're going to celebrate Niko doing so very well on his testing and his birthday." She reached out and stroked my little brother's hair as he moved past her to stand in front of Creston.

"Please come," my brother begged, grabbing the bottom of Creston's shirt. "Dad says that now that my powers are settled I can start learning to fight with them and you're a Guardien. So you could teach me." He practically vibrated with excitement as he looked up at him.

Creston laughed and shook his head. "I don't know about that, Niko, but I do know I'll come to help you celebrate your big day. You took your tests like a pro."

He beamed up at him. "I did, didn't I? It was so cool, I didn't even mess up once."

I smiled down at him as my father joined us. "Let's move this gathering back home, shall we? We have food and drinks waiting for us there." He stood behind my little brother and rubbed his shoulders. "What do you think, Niko?"

He didn't need any more encouragement than that. "Last one home has to do all the chores," he cried over his shoulder as he took off in a dead run towards home.

Zavier and I shared a look before taking off to humour our little brother in a race, knowing that Creston and the rest would soon follow for the celebration.

Neither of us wanted the chores.

CHAPTER 22

I pressed my back against the cool stone wall outside my bedroom and watched my brothers as they caught their breath. I took some satisfaction in my lack of breathlessness, proof that my efforts with Creston were starting to pay off.

Zavier eyed me suspiciously from where he stood hunched over, his hands on his thighs, as he caught his breath. "Since when are you so fit, little sister?" he huffed as he straightened and ran his hands over his short hair.

I grinned. "It's been a long time since we last raced. I, however, race him all the time." I shrugged it off and glanced over at Niko.

His face was flushed from the run but otherwise he was grinning ear to ear. It really was his day. The look on Zavier's face told me he didn't believe that excuse, but he didn't press.

"Well little man, you won. And looks like Zav is the loser and therefore stuck with the chores for the week," I gloated.

"Hey! There is no way I was the loser, it was you!" Zavier objected as Niko giggled.

"No way, it was all on you. I got here first."

Our brother's giggles continued as we argued, and we remained like that for the few minutes, before everyone else arrived; Niko laughing,

Zavier and I bickering over where the finish line was and who got there first. I was about ready for a hand-to-hand resolution when the others began to arrive.

I punched Zavier's arm gently. "We'll share it all."

He begrudgingly nodded in agreement, glancing at the arriving people before disappearing inside the house. My elder brother had never enjoyed crowds.

While he disappeared, Niko directed people around the house, showing them to where they'd set up a fire pit for the celebration of this day. The day my brother was safe from the Elliphir.

My parents stood close together, fingers interlocked as they watched Niko corral the guests, peaceful expressions on their faces. They were finally without fear their youngest child would vanish.

I smiled for them, glad that they could have this time again. I could hardly imagine carrying such a burden, so much fear to shoulder with each child they raised. Part of me wasn't sure it was a weight I could carry.

"What are you thinking?" Creston asked softly as he stopped beside me, following my gaze over to my family and the guests moving around the house out of sight.

I turned to him, as my parents too disappeared out of sight. "That my parents can finally sleep at night without the fear that their child may be gone when they wake." I tucked some stray hair behind my ear as I spoke, more out of habit than necessity.

Creston smiled, but it wasn't right, I didn't see it in his eyes, and it faded far too quickly. Those sapphire pools were dark with something else again.

I frowned. "Cres?"

He looked away from me and ran his fingers through his hair roughly. "It just occurred to me that my parents never got that day. I don't even know if they ever expected to." He shook his head. "I don't know that my father really paid attention to the fact that I was still there."

My stomach dropped, realising too late who I'd been speaking too. I didn't know a lot but I knew enough to remember that Creston's older brother had been taken mere weeks before his testing. I didn't know what happened to his parents after that, but I knew they were gone. I reached out to him, touching his arm, drawing his attention back to me, "I'm sorry."

He looked at me for a long time, pain in his eyes even though he managed to keep his expression blank. He swallowed and let out a harsh breath. "I-I haven't....talked about it in so long. Some days I can almost forget." He closed his eyes for a moment. "Today seems to be keeping it right on the surface."

"Come on, they won't miss us for a while." I tugged his arm and led him into the safety provided by the stone walls of my bedroom. The candles and fireplace lit as I dropped his hand and stepped inside ahead of him, holding the door open for him.

He hesitated for a moment before following me inside and crossing the room. He pressed his back against the wall and slid downwards, vines appeared from the ground around his feet and rose up to meet him halfway, winding themselves into a seat before he reached them.

He startled when his thighs hit the new piece of furniture, as though he hadn't been aware he'd summoned it. When the vines settled he leaned forward, pressing his elbows into his thighs as he dropped his head in his hands.

I felt a pang of jealousy at his absentminded use of functional magic as I closed the door gently, silently moving over to sit on the edge of my bed. Crossing my legs to sit facing him, I stayed silent to leave him to his thoughts for the time being, knowing he would decide when, and if, he wanted to talk about his family.

CHAPTER 23

When he eventually looked up it wasn't at me, but at the tapestry that hung on the wall across the room. "I never really understood, when I was a kid, why my parents were so afraid to say goodnight to us, and so happy in the mornings to greet us. I thought it was some sort of exciting game. I can remember thinking that. That Raphael and I must have gone on adventures while we slept. And that's why it was such a big deal. I was so, so wrong." His voice cracked.

My heart lurched, realising what he was about to tell me, the door he was about to open inside himself to help me understand.

"One morning I woke to the sound of screams. My mother's screams. I didn't understand at first. They wouldn't speak to me, my mother wouldn't stop crying. I needed my big brother to give me the answers. It was only when I looked for him then that I realised he wasn't there. That he was why my mother wouldn't stop crying. My brother was gone. I saw the mark that meant they'd taken him, there was no warning before that night, he was just gone. For months I asked my parents *Where's Raph? Why can't I play with Raph?* My mother hardly spoke after that day, I don't really remember seeing her eat either. She barely ever looked at me, or anything else. She was young, barely older than I am when she had him. So young to be a mother twice, at least for our kind. Some piece of her broke losing her first child, and it never healed." He finally looked over at me then, just for a moment.

Long enough for me to see it, the pit of agony that lived within him.

He turned back to the tapestry as he continued, "One day I woke up and she was gone too. I was only seven then. My father was around until I was ten, but losing my mother was something that he never really recovered from. He was there, but rarely left his room. After he too disappeared, it was just me, cared for by others who had no obligation to be what I'd lost." He hung his head again and held it in his hands. "I shouldn't put this on you," he muttered towards the floor.

I got up from the bed immediately and went over to him, kneeling in front of him. "Your pain isn't irrelevant just because you think no one else wants to hear you talk about it." I reach out and take his hand. "You've done so much for me, the least I can do is listen to you." I squeezed his hand gently. "I'm so sorry that you lost your family."

He looked up at me again and I could see the unshed tears in his eyes. "I'm just....I don't do this, I'm never around for these events. I make sure of it, Phi, I find a way to be anywhere else. I didn't expect that it would bring so many things up. Watching Niko..." He swallowed. "He's so happy. That's what this day should be like. I walked home alone, Dad didn't even come to watch me. I don't even know if he realised it was happening." He blinked and wiped his face quickly. "Fuck. Sorry." He leaned his head back against the stone wall. "I can't believe I let this overrun me, especially while there's a fucking party happening. That's twice I've snapped today. You must think I'm losing it."

"You're not the only one in this room who has had a family related breakdown today," I reminded him gently.

Even though he'd leaned away, he still didn't drop my hand, squeezing it absentmindedly as he tried to calm himself.

"It's okay, Cres, I promise. I'm here for you, even if no one else wants to hear you talk about it, I will."

He choked out a bitter laugh. "No one wants to hear it, because it's every parent's nightmare, and I'm the one who had to live it." He lifted his head to look down at me again. "There's a reason I stepped in that day, when those kids were hurting you. I couldn't stand it. I'd gotten into so many fights with kids who teased me because I was basically orphaned, and they were doing the same thing to you, but you weren't fighting back, I could see then that you were afraid of hurting them. That's the day I truly decided to become a Guardien, because of the way you looked at me at the end." He reached up with his free hand and stroked my cheek gently. "I think I have you to thank, for a lot of choices I've made, Firefly."

I flushed at his admission. "I didn't do anything. You would have gotten there eventually, I was just the first damsel you had to save. You're returning that favour already, by teaching me to save myself."

The ghost of a smile pulled at his lips as his thumb strayed mine. "Maybe I'm doing it so no one else gets to save you." He dropped his hand from my cheek, letting go of my other hand as he stood up, rubbing both his hands over his face. The stool disappeared back into the ground as soon as it was no longer needed.

As I looked up at him, he seemed to regain control, to centre the chaos inside himself. "Now that I think about it, my emotions have been all over the place since the morning you caught me beyond the Divide," I said, toying with my hair and standing too.

Truly, they had felt off from the moment I woke that morning weeks ago, from the nightmare I'd had and the following arrival of the Reaper and its mortal cargo. Something about that day simply felt wrong in my memories.

"You're right, that was an odd day for me too," he said thoughtfully, rubbing his thumb over my knuckles seemingly without realising. "I'm sure it's nothing, we're probably just overthinking all of this, our pasts weighing on us a little more right now." He shrugged. "Let's rejoin the party, Firefly, I'll be okay now. This is Niko's day." He squeezed at my hand, before moving around me towards the door.

I scanned him as he pulled it open and waited for me. He still looked ragged but he was right. It *was* Niko's day, and we needed to be there for him.

And yet, thoughts of the Reaping day still sat in the back of my mind, gnawing at me as my conscious mind tried to catch up with what my subconscious already knew and had tucked away out of sight. Part of me wasn't sure if I wanted to know.

I tried to shake myself out of my thoughts as I walked through the door past Creston, stepping onto the pathway leading from my room up to the house where, faintly, I could hear the sound of laughter and the echo many voices speaking at once. I glanced at him before continuing away from my room and around the house to join the celebrations already in full swing.

Celebrations that would, undoubtedly, last well into the night.

Creston and I melted into the crowd, our absence totally unnoticed in the happiness of those who now surround us, it was contagious. Soon each of us had a goblet of rich wine in hand, just as every other guest did.

It took him longer than me to relax, but eventually the tension in his body seemed to unwind, and for a time, that's all we were. Guests at a celebration, free of the weight of who we were and what we had been through in the past.

CHAPTER 24

His eyes were an ocean. No. Not an ocean, they were sapphires. Pools of midnight blue as he caught me, pulling me against his body with a broad grin.

"Caught you, Firefly," he murmured before he leaned down to claim my lips with his.

I giggled and kissed him back, slipping out of his grip just as the dream shifted, the sun and world vanishing from around me just as suddenly as it had appeared.

Running, running, I was always running. But it wasn't Creston urging me onwards in the darkness. No, there was no warmth in the thing that pushed me onwards. I had to get there first. I didn't know where there was, but I knew it was important. The laughter began as I stumbled.

"You'll never run fast enough to escape it. You're already lost and you don't even realise it yet." The words tore through my body like an icy wind.

I screamed as, for the first time in my life, I felt truly cold. A weight slammed against my abdomen and dug inside me, the ice settling inside my stomach, rendering me motionless, as I collapsed to my knees, blinded and unable to identify what I had run into in my haste to escape the things behind me.

The laughing started again.

I was trapped between ice and darkness. Fear tore through me. I couldn't find my magic, couldn't clear away the dark. There was only pain and nothingness to swallow my screams.

I woke with a cry, jolting upwards in my bed and wrapping my arms around myself, as the icy feeling stayed with me. I reached for that place inside myself that I knew held the warmth of my gift and drew it forth, warming myself until I was no longer shivering.

My stomach churned, forcing me to move off my bed and out of the room. I was on my knees outside when the pain became too much, and my stomach turned inside out, purging everything I'd eaten the night before. I gagged as the contents found its way out, closing my eyes until the spasms stopped. My throat burned and as I swallowed, I tasted a metallic tinge that shouldn't be there.

My eyes snapped open and I stared down at the ground before me.

Bloodied ice, that was quickly melting, was the sight that greeted me.

I'd vomited blood and ice. I scrambled away from the mess until my back hit the cool stone wall behind me. I stayed on the ground and held myself tightly, staring at the ice melting away into a pool of dark blood.

Pain throbbed in my abdomen as I sat there, pulling my attention away from the pool of blood with its insistence. I carefully pulled up my shirt, looking down it see the skin beneath, discovering that it was mottled with blackening bruises. Lines of black snaked out from it, looking sickeningly like they were creeping through my veins. I tentatively poked at the skin, hissing as the touch sparked a flush of pain.

The attack in my nightmare hadn't remained within the confines of dreams. It was as real as the blood on the ground a few feet from me.

I pulled my shirt back down gently, laying my shaking hands protectively over my abdomen. I could barely move, my mind racing to catch up with everything in front of me.

I don't know how long I sat there, going over each second of the nightmare to try to understand, but it was long enough for the sky to begin to lighten and the sun to illuminate my reality. I knew that my family would wake soon, that I didn't want them to find me like this, or to see the blood, but I couldn't bring myself to do something about any of it.

A pair of black boots appeared in my line of sight, as I realised too late someone was saying my name.

I looked up in confusion as a hand touched my arm, my gaze met with a pair of midnight eyes. *My favourite eyes.* The thought escaped before I could suppress it, my mind struggling to overcome the panic and fear that surged through me.

"What happened? Are you okay? Fuck, you're bleeding." Creston spoke in a rush as he reached out and wiped my chin with his sleeve. He frowned deeply, as I blinked to focus on him properly. "Where did the blood come from? Is it yours?"

"No, it's the grass's blood. Of course it's mine," I tried to scoff, tried to sound unruffled, as I looked down to where I clutched at my torso.

"The grass?" He looked around quickly, until he spotted the puddle of blood, his mood darkened as he put two and two together. "Fuck me." When he turned back to me, he was all Guardien. "Seraphine, who did this? Who hurt you?"

I shook my head. "I don't...it was a dream. When I woke I was cold, and I've *never* been cold before. I knew there was something wrong. I barely made it outside before that happened." I gestured towards the blood. "I didn't realise what had happened until I tasted the blood." I slowly lifted the hem of my shirt so he could see the bruise blackened skin beneath.

He cursed and reached out as if to touch it, but stopped himself before he made contact with the skin, instead taking my hand and helping me pull the shirt back down. "You're saying this happened in a dream? Firefly...that's...that's impossible...it doesn't happen." He frowned, deep lines forming between his brows. He seemed to stumble over the words as if he didn't quite believe them either.

"I know what I felt, Creston, and the proof is right there," I insisted, pointing to the blood. "But it's wrong. So wrong. The hand that reached inside me was so cold and dark, I could feel the wrongness in it. Like it was diseased." I shook my head, trying to create some clarity in my mind. I found little. "I need to get changed, and I need to clean up, before someone sees it."

His nostrils flared. "A hand...reached inside you?" He scanned me from head to toe, looking sick, and squatted down to be eye to eye with me.

"We don't need to talk about it," I said quickly, not wanting to remember the feeling. It was a violation I was trying very hard not to think about.

"Phi," he said softly, reaching out a hand.

Ignoring it, I touched the ground beside me and reached out with my magic, seeking out the pieces of me scattered on the grass. It took a great deal of focus and attention for it to burn away, but soon enough the blood was gone, along with a sizeable patch of grass.

He sighed, turning his gaze to the crackling grass, shoulders tight.

I looked back to Creston. "Can you please fix the grass I burnt away? I don't want anything left for my family to see." When he hesitated, I frowned. "Please."

He sighed again and nodded, going over and carefully touching the newly scorched piece of ground. As he touched it, the grass and other plants came to life, growing back in their vibrant greens. "Go wash and get dressed," he said, searching our surroundings for any sign of a threat. "I came to check on you, not for training. There was an attack during the night, and there are children missing. They're saying it was another raid. I wanted to make sure your family was okay. I know Niko passed his testing, but I was still worried."

"Why aren't you on duty? They should have extra patrols," I muttered.

Elliphir raids were once unheard of, but lately they were on the rise. The Elders had implemented protocols to follow, so I was surprised that Creston was in front of me instead of where he was needed.

"I dismissed for the day, I was on duty overnight." His expression darkened, like he blamed himself for the raid occurring. "None of us saw it happen."

"I have to talk to Cleo and Trae, I need to know what else they've found in those books. Maybe all this is just something to do with me, but if it's not, then I was attacked. Maybe in the dream, maybe in reality, but either way these bruises didn't come from nowhere." I pushed myself to my feet using the wall for support.

"Can Trae heal? I can't, but I know he's Earth-Blessed too." He held his hands out towards me cautiously as I slipped against the wall. "You need healing."

I scowled. "I'll be fine, I just need to get dressed before my family wakes up and finds me like this. And I need to talk to Trae without him trying to heal me first." Keeping one hand across my throbbing torso, I stood up straighter. "Just wait here, okay?"

Creston groaned. "You're in pain, why are you being so stubborn?" He tore his fingers through his hair as he watched me move towards the door of my room.

"Just leave it alone. I will tell him if I need to," I snapped. "No one needs to worry needlessly, and we don't need him freaking out instead of sharing what he knows." I shook my head and pushed through the door, swinging it closed behind me as I went in search of something I could put on without too much stress. I found a tunic and pants of sturdy fabric, reassuring when losing my temper could cause me to lash out and singe thinner clothes off my body with little to no warning.

Once I was dressed, after taking too many breaks to keep from fainting due to the pain, I felt less frazzled. I emerged from my room, finding Creston leaning against the wall beside the door. He straightened, shooting me a look that more than expressed his displeasure.

"Let's go, I don't want Niko to see us before we have a chance to leave." I moved past him, heading away from my home and in the direction of Trae's.

Creston said nothing but after a few moments I heard him begin to follow.

CHAPTER 25

Trae's house was closed off like a fortress once again, doors and windows completely sealed.

I had no patience for waiting today. Panting from the pain in my stomach, I summoned my fire and sent an explosive blast at the doorway, the flames tearing their way though the vines in moments, leaving a gaping hole more than big enough to substitute as as door. I waited a moment for the dust and debris to settle before continuing forward.

Creston made no comment at the destructive act, simply following me inside as I pushed my way into Trae's home, calling his name as I left the now charred remains of his opened doorway behind me. I'd have the patience to deal with the mess later, right now I needed answers and maybe a touch of healing.

Trae skidded to a stop at the end of the hallway ahead of me, shirtless and somewhat breathless. "Phi? What the fuck! Did you burn down my door? You could've at least tried knocking first!"

I waved him off. "You can grow another one, we have things to do. I need to know everything you think you know about whatever the hell is happening with my powers. A *Phoenix* you called it?"

His shocked expression darkened, visibly frustrated as he ran a hand over his dark hair.

As I calmed down a little, I started to pay attention to Trae, running a cursory look over his appearance.

He looked ragged, with deep circles beneath his eyes and clothes that barely counted as clothes, in only a pair of low slung pants. "Phi, I found more, but not all of it's good. The books I'm dealing with are far from kind."

"What the fuck does that mean?" Creston demanded from over my shoulder, radiating all the anger I was sure he wished he could have pointed in my direction.

Trae sighed. "Sit, I'll go through what I found with Cleo, but just me. She's asleep now and I don't want to wake her as well." As he turned and walked towards his living room the walls seemed to follow him, vines and branches rippling as they acknowledged the presence of their creator.

I frowned, glancing back down the hall he'd appeared from. The way he'd said it made me sure that Cleo was sleeping here, not in her own home. I shook away the thought and headed in after him, hand pressed tight to my stomach.

When I moved the walls around me seemed to have the opposite reaction, shying away from the heat my body radiated as I moved through. I sank to the floor in the living room, choosing not to sit on any destroyable furniture, just in case.

Trae climbed into the centre of a scattering of books, papers and sheets of aged parchment. Tugging at his eyebrows, a habit he had when he was feeling particularly overwhelmed, he settled in and picked up what looked to be a notebook of his own.

How touching, I warrant my own notebook just so he can keep up with whatever kind of freak I am.

I glanced at Creston as he sat on one of the armchairs, conveniently directly between Trae and I. Perhaps so he could leap at Trae, or so he could offer me support if the answers my friend had upset me.

I wasn't sure I wanted to know what Trae thought he knew, now that I was here.

We sat there, the silence only cut by the sound of our breathing, the creaking of the vine chair beneath Creston, and the rustling of Trae's papers as he shuffled this and that around as though it would all suddenly make more sense in a different order.

It didn't take long before I was beyond irritated. "Just tell me what the fuck has you looking like you haven't slept in a month," I snapped at him, the pain I was in whittling away my ability to even attempt to be patient.

But Trae knew me, and somewhere in my mind I knew he wouldn't hold it against me. "I'm sorry I just don't quite know where to start," he sighed, running his hand over his forehead as he stared at the papers in his lap in dismay. "As far as I've found your extended fire abilities have something to do with your Blessing, all pointing to you being what they used to call a Phoenix. The Phoenix children were taken away at a young age and trained to use their bodies and magic as a weapon, but then something happened. There's no record of the change, but all of a sudden records started being removed, as well as all these books." He gestured around himself widely. "Any reference of Phoenix warriors, and their gifts, have been rotting away for hundreds of years. People forgot, the Elders probably did too." He looked up at me. "But I managed to find enough between all the books to tell you where it started." His gaze flickered to Creston before he looked down at his notebook. "We all know the lore about our beginnings. What is less spoken of is the beginnings of the Elliphir, their beginning started with one child, Samil. With his existence they were born, according to every piece of our history I have ever gotten my hands on. But this text." He picked up a heavy, well worn leather bound text. "This one tells another story. Samil was not born alone, he was half of a whole." Trae looked up at us again, to ensure we were following.

Glancing at Creston, I saw that we were both wearing mirrored looks of confusion and frustration, which ensured Trae's pauses did not last long.

He cleared his throat and continued. "Samil was a twin, well had a twin, they named that child Silas, and it seems he was the very first Phoenix Blessed, *if* that's what it is called. He was taken by the first of the Elders and raised, trained to kill his own blood. If we were to talk in mortal science, then I would say that the twins were mutations, each half of one whole of our magic. In Samil was the darkness and corruption and in Silas the ability to wield magic without restraints. Samil held all the limitations of their magic and Silas inherited none. Which is why the Elliphir cannot wield any elemental magic, it's all drawn away to create the balance, leaving them to wield darkness, a sort of death-magic that can drain life from around them. Well that's what the books say."

I raised my brows in surprise. "Magic? I thought they were just insane? Why would the Elders lie to us like that?" I asked sceptically. *Magic? The creatures of our nightmares all of a sudden had magic?* "Trae, what kind of things are we talking about here?"

"Um..." He flicked through some sheets of paper and books until he found what he was looking for and leaned over to hand the list to Creston who held it carefully, as though it may bite him. "Those are all the things I've found mentioned in any lore or history I've gone through so far."

I watched Creston expectantly as he read through the list.

With each flick of his gaze over each line he read his expression seemed to darken further and further until he was scowling at the paper in his hands. "This can't be true," he growled, handing the list to me.

I took it eagerly, reading the words Trae had scrawled on the page.

Possible abilities of the Elliphir;
Consumption of life
Corruption
Compulsion
Camouflage (shapeshifting?)
Dreamwalking?
Shadow creation/control?

I struggled to fathom the information laid out before me as it fought against everything I had ever been told by those I trusted without question. I gnawed at my lip as I read and reread the list, hoping the answers would somehow appear with familiarity to the text. No such luck. I looked up and met Trae's concerned gaze.

"The way they're described in all the texts, those were the best guess I could make. I don't know how accurate they are but they're the best leads I have," he explained.

"I don't know what books you're reading here, Trae, but half of that doesn't seem possible, or make any sense." Creston looked as torn as I felt, tearing his fingers through his dark hair over and over. I didn't think he was aware of the action but simply needed something to do with his hands.

I looked back at the list before setting it down on the ground, trying not to wince at the pain in my stomach the movement caused. "You wrote dreamwalking, what exactly does that mean? And how much power are we talking here? Is it just over a person's subconscious or is it a physical presence?"

Trae sighed again, his shoulders slumped in exhaustion and the defeat of not having the answers we needed. "The books weren't clear. These are old pieces I'm dealing with, it's like all of a sudden they just stopped talking about everything they could do and just focused on making us all afraid of them, until we actually had no clue why we were afraid anymore."

I looked up at Trae as I laid my hand against my bruised stomach. "I need you to find out, because I think I was attacked in my sleep."

"Phi." Creston's tone was sharp, wary as he frowned over at me.

"No," I replied, just as sharply. "I was attacked in my sleep, in a dream. Someone did this to me." I stood and carefully moved to lift my tunic to show the blackened flesh the fabric hid.

I heard a hiss from the side and turned my head to see Cleo standing in the doorway, her hair disheveled from sleep as she clasped a hand over her mouth in horror, making the shirt she was wearing, the one that Trae was clearly missing, rise dangerously high on her thighs.

"Phi, who did that to you?" Her voice was muffled behind her hand as her gaze immediately flickered towards Creston. He received a cautious glare as she stepped towards me protectively.

CHAPTER 26

I let my shirt drop back into place, figuring everyone had seen enough of what was happening beneath it.

Trae looked pale, and Creston looked ready to punch someone or something. If he did decide to, at least Trae had the ability to heal both himself and the furniture around us so he wouldn't cause too much long term damage.

"That's what I'm trying to figure out," I said. "I woke up from a nightmare this morning and when I looked at where I'd been touched in the dream, those bruises were there." I left out the unpleasantness involving the contents of my stomach being frozen blood. The bruises were enough of an establishment of my injuries.

As everyone stared in horror at my now covered stomach, I started to take notice of Trae and Cleo in earnest, their matching disheveled appearance as well as the fact that they were wearing a barely complete outfit between the two of them. I felt my cheeks burn as I pieced together what I had been too preoccupied to figure out when I first arrived.

Cleo, realising where my mind had landed, shook her head frantically, but she was too late.

"Oh shit. You guys weren't sleeping when I busted through the door, were you?" I covered my face and groaned. When I dropped my hands they both looked flushed with embarrassment.

"We weren't exactly expecting company," Trae muttered as he glanced towards Cleo then back at me. "But it's really none of anyone's business. And has nothing to do with any of this."

Creston cleared his throat, looking uncomfortable. "Look, everything aside we need to be headed into The Square. There were raids during the night, all off duty Guardiens will be called back in soon, including me. We need to know the damage and I need to know that you two will stay with Seraphine, at least until we know what happened to her for sure."

I nodded and crossed my arms over my chest loosely, careful not to rest too much weight on my stomach. "That means you two need more clothing."

Trae and Cleo both moved to get dressed properly, needing no more prodding in their flushed states to get their asses into gear, disappearing back into his bedroom to dress.

I glanced towards the mess of paper and books that coated the floor once more and shuddered slightly. Within so much forgotten scripture was answers to questions I didn't even know how to ask, and likely some I didn't want answers to.

Creston got to his feet and stretched. "I should probably go on ahead of you, check some things out like I got the alert to return, and all this," He gestured to the room around us, "Doesn't exist as far as I know. Whatever weight it may or may not have."

I bit my lip and nodded. "Yeah, probably best if you're not seen sneaking around with me more than usual if this isn't something we're supposed to be learning about."

He nodded. "Things will be fine. You're magic is just a bit stronger than you thought. I'll find you later and tell you all I can about the raids." On his way past me out the door, and he brushed his fingers down my arm, leaving goosebumps in their wake. "Don't get too much in your head about all this until we have more answers." He flashed a half smile and headed out of Trae's home, disappearing around the healing corners of the hallway, still singed from my entrance.

Staring at the smoking parts of my friend's home, it was nice to know I couldn't be locked out of places by other magic at least.

Even though Creston's words were comforting I could still see that he was seething with unallocated anger, with nowhere to focus it. In that moment, I wished I had the answers, a place to direct us all to with both our questions and our frustrations, but I didn't. I had all the questions and no one to give me the real answers.

I stood there, my mind in a whir, staring down the damaged hallway until Trae emerged from a doorway down the hall with Cleo in tow. I half turned towards them as they returned, both fully clothed, looking tired and lost. "Look, you guys don't have to babysit me," I said, taking pity on them. "I'll be fine, I can go to The Square and find out what's going on if you'd rather stay here. Plus, I kinda made a mess that needs fixing with the front of the house."

Cleo shook her head. "No way, too much weird shit is going on with you, we're coming."

Trae nodded and stepped forward. "She's right, but first you need some healing." He held out his hand with his palm facing up, an almost universal gesture all Earth-Blessed did when wanting to heal someone.

Nodding, I took his hand and immediately felt the gentle wave of his magic flow into my body. It was like having pins and needles, except it was calming. I could feel the magic as it sought out the injuries in my body, it felt as though my stomach was crackling with the magic.

Trae's face went from relaxed to confused, his fingers twitching against my own.

"What?" I asked immediately.

He scanned my body from head to toe, eyes lingering on my stomach. "I...I can sense the injury but...I don't think I can heal it. It's like there's a...." His eyebrows furrowed as he clasped my hand in both of his and focused. "There's some sort of drain and the rest of my magic is being sapped away by it. I can't heal it all."

I pulled my hand back and strode down the hall to find a mirror, and tugging up the fabric of my tunic, I saw what he meant.

The bruises were no longer black but mottled purple and blue, darker in the centre in an odd way, like some sort of artwork with a splatter in the centre.

I tilted my head as I stared at my stomach and it slowly dawned on me.

It wasn't a spatter. One, two, three, four and then a fifth, the number of darkened spots that reached out in the centre of my stomach.

A handprint.

A wave of nausea threatened to overwhelm me as I dropped the fabric back in place, stumbling back from the mirror in horror. *Had someone really shoved their hand inside me in my nightmare?*

It had been one thing to repeat the nightmare in my head, and explain it to my concerned friends, but it was another thing entirely to have the proof I was right marking my body.

Someone had done this, someone was behind this, and I had no idea who they might be or why.

My stomach churned dangerously and I fought to keep my breathing normal. If I let this panic overwhelm me now I wasn't sure I would ever recover. I needed it to go away, to lock this feeling in a box until I was ready to break.

It took me a few long moments, but I eventually regained control, locking the image of my stomach away with the panic.

Cleo made me jump as she cleared her throat behind me. "Is it okay?" she asked softly.

I smoothed out my clothes and nodded. "Still a little bruised but fine. Trae helped, I'm sure it'll be okay." I forced a smile. "Let's get going." I pushed by her out the doorway and headed past Trae who stood anxiously at the end of the hall. "I'm all good, Trae. Let's go find out what happened last night."

I knew that neither of them believed I was okay, but I didn't have the patience to tend to their fears *and* hold down my own all at once. I moved out of the house and headed towards The Square, trusting they would follow behind me.

CHAPTER 27

The Square was flooded with people when we arrived, all waiting anxiously for the Elders to appear. The sheer mass of the gathering was enough to turn my stomach.

Raids were serious, but never had I seen so many of our people gathered for news. We usually maxed out at one person per household taking the information back, but not this time.

How many were missing this time to have created such panic?

I couldn't see deep enough into the crowd to find my family but I spotted Cleo's nearby. I ducked away to the side as she gravitated towards them, searching the edges of the crowd where the Guardiens stood, dressed in their usual attire rather than their on duty uniforms, another sign of the urgency of events that had unfolded. I couldn't see Creston either, but I knew he had to be there somewhere.

I worked my way slowly into the crowd, enough so that I could see the platform the Elders would address us from. The crowd was full of quiet murmurs, no shouts, no laughter in the back, and certainly no children running through the legs of those standing around waiting.

There was something different, from whatever had happened. One sound I hadn't noticed upon my arrival seeped through the quiet murmurs. It was the sound of sadness.

Crying.

I looked around, and the more I looked the more I realised that the murmurs were not frivolous time passings. No, they were murmurs of calming, words of comfort for those who needed it.

All throughout the crowd people were crying.

Something is wrong, very wrong.

Reapings were normal, they were part of life, an accepted price for the magic of our blood. A reminder of the risks that came with it all, as well as the rewards of being so blessed in our ability to control our magic. Knowing loss was a risk strengthened familial bonds with age, as we all grew to value those we had not lost. Those who did suffer the losses found strength in each other, as they mourned and relearned how to live life with that pain. The grief they felt was the kind that never truly eased, they only got better at managing it.

I pushed my way further into the crowd, needing to find a familiar face, hopefully of someone who knew what was happening. Someone I could trust to be clear, without any projections of the growing hysteria pulsing in this crowd. I craned my neck as I scanned the faces I passed.

There were so many faces, so many wide eyes and quiet sobs, so many people pressing against me I was starting to feel overwhelmed. I hissed when someone accidentally hit my stomach.

A hand grasped my arm tightly and yanked me between two people, and I found myself face to face with my brother.

"Zav," I sighed in relief. "Please tell me you know what is going on? This isn't right."

My brother frowned at me and pulled me further towards the edge of the crowd, "There was a Reaping."

I blinked at him, waiting for him to expand. A Reaping never drew this level of attendance.

He glanced around before continuing, lowering his voice so as not to be overheard. "They didn't just take children with Elliphir traits, they took older children, six of them. All tested and specialised Elliphae." His voice was gravelly, his eyes haunted and his hair disheveled. Stress was clear in his tone, despite how softly he spoke but I could still hear his fear, buried just beneath the rest.

I looked around with new eyes and what surrounded me began to make sense. We allowed the Elliphir to take with them their own kind in Reapings each season, an agreement struck centuries ago, but they had never before betrayed the treaty in such a way.

I turned back to my brother. "I don't understand. How did they get past the Guardiens? The families?"

"Nobody knows. No one saw them, not one soul. We only know it was them because they left their mark on every house that lost a child. As a taunt." Jaw clenched, he looked out over the crowd, eyes faraway and unseeing.

I cursed and looked around again. There were many familiar faces in the crowd in mourning, clearer now that I knew the circumstances. We turned as the Elders started to appear through the doors to a balcony that looked down on The Square.

The crowd silenced and all faces turned to the balcony where thirteen Elders appeared, dressed in what was considered the Elder uniform, each one in a robe that held the symbol for the Original Elder they represented.

Derlinic stepped forward. "We know there is panic, but we must remain calm and together," he called, raising his hands against the protests to silence them. "It is true the Elliphir have taken more than their share of our people, but we will not let this go in silence. We have sent Rangers beyond the Divide in search of them, and we will bring home those beloved by us. We assure you of that. We do not yet know why the children were taken, but please return to your homes and work. We will call for you all when we know more." With that the Elders began to disappear inside, dismissive of all who had listened to them.

There were murmurs within the crowd as people turned to one another, outraged. None of them were content. As if their anger had waited below the surface until the Elders confirmed that the children were truly gone. There was a shift in the air. Powers were stirring alongside anger, so thick you could almost taste it.

The shouts started before the Elders could slip out of sight, and just as they shut the door, the first rock cracked against the wall where they'd lined up.

I looked to Zavier with childlike hope that he, as my big brother, would have answers where the Elders did not, seeing that Cleo and Trae had joined us now. We all shared the same look of sadness. I shook my head and shoved my way out of the crowd as the shouts grew, families demanding more action. More answers.

We reached the edge of the crowd as an Elder tried to calm the crowd from the balcony, but I paid no attention to who it was. Chaos descended behind us.

We pushed through it carefully, only stopping when we were far enough away. I turned to my brother, suddenly worried. "Are our parents here? Niko?"

He shook his head immediately. "I came when we got the message, but there wasn't any urgency in the message any more than there normally is. This hysteria is new, created by word of mouth." He glanced back in the direction of the crowd.

I wrapped my arms around myself and looked at my friends, speechless.

There was a pause in all of us, no one really knowing how to handle such an event. We stayed like that for a little while, quietly contemplating what to do next.

I was still trying to catch up emotionally. There were children missing, children who were supposed to be safe from anything like this. If they were no longer safe after their testings then were any of us safe?

It wasn't until another joined us that things changed. He cleared his throat behind me.

I turned towards the sound, my eyebrows shooting up.

"Hi, uh, Seraphine, right?" Kylan stood a few feet away, dressed in clothing clearly made by us. It looked odd on his body.

Trae nudged me when I said nothing, simply staring at the male as unease settled over me.

"Oh, right, yeah. That's me. Can I help you?" I let my arms relax to my sides, but the action was forced.

"Elijah sent me to you. He's too busy to facilitate today, so he told me to find you so I can learn my way around here." He glanced at my brother, quickly, as if appraising him, that gaze then flicked over both my friends. He flashed a shy smile. "Uh sorry, I'm Kylan. I'm new here." He held out his hand to Trae first as he was the closest.

He stepped forward and shook his hand. "You came in on the boat, right? I'm Trae. That's Zavier, and this is Cleo." He wrapped his free arm around her waist as he introduced her.

She smiled at the action, then glowed at Kylan in a way that only she could. "Welcome to Keinteris. I promise there's not normally this much drama around here. It's usually extremely peaceful."

He smiled more, but it still never reached his eyes. "Thank you for the welcome. I'm eager to learn about this world. It seems magnificent. Truly. I never imagined a place like this existing."

Her smile brightened. "Nor should you have. That's the entire point. But you're here now."

"And under the charge of Phi, right?" Trae added dryly.

I resisted the urge to scowl at him. "Uh. Yeah. What is it Elijah wanted me to do with you?"

Kylan shrugged. "He really just said to follow you, learn the area properly. Meet new people." He nodded towards the others. "I'm happy to just tag along with your day, until I have to report back to Elijah."

I did scowl then, not bothering to hide it. Of course Elijah had him reporting his days, all so I couldn't ditch him.

CHAPTER 28

I glanced at my brother as we all stood there, noticing that he hadn't said a word since Kylan's arrival.

He met my gaze briefly, cocking an eyebrow. It was a curious action for him, but I had no time for explanation, not here at least. Cleo was shining at the new addition, her warmth enough to distract him from my coldness, I hoped.

"Well, we were about to go towards the learning houses. Away from this. You can come with us." I glanced at my friends again. I knew I had no right but I didn't want this newcomer near my family.

Cleo nodded, swiftly adapting to the new plan. "Yeah, I just have to get something from my tutor if he's there."

Kylan nodded. "Sure. Which tutor do you work with?"

"Veneficus," she answered as we started down the road. Oddly, Zavier stayed with us.

"Veneficus?" There was a slight change in Kylan's tone as he repeated the name. "I think I heard about him. From Elijah. It's an unusual name, hard to forget."

Cleo glanced at him as we walked. "Oh, he's a great teacher. And you'll adapt to the names." She began to prattle on about the things she was being taught.

As she spoke with Kylan, I fell back beside my brother. "What was the look?" I asked him softly. The others were ahead, but not far enough that I wasn't going to be cautious.

"I don't know." He rubbed the back of his neck, his voice just as low. "Just a feeling, like I know him from somewhere."

I looked towards the front of our little group, where Kylan seemed deep in a conversation with Cleo, Trae close at her side. "Maybe it's just the clothes. They're probably someone else's hand me downs." Though I truly couldn't deny he looked as though he belonged right by my friends as they walked. Usually there was more hesitation from mortals who arrived here. But then again, he had arrived weeks ago.

"They don't normally take to our kind so quickly. Normally they're like frightened animals, you can taste their fear. He has none," Zavier said, his eyes never leaving the strange male in front of us.

Following his gaze, I shrugged. "Perhaps to him, whatever he left behind is far worse than the living around magical creatures."

My brother withdrew into himself thoughtfully. The talk ahead continued, but I too paid no attention, staying silent beside my brother as we walked a little way behind them.

When we arrived at the study hall Kylan was still glued to Cleo's side, insisting on coming with her to meet her mentor, who he seemed to find illustrious. The rest of us waited outside, watching them walk into the building while still chattering away non stop.

Trae fidgeted from foot to foot. "That guy is clingy." He frowned at the door they'd disappeared through.

"You can't be jealous of someone with her already." I nudged him in the ribs. I wasn't happy about them disappearing from sight either but that was for me to feel, not for Trae to worry over. "But she does need to get that book back."

Trae shook his head, a troubled look taking root in his features. "She needs another one. She needs to do a swap for me. I didn't anticipate an audience." So it wasn't jealousy, it was concern about a book.

I stopped from rolling my eyes at him as I glanced towards the building. "Hey, maybe the new guy will distract V," I offered, trying to ignore the incessant pain in my stomach. "Or is it one that she could borrow without suspicion?"

"It's an age old Fire Magic history, she couldn't know to ask for it, not without him questioning it. She needs the space to swap it." He sighed before falling silent, staring after Cleo, chewing one of his fingernails.

I glanced back at my brother as we waited. "You don't have to hang around, you know."

He shrugged. "Better here than home right now. I'll bring the ill news later."

"Do you think Dad will go back to the Guardiens, with something like this happening?"

He rubbed at the back of his neck. "I don't know, he seemed truly done when he left, but you can never be totally sure with him."

"I suppose," I murmured, trying to ignore the pulsing ache in my stomach as we fell silent, wandering away from the entrance of the building to keep from drawing attention to our group.

A small eternity later Cleo reappeared in the doorway, looking around quickly, she spotted us and hurried towards Trae, and a few moments later Kylan followed her. Cleo winked at Trae flashing the book in her satchel as she stopped beside him, looking at me. "Where to next, guys?"

Kylan's presence was like a constant hum in the back of my mind, something I wanted to shake but couldn't. I still didn't particularly want him near my home. "Why not the falls?" I suggested. "It would be empty, not for good reasons, but we can't do anything right now, so why not relax? Plus, we can show Kylan."

Trae and Cleo exchanged glances then nodded. "Sounds like a great idea." Cleo grinned. "And we can show off some magic. We have almost all the elements, enough to give him a good show."

The male nodded enthusiastically. "I'd love to see the kind of magic you guys have. From what I've seen so far I can only wish I'd been born here, and not as a human."

I watched him, frowning. Something about what he said was ringing alarm bells, but I couldn't work out why. He was harder to read, projecting more awe than felt right. I cleared my throat. "Let's go."

The others agreed, though they didn't seem to notice the strangeness that I did, and we started skirting around the village and towards the half hidden waterfall at the edge of the island.

Chapter 29

The falls were as deserted as I had hoped they would be. We hadn't rushed there, and despite what he'd said, I was still surprised when Zavier came with us, having half expected him to regret the decision and leave on our way.

Not so surprising was the fact that Cleo had headed straight for the water's edge, Trae and Kylan followed after.

I stayed back, perching cross legged on a large rock that had been smoothed out over time by either magic or higher water. Around here, perhaps it was both.

Zavier settled nearby, and we both watched the others as they talked and laughed by the water.

Cleo was explaining something to Kylan with a huge grin, Trae laughing at something she said while Kylan seemed to remain serious as he took in her every word.

I glanced at my brother, noting he seemed to be staring at Kylan with a similar intensity that Kylan was paying Cleo. I cocked an eyebrow. "What's wrong?" I asked him quietly as I shifted into a more comfortable position. "You've never shown interest in hanging out with us before, even with other turmoil. What's different?"

"Huh?" Zavier asked, obviously distracted. He shook his head, as if clearing it. "Oh... I don't know. Just can't shake the feeling that something about him seems familiar. I just can't place it."

Sliding my eyes over towards the others again, before I looked back at my brother, I scratched my chin, trying to understand why the stranger made me so uncomfortable. "I guess I can understand that, I got a similar feeling when I first met him. Maybe it's just that we've met so many people from his world now."

He shook his head. "No, it's not that. I don't know. I'm sure the answer will come to me, or maybe I'm just going mad." He flashed me a halfhearted grin before glancing back at the others.

Cleo had moved into the water and was showing off with her abilities, something she'd always loved to do around those new to magic. We watched as she summoned the air around her, creating a vortex that drew water into her show with a flick of her wrist. If one hadn't been paying attention they would think it was the water she controlled, instead of the air carrying it.

I knew the other reason she was showing off was because of all the work she had been doing with Veneficus. Her control over her air abilities had increased sevenfold in the shortest time I'd ever heard of, which is also how she could now dive into someone else's mind so easily.

Trae didn't seem inclined to show off any of his abilities, letting Cleo have her fun instead, watching her graceful movements with a light in his eyes I'd not seen before. I knew he likely wanted to be at home, poring over the book they had just taken.

Zavier stood suddenly. "I should go. You're right to question me, there's so much more I need to be doing today, rather than following you and your friends around." He brushed himself off, more out of habit than actual need to clear any dirt from his body.

I stood as well. "Agreed, I want to check on Mum and Dad, Niko too." I slipped down from the rock and looked at the others.

Trae had noticed our movement and twisted towards us, a questioning expression on his face as he made to stand too.

"We're going to head home," I called out to them.

Trae frowned a little but nodded, sitting back down. Having my brother with me meant they didn't need chaperone me as Creston had demanded. Plus, Cleo and Kylan were still far too engrossed in a further magic display to notice anything else.

We walked away and headed towards home, leaving Trae to tell Cleo we had left when she paid no attention.

Somewhere along the way, with only a glance at each other and challenging grins, we decided to race back to the house. It was faster and I think we both wanted to be closer to our family, heading straight into the house as we arrived, seeking out our parents, panting. We found our mother and father in the living room with Niko.

He was trying to build something with his magic, both of them giving him instructions as we came into the room. Niko and our father didn't notice our return, their backs to us, but our mother smiled when she saw us.

We moved to opposite sides of the room to watch our baby brother harness his abilities, trying to keep our ragged breathing as quiet as possible.

I looked away. I'd seen this show many times before, with Zavier as well as Niko, but I had never experienced it myself. They hadn't known how to toy with an element that was destructive in its power, so I had been sent to the house of other fire users in order to help me learn.

My parents had supervised the first few times but eventually stopped coming as I had too often looked to them when something happened, and with them unable to help, they decided their presence only made it harder for me.

I'd heard them talking about it once, sharing their distress at the inability to help me grow. I'd tried not to use my powers at home after that, unless I was alone. If I didn't use my powers then I could almost pretend I was the same as they were. I could still feel the magic, the life in each other element, but I was cut off from all but Fire.

It was the same for all of us. We could feel each element, in nature and in each other, as the life of the magic called out to our blood, but we could do little more than use that to guess another's blessed element.

My attention was pulled back to my family at their sudden cries of celebration.

Niko had achieved what I could only assume was his goal, an intricately woven stool that moved ever so slightly. I even caught Zavier grinning and congratulating our brother.

Niko got up and sat on the stool, rocking back and forth on it to check its sturdiness. "I did it!" he said, glowing with pride.

Our father ruffled his hair. "Yes you did, my boy, and we'll make sure to practice every day, until your powers are as strong as they need to be." He stood and looked between Zavier and I. "The news?" he asked as his gaze landed on Zavier.

My brother glanced at Niko, jerking his chin towards his room.

Our father was no fool. "Niko, why don't you take your stool to your room? We'll work on a set over the next few days."

Niko was too overwhelmed with his excitement to notice the change in atmosphere as he rushed off with the stool, still calling out how he could change it or make it better on his way to his room.

Zavier cleared his throat when he was gone. "There were children taken overnight. Eleven in total. Six of those children were Elliphae tested, and specialised. Well beyond the traits of Elliphir. They have no idea how they were taken or how their captors remained unnoticed.

All Guardiens are on alert, they have sent Rangers in search of the others but our people are in a state of grief and panic," he rattled off with little emotion, just as our father had taught us. He glanced towards me and then to our mother as she moved to her husband's side, taking in her worry pinched features. "They have nothing more to tell us."

Our parents shared a look, the same fear I had seen in the crowd finding its way to them finally with my brother as its harbinger.

"Do we know what children were taken?" our mother asked first, shaking her head in disbelief.

Zavier simply shook his head. "They didn't say, Mum, they kept everything close to their chests. They don't want more panic. People are terrified and grief stricken. They want the children home and to know why they weren't defended."

I wrapped my arms around myself, heartbroken for the families that had been torn apart so unfairly.

My parents looked to each other again, a silent exchange passing between them, as though they could read each other's minds. Whether they truly could I didn't know, but they seemed to sigh at the same time.

"I will visit with your great grandfather, he may not see us often but he is an Elder and will have answers to give me," my father said, not looking away from my mother. "Even if they're just answers on whether or not more protection is needed for our settlement. If help is needed, we are Earth and we can build a stronger Divide. Fates know it's become riddled with gaps over the centuries." He pinched the bridge of his nose.

I felt a new twinge of fear, my stomach sinking. A strengthening of the magic that held the Divide in place would make it harder for Creston and I to pass through it for our training. It was selfish of me to be more concerned about making sure there was still a way for me to breach the Divide to keep my sessions with Creston, but I couldn't help it. They were one of the very few things helping me feel more in control in a world where I seemingly had none.

Yes, Creston could create pathways for us but if the magic was being maintained by many users, the likelihood of our movements getting noticed increased by odds I did not care to challenge.

"Surely the Divide has become only symbolic now, Dad," I said, barely keeping a lid on the panic. "The magic of the Divide has never *really* held the Elliphir back, only marked the boundaries of land they are not invited into." I managed to keep my tone calm and balanced as I spoke with him.

He seemed to consider it a moment and then sighed, dropping his hand from the bridge of his nose. "Perhaps you're right but seeing Eledrie anyway is going to be our most reliable option for the next steps ahead with our people. And to get the names of the families so we can assist them."

Mother nodded beside him, expression firmly set into one of grim readiness. She'd been alive long enough to know an act of kidnapping children that had been tested and assigned a Blessing was almost akin to an act of war.

Zavier looked as sick as I felt as he spoke. "What can I do to assist, Father?"

"Remain here, perhaps work on our home's boundaries a little, for peace of mind. I will go to Eledrie alone." He moved away, his clothes shifting into something more formal.

My father was a fine craftsman of all kinds, including his own and much of my family's clothing. Without gifts, you would almost never know he was creating such fine garments with nature alone. He made more for me than anyone else because he liked to ensure I had spares, in case things were damaged by my abilities.

I'd always cherished that.

He gathered himself, kissed my mother's forehead and then mine. "I will return soon with what answers can be gleaned from our grandfather. Do not inform Niko just yet, we don't want him to fear," he said firmly, meeting each of our eyes until we nodded in agreement. "Keep him here until we know more about who was taken, should they be someone close to him."

"Be careful, my love," my mother said quietly.

Father stared at her for a long moment then disappeared out the door without another word, leaving us standing silently in our home, unsure of what we should do next.

Niko saved us from having to say anything else, running back from his room, still excited about his new stool. He started to plead with Zavier to help him make something else in Father's stead.

Zavier caved easily to our brother's wishes, so my mother and I settled in chairs to watch them attempt to create another stool from nothing but their gifts.

It was calming, and for now it was all we had.

CHAPTER 30

Three days passed agonisingly slowly, while we stayed close to our homes, unwilling to leave the children of Keinteris alone, waiting to know exactly who had been taken. We waited for more kidnappings and waited for our Rangers to return. None of which bore fruit.

The fact that Rangers hadn't returned had caused further unease for us all. They were the best of us; a battle-honed, trained, secretive force that should have been back on the first day. When they didn't return, the Elders ordered everyone to obey a curfew.

Guardiens were out in full force around the settlement, enforcing the curfew and maintaining a visible presence. I couldn't get near the Divide, much to my frustration.

I had seen Trae and Cleo around, strangely enough with Kylan in tow, following them intently. Creston was buried somewhere within his Guardienship, unable to answer my questions, but I knew he would resurface when he could. Hopefully with more information.

At the end of the third day I wondered how long this would last.

We had never been hit so deeply by the Elliphir in our history. They had never taken more than their children from us before, and it was an unprecedented shift, something that had the remaining parents on edge, eyeing people they used to call their friends with suspicion.

On the third night, I curled up in a ball and tugged my blankets up around me, pulling my hair back and blindly binding my curls into a braid. Each night I waited until my whole family went to bed in the main house before I retreated to my own space, as if somehow my presence made any difference to the situation at hand.

Nightmares followed me down into sleep each night, but they had changed. I wasn't always chased.

The voice returned each night, asking the same thing. *Where are you?*

I yawned and rolled over, letting my magic flow out from my body to dim the lanterns and reignite the fireplace.

Sleeping in total darkness was never something that had sat well with me, so the fireplace always remained lit, regardless of the season. The heat never bothered me, in fact, I found it comforting.

I watched the new fire crackle then burn to life. The use of the magic brought a flush of peace and warmth through my body like always, a reminder that the magic was just another muscle within my body that I enjoyed stretching.

My eyes were growing heavy and I was about to surrender myself to my exhaustion when my door creaked slowly open. The lanterns flared back on as my eyes snapped wide open and I sat up in my bed, my hands out in front of me, flames in my palms as the figure at the door pushed back his hood and held out his hands.

"Cool it, Firefly, it's just me." Creston grinned at me, but it didn't sit the way it should. Exhaustion showed in his posture and had reached his eyes.

I sighed and extinguished the fire dancing at my fingertips. "Don't screw with me like that."

He edged into the room, letting the door close behind him, a chair developing in the centre of the room by my bed as he walked towards it.

"I thought you'd be asleep by now. I was going to wake you gently. My apologies." He flopped down in the seat he had created with a groan, and rubbing his face roughly, he sighed before looking at me again. "So..."

I cocked an eyebrow. "So?"

He grinned again, and it was slightly more authentic this time. "Oh, I was waiting to be bombarded with questions."

Ignoring the way my heart stuttered at how well he truly knew me, I rolled my eyes. "Honestly, if you hadn't pulled the chair from your magic I was going to be concerned about you collapsing. You look exhausted, Cres."

He shrugged. "Things have been...tense within the ranks the past few days. All Guardiens are on edge, because we still can't figure out how the Elliphir got so many of our people out without anyone seeing anything. One or two could be smuggled out without us knowing, but so many? At various ages? Not a sound, not a witness or trail to follow? It's so frustrating." Creston threw his hands up in the air, shaking his head.

"There aren't any answers then? Nothing more than what we've already heard? Who was taken?" I asked, frowning at him.

"The Elders have sequestered the families with missing children," he said, folding his hands behind his head.

I refused to let my eyes dip to where his shirt rose, showing a sliver of his toned stomach and the edges of where the vines tattooed on his arm continued down his left side.

"We don't even know the names or levels or real ages of everyone who was taken across the Divide," he continued, oblivious to the distraction he'd offered. "Add that to the fact we have had to send a scouting party to find the original group of soldiers sent when the alert was raised. And they want to keep as much of it confined to those who need to know, to keep people from panicking, even though we don't know what we would need to be panicking about." He slumped further into the chair and sighed, looking away from me and towards the tapestry on my wall.

I gnawed on my lip as I watched him. "This really is beyond what the Elders have prepared us to expect from the Elliphir, isn't it? They've always told us we were safe here, that there was a balance in place. That the treaty would keep us safe."

Creston met my stare evenly. "I know."

There was something he wasn't telling me, that much was clear. "Do you think the treaty is still in place now? The Elliphir have done this for a reason. We just have to find out how serious that reason is. Maybe they just took the wrong children?" I suggested, though the knot that refused to loosen in my stomach warned me it was a childish hope. "They are known for their madness, it could be anything at this point. They could have dumped the unwanted children somewhere before they returned home, when they realised they weren't part of whatever hive mind they possess." I sat up and crossed my legs, feeling like I was going to go crazy if I didn't hold myself together.

He leaned forward, resting his elbows on his knees. "We are being told to act as though the treaty stands," he said delicately. "We can't go crashing through the Divide until they give us permission. As much as I might want to," he muttered. "We have to wait until the Elders tell us more or the Oracles have new answers. Their doors are also sealed."

"So basically we know nothing and can do nothing. Marvellous." I shook my head and rubbed at my face in frustration, my frown deepening as something occurred to me. "Your friend, the one you were worried about doing something stupid, where is he?"

The colour drained from his face. "Hyatt is with the missing Rangers." His voice was almost too soft, as though speaking the words were a curse.

I wanted to reach out and touch him, to offer some sort of support, but I couldn't, not without shattering the peace between us. "I'm sorry."

"He will be fine." The way he said it was unwavering, as though there were no other options, and I didn't know what else to say. He watched me for a moment with an odd expression on his face then got up and moved to sit beside me on the bed. "Can we talk about something else?" he asked in a low voice.

I nodded slowly, heart pounding as he crossed the line I hadn't been able to, somehow listening to the thing inside me that demanded I be closer to him, perhaps he felt it too. I shoved the thought aside. "Yes, please."

He nudged my shoulder with his. "Have you got any more answers from those history books Trae is likely still buried in? If Cleo isn't keeping him too busy." He chuckled.

It was hardly the topic change I expected, but he had a lot on his mind, so maybe all he needed was a distraction. *And not for me to push my growing feelings and needs in his face.*

I groaned. "Shit, I forgot about that. I did not see that coming when she told me she had a date...but they do fit, he's calm where she is wild."

He smiled, knowing exactly what I meant. There had been many a time where Creston stopped Cleo and I from getting ourselves into trouble, or helping us get out of trouble we had already caused.

"But no," I continued, "I haven't really seen them since the morning the missing were announced. I have seen them with Kylan, you remember the arrival that Elijah introduced us to and seemed to assign to me?" Creston nodded in acknowledgment. "Well, he showed up after you left us the other day, and from what I've seen it seems he's clung to them rather than me, which I'm not mad about."

"Small kindnesses, I suppose," he said thoughtfully. "But that research can't be forgotten in all the rest of this. I still want you to be careful, until we know more. Agreed?"

"Agreed. I hardly think that the questions I have about my magic are going anywhere." I half smiled at him.

He yawned and leaned back against the stone wall beside the bed, "Good, glad you agree." He closed his eyes and relaxed against the wall, rolling his shoulders to try and find a comfortable position.

I usually agreed with him, but I didn't need to admit that.

"And your stomach?" he asked without opening his eyes. When I hesitated, he opened them to squint at me, waiting.

My hand drifted to hover over the fading bruises, hoping he wouldn't notice the movement as I plastered a smile on my face. "Trae healed it. Good as new."

Creston cocked a brow, looking pointedly at the hand pressed against the part of my stomach that still ached if I twisted the wrong way. "Good as new," he repeated, almost sarcastically, meeting my eyes as he stifled another yawn.

Taking a chance, I said, "You're exhausted. Come on. Lay down." I shifted back to give him room on the side of the bed he was already on by the wall.

He gave me a sidelong glance. "Here?"

"No, on the floor," I said, hoping the dim lighting hid my blush. "Yes, of course here, now hurry up. I'm tired too." I gestured to the bed beside me as I kicked at his legs so I could slip back underneath the blankets.

He stared at me for a few moments, waging a war with himself, before the part of him that was beyond exhaustion won.

He kicked off his shoes and crawled up beside me. I tossed some blanket over him as he settled in. He yawned again and scanned me from head to toe. His gaze changed, eyes darkening from exhaustion into something else as he looked at me.

I flushed under the new weight of his midnight gaze, clearing my throat and shifting beside him. "Comfy?" I asked softly, in a weak attempt to break the intensity of his gaze.

He grinned at me, this time his eyes glittered with some joke I wasn't part of. "Very."

I nodded and reached out with my magic for the second time tonight to extinguish the lanterns, leaving just the fireplace creating a dim flickering light within the room. There was a slithering sound from behind me, but I didn't need to turn all the way see what I knew it was. Creston was releasing the chair he had created back into the earth.

I looked back to him when it was gone to find, he was still watching me. I smiled. "Close your eyes and go to sleep, Cres."

"Fine." He screwed up his face then closed his eyes. I watched him for a moment as he relaxed to welcome sleep, he opened one eye and grinned. "Go to sleep, creeper."

I flushed again and laughed, laying against my pillow and yawning, closing my eyes. "Goodnight," I murmured after a few minutes, trying to ignore everywhere his skin touched mine.

I felt Creston tense for a second and then move closer, then his lips pressed gently against my forehead as he drew me in against his chest.

I froze, heart pounding in my chest. What was he doing? We'd been skirting around each other for what felt like years, but he'd always been affectionate. Always finding excuses to touch me, my hair, my face, and in return I'd always found excuses to seek him out, sometimes unnecessarily.

"Stop thinking so hard," he said sleepily. "It's keeping me awake." Once I relaxed into him he nuzzled against my hair and murmured.

"Goodnight, Firefly."

I eased into his chest more and allowed myself to drift off to sleep.

CHAPTER 31

Running.

I was always running.

I ran in darkness, and the shadows reached for me but no hands landed upon me. There was something I needed to reach, something ahead.

An escape.

Just as the thought formed, I slammed into a wall in the darkness but instead of forcing me to a stop it moved, morphing into something malleable and slithering around my body, pushing me through to the other side.

I squinted as I emerged in a vibrant autumn forest. I wore a dress that matched the changing greenery around me.

It was made of magic, that much I could feel. Red reached from the lowest hem in the dress as it changed to yellow and finally green around my breasts, almost as if I stood in it too long, it would change entirely to red.

I turned, looking for the wall that I had fought through and instead found two trees that had grown towards each other to form an archway. Darkness consumed the opening between them. I stepped back from it as tendrils of shadow reached for me from within it.

"Finally," a low voice purred from behind me.

I spun on my heels, seeking the source of the voice in the forest around me.

A hooded figure stood across from me, leaning against the broad trunk of an old oak tree.

There were fresh marks on the tree. Runes that were unlike anything I had ever seen. I could only assume they had been created by the black blade in his hand. It glimmered with more unfamiliar runes.

I frowned as I sought out his face, but it was too deeply shrouded for me to get any grasp on his appearance. *"Who are you?"* I hated that there was an audible edge of fear to my voice.

"You've really taken your time getting past the door, haven't you?" he asked, ignoring my question as he strode forward away from the tree, spinning the blade in his hand as he walked, almost as though it was an idle movement.

I held my arms ready at my sides, my palms burning with the magic I kept just on the brink of use. Something about the male seemed to give me pause, leaving me on edge. *"Door?"*

"Let's not dwell," he said, brushing my question aside again as he stopped a few paces from the tree and used the tip of his blade to flick the hood of his cloak away. His hair was almost as dark as the cloak he wore, flowing in trimmed curls towards his delicately pointed ears. His features were sharp and angular, his skin a warm shade of brown. But his eyes, they were the true draw. Pools of liquid gold complimented by his dark features. He drew his full lips into a smirk as he watched my reaction. The expression came complete with dimples, and their appearance was somehow the most at odds with the way in which he held himself. *"Now that you've finally arrived, we can speak."*

"Who are you?" I repeated. He didn't look familiar in any way, except for the points of his ears. He was Faerie, or at least half Faerie.

He went to step forward again, but the world around us shuddered, inciting a growl from deep within his chest. "Damn it. It's too soon. I finally found you," he snarled, lunging towards me but he never reached. "Next time." The words followed me out.

I woke with a gasp, trying to sit up but my way was barred. It took me a moment to realise why.

Creston.

His arm and his leg were draped halfway over my body, keeping me pinned down to the bed. His leg perilously was close to my stomach and the bruise.

I squirmed, growing increasingly anxious under the weight of him, feeling claustrophobic. I was sweating and needed to breathe cool air after the nightmare. I jabbed Creston until he groaned and rolled just enough in his sleep to release me from my capture.

Slipping out of the bed, I moved towards my door. I reached out towards it only to turn away, suddenly changing my mind, planting myself on the floor, crossing my legs beneath me.

For what felt like hours I sat by the fireplace, admiring the flames, when I remembered I had wanted to be outside, had wanted the cool air on my face to help chase away the nightmare.

I looked towards the door again, an overwhelming sense of repulsion rolling through me. I knew it was still dark outside, but I had never before been so sickened by the idea of stepping out into it. I yawned as I looked back to the flames, curling my knees towards my chest, watching the fire dancing until my heartbeat calmed and I grew uncomfortable enough on the floor to want to get back into the bed.

I wasn't sure how long I'd spent on the cold floor, but as I got back into the bed Creston stirred. "Morning," he muttered, his voice deepened with sleep as he rolled towards me and rubbed his face. It took him a few moments before he looked at me properly. "You okay?"

I nodded, avoiding his eyes. "Just had an odd dream. Nothing to worry about, just didn't want to set you on fire if I fell back asleep." My attempt at a joke fell flat when he stilled. I glanced back at him.

His eyes were wide. "Fuck, I didn't think about that." He cleared his throat and sat up slowly. "I'm really glad you didn't set me on fire during the night." He stretched and examined the bed. "Despite the non living parts, this bed is quite good."

"Glad one of us slept well, but given how you looked last night, I could hardly let you leave when you were so run down." I nudged him. "Though you nearly crushed me throughout the night," I teased, smiling a little, needing to make light of something this morning to keep snarls and golden eyes from my mind.

Creston rolled his eyes. "I would have survived. They teach us how to deal with lack of sleep early on as a Guardien." He yawned and stretched some more, then pinned me with a harder stare. "So you're lying about it just being a dream, right?"

I squirmed a little under the intensity of his gaze. "Maybe."

He crawled above me, kneeling on either side of my thighs and holding himself with his arms on either side of my shoulders, so his weight didn't pin me to the bed, but his presence was more than enough to still me. "Want to tell me about it?" His voice was softer now, not urging but just offering me the ability to release the burden of fear onto him, instead of burying it like I usually did.

I opened my mouth to speak again, the words forming, when a scream tore suddenly through the air, the sound like a knife being scraped down my spine. My whole body went rigid as a coldness spread throughout it.

Creston reacted faster than I could, on his feet, with a blade appearing in his hand as he moved. He stalked towards the door as the screams seemed to turn to cries.

I was frozen, and it took me time to realise why.

The screams were close, too close. They were female, and had to be coming from my mother. She was the only other female close by.

I moved from the bed once my thoughts formed coherent pathways again, flames at my fingertips as I shoved past Creston, who was still standing in the doorway.

"Seraphine, wait!" he snapped, but didn't grab for me, obviously having noticed the flames. He'd learnt that lesson.

I didn't wait, but he kept close by me. I tore across the yard leaving a path of singed ground in my wake. I did my best to reel my magic in against my panic as I barrelled through the front door.

Everything in the kitchen was the same as it had been when I had left for bed the night before, nothing had changed or been touched. No one had risen yet for breakfast. The sun had barely cleared the horizon, as even the birds were only just waking with their morning songs.

I turned as I heard the first sobs and had a renewed sense of direction, racing down the hall and skidding to a stop at the doorway to a bedroom.

My mother was inside, on her knees at the foot of the bed with my father beside her, pulling her into the safety of his chest. Her hand was pressed against her heart as she wailed, a heart wrenching cry that made the flames in my hands gutter out. Her eyes were squeezed shut, but the tears still leaked out with her sobs.

Staggering into the room on shaky legs, I couldn't make sense of it, none of it connecting. I looked around the room, trying to understand. What had happened? Who had been hurt?

Zavier was there too, on his knees beside the bed.

All at once I caught up.

This was Niko's room.

My father was crying too, his sobs quieter than my mother's although just as pained, and Zavier's shoulders rocked as though he too cried, even though his lips were pressed together. It looked like he was trying to be the rock my parents needed at that moment.

My mother was not crying incoherently anymore, what she said I could now hear through the blur of my mind. "Not my baby," she was babbling, voice hoarse. "Please no, they took my baby." Over and over, as though the words could change things.

I sought out what all their eyes were glued to, on the wall above Niko's bed.

There it was. The mark. The Elliphir mark.

My knees lost all strength beneath me as the full weight and realisation of what I stared at was suddenly clear.

Niko was gone.

CHAPTER 32

I never made it to the ground.

Creston's strong grip caught me before I could get that far, his reflexes still sharp despite the scene we had entered into. He pulled me to my feet smoothly, even though my legs weren't up to holding my weight anymore. He dealt with that just as swiftly by moving me out of the doorway and leaning me against the wall, momentarily taking away the sight of Niko's empty bed and my mourning family members, but my face remained turned towards the sound of their mourning even with it out of sight.

"Seraphine. Look at me." Creston held me in place as my legs shook, trying to regain the ability to hold my weight on their own. When his voice gained him no reaction he gripped my chin firmly and forced my gaze in his direction. "Look. At. Me," he growled, demanding my attention.

Somehow, I found a way to focus on him from some depth of the grief swelling within me, like a wild storm at sea. The thought of my baby brother, scared and alone, threatened to overwhelm me. I stared into his fierce blue eyes, knowing that where I saw strength in his, he would see nothing but pain in mine.

"This will not help," he said in a voice I barely recognised. "You need to focus, okay? I need you with me on this, let the others mourn. We need to do more." He kept his grip on my chin, holding me in place as he watched me, waiting for some sort of recognition.

Trying to fight my way through the fog of fear and pain, I frowned at him after a few more slow moments, nodded. "Okay." The word was harsh and thick with emotion, so much so that I had to clear my throat and try again. "Okay." The word was clearer the second try.

He was right, and I knew he was right. It was barely dawn, there had to be a chance there was something we could do.

After a few moments he stepped away from me, trusting that I was stable enough on my own now, although he kept a hand extended in case I wasn't. I moved off the wall and took a deep breath to centre myself.

Once I felt steady enough, I moved back into the doorway. No one inside the room had moved, but my perspective had changed, my pain slowly burying itself below the warmth of growing anger. I stepped further inside, looking through the room beyond my family, focusing on the smaller details.

None of Niko's things were in disarray any more than they would usually be. It was as though he hadn't struggled at all, perhaps taken while he was still asleep.

I frowned as the mark on the wall drew my attention, striding further into the room to get closer to it. Without realising what I'd done I was standing on Niko's bed. I heard a mutter of surprise behind me that sounded like it came from Creston, as I reached out to touch the mark.

Before my fingers reached it, the air above it seemed to shiver and after a moment, the mark lost its form, shadows sliding down from it, slipping along the wall towards the window.

Seeking escape from me.

I glanced over my shoulder to where Creston stood by the door. He stared back at me with a mixed look of horror and fascination. "We have to follow it." The need to follow the shadows as they slid out of the window was like a ringing in my ears growing louder the further away it moved.

As it slipped out of sight, I launched after it, suddenly on my feet outside.

It slithered along the ground, leaving a path of half withered life in its wake. I didn't look back to see if Creston followed me out the window as the shadow shivered again and started to slip away faster. I was soon running to keep up.

I was racing after it at full speed when the shadows reached the Divide and vanished through the branches of the trees out of sight. I looked up as Creston stopped beside me barely out of breath. "We have to keep following it," I insisted, panting. "It's going somewhere, otherwise it would have just disappeared. Open a path, I can't risk burning it." My lungs burnt as I spoke.

"Burning it?" he asked, frowning at me, but despite the confusion in his tone he still opened the Divide quickly.

"In my nightmares, fire destroys them. That thing, whatever it is, is just like the kind of shadows that I see in every one of my nightmares," I explained as I moved through the path he had created, brushing aside the branches and leaves that clung to my clothes. I looked around frantically, hoping I hadn't lost the shadow, but found the trail of withered plants the mass left behind.

He didn't reply but I could hear the Divide close behind us as we moved further away from it and deeper into the woods.

The shadow seemed to follow a clear path, and no matter how close to it I got, it never reacted. I considered blocking its path with flames to see if it would change course, but did not dare risk destroying it altogether, knowing without reason that it could lead us to something more. I wasn't sure where the knowledge came from, perhaps it was desperation, my mind grasping for an answer whether it was viable or not. Just so I could feel as though I hadn't allowed my baby brother to be taken from us.

But I did know if I hadn't triggered this shadow, it would have remained, perhaps until darkness, as the reminder my brother was gone. It was the fear.

The marks had always been left to cause fear, at least for the first few days, then the sensation of unease they created faded. Perhaps this was why, because these wisps of darkness were left to taunt us, as if a stolen child wasn't enough.

We followed it deeper into the woods than I had ever been, when a sudden violent wave of nausea stopped me in my tracks as the shadows slipped between two trees and out of sight. I pressed my hand to my stomach, ignoring the icy feeling where the bruises were.

Creston moved up beside me, having been lingering behind me until now. "What is it?" he asked softly as he looked around, in full Guardien mode.

"Something's wrong." I stared at the trees ahead of us. The nausea continued to roll over me, making me to step back in an attempt to make the feeling stop. "Whatever is on the other side of those trees is making me feel sicker the closer I get," I said as I took another step back.

He frowned and stared at me for a long moment, concern flickering though his gaze before he looked away from me. "Wait here," he murmured, slinking forward, ducking lower until he was crawling to the edge of the tree bases.

I watched him, remaining still and silent as my stomach continued to churn. It occurred to me that his movements were completely silent.

He was manipulating the nature around him into silence.

Beyond impressed, I snapped my mouth shut to keep from asking the question. Where did he learn to do *that?*

Creston's body stiffened completely as something beyond the trees caught his attention, and he halted, tilting his head to the side to listen.

I tried to step closer but was pushed back by another wave of unease. I gritted my teeth and took a breath, trying again, dropping down on my hands and knees to crawl towards him, not nearly as quiet as he had. I made it to his side, my whole body shaking with the effort, but the nausea began to ease the further I pushed past my revulsion. I needed to see what he could.

He reached out and put a hand on my back as I settled against the ground. The gesture felt calming, but I didn't know it was to keep me firmly in place until I moved enough to see beyond the crest of the hill. I sucked in a breath and felt my eyes widen.

In the small valley below us it was clear where the shadow I had stalked had returned. A mass of darkness filled the space, more shadows slithering to the centre.

The cage was made of pulsing darkness, menacing the centre of the clearing below, but everything around it was dead. Every plant and flower had withered in its presence. Death seemed to seep from its confines, devouring any life it found in its path.

My stomach flipped again as I watched the shadows shudder against themselves, pushed by forces from within. It took me a few moments to realise that as the shadows moved there were glimpses of what lie inside.

Hands. I could see hands gripping at the shadows fighting them from inside. Fighting to escape the dark confines that engulfed them.

The desperate fearful grips of stolen Elliphae children.

CHAPTER 33

Creston pressed his hand harder into my lower back as I tried to push up from the ground and move towards the cage. "Don't," he warned softly, his hand keeping me firmly in place. I shot him a frustrated look but his eyes weren't on me. They were fixed ahead of us, scanning around the cage.

"They're right there, Creston. We can't just sit here," I breathed as I turned back towards the cage.

"Quiet," he hissed, his focus elsewhere, his whole body tense.

I began searching for what he saw. My attention had been so secured on the writhing mass of the cage that I hadn't felt the need to look elsewhere. I scoured the area but couldn't see anything in it other than the snakelike shadows. I looked to him again, studying him instead.

His free hand, the one not on my back, was half buried in the dirt in front of him, but his eyes had never left the clearing.

Following his line of sight, my gaze caught on the far side of the clearing below, halting on a small unusual bundling of trees.

The trees were out of place with all the dead life that lingered around them, their leaves still lush and green, where everything else had become a strange withered brown or grey.

Creston shuddered beside me. "Those trees," he breathed, just loud enough for me to hear.

I looked back at him, confused. "What—"

"Focus on them," he interrupted, barely above a whisper.

I frowned at him, and when I didn't turn back immediately, he glanced at me, deep eyes piercing.

My friend was lost somewhere in that blue stare. It had hardened, become something else. A Guardien's stare. "Do it. Tell me what you see."

I turned back to the trees, looking at them properly, trying to make out the finer details I should be able to see. Each time I tried to pinpoint a specific detail, they seemed to shift, distort a little, then return to normal with a blink.

When I turned to Creston, he was still watching me. "They're not really there." He nodded towards the trees then to his hand buried in the soil. "I can feel every thing here, living and drained. But those trees, there is nothing there." He paused, his fingers flexing in the soil, as if he was searching for something. "Well, not nothing, there is something there. Elliphir perhaps. I can feel them moving through the soil, feel the way the drained plants crunch under them. But I can't see them."

"But how? That doesn't make sense," I whispered back, trying again tried to see the trees properly. This time, as I focused harder they seemed to waiver deeply, almost disappearing entirely for half an instant but then they righted themselves. I glanced back at the cage. "What if I burn it?"

Creston shook his head. "It's too much risk, you don't know how many children are actually in there. You could hurt them. You could hurt Niko." His hand stroked my lower back gently, trying to comfort me, while still keeping me in place.

I grunted, frustrated by his doubt. "I have more control than that.

It'll never touch them." Turning back to the cage, I reached for my fire, only to falter, realising I didn't know how I was going to get it around the cage safely. I may be in total control of my magic, but the children could panic, run through the flames before I could react.

"This is not a good idea," he said warningly.

I felt the magic build, the flames burning within me as they waited for their orders. For me to send them out from me with a purpose. I stared at the writhing cage and gnawed at my lip, trying to decide where to begin. I didn't know if it would even work, but if the nightmares I was having were reaching into my reality, then there had to be truth to them somewhere.

Creston hissed and quickly removed his hand from my back, shaking it by his side. He cursed softly at the sight my hands covered in blue flames, singeing the earth around me. Still waiting.

I glanced towards the trees that didn't really exist and decided to try something else. I pressed my burning hands against the ground watching as, in the same instant, a trail of fire rushed to create a ring around those trees. It took a few moments before they flickered out of existence, revealing the sounds and beings that had been hidden within the illusion.

Three Elliphir males stood within it, clambering to remain as far away from the flames as they could. All were dressed in dark clothing, tattered as it was, torn from unknown sources. I could see their faces through the flames. None were remarkable but all held the same look of disgust and fear. They did not like fire.

Other than their initial outbursts of shock, none of them spoke, but they shared looks with each other that held more meaning than they should have.

I looked to Creston. "Better?"

"We'll discuss your recklessness later." He got to his feet. "Stay here, keep the flames as they are." He stepped over me carefully to get on the correct side of the flames.

Like I would ever let them hurt you, I thought with an edge of annoyance, but watched him carefully as he made his way towards the newly trapped males.

"Well guys, seems you got yourself into a bit of a hot spot, didn't you?" Disdain bled into every word as Creston spoke, clear to me even from a distance.

Heightened hearing was a gift from our Fae ancestors that usually left me annoyed, but today I was for once grateful for it.

The males inside the ring stared at him but said nothing, so I tightened the circle around them a little, forcing them even closer together in the centre.

"Now, we're going to have a little chat," Creston said, face twisting in anger. "Because once I get that cage open, I can assure you those children won't be of your kind, and that violates any peace I may have oaths to uphold." He stalked around the flames as he spoke, forcing them to watch him.

There was a shout from inside the circle, and it took me a few moments to figure out why.

Creston was using his abilities too, inside the flames where it was much harder to tell. Vines were finding their way up the bodies of the men inside, holding them in place, meaning they could no longer shift as the flames did.

I pulled the flames in closer to help emphasise Creston's menace, not that he seemed to need it. I watched his face as it appeared and disappeared behind the flames.

There was a wrath to his expression I'd never seen before. A raw, pure hatred. It darkened everything about the male I so often relied on for light and warmth.

"Watch yourself, earthen one. We are not alone in these woods and you are on the wrong side of your pathetic little wall of trees," one of them sneered through the flames.

"And you are trapped within a wall of flames you have no way of escaping, especially not in order to call for the help you may need, so why should I care?" Creston snapped back, crossing his arms, eyes spearing onto the side closest to the one who had spoken. "For all you know I came with an army of my own, waiting out of sight for more to arrive."

"Only one other touches the shadows here besides you," another voice inside the cage of flames spoke, his voice was blank, as though he wasn't really focused on what he was saying.

Alarm flashed in Creston's expression quickly, before it vanished behind that mask of rage once more. He called to me without his gaze moving. "Phi, make it a bit more cozy."

My eyes widened at his request. There was little space left to move the flames now without real risks. I got up from my stomach and crouched in the dirt, catching his eye as he looked towards me now, both because of my movement into sight and because the flames had not yet moved.

"Do it, Seraphine," he ordered. "One of them controls that cage somehow, and his death will surely cease the magic." He turned back to those in the flames. His vines had disappeared now, leaving them exposed.

I gulped and slowly started bringing the walls in closer, closing them in tightly. I could feel the space between their skin and my fire, the sliver of air that kept them from being engulfed. Sweat ran down the side of my face as the control I had on the fire slipped, unused to dancing it inches away from a living thing.

As the flames licked out against the arm of the male who had, so far, remained silent, he cried out in pain. His screams echoed the shadows of the cage and they reacted to it, shuddering and writhing, before they slammed to the ground in a wave of blackness, pooling across the small valley and vanishing into the normal shadows of the nature around us. After a moment there was a clear view of the children who had been trapped inside, four of them.

I got to my feet as I searched their bruised, bloody faces while my heart leapt in my chest. The girl seemed the least injured, but the boys were older and looked like they had fought harder, leaving them with torn bloodied clothes and darkening bruises on their faces and arms. My heart ached with new agony.

I looked back towards Creston, tears stinging my eyes at the face that wasn't there.

He nodded. He had seen what I had.

Niko was not there.

His eyes met mine with a brief softness, a wordless apology that my brother was not yet safe.

A new rage awoke in my chest. They had not just spirited them away at night. They had beaten them too. It was too much. I walked towards the ring of flames, the ground burning beneath my bare feet with every step. My anger and pain fuelled the flames around them, turning from an amber hue to a violent, and almost invisible, blue.

I met the gaze of the male closest to me through the flames, the one who had spoken first. "Tell me. Why are you stealing our children?"

His lips pulled back in a snarl, flashing teeth that it took me an instant to register. They were pointed, filed, sharpened to tips. Like a shark.

I reached out as if to touch him, but instead let the flames caress his skin.

He glared at me but made no sound, the muscles in his jaw spasming as his mouth clamped shut with the pain he must have felt.

"Tell me where the rest are," I whispered, pulling the flames closer to the males once more.

His eyes darkened and he leaned forward, watching me for a moment before he smirked slowly, the pain fuelling something vicious and animal in him as he stared at me. "Are *you* are supposed to save them?" He laughed then, deep and victorious. "You'll never find them."

The rage in me spilled over as he laughed at me, the sound grinding against something deep and cold, awakening it.

I was resolved then, to do what was needed, and the flames began to descend.

Screams tore from the others, but the one who laughed returned to silence, eyes so dark they were almost black staring at me endlessly through the flames that licked at him and his companions.

I was barely aware of his presence as Creston grabbed my shoulders, spinning me to face him, too lost in the sight and feel of the flames being allowed to do *something* constructive. I'd always had to hold myself back, keep that thing inside locked away, but these males had taken my brother. They'd broken the peace we'd lived with, the agreement we'd struck so long ago. For that betrayal, they would be the first to pay the price.

"STOP!" he shouted, shaking me until I looked at him.

I knew his hands were burning as he touched me, but he didn't let me go and I was beyond trying to stop it happening. I turned my gaze back to the Elliphir, lost in the darkness I'd always known existed in me, hidden deep within me.

The males were the cause of my mother's screams, the pain she felt. They were the reason I could see my father's heart breaking on his face, had witnessed my normally stoic older brother break down in sobs over Niko's fate. No, the three Elliphir would not leave this clearing. They didn't deserve to li—

"Firefly, stop," Creston pleaded, trying to find me within the depths of my rage.

Some part of me finally reacted, and slowly, so very slowly, I felt a piece of me rise from the rage, snapping back into place, into myself.

I stepped back, out of Creston's grip, letting the flames drop away from around the Elliphir.

One collapsed instantly within the ring as the flames fell back.

I didn't allow myself to look. I didn't want to see what I had done, what happened when I lost control. I closed my eyes and took a breath, securing the magic that held the flames in place. Once I felt calmer, more myself, I looked to Creston where he stood, face inches from mine.

He sighed a breath of relief, as whatever he saw when I met his gaze calmed him, lowering his hands.

I flinched at the sight of the raw reddened flesh that remained and I opened my mouth to speak but he shook his head.

"Go get the children. We need to leave now. These screams will have attracted others if they're nearby." He stepped back from me, turning to the three males.

Some of the children were friends of Niko's, and they were relieved to see a familiar face, clamouring to tell me what had happened since they'd been taken. As kindly as I could, I shushed them. "We're going to take you home, but you have to be quiet, okay?"

The one who looked to be the oldest nodded sagely, wrapping an arm over the trembling girl's shoulder to comfort her.

I gathered the children quickly, despite their fearfulness, and moved them out of the valley back towards the path we had used to find them. I turned towards where I had left Creston.

He stood watching the Elliphir, until the children were out of reach. Only then did he turn to leave, catching my gaze as if by accident. He looked down as he moved towards me. "Let's go. We need to return them to their families."

"What about them?" I asked softly, nodding towards the three males I had almost scorched. *I would have killed them, if he hadn't stepped in.* I could feel that now. I had wanted them to burn. To have them feel some of the agony they had inflicted upon others.

Creston grabbed my arm, wincing as he agitated his injuries. "They are not our concern. I will send others to find them if my bindings hold once your fire fails."

I realised then as he nudged me away what he had been doing while I had gathered the children. Binding them in vines to keep them captured. He had never intended their deaths, just the threat of them.

I was the one who had taken his threat too far and almost made it a reality. I flinched at the thought, turning away and trudging forward, putting space between Creston and I, as he watched our surroundings vigilantly, looking for any sign that more Elliphir would get in our way.

None came.

We made it to the Divide quietly, safely, and Creston opened a doorway for the children to rush through, turning back to make sure we followed close behind them. They were all still terrified, but I could hardly be of comfort to them. I had closed myself off.

The reality of what I'd almost done weighed on me with each step I'd taken away from the Elliphir, largely because there was still a piece of me that wanted to go back and finish what I'd started. Only Creston's presence beside me stopped the feeling from becoming overwhelming.

I paused and waited as he closed the wall once we were all through, trying to think of something, anything, to say. No words came.

He brushed past me and looked over at the children, glancing back at me over his shoulder, refusing to meet my eyes. "You should go home. Check on your family," he said roughly, more emotion to his tone than I could understand with my own clouding my thoughts.

My mouth dropped open, ready to protest, but I couldn't find the words. I cleared my throat and nodded, settling for agreement instead as my stomach churned. "Sure."

"I'll get the children back, and I'll alert the other Guardiens. I'll find you later." His tone was sharp, distant. A soldier's tone. He turned away from me briskly, moving to the children, speaking to them in soft hushed tones I didn't care to listen to, before leading them towards the centre of our settlement. I knew he'd take each one where they needed to be, knew he didn't need me to know who each child was.

I waited and watched until they disappeared out of sight, Creston never looking back.

I was completely alone.

It took me some time to realise I was shaking with the leftover adrenaline, the residual anger, the hurt at Creston's attitude and absence, still coursing through me. I couldn't seem to still my hands. I balled them into fists and took a step towards home before stopping short. I couldn't be there. Not when I hadn't brought Niko home to them. I turned and looked back towards the wall. I knew Creston would look for me, but not for at least an hour. I had time.

With the decision made, I was back on the other side of the wall, my feet carrying me forward with emotionless determination. I just needed some peace. Some space. I knew where I needed to go.

I had nearly made it all the way to clearing when I heard their voices.

CHAPTER 34

I slowed cautiously as the sound reached my ears.

Walking carefully, I quietened my footsteps and slipped off the path as best I could, keeping my presence quiet, unknown, crouching down, as much out of sight as I could be without knowing exactly where the source of the voices was.

"I have forgotten nothing, boy," the voice spat. "You may be a soldier on the inside now, but you are disposable if you become a threat and I'm the one who gets to decide if you are that threat. Is that understood?" There was menace in the first voice, and even though it wasn't directed at me, it sent a shiver down my spine and had my full attention.

It was clear who the more powerful of the two must be.

There must have been an interaction I couldn't see as the voice continued. "Good. You have a role you should be focusing on. You were not assigned to be hiding here playing house, so do what you were told. You seemed sure it would be an easy role for you to play, given what you intend to gain."

"I wasn't aware you were informed of the... intended benefits to my role here." The second voice sounded unsure now.

"I know everything about your foxy reasons for volunteering yourself," the first voice said dismissively, uninterested. "I'd have you keep that in mind from here on out."

The first male seemed to be moving then. "We will speak again later, in less compromised positions. Go separately to where you should be found."

There was no reply but I remained where I was, keeping as still as I could, listening to the rustling of the undergrowth, a trail of sound that marked them moving further from me.

I tore my fingers through my hair in frustration. Both voices had sounded familiar but I could place neither, perhaps due to the malice that was being used between them. No one I knew spoke with such disdain, at least not that I'd ever heard.

I waited until it felt truly safe then pulled myself up from my prone position in the dirt, sitting with my legs crossed in the underbrush. I was out of sight from all directions for now. I took a breath as the sudden silence reeled in the pieces of reality I was pushing away.

Niko is gone.

I pictured him in my mind's eye, heard his laugh, envisioned the way he would smile at me before he ran off on some ridiculous mission. He was not old enough to be gone. My eyes stung.

By our perspectives, yes, he was just eight, but within the terms of humanity he appeared to be much younger. Six. I think that was the age the Enlightened had settled on as the equivalent size. Until our magic was confirmed our growth was slowed, but after that we grew at what seemed to be the same as our human counterparts. That is, until we reached our twenty-fifth year, then ageing slowed drastically during our Settling, a gift of our Fae blood. Such were our milestones.

I let myself cry then, for all the things my brother may miss if we could not get him back. For the fear he was already taken from this world.

I buried my head in my hands as my misery broke the silence around me. Fear of being gone too long faded into numbness as I sat there, and only when a chill started to permeate the air around me did I notice darkness had begun dominating the forest around me. I shuddered, no longer feeling at peace in it. I pulled myself from the underbrush and made my way along the inside of the Divide wall, arms wrapped around myself. I found my usual crossing and burnt away enough room to pass through, my unease at facing more shadows far outweighing my fear of being caught.

I didn't pass anyone as I made my way home, the evening sun much warmer on this side of the Divide. I paused in the trees surrounding my home, on the edge of the pathway that would take me directly to the front door. I could see light in the windows.

Someone had lit the lanterns inside.

I looked away from the house, pushing back the images of my family collapsed by my brother's bed. It wasn't a sight I could face yet, and neither were they. I slipped off the path and went towards my room. It was far enough away from the windows that I knew there was little risk I would be spotted before I made it inside.

I had barely pushed the door open when hands grabbed at me, yanking me inside and slamming me back against the door as it closed with a thud. Breathlessly I found myself staring into furious midnight eyes.

"*Where. The. Fuck.* Were you?" he growled as he pressed me further against the door, his palms splayed on either side of my head.

No words or explanation came to mind. And I could feel the wooden door ripple against my back as the silence stretched out, his rage allowing his magic to seep into his touch involuntarily.

"I told you to fucking come home." I flinched at the anger in his tone and looked up at him, heart beating erratically in my chest. "Why was that so hard?"

"I'm not a child, Cres. I can actually decide where I go. And I didn't want to be back here yet." I put my hands up and pushed at his chest, attempting to get him to move back.

He didn't. Instead it seemed to make him angrier. "Yeah? Poor you," he snarled. "You're not the one who had to lie, to your already frantic family, about where you were." He moved closer to me, every line of his body pressing against mine. "Imagine how surprised I was when I got here to check on you, and your family had no clue where you were. Because you never came home today." He glared down at me as he straightened his shoulders, using his height to look down on me. "So I'll ask again, one more time, where were you?"

"I think the sentence you used actually included 'fuck' for emphasis." I pushed on his chest again, harder this time. "I went to get some space. I needed time alone to breathe."

He shifted back ever so slightly but kept me pinned with his arms on either side of me. It was space enough.

I ducked under his arm to move around him. When he turned and grabbed my arm to stop me, I twisted using his momentum to drive my knee into his stomach, eliciting a surprised grunt of pain from him as it slipped through his defences, something in me snapping as he growled and pushed me backwards, catching the new look in my eyes.

"Don't," he warned.

I tried to find one of the defensive positions he'd taught me in past weeks as I faced him. "Don't what?" I cocked an eyebrow.

"Start a fight you will not win." Despite the warning in his tone, he mirrored me, his whole body tensed, ready to pounce.

My eyes narrowed. "You want to know where I was, *boss*? Earn it."

CHAPTER 35

There was a subtle flicker in Creston's expression before he moved, feigning a punch towards my head that I blocked as we began to circle one another. We had been practicing for weeks now, I wasn't as skilled as he was, I probably never would be, but I was learning. Fast.

He lunged towards me again, landing a blow to my ribs when I blocked too high. I glared and lashed out at him. He blocked the first swing but missed the second I aimed at his stomach. He grunted but smirked at me as he stepped forward again.

I was so distracted rearranging my footing that the leg he swept beneath me went unnoticed. I landed on my side with a thud, barely having time to roll away as he came for me again.

I moved onto my back, swinging my leg into a kick to gain some room to move, and as he dodged the kick I crawled forward enough to grab his ankle and yank. It was weak but it was enough to throw him off balance as I scrambled to my feet, able to use his momentum against him.

I landed on top of him as his back thudded against the ground, moving to pin his arms as my weight settled, but he reacted before I had the chance. He knocked my hands to the side in a swift motion and pulled me down against his chest roughly, his left leg hooking over my right to trap me in place as he flipped us.

I wheezed when my back hit the ground again and his weight pressed down on me from above, my arms pinned between our chests. Furious blue eyes stared down at me.

"Are we done now?" Creston asked roughly.

I sighed and blew strands of curls out of my face, glaring up at him. "Fine."

His eyes narrowed as he watched me, assessing whether or not I was telling the truth, before easing his grip just a little.

I cleared my throat as the adrenaline from the scuffle wore off, replaced by a different kind of rush when I shifted beneath him. I met his gaze, watching his anger bled out into another kind of darkness.

His gaze flicked down to my lips when I ran my tongue over the lower one.

The motion seemed to be enough to snap something inside him. His lips crushed against mine in the next breath, his hands no longer caging me, instead sliding along the side of my body, his hold on me melting into a needy grasp. My arms freed from between us, I slid one to the back of his neck as I sank into the kiss, drawing him closer with a soft groan.

Creston hooked my legs around his waist, and sliding his hands under my back he lifted us up off the floor, lips only breaking contact with mine as he drew them down my neck. He laid me down on my bed gently and nipped at my neck, drawing another groan across my lips when he seemed to target the most sensitive part of it. His fingers trailed beneath the edge of the chemise I wore, his lips finding their way back to mine.

I slid my fingers into his hair and pulled him closer, biting his lower lip gently, earning a breathy moan from him in return. His lips parted as he pressed down against me more, grinding into the curves of my body, kissing me hungrily. I tugged at his shirt, and he pulled back just enough so I could tug it off over his head.

He broke away from my lips to look down at me, breathing heavier now. "Tell me to stop," he murmured, stroking my cheek, fingers sliding to tuck stray curls back behind my ear as he watched me, looking for signs of hesitation. He found none.

"No," I breathed, pulling him back down towards me, moaning softly when he bit my lip before drawing me into another hungry kiss that left me breathless.

He ran his hands over the front of the chemise, ripping it away, using his magic to destroy the fibres. He tugged it open roughly, pulling it from beneath me and tossed it towards his shirt on the floor.

If not for the heat that roared through my body I would have felt shy beneath him, with my stomach and breasts exposed. But Creston left no time for me to try to cover myself, even if I had wanted to. His lips traced over my skin, as if he knew exactly what I was thinking.

When his teeth tugged at my sensitive breast I couldn't help the moan that crossed my lips. I arched beneath him, eliciting a throaty chuckle from him while he continued his path of lips, teeth and tongue over my breasts until I could think of little else. I'm not sure when he took them off but my pants were gone too, soon I was naked beneath him and he was following closely.

He moved above me, breaking away some of the contact between our heated flesh, his eyes dark and lips swollen. I flushed as he shifted his hips against mine, his breathing piqued. He smirked at me, and I felt more heat rush to my face under the weight of his gaze.

I had been with others before, as had he too, no doubt, but no touch had ever felt so much like fire as his did.

He bent down and rested his forehead against mine. "Oh Firefly, you might just drive me insane one day." He took a breath before drawing me closer, one hand sliding to grip my throat, claiming my lips with his. I slid my hands down his back, tugging him closer as the kiss deepened, my legs drawn up on each side of his hips to nestle him closer against me.

I heard the crack of the door shattering open, in the same instant Creston shifted, rolling so I was behind him, his body shielding mine from view.

"Oh, what the fuck," Trae exclaimed from the direction of the doorway.

I peeked over Creston's shoulder to find my friend halted halfway across the room, standing completely still as he absorbed the state we were in. I hastily pulled a blanket across my naked body, thankful Creston had shielded me from most of the exposure without blocking my view of the doorway.

I sat up slowly, my face burning no longer with lust, but with anger swelling within me. "What, you just smash through doors now?" I snapped at him.

Trae cocked an eyebrow at me. "Returning the favour," he countered with the same clipped tone.

Creston tensed even more as another figure stepped into the room. He slid a hand back to touch my thigh where the blanket covered it and I felt the fabric shifting with new life, curving itself over my body, the seams knitting together quicker than I would have expected. Creston used his gift to redress me as I stared in shock at the other presence in the room.

CHAPTER 36

"Get up. Now. Both of you." Veneficus towered over us from where he stood by the doorway, a small male by no means. He kept his scalp free of hair, his shortly trimmed beard at odds with the lack of hair elsewhere. It was said he kept his hair cut to show off the delicate point of his ears. And as one who taught classes on the strongest Magics, he was not to be messed with.

He was also not one who should have been barrelling through my doorway for any reason.

Unlike Cleo, I was no longer a student under his tutelage.

"I said now. We do not have time for this. Guardien, get out." His tone was edged with something that made me shudder, far more forceful than it ought to be for an idle visit.

Creston straightened, bristling at the interruption and the command. "No. Whatever business you have barging in here, I will be part of it." He had dressed himself now too, getting off the bed to stand but keeping his body angled so I was behind him as I too stood up.

Veneficus' eyes narrowed at Creston. He seemed to evaluate him for a time before he spoke again. "You will not start a fight that you will lose, boy, that is the only warning I will give to you." He glanced between us, apparently realising it was a fight he wasn't going to win.

"I will allow you, only because I deem these two have not kept secret the reasons behind their recent thievery of ancient resources."

"I put it back," Trae muttered, running a hand over his hair. He seemed cowed, like a child scorned for some deviant trick that had only meant to be funny.

"You should never have meddled in such things," Veneficus hissed. "Now you have forced my hand. Let's go. All of you." He turned and gestured towards the destroyed doorway.

Creston reached back and took my hand, guiding me beside him out the door. I shot a glare at Trae. "New door. Now," I growled at him as I moved through the shattered remains left hanging from the framing of my doorway.

We hesitated outside, glancing at each other anxiously as Veneficus took the lead. He stormed ahead, not bothering to see if we followed.

We did. Creston's entire body was fraught with tension as he hurried behind the imposing male. He never spoke as he led us further from my home.

I quickly realised where we were headed. The Divide. I glanced at Creston, his jaw clenched. He knew too. I looked behind us to Trae, whose expression was grim with knowledge he clearly hadn't shared yet. Perhaps knowledge as to why, beyond our borrowing of resources that were so limited to us, we were following Veneficus through the early evening. I frowned at him in inquiry but he simply shook his head.

A shiver smoothed its way down my spine as we came to a slow stop at the edge of the Divide.

"Vaelle. Open it." Veneficus gestured to the trees before him, barely turning to acknowledge us.

Creston dropped my hand and stepped forward without hesitation, perhaps in the hopes that quick obedience would lead us to answers faster. He brushed his hands through the air in front of the Divide, and the vines and branches shuddered, rolling back to create a small living doorway for us.

"Through you go, Seraphine. Quickly now." Veneficus stepped aside to allow me the room to pass.

I took a step forward and then glanced back at Creston, waiting for his response, for him to say it was safe or to interject.

But he didn't look at me. In fact, he hardly seemed to be looking at anything at all. With a frown, I looked towards Trae and found him in the same state. I watched their eyes glaze black as they both settled into complete stillness. I turned an accusatory gaze on Veneficus.

He just smirked and shook his head. "As I said, quickly now. I don't have time to play these games."

"What's wrong with them?" I asked, backing away, wanting nothing more than to be as far from him as possible.

"They're seeing what I want. Now move, or I will make you. I told you, I do not have time for this." Something in his tone darkened enough to make me step forward. He gestured towards the doorway Creston had created.

Neither of my friends moved as I went through, nor did they speak. Veneficus quickly followed.

I shuddered as shadows swelled towards me, stretching and reaching from the forest as I passed the safety of the Divide.

A strong hand gripped the back of my neck and yanked me backwards against a hard chest, a second hand burying in my hair and pinning me in place with a startled yelp.

"Nice to see you again, bitch," a voice hissed in my ear.

I froze, watching as Veneficus strode away from the opening without flinching, my sudden containment no surprise to him.

He regarded my shocked, fearful gaze with amusement. "What?

Don't recognise his voice without his screams of pain?" He raised an eyebrow at me, as if in a challenge.

The reality of who held me suddenly dawned, and in the same moment the realisation hit, I reached for my magic, burning at the hand on my neck and twisting away so I could see my captor.

He released me quickly enough, though I felt as though some of my hair stayed with him. One of the Elliphir I had caged earlier stood before me. I stepped further from him and looked between both men in confusion. "What is this?" I demanded as I took another step backwards, eyes bouncing between the two males, not wanting to draw my attention too far from the Elliphir.

"Kinder introductions, of course," Veneficus drawled, as though he were introducing two people at a ball. "Seraphine, this is Elonis. Elonis—"

"This is your flaming whelp," the male spat towards me.

"Language!" Veneficus chastised with a shake of his head, the interruption seemingly having offended him far more than it should.

"Firstly, I'm not his anything," I said, trying not to panic and to remember what Creston had taught me. "He's a teacher and not even mine." I backed up a little more from them both, earning a dark laugh from Elonis, despite the sharp look he received from Veneficus.

"Now now, don't be rude," Veneficus sighed, brushing a leaf from his sleeve. "I haven't got much time here, Seraphine. Answers are required and swiftly. I don't have the patience left for gentle pretence. How often have you passed onto this side of the Divide, and for how long?" he asked.

I continued to edge away from them both, looking for just enough space to give me better grounds to either run or fight, whichever I might need. He did not seem to care that I was creeping away from them in the slightest.

He just stared at me expectantly.

Elonis, on the other hand, watched me with a small smile, as if challenging me to attack or run.

Finally remembering something Creston had told me, I stopped and stood still, watching him in return, realising that the more I acted like frightened prey, the more likely it was that he would treat me that way.

He scoffed. "Fine." He strolled away, hands in his pockets, and leaned against the trunk of a nearby tree.

Veneficus snapped his fingers at me with two sharp clicks. "Seraphine, answer me. Now."

I turned my attention back to him with a frown, before looking between the two males again, trying to gather which one was truly more of a threat to me. "A few times, for some years now."

"All that work warding this place wasted," he sighed heavily. "The nightmares, have they started?"

Jolting in surprise, I fought to keep my expression neutral. "How do you know about the nightmares?"

"At what age did they begin?" He held up a hand the instant after he spoke, waving away whatever answer I might have had. "Never mind, it doesn't matter. Your little show with the children has made you quite the target now. You are not to be involved. I'm sure Elonis and his friends would love to tear open your throat, but they know their place well enough to know it would be not worth their own lives."

I glowered at him. "They stole my *brother*. What makes you think I'm going to just let that happen without doing anything?"

His eyes flashed with a surge of anger. "Do not push me further, Seraphine, you have done enough irreparable damages as it is. Your stupidity is only excusable due to your naivety, which is my own fault. I should not have assumed the draw would be weak enough for you to ignore." He turned to Elonis. "Go. You know your role. Carry the news to him, I know he is angry."

"More than you know," Elonis grunted as he straightened. "What of her?"

"She stays where she is. Now go, there is much to be done." He waved the male off and he moved into the shadows. They consumed him almost immediately as he stepped away.

The sight of the horrible male slinking back into the shadows made me shiver.

Veneficus turned his attention back to me after a moment, after making sure he was well and truly gone. "Back across to your friends. I have damages to repair. Give them a little singe, it should wake them." He stepped aside to give me a clear pathway to return through the doorway Creston had made earlier.

I hurried past him, eager to be free of the feeling of being watched by unseen eyes.

"Oh, and, Seraphine? If you or your friends steal from me ever again, the price will not be worth whatever you gain from the item. I promise you that."

I stiffened for the briefest moments before I slipped through the wall, darkness slithering over the opening, blocking it the instant I was on the other side.

Creston and Trae waited where they had been left, like breathing statues they stood with their blackened gazes far beyond this reality.

I rushed towards them, calling my magic, hands flaring with heat as I reached out and touched each of their hands. I frowned when neither reacted, summoning more fire and trying again, a bead of sweat rolling down my face.

Their bodies shuddered and both men collapsed to the ground with a thud. My knees went weak with relief that they were okay, that

Veneficus hadn't lied.

"Fuck, that hurts," Trae groaned, cradling his hand before looking up at me.

"What the fuck was that?" Creston, true to his soldier nature, was already getting to his feet beside me.

"I don't know," I said, wishing I had something more to give him. "You two were playing dead eye statues while Veneficus took me through to reconnect with one of the Elliphir I tried to kill today. Can we please leave? He's still over there and I'd rather not hang around until he decides to come through. Can you explain that?"

Creston leaned down to yank Trae to his feet, as he cradled his still singed hand. "You're a healer, deal with it," Creston muttered to him before nodding for me to move. "He shouldn't be free, someone clearly let him go. Let's go to Trae's. I want more from this book."

I nodded and turned, leading the way from the Divide and the new feeling of fear, where before it had brought comfort. The need to get as far away from the Divide as possible was overwhelming. Creston and Trae said nothing more but quickly followed behind me.

CHAPTER 37

Trae opened up his home once it was in sight, and we hurried inside as the walls sealing us in.

Creston turned on me the instant we were closed away within the safety of Trae's magic. "Exactly what happened while we were standing there watching happy memories?" he asked, crossing his arms over his chest and waiting, watching me with eyes that were once again their usual midnight shade.

"Happy memories?" I cocked my head at him in confusion.

"Kinda like a highlights reel of distraction from reality," Trae called, striding into the house, leaving us in the hall.

Creston shot me an impatient look.

I tugged my fingers through my disheveled curls as best I could without my fingers tearing through knots. "He took me through the Divide to scare me. I think," I explained slowly. "One of the Elliphir you stopped me from killing was there, they knew each other but don't ask me how. Half of what they talked about made no sense to me, but Veneficus was very interested in the fact that I had been crossing across the Divide. And he knew about my nightmares."

He frowned. "Veneficus knew an Elliphir?" His brows rose at the implications.

"Quite well too. His name is Elonis. They wouldn't talk about Niko, they were only worried about me," I said, frustrated that I still had no answers about my brother. "He left me with a warning, to stay out of things, like I've somehow ruined something. It all started and was over too quickly for any real answers, they acted as though there was some sort of rush in the whole thing." I wrapped my arms around myself, still shaken.

Apparently realising I was not far off losing it, Creston stepped towards me, reaching out and touching my cheek gently. "Are you okay?" he asked, his demeanour changing into something softer as I leaned into him, concern overwhelming his features. As if he had just realised who he was talking to. Not another Guardien, but a... friend.

I nodded, looking up at him. "Confused, a little scared, but I'm okay."

He watched me for a few moments before nodding and stepping back, looking over my shoulder. "And uh..." He cleared his throat. "About what happened earlier?"

The grin crept onto my face before I could stop it. "What happened earlier was great," I said in a low voice, feeling the ghost of his touch brush down my body again.

His eyes shot back to mine, nostrils flaring at whatever he saw on my face. He cleared his throat again. "Let's see what Trae has, there has to be something in that book he wasn't supposed to learn." He rubbed the back of his neck, a blush appearing on his cheeks, and headed down the hall to where I could hear Trae searching through papers.

I followed him, smirking at his reaction.

Trae was on the floor surrounded by books and pieces of paper once more. It was like a bucket of cold water had been thrown over me, reminding me of what was happening.

As I had days before, I sat waiting, letting him work. He and

Creston talked but I barely heard them, my mind churning over and over. *Why did my nightmares matter? How had he known about them?* A torrent of unanswerable questions consumed the entirety of my thoughts.

"Phi?" Trae's voice snapped me from my thoughts. He held out a small leather bound book. "You need to read this. The book I borrowed from Veneficus helped me find it."

I reached over and took the book from him, running my fingers over the aged leather. Whatever had been stamped over the cover had long since faded. "What is it?" I asked him before opening it up carefully. I gently flipped past the first few pages, but on the third page, I froze.

Covering the page, scribbled as though repeated frantically over and over, was the same rune I'd only ever seen in one place before. The tapestry that hung in my bedroom. I ran my fingers over the grooves in the paper where it had been repeated over and over again.

"It's a journal, I think," he said. "All I know is that its old, older than Keinteris I'd wager. But the rune is what made me realise it was relevant."

"What's in the book?" Creston asked me from his seat across the room.

"That's the problem, I can't read it," my friend replied, frustrated. "Not yet, at least. It's in the old language, or an old language of some sort." Trae went back to going through the papers and books he had around him. "I just can't figure out which language. I've compared all the ones I can find so far. None match, but some get close."

"So we get more resources, without stealing them from Veneficus. There has to be a way to read it." Creston got up and moved seats, holding out a hand for some of the papers Trae had collected.

Together, they launched into further conversation about where they should look. As they did, my attention returned to the book in my hands.

I slid my fingers to the edge of the pages and turned beyond the rune covered page. It was handwritten but somehow the ink still looked fresh. I ran my fingers over the first lines, glancing at my finger afterward just to check and make sure the ink hadn't actually transferred. My finger was clean. As I looked back to the page it all seemed to shudder, the runes slithering out of alignment and after a moment reformed into...words.

Greetings to the next of us, it began.

I have hope this has reached your hands through the pathways I have set in place. With clarity, know you may only read what is within these pages with the burden of Phoenix fire in your blood.

We now grow without guidance, or enough understanding. I am trying to cure us of that.

The knowledge is yours to claim, and no others may decipher what I have charmed to be revealed by the touch of a Phoenix alone.

I don't know what age this will reach you, nor how much you may understand. But I do know that a lack of understanding will be present, unless our kind has been returned to what they once were, powerfully trained and held in the highest regard. But given the fear present as I charm this, I doubt that is the world that you exist in. I am sorry I wasn't able to change things in my time, but I can only hope that what I can offer within these pages is enough to make up for it.

CHAPTER 38

I read the page over and over, not quite sure what to do with the information in front of me. I'd been around magic my entire life. It was within me, part of my very being, but this magic was new. New to me, at least. It was old magic, older than I'd ever felt before, even from the Oracles, whose magic unnerved me. Far more powerful than I'd ever seen. Cloaking an entire book into a language, that is only decipherable with the touch of a specific carrier, was a lot to process.

I looked up from the page in front of me.

Creston and Trae were still arguing over options. I didn't think either of them had looked up since Trae sat down.

Creston was on the floor now, having cleared a space for himself. A book lay open in his lap and he was handing other pieces of paper to Trae for verifications.

From what I could catch up with, some of the pieces Trae had been working with were in the ancient languages. Creston apparently knew some of them but clearly others were beyond him.

I glanced down at the book in my hands. There the words remained. "You really can't read this?" I asked no one in particular as I stared at the words some more. They held steady with no sign they'd ever been anything else.

"It's in a language I've never seen before," Trae said, brows furrowed.

I looked between him and the book, no longer confused. "It's charmed. I don't know how or with what, but I can read it. When I touched the page it changed for me. It's a journal I think."

They shared a dumbfounded look before they rushed over to me, looking at the open book in my hands. After a moment, they exchanged glances, frowning deeply.

"I don't see anything different," Trae said, sounding disappointed.

Were they not listening to me? "I know," I said, exasperated. "It says that I can read it because of my magic. Like I said, it's charmed."

"I've never seen anything like that," Creston murmured, crouching beside me. There was an edge in his voice, something like awe. "You can really read it?"

"I can. This page is an introduction." I looked back down at the book again, turning the page over and skimming through what waited there. "It's addressed to anyone who's like me. It's explaining the Origins of the Phoenix, all the way back to the Seventeen. Listen;

When our race began, the creation of half mortal and half fae children wasn't unheard of. But the birth of our race, as more than random children of mixed magic, was never meant to happen. We could not be easily removed from humanity and returned beyond the veil to the Fae realms the way a changeling or halfling normally was.

We began an imbalance within nature and magic in this realm. We were not born by the Seventeen, as the histories now favour. Instead, we were magically manufactured by them, in ways that were not balanced by nature or magic. So, as nature and magic do, balance was demanded.

That balance brought about the first of us. A set of twins was born, not unusual for a birth of our kind, but as they grew, and their powers grew, something was different.

The first child no doubt you are aware of. Samil. The first of the dark children. But that was only one child, and just as his power grew, so did his twin's. His name was Silas. Our histories really don't talk about him much anymore, but he was the first of us. The first Fire child of Shadows and Earth. His powers grew alongside his brother's.

Both were nurtured. But as fear grew to the darkness and violence within Samil, the Seventeen decided their time was up here.

They knew Samil belonged beyond the mortal realm as he began draining life around him. Yet Silas was left behind, and over time he grew more and more powerful. Those who saw his power began to revere him. He was a leader of our people for a time. And while he didn't have his brother's darkness of magic, they shared common temperaments. He searched for his brother as he got older and more powerful, desperate to be reunited with the other half of his soul. Eventually he began burning down our cities as he did everything he could to bring back the Seventeen. His madness worsened when other dark children continued to grow in this world and none came for them.

He started taking them, and there is only rumour of what he did to them, none of it was kind. In the end, it was our own kind who decided to stop him, as the Seventeen could clearly not see the destruction they had created in the separation of two halves. His story is our burden. He was drowned, killed by his own people who learned to fear him so truly. People who loved him still helped with his death. Fire could not take him from this world, but water did.

But the balance had to remain. Our births continued, though fewer as the Dark Children vanished from our colonies, and we too were often hidden. Left untrained and dulled to be kept out of the fears of others. We are born of Shadow and Earth only, and so our existence was rare and powerful, but we maintain part of the balance that nature forces upon all our magic," I finished and looked between the two of them.

Trae ran his hand over his hair and as he blinked with wide eyes.

Creston's frown had deepened to a rigid curve between his dark brows.

"None of this is in any history I've ever read, and I've read a lot of history books," Trae muttered, wandering back to the books and paperwork he had scattered around the room.

His temple of confusion, I thought dryly.

Creston slumped into a sitting position on the floor. "This both makes sense and doesn't. Of course the Elliphir's madness would need balances, but why is that balance Fire? I don't understand that." He shook his head. "Why wouldn't it be clarity or clairvoyance? Why wouldn't it be our Oracles?"

"Because, as I have said, it isn't just madness," Trae interjected fiercely from across the room. We both looked up at him in surprise. "Oh, come on! I showed you the list before, does no one pay attention when I speak?" He started sifting through the papers until he found what he wanted. A vine snatched it out of his hand and dragged it over to us. "Read it again. I added more anyway."

Creston delicately pulled the page free of the vine and held it so we could both read it.

Possible abilities of the Elliphir;
Consumption of life

Hallucination
Corruption
Compulsion
Energy draining?
Camouflage (Shapeshifting? Glamour?)
Dreamwalking?
Shadow creation/control?
Emotion manipulation

It clicked as my eyes skimmed over the list again. So much had happened in such a short time that I had entirely forgotten this list. "Hallucinations? Like what exactly?"

"The books are fairly vague on that front. It's not like they're the ones writing the books I can get my hands on. It's all secondhand or third party information." Trae waved me off as he moved away from the paperwork and headed down the hall. "I'm hungry," he announced, disappearing from sight.

I closed the book in my hands with a sigh and looked to Creston.

He met my gaze after tracing his eyes over the list for a moment longer. He opened his mouth, then frowned again. "How's your stomach?"

CHAPTER 39

I cocked an eyebrow at him, the question taking me by surprise. "That's a hell of a subject change." Nonetheless, my right hand drifted to my stomach and pressed, and when no pain gripped me, I shook my head. "It's fine."

"There were no bruises. When I..."

Stripped you naked, I finished for him in my mind as he glanced towards the hall quickly.

"The bruises were gone. I expected them, I expected to have to control my emotions seeing them, but they weren't there," he said, his eyes dropping to the hand on my stomach.

I blinked at him for a moment, then frowned. Too much had happened in the past few days for me to have thought much about how the bruising was healing, only worried when that strange cold pain radiated through me. "Trae healed the worst of them the other day."

Creston nodded, but I could see the glint in his eyes as his mind fired, could practically hear the thoughts ticking over as he drew some conclusion he didn't share.

I sighed again. "Things are only getting weirder, aren't they?"

He nodded and rested his hand against my back. "Seems that way. I think we have a lot left to unravel about what's going on. Things have changed, and I don't know why. After centuries of existing as we do, why now?"

"I've been asking myself the same thing," Trae said as he returned, wiping his mouth of whatever he was chewing.

Creston removed his hand from my back, his fingers trailing over the skin as if hesitant to let go. We both turned our attention to him.

"We all know the histories, or we know them the way they're taught. We know about the Faerie who created us. They attest it as the Seventeen, but there were far, far more, but you have to go deep into the histories to find the details. The Elders enjoy the tales they tell us," Trae muttered, a dark looking passing over his face. "And we haven't had reason to see them as anything but true histories. We know so little about our own half race. The humans here know more of Faerie than we seem to." He sank down on the other side of me, casting a cursory glance at the book still in my hands. "You're going to have to find some answers in there that I can't."

I screwed up my nose at his request. "You know studies were never my best area."

Trae laughed. "We are long out of school and you've been known to pass through a novel or two from time to time. I'm sure you can manage a book that specifically offers you answers. To questions we probably haven't thought of yet."

I sighed deeply. "You're right. I know you're right, but I know there will be answers we don't want."

Whatever I would have said next was silenced by the sound of a gentle knock at the front of Trae's home.

He perked up in an instant, smiling happily. "It's Cleo," he explained, heading for the door.

The moment he opened the door, everything living around us

shuddered. Vines slithered from nowhere and devoured all books, papers and notes scattered around the room, all of it disappearing in a wave of nature, vanishing beneath a new floor.

I frowned deeply and glanced at Creston.

He was already on his feet, a wary expression on his face. "I don't think she's alone," he said under his breath, reaching down to pull me to my feet. "Hide the book." He nodded to my hands.

I looked around frantically for a hiding spot, before striding over to the couch and sliding the book between the hand spun silk pillows before settling myself against them.

Creston followed, sitting on the couch beside me in a stretched and forcefully relaxed position.

"Will this day ever end?" I asked, stifling a yawn, not looking to Creston as we waited.

His reply came in the form of a grunt of agreement.

Moments later, Trae rounded the corner into the sitting room, Cleo's fingers twined with his as she appeared beside him, a halo of pale blonde hair free flowing over the icy blue summer dress she wore.

It made me smile a little to see them so close to each other. They balanced each other, something I'd never noticed it before. Like mirrors of reversed energies, they were made to fit.

Cleo gave me a saddened look. "There you are. We've been looking for you."

"We?" Creston beat me to the question, keeping his tone deceptively light and with an edge of idle curiosity, though I knew it was far more than that.

Cleo didn't need to answer as Kylan slowly walked around the corner behind them. He smiled, but it never reached his eyes. "Cleo has been showing me around again today. I went to find her after you weren't home." His gaze fell on me almost accusingly.

It took everything within me not to straighten out of my relaxed position on the couch. I rolled my tongue in my mouth before speaking, taking the acid out of my tone. "I'm sorry, I didn't realise you'd be looking for me this morning, I'd imagine that news of my brother being taken would have reached everyone quickly. Plus, I'm sure Cleo is a much better guide than I could ever be."

"I was sorry to hear of the loss. I was informed it was not unusual to lose children to the...Elliphir?" He looked at me in a curious way as he said the word, like it tasted odd across his tongue.

"The loss of a Tested Child is far more serious, and my brother was one such child. He will be returned, be sure of that." I shifted a little in my seat, uncomfortable with this stranger talking about my brother, and Cleo shot me a sympathetic look.

"Well, I'm always happy to play guide around here," she said, trying to diffuse some of the tension. "And she's right, she's an awful guide. She forgets too much." She flashed me a tight smile and I was grateful for the change of topic.

My heart ached to think that just this morning my brother was taken from us. I had too much chaos in my mind to focus on my grief for an extended period. I was so tired. I wanted my bed, and would even settle for a nightmare to escape the roiling emotions I was desperately trying to stifle.

Kylan took the change of tone in stride, suddenly smirking at me. "Then what is it you're good at? Perhaps there are other talents you have that would be useful to my adjusting into this world." There was an edge to his voice as his eyes then slid down over me slowly. "Or I could suggest a few."

Creston stiffened beside me, turning to look towards Kylan, a wave of malice rolling off him. His movement drew Kylan's gaze from me, but the smirk remained in place. "If I were you, I would watch your tongue. Lest you lose it."

The smirk slipped from Kylan's face and his gaze flickered between Creston and I. He clicked his tongue. "I see. My bad. I didn't mean to upset, only trying to...connect."

"Connect in other ways, or with other people." Creston's tone was dark, the warning clear.

It took all I had within me to keep my face neutral. Creston had been protective of me all my life, but never quite in this manner. *Did he too feel a churning unease around Kylan? The same way I had since I had found him staring at me from across the field at Niko's testing?*

Shooting an alarmed look at Cleo, I saw that her eyes were practically alight as she glanced between the two males. The tension in the room rose as neither looked away from the other.

Trae clapped his hands, making me jump. "Okay..." he said, drawing out the word slowly. "I think you both came here in the middle of the night for a reason?" he asked Cleo, trying in vain to distract the others.

She cleared her throat and shook herself, reigniting the usual vibrant expression she toted. "We really came to see if you guys wanted to come to show Kylan more of our home. I was thinking we could all show off some of our magic tomorrow, to help acclimate him around its usage. And maybe relieve some pent up stresses," she added, raising her eyebrows at the males.

I stared at her, warning bells chiming in my head, but I wasn't sure why. Her suggestion wasn't outrageous by any means. It was a normal progression of introduction of humans into our lives. They were less likely to fear our differences if they were in awe of the things we could do with our magic, rather than worrying what they couldn't do against it.

Standing, I looked to Creston, tired already of being around Ky-

Ian's strange presence.

He met my eyes immediately, brows still furrowed. The tension in his shoulders remained, making me think he could do with letting off some steam as well.

It had been far too long since I just let my fire burn for fun, and with so much already weighing in my mind, Cleo was offering an escape, however brief, and I intended to take it. "Alright. Tomorrow morning. We play."

CHAPTER 40

The moon was still bright and full in the sky above us as all five of us stood by the falls. Dawn threatened at the edges of the horizon but the season kept the moon bright. We had all agreed to the early morning, so that we didn't attract too many others wanting to play with their magic and ruin the relaxation of it all.

The rest of the night before had passed simply. We had all said our goodbye, Creston had escorted me home but left quickly after making sure I ate, heading to attend to some Guardien duties.

I'd let him go, too tired to do anything but crawl into my bed and drift into unconsciousness, blessed with a strangely, but welcome, dreamless slumber.

I hadn't gone to my family. The thought of seeing them without Niko made my heart ache too much. I would see them later. They wouldn't let me hide forever, no matter how much I wanted to, and I knew if I didn't go to them, they would certainly come to me.

Creston had crept into my room in the early hours, woken me gently and walked with me in silence to meet the others. I wasn't sure what was on his mind but I felt no urge to push. Whatever it was, if it involved me, I knew he would tell me eventually.

I looked around the falls, an ache building in my chest.

Less than a week ago I had been here with almost the same group, although much merrier, despite the burden of other lost children. But then, my magic had remained neatly away. I hadn't been in a mood to entertain then, and in truth I felt even less inclined now, but I longed to use my magic.

Fire was destructive by nature, so I was not able to use it anywhere near as much as the others. Trae and Creston were able to use their magic constantly, as was the benefit of earth magic. It was very useful in all of our day to day lives. The greatest things I achieved daily with my magic was keeping my family warm and heating water for them.

We fell into a rough circle, Kylan following suit quickly, and Cleo stepped forward first, the air around us picking up, a breath of wind quickly turning into a gust.

She focused the energy into the centre of our group, spinning leaves and flowers into the circle as she created a whirlwind. The air twisted faster and faster, growing towards the sky. Then, it was gone. Cleo grinned, eyes sparkling with the rush of flexing her magical abilities. I clapped at her display, watching the flower petals drift back to the ground.

Without a word, Trae closed his eyes and held out his hands, the ground around us suddenly overflowing with greenery. It rolled like water across stone, filling the empty space. From the greenery grew tall stems, they rose above our heads and blossomed into magnificent sunflowers. He opened his eyes and grinned at Kylan.

Creston took his turn next. The ground beneath my feet shuddered, making me crouch to keep my balance, and the others did the same. The earth beneath us lifted, pushing us all higher in the air, curving around us as vines slid through the air, slithering into a large throne like chair for each of us to sit back on and rest, now sitting with the sunflowers at our feet. Small flowers blossomed from the chairs we sat in, filling the air with their heady fragrance.

"Impressive." I smiled over at Creston.

"Everything I do is impressive, Firefly." He winked at me, the vines around me briefly tightening, as if in a quick hug.

Kylan had watched each of my friends intently as they manipulated their magic, but his strange eyes were glued to me now. Expectant.

I looked away from him and towards Creston. "Stone?" I needn't say more than that.

He knew what I was asking, and nodded, drawing on the earth forging talent he had grown into in recent years. One I only knew about because it was a power my father also harboured. In the next instant the nature that created my seat changed. The vines melted away and were replaced with seemingly carved stone.

I smiled at him in thanks, turning back to the centre I pulled my legs up and crossed them beneath me.

Where to begin? What show to make of my magic without destroying too much of theirs?

I laid my hands open on my thighs, palms up to the air. Flames ignited over my skin as I focused. Around us, outside the space the others had used for their magic, coiled ropes of fire. They rose from a star above us, stretching their way to the ground and circling, leaving us in something akin to a giant bird cage. I clicked my fingers on both hands, and hundreds of single flickering lights appeared in the air around us.

The flames were no more than that you would expect from a candle's wick.

Cleo giggled softly, raising her hand to reach for the tiny fires.

I twisted my right hand and with a flick upwards the droplets spun in their places.

No flame was close enough to any of them to cause them any harm, but they would feel their warmth as they hung in the air.

Proud, I glanced around the circle, feeling the relief at finally being able to get some of the strain of my gift out of my brain.

Trae and Cleo watched the me with small grins. It was not their first time to see such a show from me, but they always enjoyed it nonetheless.

Creston, however, had never seen me make a show of my magic in all the time we had known each other.

I don't know why I've never shown him before, I thought to myself.

He stared at the flickering flames with awe in his gaze, the glow from them highlighting the raw angles of his face and revealing flashes of colour in his onyx curls. His eyes sparkled with the reflection of the fires like hundreds of tiny stars in his dark gaze.

I smiled as he looked at me, sensing me watching him.

He flashed me a grin, admiration in his eyes as he looked me over, perhaps noticing me by the firelight the same way I had seen him.

I flushed and looked away, instead looking up at the flames, putting off looking to the last person with us.

Kylan sat almost directly across from me. He was not watching the magic, his gaze instead intensely focused on me. A slow smirk slid across his lips, but quickly twisted into a far more animalistic snarl.

My turn.

CHAPTER 41

The words pressed into my mind, rolling though my consciousness like the echo of words shouted into a cavernous space.

His grey blue storm eyes bled to blackness, inky shadows dripped from his hands the same way flames dripped from mine.

My heart pounded. "No!" I cried, as shadows tore through the air, not towards me, but towards my friends.

Creston reacted the fastest, but we were all suspended above the ground on the raised chairs he had created. It left very little room to run, without just flinging ourselves at the ground several feet below us.

The shadows caught each of my friends in a tight grip, chaining them to their false thrones. Cleo and Trae cried out in shock as they were immobilised.

My body vibrated with both fear and anger, my magic reacting as vivid blue flames spread up my arms. "You aren't mortal, are you?"

Kylan laughed, and it was an icy sound, tearing through me and making me shudder. He pushed back his hair to show off his delicately pointed ears. "Technically, in part, but I am no more mortal than you are." His eyes were still pits of blackness, nothing left in his gaze but shadows. He looked around the circle.

The sound of his laugh woke that cold thing that seemed to slither around inside me now, and I couldn't help but press a hand to my stomach, as though I could stop the sensation by protecting the spot where the bruises had been. My heart pounded in my chest, my mind flitting through all the escape options I could use. I wanted to act, but I couldn't think clearly through the panic that threatened to overwhelm me.

He and I were the only two unrestrained, and Creston looked between the two of us, unusually calm. Trae and Cleo too were still. Whether the shadows held them that way or it was the shock, I did not know.

"Do you have any idea how boring it is pretending to be powerless?" Kylan snarled. "Watching you all act so superior? To hear the beliefs you have of my kind?" He clicked his tongue and shook his head. "It's sad, really, how wrong you all are." His eyes returned to me. "But you were starting to figure some things out. Your little stunt with our professor yesterday freed me from the confines for my guise. I no longer have to play moron, or toy. Instead, I get to stretch. You forced his hand, now I get to make sure that above all, you stay silent."

I gripped at the chair I sat in, the stone blackening beneath my skin. "If you are here for Veneficus, then my friends are of no value in whatever annoyance he holds for me. Leave them alone." The flames that still hung in the air were growing, expanding as my anger and fear influenced my magic.

The flames flickering closest to him made him flinch. "Remove them," he demanded, clenching a fist. Cleo cried out. "Or I'll start pulling the shadows *through* her."

I stared at my friend.

Cleo had paled at the threat.

I knew I could burn through the shadows if need be, but perhaps he didn't know that. Maybe I still had an advantage, given the right leverage. I flicked my fingers and just as quickly as they had appeared, the small flames around us in the air vanished.

He relaxed a little as they disappeared but the cage around us stayed. "Much better."

"You're Elliphir." The accusation came from Creston. He had spoken aloud the assumption my mind had quickly formed. I realised then he had never truly spent much time around Kylan. He had been absent from our last trip and had only seen him in passing, and yet he was the first to realise what he was.

"Correct." Kylan watched Creston with his black eyes for a long moment, as if waiting for more. When Creston only frowned, he rolled his eyes and turned back to me. "So you're the lucky number fire then, aren't you? I can't tell you how glad I am that you never minded your business and stayed where you should have, because you're about to release so many things. Long, quiet things." He shifted in his seat and a thought occurred to me.

We were all still seated above the ground on these chairs, with Creston's magic holding us up at this male's mercy. Creston shot me a pained look when I glanced at him.

Kylan barked a laugh. "He can't. None of them can. Almost any magic is rendered worthless where the midithrias are involved."

I looked at him, curious. "Midithrias?" I drew the word out slowly. The shadows seemed to shudder on my friends as I said the word.

"Really, did you think we would just call them shadows?" he asked, annoyed now. "They are far more than that. You have been touched by them before. You of all people should know they are no mere tricks of light and space." More dark inky tendrils flowed from his hands, but this time they sought out the garden of sunflowers at our feet.

Everything they touched quickly withered, turning to greyish husks against their former beauty.

"They take much, but give much more," he said, staring at them feverishly.

Frustrated that we'd been played and trapped, I swiped my hand in the air, igniting the dead husks, and stared across at him. "I'm tired of this. You've made your point. You are not what we think you should be, but the things we're taught by the Elders are hardly something we can be blamed for."

"You can be. It was your kind that started our isolation. Once, we all lived together."

I frowned, unsure how we could be blamed for that, but then my eyebrows shot up.

Silas. Silas from the journal still shoved in Trae's couch cushions. The first of my kind. The one who had taken the first Elliphir away from the Elliphae, before our races found our names.

"And how am I to blame for events centuries past?"

"You shouldn't be the one with the gift of fire," he spat, glaring at me. "You don't deserve it. You're weak, you're idle and you know too little about the reality of our kinds."

"Because I was taught lies!" The flames around us flared with my anger. "I was taught by those I had no reason not to trust. And who are you to make any assumptions about me? You know nothing about me."

"I know more than you think I do," he said slowly, looking to be on the verge of giggling. "I know what you are and I know why it's important. I know what they want from you. I know why the shadows call to you. Maybe I'll even tell you. For a price."

I groaned. "I'm over this. Let my friends go. If all you wanted was to corner me then you could find plenty of opportunities."

"That's where you're wrong. You're rarely unguarded." His gaze flickered to Creston then back to me. "And I feel this has more dramatic emphasis. See, you have to listen to me when there are other people on the line. If not for them, I think you'd have covered me in flames, the same way you threatened the others yesterday. And I would rather not be caged."

"You already are." I gestured to the flames around us.

"Ah yes, but so are your friends. And hurting me would mean me hurting them, so neither will happen so long as you keep your pretty little fires to yourself."

I leaned back against the stone, now hot from the flames stretching from my body. "Fine. No harm will come to you so long as no harm comes to them. Get on with whatever it is that you need from us now. But when we are done, you will stay away from all of us."

He barked out a laugh at that. "That is where you're wrong. You see, there is at least one person here that will very much want me close from here on out. And you will have no say in the matter, regardless of who you are." His attention again turned to Creston, who's gaze had remained steady on the male the entire exchange. "Well? Have you caught up yet?"

Creston's brows furrowed. He looked as though he were in pain. He opened his mouth then closed it again, shaking his head.

"Come now," Kylan said, almost rolling his eyes. "The dreams have not been enough? You have not been reminded enough?" As he spoke, his eyes bled back to their storm blue.

"Dreams?" I asked Creston but he avoided my gaze, keeping his trained on Kylan. They stared at each other for a long moment that seemed to last an eternity.

It was Trae who snapped the tension. "What the fuck is going on here?" he demanded, trying to wiggle against the shadows that held him in place. He groaned as they tightened.

Kylan shook his head. "Come now, *brother*, am I really so lost to you that you do not recognise me?"

CHAPTER 42

My head snapped around. I stared at Kylan, whose face seemed to have changed in the firelight, his ears now pointed and cheeks more angular, hair lighter.

He looked more like... Creston.

My chest constricted as I looked at Creston's face, watched as it paled in the mixture of dawn and firelight. "Brother?" I echoed.

Kylan held up his hand. "Shut your mouth, bitch, this is nothing to do with you now."

"Don't speak to her like that," Creston growled.

Kylan cocked an eyebrow at him. "Then speak to me, *brother,* I'm sure there is much to say." He relaxed in his seat and smiled, as though a sudden weight was lifted off him. "And I have much to ask."

"Then we will speak. *Alone.* At home. You do not need this show anymore. If the fact that you have returned is all you needed, why could you not just come to me? Why not use your true name?"

"Because I needed time for other things, it's why I have not allowed you to see me clearly until now. I needed the time I needed." Kylan shrugged, unfazed. "And I wanted to know who you were first. Cleo has been very helpful in that aspect. She's quite the talker."

She made a soft exhausted sound, realising she had been used for her warm and open nature.

Creston sighed. "Let them go. Or let me go enough to let them down. They can leave and we will talk. Isn't that what you want?"

Kylan watched him for another long moment and then nodded. "Yes little brother, it is some of what I want. But I also want a guarantee that none of you will speak of me, or any other who knows what I am, and that you will swear it. We have work to do and each of you have a part to play. So I will hear it. Do each of you swear you will say nothing?"

"For what benefit?" Trae asked, cocking an eyebrow at him.

Kylan smirked and looked directly at me. "Because I know where your brother is."

I sensed both my friends staring at me as I went still. Even the flames guttered, almost going out.

"I swear it on my being, I will say nothing of this dawn to any not within this circle." Cleo said the words first, recited in the way we were taught to swear our oaths. Our word had power after all.

Trae quickly repeated the words.

Creston too.

Kylan stared at me, waiting.

I swallowed, feeling like one of Creston's vines had wound its way around my throat and begun squeezing. He had us cornered. There was no way out except to do what he wanted. "I swear it on my being, I will say nothing of this dawn to any not within this circle. So long as my brother is returned in peace and safety to his true home." I glared at him as I added the last part.

He only laughed and flicked his hands, the shadows slithering from my friends, giving them access to their magic again. Creston stretched his hands out, the thrones shuddering as the earth that held us up started to fall away, quickly lowering us all to the ground. I put out the flames around us, reeling the warmth back to myself.

We all stood as the thrones disappeared into the earth from which they had come. Trae and Cleo strode to my side the second they were able. I looked to Creston, but he stayed rooted in place, avoiding my gaze and remaining focused on his brother.

"They leave. Without your interference," he told him firmly, still without looking at us.

Kylan nodded once but said nothing, apparently satisfied now.

Creston dipped his head towards us but still did not take his eyes off his brother. "Go. Now."

Trae set his hand on Cleo's back with a nod, pushing her forward.

When I didn't move Cleo grabbed my hand. *'Come Phi, this is his choice'*. The words were a whisper in my mind. A whisper was all the access she could get but it was enough.

With heavy feet I moved, allowing my friends to pull me away through the woods around the falls, to pull me back to the world that was now waking with none of the knowledge we had just gained. I said nothing, my mind still beside Creston and Kylan.

His brother.

His brother whose loss had caused the destruction of his entire family and left his heart an open wound most of his life. His brother whose true name almost escaped me, I had heard it so rarely.

Raphael Vaelle was returned.

Trae took us all back to his home and sealed us inside, resting a hand against the front door. More vines crept across it from the walls, weaving amongst each other, adding extra security. "Sleep. All of us need more sleep," he announced as we stood idle in his hallway. He turned to Cleo and stroked her cheek. "Go. Bed. I'll be in soon." He kissed her forehead and she headed down the hall after a tired half smile at me. He looked to me. "You're exhausted. We'll deal with this all later, and you need rest. Those few hours weren't enough for any of us, especially not you."

I sighed. He was right. "Okay." My whole body felt suddenly heavy. I turned and trudged into the living room.

Trae followed me. "Here," he murmured, touching his fingers to one of the walls, vines snaking and twisting together to create a small bed. He grabbed a blanket from a nearby chair. "The silk is harder to replace, so try not to burn down the house, okay?" He nudged me with a smile.

I barked out a tight laugh, unsure if we were at the stage of laughing about my dreams yet. "I'll do my best. I could always go home where I'm less likely to cause excess damages." I pulled the blanket against my chest.

He just shook his head. "You're better here for now. Go home when you're ready, but rest first." He rubbed my arm gently and then turned away, heading up the hall to join Cleo in his bed.

I watched him leave and sighed, looking around the room. It occurred to me the journal was still hidden between in the silken couch pillows. I padded across the room and slipped it out from its hiding place, returning to my new bed with the book in my hands.

I wriggled beneath the blankets and opened it, reading over the first pages again, afraid to turn beyond them but also unable to get the look on Creston's face out of my mind. Tracing my fingers over the words on the pages, reading them over and over, eventually lulled my thoughts into quiet. I set the book on the floor beside me and rolled over, closing my eyes and forcing myself not to think of Creston and his brother so I could fall asleep.

For the first time in days, dreams consumed me the instant they were able.

CHAPTER 43

It burned.

Even in my dreams, the way he touched me burned, in the most delightful way. Like nothing else could burn me.

He kissed and bit my neck, drawing me closer to his chest, pinning me there as I moaned, fingers buried deep in his dark hair as his lips returned to mine.

I bit his lower lip, enough to make him pull back. Breathlessly, he looked down at me. "Firefly," he breathed against my lips, sinking back towards them.

But the touch of his lips never returned, leaving an ache in me, as my dream changed.

There were no shadows to be chased by this time.

I woke in the same forest I had stepped through to in my last nightmare. I glanced behind me.

The seething dark portal was exactly as I remembered it, but this time I had no memory of passing through it. I turned forward, looking around. I was alone. The male with his vibrant yellow eyes was absent from beside the rune marred tree.

I looked down to see I wore the same dress, but as I had expected the colours had changed. Almost all the green had left it now as the red had drawn upwards. I stepped further from the doorway of shadows.

Birds were singing high in the treetops and old dry leaves crackled beneath my feet as I wandered further into the forest. The trees never seemed to end, stretching in every direction, drawing me deeper into the forest, my feet finding a direction for me all on their own.

Everything around me seemed to vibrate with a magic I'd never felt before, but in a way that made me feel calm.

I stopped suddenly, looking around, as I no longer felt the need to walk, instead sitting down in the fallen leaves and grass that lined the forest floor. My dress and hair fanned around me as I laid against the cool earth, staring into the forest ceiling, watching the branches and leaves sway in the wind. It was almost meditative.

"Beautiful, isn't it?" a voice asked from beside me sometime later.

I sat with a start, finding a set of golden yellow eyes staring at me with amusement.

"No need to get up on my account. In fact, you weren't expected, so technically, I believe you are intruding on my space." He pushed the sleeves of his dark tunic shirt up his arms, revealing more strange runes, this time in tattoos.

"Your space? This is my dream," I argued, pulling my knees towards my chest, keeping him where I could see him.

Close up, his eyes truly were liquid gold and his hair seemed to shimmer, new colours revealing themselves each time the light caught it through the canopy above us. "Is it?" He tilted his head to the side. "Because last I checked this was my home. Not your dreamscape."

I frowned at him, looking around again, then back to him. "I don't understand."

He laughed, a rich warm sound that sent a shiver down my spine. "Made of magic yet you understand so little of it." He shook his head and grinned at me. "I could help you change that, Phoenixling."

It was my turn to tilt my head at him, blanching at the name.
"Phoenixling?"

"Well, you are a Phoenix, but you are untrained so hence the 'ling'
addition. Perhaps it is much too much a mouthful," he mused thought-
fully. "How about Nixling?" He nodded to himself as he looked me over,
not waiting for my answer. "Yes, I think that suits. After all, there are
many who don't know what you are or are capable of."

"And you do?" My back straightened a little, excited by the idea that
someone might actually have answers for me.

"More than you know. Much more." He looked around as the world
shuddered. "But once again, we are interrupted." His molten gold
eyes burned into mine as his attention returned to me. "Wake well,
Seraphine. We will speak soon." He winked at me in the last instant
before everything went black.

I woke with the sun streaming through the windows against my
face, to the sound of clattering and voices coming from the kitchen. I
groaned softly and pulled the blanket up over my face, briefly blocking
out the light, and reality. But slowly it trickled back in.

Dawn. Kylan.

Creston.

I shoved the blankets down, rubbing my face as I dragged myself
from the bed, still fully dressed from the morning. I guessed from the
sun that it was late morning, sometime close to midday. I narrowly
avoided stepping on the Phoenix journal as I got up, forgetting I'd left
it on the floor before I slept. I bent down and picked it up, taking it
with me as I sought out my friends.

I found them in the kitchen, laughing and teasing each other as
they prepared a meal of some kind. Their happiness made me smile. I
wondered why they had waited so long to allow themselves to truly be
like this.

They had always glowed in each other's presence but they had shied away from it, hiding in other relationships. *What changed?* I meant to ask no one in particular but when Cleo turned towards me I knew I had not.

"Hey," I said, drawing Trae's attention too, stopping Cleo before she could answer the question I hadn't asked aloud, and was not my business to understand.

"Sorry, we tried not to wake you." He half smiled at me apologetically.

"It's fine, I should probably head home anyway. My family are going to start worrying because they haven't seen me in days." I scratched at my head idly and looked between them. "I'll see you guys later."

They both nodded. "Come back if you need," Trae offered as I turned away.

"Thank you. Let me know if you find anything more in your research. Just no theft for now." I gave them what smile I could muster before I left, making my way home slowly with the journal in hand.

Everything seemed almost normal as I walked home, even though it was anything but. I smiled and greeted any whose path I crossed, and some gave me a sad look or word of mourning but I paid little attention. I could almost pretend things hadn't changed until I stepped onto the pathway that led to my family home.

The trees seemed duller here, as though they too mourned my brother.

I took a breath before I headed towards the main house, and as I rounded the corner I noticed a figure standing by my door. My heart leapt for a moment until the figure became clear. "Zav?" I changed my path and headed towards him.

My elder brother looked me over. "I wasn't sure you even lived here anymore."

I sighed. "Don't be dramatic. I've just been out. Things here aren't exactly easy."

"You think I don't know that, Seraphine?" he asked coldly. "I'm the one in the home with our parents while they mourn our brother and worry over your constant absence." He pushed off the wall and stood in front of me, hands crossed over his chest.

"I was coming now, to see how they are. To see how you all are. I've been trying to find him, Zav," I protested weakly, knowing he was right. Guilt hit me like a wave, churning in my stomach.

"Oh yes, I heard about the children you and Creston brought back after you jumped out the window. But what makes it your role? Why is it not enough that the Guardiens are looking?" he asked, furious.

"Because they won't look for him the way I will!" I almost shouted. "They'll stop! I won't. He's our brother and he's out there somewhere scared. He needs us." I crossed my arms across my own chest, mirroring my sibling as we glared at each other. "I can't just do nothing. Getting those other children back means there must be a way to get him back too. There's more going on here, Zav, I need you to trust me on that."

"Why?" he demanded. "Why should I trust you with anything when you don't trust me with whatever it is you know? I am not Niko. I don't need protecting in the same ways. I am far beyond that."

"I know that, Zav," I sighed, shaking my head. "But truly the more I learn, the less I feel I can say to anyone. Even you. Maybe part of it is to protect you."

"If you keep things from me, things where I can help, then you will lose me, Seraphine, because I will find out whatever it is you are hiding, even if it takes time. Do not underestimate my own need to keep my family safe. You are not the only one here who cares." He jerked his head towards the main house, refusing to meet my gaze any longer. "We need to go in, Mum and Dad need to see that you're okay with their own eyes."

I turned to head into the main house, content on leaving this conversation behind, when he grabbed my arm in a vicelike grip.

"And the next time you leave, I'll be coming with you," he growled.

I cringed. "Fine. Trae can give you the run down. I don't have all the answers, Zav. Not even close. All I know is our brother was taken and it isn't because he is Elliphir. That we know for certain, the actual why is much harder." I stepped back towards the pathway to our front door.

My brother followed suit, hot on my heels. I could feel his anger in the silence he sank into. I knew he hated being left in the dark, but he had never given me a reason to seek him out.

He was my brother, yes, but while he looked barely a year older than me his true age was much closer to thirty years above mine. The only reason he lived in the home our parents had created was because of Niko. He had returned solely to help watch over and guide his magic.

After my birth had been followed by the torment of Nicola's death for my family, and then later the complication of my magic, our younger brother's birth had stirred fear of a repeat. Often, I forgot he had so much of his life on hold these past eight years as Niko had grown.

I put my hand on his chest as we reached the door. "I'm sorry, Zavier. I know this was everything you came home to prevent. I'm sorry I forget sometimes."

He scoffed. "You aren't the only one who forgets. I do too."

"So what is waiting for you beyond this?" I asked, trying to change the subject.

My brother flashed me a dark smile. "I have no idea, I hope to find out someday soon, after our brother is home again." He opened up the front door for us, waving me inside.

"I think if I'm to tell you my secrets you should share some of yours. Being closer will be easier then," I muttered as I walked past him into the house, surprised to find it silent.

It was quiet inside, the usual vibrancy my family brought to the home with their magic absent. No flowers bloomed anywhere as I walked deeper inside, stopping in the kitchen. There were no bowls of fresh fruit lining the counter. My stomach growled softly, and I couldn't remember when I last ate more than a few bites of anything.

My parents were not lounged in their usual place in the living room.

I turned to Zavier. "Bedroom," he told me softly. "You go talk. I'll get you something to eat." Clearly I was not the only one who noticed my stomach's lamenting.

I nodded, setting the journal on the bench before heading down the second hall that led to their room. Their door was ajar when I reached it, and I knocked gently, pushing it open.

My mother lay in bed, curled on her side facing away from me. Everything about her was dull, drained of her usual lustre. My heart ached in my chest at the sight of her tear-streaked face. My father sat in a chair by the bed that looked new.

I had never seen it before but recognised enough about the design to know it was made with his magic. He looked to me first, dark circles under his hazel eyes.

Some days I could see my own green in his eyes, or dreamed I could.

He relaxed a little at the sight of me. "Seraphine," he breathed, getting up from the chair to embrace me, crushing me to his chest tightly, stroking my hair down the way he had done so often when I had cried in his arms as a child.

My eyes blurred and burnt with unshed tears. "I'm sorry," I whispered against his chest. I didn't know what else to say. In pushing myself through so much else, I had pushed away how my parents must have felt during this time.

He squeezed me before pulling back to look at me, cupping my chin. "You don't need to be sorry. We all mourn in different ways, but your mother and I just feared for you," he said, shooting me a look that said he knew I hadn't been behaving myself. "We know how you love your brother." He stroked my cheek and stepped away. "Sonia? My love." He stroked her leg as he sat on the edge of the bed beside her. "Seraphine is here."

I slipped around the bed to be closer to my mother. She didn't move as I came into her eye line. I reached out and took her hand. "It's okay, Mum, we'll bring him home. I promise you that," I told her softly. My father shot me a warning look but I ignored it. "He'll be okay." I squeezed her hand gently as she looked up at me.

"We named him for her, and we lost him too." Her voice was rough, and there was a sadness in her gaze, like a pit you could fall into if you stared too long. It made me shudder. Their loss of Nicola being parallel with their loss of Niko too much to shoulder. I kissed her hand and moved away as she curled into herself again. My father watched me closely.

"I'll come back later," I promised him, but later could be at any time. I didn't want to be in this room, with sorrow raw and catching. I mourned for my vibrant happy mother. I headed back to my brother.

He wordlessly handed me a bowl of a fruit mix that I devoured greedily, his gaze lingering on the silent room, on our parents.

"Thank you," I told him when I was done, drinking the juice from the bowl. "I needed that."

Zavier nodded and set a bag on the bench. "I forget you can't grow your own sometimes, so I filled a bag for you of your favourites. I'd wager that your friends also forget you cannot grow your own. Apart from your air friend, of course."

I took the bag and set it in my lap. "Earth magic is by far the most valuable, really, you can provide yourself with everything." Even the bag in my hands was made from weaving magic. "Having magic that is destructive is much harder."

"I know, it's why I have tried to ease your burden growing as much as I could. But you do well enough for yourself even without that help." He smiled bitterly at me. "You're no child anymore. You're less than a year from your Settling. If you want it, I'll make a home for you. I'm sure Creston and Trae will help maintain the magic where I can't."

I looked to him in surprise. The thought of moving out of my family's home had rarely crossed my mind, let alone that he would be the one to help me build one of my own.

He nodded at my unasked question. "I know you have to have thought about it, the room you're in now is separate yes, but it's hardly a full home for an adult."

"I had, in the past, but I can't leave now," I protested. "Mother looks the oldest I've ever seen her."

Zavier laughed softly. "Phi, she's closing in on over half a millennia. She is hardly a child either."

I smiled at him. "I am aware." I looked away from him, uncertain of our new standing with each other. "Do you think they sent for the others?" I asked, changing the subject.

"Our older siblings? I can't see why," he replied. "They don't know us, let alone Niko. They stayed on the mainlands when Mother and Father came to settle here. I'm not even sure that they hear much from them lately." He sat down on the stool beside me. "They are from a different world altogether. We were raised in safety, they were not."

"Lately it doesn't seem we were raised in safety either. Just on lies."

He shot me a confused look at the comment.

I just shook my head, not at all ready for that conversation. "Ask Trae. He's a better teacher than I am." I picked up the journal from the bench and slid it into the bag with the fruit.

"I'll assume that unreadable thing has something to do with it all?" He cocked an eyebrow at me. Of course he had looked.

"Yes. But again, ask Trae," I said tiredly. "I barely have enough space to process what I know, let alone pass it along." I stood up from the stool. "I also have research to do. I'll check in later. Take care of them?"

"Of course. Don't stay away too long. I'll go to Trae's when I can. They held no summit in The Square after Niko was taken, just so you know. They know we all know but they want to calm some of the panic."

I nodded. I had been too distracted by everything else to really pay much attention to what the Elders were doing to address the situation, as it was. I knew too many lies that we had been fed by all of them over the ages. I wondered idly if my uncle or great grandfather knew the truth, given their positions. Or Creston's grandfather for that matter.

Perhaps the lies had been told long before they were allotted their Elder roles.

CHAPTER 44

I headed out the door with the thought on my mind, realising as I shut myself away in my room that I hadn't felt truly alone in the longest time. I sat on my bed and pulled the journal from the bag of fruits.

I leafed past the first few pages I had already memorised. The words didn't shift anymore. They came to me with ease.

I must start with more on our counterpart, as with each passing day, all that we know about them seems to be buried deeper and deeper beneath other tales. You are not to be fooled by them. They are just as we are. But their magic... it is twisted. Their magic is the darkness of our ancestors. Nature was vengeful, for it raged against imbalances. It took that vengeance out on them, making their magic steal from nature to survive, rather than creating from it as much of our magic does.

We are fleeing even now. They attack more and more. But it is the divide between us that is the problem. We are one race, not two. But so much of the fear has turned to hatred. They hate us because we leave them to starve. They are forced into brutalities to ensure their own survival. In the beginning, they were no risk. They are mastered now, from where I do not know, but they hunt us, seeking something from us. The children disappear before they can truly be nurtured, before any can showcase their magic in a controlled way. And they can control it. I have seen it. I have watched them trick, torment and terrify with their magic. Humans and Fae Born alike. Their hatred and misunderstanding makes them cruel. The reversal will be no easy task.

A unification is required. And it is a task that will only worsen over the ages. I regret that, and I hope that the knowledge reaches you before the ages have hidden even more from all of us. I've done all I can here, I have gathered as much about their magic and what is needed as I can.

Good luck.

I closed the book again after staring at the final introduction pages for what felt like hours.

There were pages of diagrams, lists of the possible magics, and from what I could tell from there, instructions on how to broaden my own magic. It was a lot to take on. There were notes scribbled in margins, notes that did not come from the author. They made me wonder how many others had held this book, sought to learn from it, yet had done so very little with it. Perhaps they read it as I did, hidden away from the world. And that's where they'd remained with the knowledge, hidden.

I looked up to the tapestry on my wall.

Dreams.

My mother had dreamt of that image. A girl with flames for hair, sitting beneath a burning autumn tree, surrounded by a strange rune she had never seen before, but nevertheless she included it in a tapestry she had kept near me my entire life.

Feeling restless, I glanced around my room, looking for a distraction. My door was replaced but there were still some splinters around from its broken predecessor. I got up, gathering the mess and putting it into the dormant fireplace. I would burn it later, not that the fires I created required any fuel to keep going, but sometimes I enjoyed the sound of a true crackling wood fire.

I extended my cleaning beyond just the splintered wood, picking up my discarded clothes and blankets, going through my room until I felt calm again. Until I had nothing else to distract me from the hours that had passed since I'd been made to leave Creston alone with a possibly insane member of his family.

Not insane, I reminded myself, *just dark.* Full of magic none of us seemed to truly understand just yet. But maybe they did. It was their magic after all.

I didn't go back to the house for dinner. Instead, I picked at the fruit my brother had given me and curled in my bed with an old novel from the mortal world that always improved my mood. I didn't know when my exhaustion won, but I must have drifted off, and the next I knew I was dreaming again.

The shadows reached for me.

I could see them.

Hands of darkness, gripping at the air around me, stopping just short of truly touching me.

There was light from somewhere, and I turned to find it but saw nothing but shadow. It took me time to realise the light was coming from me.

As I reached my arm out towards the writhing darkness I saw the way my skin glowed, like the dull light from a candle's flame, it stretched from within me.

The shadows shied away at first, then surged.

I screamed as they covered my skin, devouring my glow with their touch, the light dying out, leaving me in darkness as the shadows stretched over my body. They dug into my skin, as if clawing at it, trying to rip away the light. I tried to pull away to no avail.

I reached for my magic, letting out a cry of alarm as flames roared from within and destroyed each shadow where it touched me. As the darkness disappeared I saw that I stood in the autumn forest again.

"They were only trying to dress you. If there were a need for screams, you would have known it," a newly familiar voice muttered from behind me, tsking.

I turned, looking down as I did so to see I still wore the clothes I'd fallen asleep in. "Maybe I didn't want to be changed," I said and stepped out of the smoking remnants of the forest floor that had been caught in my mini inferno. I met the golden eyes of the male in front of me, crossing my arms over my chest. "The clothes I'm wearing in reality suit me just fine."

"Ah, but that's where you're wrong. You should be in much finer things than that at all times." His lips curled into a smirk.

I frowned at him. "Who exactly are you? And why are you in my dreams?"

He clasped a hand over his chest in mock injury. "You scorn me." He laughed, taking me aback with the sudden change. "You truly do not know who I am, do you?" He tilted his head, his bright eyes measuring me.

I shook my head, making him laugh again.

"Oh. Well." He paused, looking genuinely confused that I had no idea who he was. "I suppose there is reason for that. Though I'd wager you do know who I am, but have not yet figured it out. Allow me to help." He stepped back and swung himself into a graceful bow. "My name is Samil, son of many." He straightened and a shiver crawled along my spine. "But I would much prefer you call me Samil. It is after all a name

with much appropriate meaning."

My whole body was tense. I stood within a dream with the first of the Elliphir. *"How?"* I breathed.

"How do you dream of me?" he asked. *"How does the sun rise? How do the stars fall? You are going to have to be far more specific with these things, Nixling, or else I may become confused."* He seemed to take joy from my reaction, from my shock. He waved a hand impatiently. *"I have little patience for games. I have sent for you in my dreams for the greater part of a decade now. You were so far and so resistant at first. And yet now, you come all of your own accord. You are truly more than I expected."*

"All on my own? This is a dream, *you drew me here."*

"Incorrect. You brought yourself, this time and the last. And I am not sleeping." He shrugged.

"What do you mean?" I looked around again. The forest was the same as each past dream I had seen it in.

He made an annoyed sound and folded himself to the ground. *"I mean you are a Nightshade."*

"A poisonous plant?" I asked incredulously. *"Seriously?"*

"No not a plant, Nixling," he practically sighed, sounding frustrated that I wasn't as up to speed as he was. *"A poisonous walker. Sleepshade is another name, but it's hardly as powerful. You can move yourself to wherever you like. With a little training, it's a powerful trait."*

"I'm dreaming." I refused to believe the alternative. It went against everything I'd ever known. When I woke in the morning, Trae would be able to explain the loss of sanity and the strange dreams, I was sure of it.

He sighed again as I said it and got up, coming over and standing directly in front of me, his golden eyes shimmering as he looked down at me, hands on his hips. *"No, you're not. You're projecting,"* he said firmly. *"It feels like a dream perhaps. But I am awake. In the beginning, yes, you were dreaming, and I was the one creating the dreams, but now you have followed me back. You are no longer being controlled. You are present. Here with me. You are not totally physically here, but with magic you are close enough." He reached out and toyed with my hair.*

I could feel it. The sensation was odd. Not complete. Like poking at a part of your body that's asleep, you know what it should feel like, but it's behind a wall of tingling sensations that block the way.

I pulled back from him, getting to my feet. "If you are right. Then where am I, where is here?" I crossed my arms tighter over my chest, like holding myself could cure the growing anxiety I felt.

He smiled at me, a bright vivid smile full of joy and deepening the dimples that appeared in his sharp features. "Seraphine, my Nixling, you are in Faerie."

CHAPTER 45

"Faerie?" I repeated, a little too loudly.

He nodded once. "It has many names, but Faerie will suffice. The Autumn Wood, to be precise. This is my home. Well, not this spot exactly but within this wood. For now."

I looked around again. I could feel the magic in the world surrounding me, but it was dulled. I knew there had to be far more to it. "Faerie left us behind," I murmured, though the words felt strangely hollow.

"Incorrect. The Seventeen left your race behind, not Faerie itself." His tone was bitter, the words almost a snarl. "Many here did not even know our kind existed, just as I am sure you are poorly educated on the races that live within Faerie. But I am fixing that. I am bringing you all home to me."

I looked back to him then, frowning, once again struggling against what I knew and what was the truth.

He smiled at me again. "No Elliphir or Elliphae remain in the mortal world, except for the colony on your island, Keinteris. I have spent a lot of time working towards this. Hundreds are here already. Your people will be next and last to return to your rightful home. I would take you to see, but you only ever appear here in this place, by the Midithrias doorway. Ironically, the doorway you will all use to arrive here."

"You have every other Elliphae and Elliphir in the world here?"

"Yes, and really, I resent the diversion in your names," he said, an annoyed expression on his face. "You are all of the same design. We are all of the same design. But it is distinction and we require that. Perhaps as the ages pass I can reconnect the two within one, as we were when I was a child."

I cocked an eyebrow. "If my memory serves, it was your growth into your magic that caused the separation."

He growled softly at the comment. "Do not blame me for the workings of nature and balance. I could help it no more than you can. I am sure you have dealt with much given the configuration of your blooded magic and your true magic."

I flinched at the statement.

He raised his brows, as if my answer was something he'd suspected. "Just as I thought. Then you know what it is like to have others treat you poorly for aspects well beyond your understanding, and should they teach you true history, I was not present when the diversion started in our people. It occurred centuries after my magic was present."

"So I am discovering," I murmured. Sighing, I kicked at the ground. "I shouldn't be here again. There are more important things for me to be doing. Back where I'm supposed to be."

"This is where you are supposed to be," he snapped, the calm facade slipping for the briefest of seconds. His golden eyes was edged with a black ring that seemed to grow thicker. "You belong here in Faerie. In your true home surrounded by magic instead of being drained by it." Closing his eyes, he took a deep breath, holding it for a moment before releasing it and opening his eyes again. The black was gone.

My heart jumped into my throat at the anger in his voice, but I schooled my expression, trying not to show him any fear. "I don't understand." I shook my head, overwhelmed with everything he'd said, the *lies he claimed the Elders had told us, far beyond the reach of forgotten histories.*

Samil rolled his shoulders, his expression smoothing into the bland smile again. "That you clearly do not. Wake now, Nixling. I have more to do than teach you the nuances of your own history. There will be time for more later." He reached out and touched my forehead, his finger freezing cold, sending an electric current through my body.

The forest shuddered and went black as I collapsed to the ground.

I woke on the floor of my bedroom, blanket curled around my body. I sat up with a groan, looking around blearily

My room was dim, lanterns no longer lit. My novel was still on the bed, and I suddenly felt as though so much of my day had been wasted sleeping and waiting, not truly knowing what I was even waiting for.

Was it for Niko to be returned to us? Was it for Creston to show up with answers? Was it Trae with a new revelation? Kylan...or Raphael? What name he preferred, I did not know, just as I didn't know if he would arrive with a new threat as he dangled my brother's whereabouts over my head. Or perhaps I was waiting for Veneficus to show up with more threats and half answers all the while.

I paused with the thought.

Veneficus.

The nightmares, have they started? His words echoed in my mind. He knew. He had to know. Not just that the nightmares would come, but who was responsible for the nightmares being forged in my mind. That Samil would call to me. Somehow he expected it. But why? And why had it worried him so?

I got up from the floor, pacing in my room, trying to remember everything he had said, what he'd accidentally let slip.

The Divide. He had been concerned about how close to it I had been. I had been scared of it my whole life, not just of it, but beyond it. That all had changed, especially after the first night I set myself on fire during a nightmare. Right on the edge of the Divide. My magic had woken me and from then on I had been constantly drawn back, as if something beyond it called out to me, but I had never thought much on it.

As I grew, I had always just assumed it was my vein of disobedience against a world so careful about everyone in it. Everyone but me, but the girl with magic that made no sense. I didn't have to be anyone but myself while truly alone beyond the Divide.

Surrounded by magic, but not drained by it.

And perhaps that, in itself, was the answer. We were shielded here, so deeply shielded with so much magic that we couldn't be found. So much magic that it required all of us to offer some of ourself, even if we did not know we were doing it.

I sat down on my bed, lost in thought. The more strings I pulled at in my mind, the more things seemed to unravel with great ease. It made my head ache. I pinched the bridge of my nose and sighed softly.

Too much was falling apart. Or, more accurately, we had tugged on the single thread capable of unravelling the entire world the Elders had built for us.

Samil's words settled in my mind, like a stone sinking to the bottom of a lake. We didn't belong here. We didn't belong in the realm of mortality. We were made of too much magic and darkness to ever truly belong here, it was why we were forced to hide away from the world. But how could we belong in Faerie? When we were taught nothing of it?

Perhaps to stop us searching for it in the same way Silas had when he'd lost Samil to it.

Maybe it was not Faerie that the Elders feared, but the loss of power that would surely rise from us joining a world entirely of magic. Magic far purer and far stronger than any they could hope to possess.

As I sat on the edge of my bed with my mind working in tangled circles, I realised dim light was beginning to show through the gaps in the curtains over my window and the edges of my door.

Dawn. It was dawn again.

A whole day had passed. A day wasted away into confusion, although time had felt like it was moving at a snail's pace in my dream.

I got up from the bed and grabbed fresh clothes, slipping into my bathroom to wash away everything and relax. Newly dressed with my wet curls pulled into a tight ponytail, I hurried away from my home.

Once I reached the open pathways I stopped, no longer so sure of where I was going. I needed more answers, about Niko, about Samil, about the dreams, but I didn't know where to start.

Kylan had those answers, but I presumed he and Creston were hidden away in their family home. A home I had never seen nor tried to find before, respecting Creston's wishes not to have it as a place that was visited. I was too concerned for his wellbeing and for my brother's safety to respect those wishes now.

I would have to hunt for them through others, would have to ask around to see if someone had seen him out and about.

Although perhaps that was not the best of ideas, to alert others that I deemed him missing. He was a well known Guardien after all, it would be noted.

I sighed. I doubted I could gain more than further confusion from Trae.

Lately it seemed that for every question he answered, he only created five more unanswered ones. Cleo would be with him and her answers would stem from whatever he had shared with her.

As my mind ran through the steps, I started moving, my body registering before my mind where I needed to go.

Veneficus.

He was the one who seemed to know the most about how all this involved me, and perhaps would know more about my mystery dream visitor.

It didn't take me long to arrive outside his home.

It was a simple one, made of vines and stone, though it was not modified in the way most earth users would personalise the earth that grew around them. Given that his noted magic was Air, that stood to reason. He, like myself, would have to rely on others to maintain his home.

I rapped on the front door loudly. It was early morning but I had no doubt that he was awake.

It took a few minutes until I could hear movement somewhere on the other side of the doorway, right before it swung open, revealing a very alert but slightly disheveled Veneficus.

Not waiting for him to speak, I demanded, "How did you know about the nightmares?" I crossed my arms as he took in my appearance at his door.

He sighed tiredly. "Seraphine, I asked that you do not push these things. I am busy."

"I don't care. How did you know that Samil would visit me in my dreams."

His eyes widened ever so slightly at the name, and that was my chance. "You have spoken with him?" He seemed uncharacteristically shocked.

"Yes. I have. More than once. The nightmares, it seems, were a pathway to exactly that. But I think you already knew that." I scanned his face, waiting for some kind of subtle tell that I'd surprised him with my information.

It was not subtle. His expression morphed, no longer shocked but frustrated. "I had hoped I had more time. He knows where we are," he said, almost to himself, running a hand over his face. "If you have been so exposed, then you broke the ward far earlier than I though, and he knows where to come." He rubbed his forehead. "I truly should have kept you on a tighter leash. There are no reversals now."

"What does he have to do with me? Why does he haunt my dreams and no one else's?" There was pleading in my voice that I resented deeply.

He shot me an almost sympathetic look, covered immediately by a pained one. He smoothed his hand over his bald scalp. "Because of your magic. Because he sought the creation of what you are. Because you are the counterpart he lacks. There is much you do not know, much that comes from ages before you. It was easier when you didn't know."

"Maybe if we were taught true histories and not the falsities that suited the Elders' agendas then things would be much easier for us all," I said, annoyed. I squeezed my arms tighter, trying to hold in the torrent of emotion that begged to be released from inside me.

"Choices were made," he said blankly, his stare distant for a moment.

I laughed bitterly. "That's all you've got to say? 'Choices were made'? What kind of cryptic bullshit is that?"

"The kind that keeps you safe." He looked exhausted as he stared at me.

"Screw safe. Obliviousness isn't safe, it's vulnerable," I snapped. "I'm vulnerable because I don't understand who or what I am, because I was never taught. I was never even given the chance."

He sighed again as I spoke. "What you fail to understand is the why. Once your eyes have been opened to see that which you were blind to, it is almost impossible to return to blindness."

Chapter 46

"Who says I ever want to return to being blind?" The words were a challenge, and a declaration. Being held in the dark had never caused me anything but pain and fear.

He gave me a sad look. "We all wish it, at least once. There are things you will wish you never knew, I assure you. And you have many of the answers within your reach already. Trae didn't find that journal for no reason. I could never read it, but I'd imagine you can, if my memory of that particular writer serves."

My eyebrows rose. "You knew her?"

He nodded. "Many moons ago, before we came here, when Faerie started to call us home. She left it behind, with someone else. It eventually made its way to me and I put it in Trae's path. Have you read it?"

I wasn't sure if he was someone I could trust with the knowledge that I'd read most of it, but I needed answers. "I have read some, yes," I admitted reluctantly.

"Just be careful," he warned. "I know not what knowledge is there, but some will not be kind."

"If you know the history hidden within it, why not tell me?"

"Because it's not my story to tell." A shadow passed across his face and he waved me off. "Go, Seraphine. I am done chattering. There are things I must do." He shooed me backwards and closed the door in my face.

I groaned and rubbed my face with both hands in frustration, dragging my fingers through my bound hair. Taking a breath, I reopened my eyes and refocused, turning on my heels and headed away from the home behind me, to return to my own.

In all my life, I didn't think I had spent so much time crossing through Keinteris to get somewhere quickly. Life had always been simple, if magic was removed from the equation as much as could be done. But I had some answers, and the journal had more to tell, perhaps deeper within it.

Arriving back at my home without seeing anyone else I knew, I slipped into my room and found the journal, curling onto my bed as I opened it, quickly flicking past the last portions of it that I had reached.

Beyond the spells and instructions on how to increase my magical abilities, there was another passage.

The past and history are a strange thing to manage. When I learnt of what I was, of what it meant to be a Phoenix, I was blessed to have it cross the lips of someone I trusted. Of another Phoenix. Before he chose his death, he taught me all that I have tried to leave here for you, and I am sorry that there isn't more.

Your magic will define you. Just as it defines me as Faerie calls us home. I will not go to the island, I want to see what awaits me in the realm we belong within. But it means that any born here may never know the blessing of being taught who they are. You are half of a whole here, and I do not know what that truly means. Even as powerful as we stand to be, more power is locked away from us. Buried deep is a key to unlocking it, to having what Silas once did. I seek it now, and though he never made it to Faerie to find his brother, I will.

He comes to me now. Sunshine eyes in dark dreams. I wish I had more time, to learn more and leave it in this realm to be found. Perhaps you will not grow here long, and what I do learn can be found by you in Faerie, where I may be as powerful as I am promised, and may too pave the way for you.

Be well. Faerie awaits us all.

I flicked through the pages, looking for the rest. Surely there had to be more. The author hadn't left a book of riddles with no answers, had she?

They were blank except for three runes. Runes I felt I had seen before but wasn't sure where. I frowned. There was nothing else, only empty pages part of me wished had been filled.

Sunshine eyes in dark dreams.

Samil. He had clearly been walking in the dreams of others for a long time. Given I didn't even know how old he truly was, the news shouldn't have surprised me.

I strode over to my bookshelves, grabbing a notebook from it. It was filled with random entries that I ripped out before getting to work, deciding to use my racing mind to my advantage instead of thinking about Niko and what he might be going through.

This journal was only meant for a Phoenix, that much was true, but there had to be things I was missing. Things that a finer eye, and a sharper mind, would catch. Things Trae would be able to link it with.

So I went about the task of copying every last word into my notebook, to give him the resource he lacked. The task took hours upon hours as I tried to keep every detail exact, including copying each and every unfamiliar rune and symbol in painstaking detail, only shifting positions on my bed when my muscles ached or I needed to use the bathroom.

Nothing else disturbed me from the task as I copied page after page of spells and instructions beyond the two directed messages. I had given myself no small task. I thought of little else as I worked, almost relieved to be able to not think about Niko's disappearance, my mother's heartbreak and the handprint that had bruised my stomach.

A soft knock on my door made me jump.

I looked towards the door as it opened slowly, rubbing my eyes. They were sore after squinting at the journal for so long.

"Seraphine?"

I was surprised by my mother's voice, but I closed both the journal and my notebook and stood quickly. "Mum. Hi."

She entered the room with a bowl of steaming soup in one hand and buttered bread on a plate in the other. My stomach growled ravenously as the scent of the fresh pumpkin soup hit me. She gave me a small smile. "We hadn't seen you, so I assumed you would be hungry. I see I was right." My mother used her magic, a small table forming by my bed as she walked towards it. She set down the bowl and plate before looking at me properly. "Are you well?"

"I should be asking you that, not the other way around," I told her softly, my throat suddenly burning as my eyes welled with unshed tears. Something about my mother's presence tore at the walls I was hiding behind.

She stepped forward, cupping my cheek in her hand gently. "Shh, don't be absurd. We are all mourning your brother, no pain is invalid here," she said, smoothing her thumb over my cheek. "But I must still care for the children who remain, your father reminded me of that." She tucked some of my curls behind my ear.

I had let my hair loose at some point earlier in an attempt to ease the tension headache. I didn't quite remember when, but my curls flowed free over my shoulders.

"You are so beautiful, Seraphine. My littlest flame." She kissed my forehead gently.

I closed my eyes for a moment, revelling in the way her magic swept through my body. It happened every time she kissed me, almost like a reflex, as if she always needed to be sure I was okay. "I'll get him back, Mum, I swear it."

She gave me a sad look. "Do not swear to what you cannot control, Seraphine. We will all do what we can to get him home. But that starts with care," she said firmly, pointing at the bowl of soup. "Eat, rest. It is already past sunset. You never sleep enough with your nightmares so sleep now. I love you." She stroked my cheek again and left. To return to her own pain, I assumed.

I didn't stop her. I did, however, pay attention to the world outside my window. She was right, darkness had fallen on the world around me again. The whole day gone with my fixation on copying the journal for Trae.

And Creston still didn't come.

I pushed the thought away as I sat down on my bed again, quickly devouring the bread and soup, every drop gone before I set the bowl down. I considered going in search of more but as I stretched out in my bed, a battle with exhaustion that I couldn't win overwhelmed me. My eyes grew heavier and heavier. Blinking sleepily, the answer came to me. The odd taste in the soup.

Passionflower.

Mother had added the herb to the soup, likely for all of us.

Sleep came for me quickly, and I knew what would follow with it. *Dreams.* I had once feared them, but was growing to welcome them.

Dreams could offer me more answers.

CHAPTER 47

I expected the dress this time, running my fingers over the fabric as I opened my eyes in the Autumn Wood, surprised to find the night sky open above me.

I sat up, looking around in the darkened wood. Nothing else seemed to have changed, it was just pitched into night.

"No need to worry." I turned towards Samil's voice as he walked towards me, noting the light that was likely a home in the distance behind him. He stopped a few steps from me and sat down so he faced me. "You are just here at a different time than you're used to."

"Oh." I looked away from him and back to the sky above us. "The stars are different," I murmured. The clusters and constellations were off.

"And there is a second moon once a year," Samil added. I looked to him, surprised and he grinned, dimples appearing in his cheeks. "Yes, two," he supplied before I could ask.

"I think I'd like to see that." It didn't seem real.

"And so you will, Nixling. In time." He leaned back against his arms, cocking his head to the side, surveying me. "Your sleep is different. Why?"

I toyed with the dress, avoiding his stare. "My mother, she gave me something to help me sleep. She knows I am prone to nightmares."

An indecipherable expression crossed his features. "Have you told her about these dreams?"

I shook my head immediately. "My mother has enough to carry. Even I don't truly understand what these dreams are, so how could I explain them to her?" I gnawed at my lower lip, the thought turning my stomach.

"Have you told anyone?" he asked casually. Too casually.

I laughed dryly, trying to hide my nerves from the strange man. "Who are you worried knows?"

"You could tell anyone, Seraphine, I care little. But I know you have questions."

"I have more questions than I know how to put into words," I admitted quietly.

"Where would you like to start?" Samil ran his fingers through his dark hair as he watched me with his odd golden eyes. They seemed liquid in their colour, pure magic perhaps.

"The beginning, I suppose. Why were you looking for me?"

"You know about my brother. My twin," he began, looking over my shoulder with a faraway expression. "His type of magic calls to me. And I have been searching for Keinteris since I retrieved all others from the Mortal Realm. I've already told you that none of you belong there and that I want all of our people returned. You were a key to finding them. I doubt I would have gotten so close if you had not existed." He sat forward, hands clasped over his crossed legs.

"Close? So you haven't yet found us?" I couldn't help but ask. Veneficus had seemed so concerned about his proximity, what harm could it do to know how far away he was?

He pinned me with a withering look. "No, but each day I get closer to what I need to find you all." He leaned forward a little. "But I have questions for you. About the Guardien."

I jerked in surprise. "Creston?" I asked with a frown.

Samil shrugged. "His name means nothing to me, but what does he mean to you?"

I opened my mouth, then closed it again, unsure. What did he mean to me? He was one of my closest friends, but I hadn't seen or heard from him in days, which was very unusual for him. My days felt emptier without our banter in the morning, and I missed his presence.

He held up his hand. "I'll help you answer. You can show me what he means, think about it."

I wasn't sure what he meant, until the Autumn Wood disappeared from around us. I turned towards new lights. A window appeared in the darkness, and as I focused the rest of the image settled into place. There was no sound, but I didn't need it.

There I was, as a child, seven children gathered around me. I was on my knees at their centre. I could see the blood on my cheek. They were tossing stones at me, grabbing at my limbs with vines to keep me from running. I could remember it all, as I watched it happen again, I knew the rage that filled that little version of me. The fear that had me panicking, overwhelmed, terrified no one would come to help me, to save me. The desire to hurt them. But I couldn't, because hurting them would upset my family.

Then it changed. From the edge of the image Creston appeared, far younger and far more gangly than he was now. He punched the two boys who had been reaching out to hit me next and they went down hard. He took the rest down in twos and dared them to try and get back up.

He was older, he was stronger and they knew it. They complained, whined about him getting in the way of their fun. He paid them no mind, instead focused solely on me.

I stared at him with wide eyes, tears streamed down my face through the blood as he helped me up, keeping me close by his side as he led me from sight.

My heart raced a little. This was the first time Creston had ever saved *me and there was still more to be shown. I didn't know whether I was controlling it or Samil was, but I didn't fight it either way.*

The window went dark, then lit up again with a new image.

I was older now, seventeen, or close to it, standing by myself in a hallway. I was dressed in all white.

It was the night my uncle became an Elder, I realised, stiffening at the memory. A figure walked towards me down the hall.

Miles. He pulled me towards him when he reached me, and I could see the way my younger self flinched as he touched me. I pushed away from him. Once again, I couldn't hear the words spoken but they were burned in my memory.

He was telling me how worthless I was, how he had taken pity on me by sleeping with me. He'd been in the first memory too. The one who had cut my cheek. Nothing happened other than the silent shouts, and my young self cowering closer and closer to the wall.

He was drunk. I'd realised that too late then. But when he lunged forward towards me, his hand never ended up on my skin.

Creston had appeared too quickly for that, catching Miles before he could do anything more than shout at me.

They'd argued with one another. I hadn't remembered that, too shocked in the moment, realising the mistake I had made. Creston had tossed him aside like he was nothing, doing just enough to make sure he wouldn't come back.

When Creston was satisfied Miles wouldn't return, he was back with me, calming me, cleaning up my tears and holding me.

A girl with dark hair ran towards us, Lana, not Cleo, taking me from Creston as he was led away by a blond male I vaguely recognised as Hyatt.

Creston had saved me that night, but Lana had been the one to heal my heart, months later, becoming my first real love. It had been a young love, and it hadn't lasted, but she had been exactly who I needed. Kind, genuine, caring... she'd helped put the pieces of me back together. Even though our relationship ended amicably just over three years ago, it had been Creston who'd found me sitting by the sea, crying in the dark the night we broke up. It had always been him who found me.

The image blackened and I turned back to Samil.

He was already watching me carefully, trying to read something in my expression. "He's your protector then. There are more, I can sense them. More times where he was there for you, that he rescued you."

I rubbed my hands over my arms. "He has, always. He has kept me safe from things I didn't know I should have been afraid of. He's always been there."

His eyes narrowed a little. "I see."

A shout rang out in the night, before he could say any more. It sounded like his name but I couldn't be sure.

I glanced in the direction of the sound curiously. It came from somewhere by the lights.

He was on his feet quickly, tugging me to mine. "It's time for you to go again, Nixling. I have things to attend to. I will speak with you soon. Trust that."

The world around me wavered and turned back to the blackness of dreamless sleep.

When I eventually woke, it was to the sound of bird songs, not the residual fear from any nightmare I had grown so accustomed to. It almost felt weirder to wake up normally, though I was grateful my bedding had survived the night. I stretched out in bed, my body cracking in protest.

I groaned softly, reaching for both journals, needing to finish what little was left. When I was done, after a few hours, I got up, getting dressed and grabbing the newly filled notebook from my bed.

I left my room and headed into the house. My stomach ached with hunger and before I went anywhere else I knew I needed to eat. It was still early, but my father sat in the kitchen.

He looked up at me from the glass in front of him at my entrance. I knew whatever was in it was alcohol, and I passed no judgement for it. He looked more rested than he'd appeared in days.

"Morning," I told him softly as I picked up an apple from the bowl on the bench.

He nodded in greeting. "Morning, darling. I take it your mother also supplied you with a night's sleep?"

I smiled as I bit into the apple. "She did. Are the other two still asleep?" The house seemed too quiet for them not to still be sleeping, though the entire house lacked vibrancy without Niko's erratic energy.

"That they are. Are you headed out?" He jerked his chin towards the book in my other hand.

I clutched it a little tighter, taking another bite from the apple, chewing as I nodded. "Just to spend time with Trae and Cleo," I told him after swallowing the bite.

He watched me, looking like he wanted to push for more. But he didn't. Instead he stood, finishing the dark liquid in his glass. He put it in the sink before passing by me. "Just stay safe." He kissed my temple, the scent of liquor on his breath before he disappeared towards the room my mother slumbered in.

My heart ached, but I pushed the sensation away, quickly eating as much as I could justify before leaving.

Once again, I was on my way to Trae's house. It seemed to be my home now more than anywhere else. I refused to address the lack of laughter in my own home, the vibrancy taken away with my brother. Trae's home felt safe, calm, and I needed that. Despite my desire to be there for my family, sitting in our agony helped none of us. I needed to be doing something more.

I was about half way there, mind spinning through various events and realities, when he appeared in my path, quite literally emerging from the shadows, a grin lighting up his face and a dark edge in his storm blue eyes. I stepped back, taken by surprise, having been paying far too little attention to my surroundings as I walked. Just like Creston always warned me about.

Kylan swept his hand in a mock bow, his ever present smirk growing as he noticed my surprise. "Well hello again, Seraphine. So nice to have you without the constant audience. Perhaps it will finally grant me your undivided attention."

CHAPTER 48

"So what exactly am I supposed to call you now? Raphael?" I folded my arms, leaning my weight to one leg as I tried to hold myself in a strong stance. But no matter how I held myself, his presence still sent a sense of unease through me.

He chuckled softly as he looked me over, but I noticed the way his hand flexed at the name. "That name died with the child I was. Kylan was my middle name, the name I chose after here, so let's settle on that. I have explained so much of my life after here to my poor baby brother."

"I would describe Creston many ways, but poor isn't one of them," I snapped, furious that Kylan would be so cruel about his own brother. "Saddened, perhaps. But then again, you've only spent, what? A few days with your brother. Hardly time enough to know him." I clenched my teeth, inhaling deeply, before speaking again. "Where is Creston?"

"Resting. In our family home. See, while I may have only spent a small amount of time with my brother now, I have had a place in his life for far longer," he said, watching intently for a reaction. "My bedroom is just as I left it as a child. Even with both our parents gone, my brother has never had the heart to touch it." He seemed to find the fact amusing.

My heart lurched at his statement, thinking of Creston alone in a home that included a shrine. *Was that what my home was to become?* I shuddered at the thought. "Why are you even out here if he isn't?" I frowned at him. "You made yourself very clear the other day. And you owe me a debt."

"One that I will heed in time. But for now I have appearances to keep up and work to be done. Starting with you." He flicked his wrist, shadows sliding over his palm and leaving behind a pendant.

A thick silver chain held the heavy pendant. The same silver twisted in intricate swirls around the edges of a rich red stone, one that seemed to swirl beneath the surface, like liquid was trapped inside it, yet a gnawing feeling told me the swirls were made of something else entirely. I knew that the red would match the dress I wore in my dreams. The pendant was undeniably beautiful, even if it struck a cord of fear through me.

"Seeing as you are already proving your inadequacy and cannot carry gifts with you from your dreams, I was asked to give this to you." He lifted the pendant by the shining silver chain it was attached to. "I would like to be very clear. This is not a gift from me." He held it out towards me, face twisted with distaste at the idea of gifting something to me.

I hesitated. "It's from Samil," I guessed, staring at the stone. It was like nothing I'd ever seen forged here.

Kylan chuckled softly. "I see you've been educated on some things then. It is from Samil. It is a stone of Faerie. He asked me to give it to you and advise you to wear it."

"Advise me?" I cocked an eyebrow, my gaze finally drawn from the stone.

Shadows slipped closer around us and Kylan smiled at me. It was a smile that never reached his eyes, the glimmer there was something else entirely. "Advise. Or Threaten. The choice is both yours and mine. But this will hang from your neck before you leave here."

My fists clenched in response, my flesh heating as my fire flickered in the corner of my mind, waiting. I was tired of the way he spoke to me, how he taunted me and threatened the people I cared about.

He tutted at me. "Uh ah, fire bitch, let's not forget who knows the location of one precious baby brother. Two if you count my own, given that he is surely who you hoped to next see."

I dug my nails into the palms of my hands as I stared at him, taking another deep breath to calm the hot anger I felt bubbling at the edge of my mind. "If I take it, and wear it, you'll tell me where my brother is?" I asked after a moment of silence.

He pursed his lips as if thinking it over, then made a clicking sound with his mouth. "No." He swung the necklace a little. "But I will tell you where to find my brother." He watched me and waited.

I chewed at the inside of my cheek as I looked at him, glancing at the necklace again before nodding. I reached out a hand, ignoring the small crescent moons that marked my palm from where my nails had been.

He stepped forward and dropped the pendant in my hand.

The instant it touched my skin I shuddered, my hairs standing on edge as a flow of magic swept over my skin. I glanced at him with wide eyes.

He just held up a hand. "Before you ask, no I don't know what magic is within it. Just that it was made for you and you alone, so on it pops now." He made an impatient motion with his hand.

My mouth felt dry as I lifted the necklace, unclasping the chain and fastening it around my neck. The heavy weight of the pendant was cold against my chest, nestled neatly above my breasts. It sent another shiver through me as it settled in place. I rubbed my hands together as

I looked to him again. "Okay. My part is done."

He flashed one of those wide grins that never reached his eyes. "Good girl." He flicked his wrist again, a shadow sliding out with the action. It slipped across the pathway and kept moving. "Follow that. It will take you to my brother." With that, he turned and walked away.

I stared after him for a moment before hurrying to catch the shadow that hadn't stopped to wait for me. It took a minute to find, but I soon eased back into a steady walk. I was led further away from the main settlement, towards the woods that edged the other side of the coast's cliff line. Creston had found me once here, and I'd always wondered why he'd been so far away from the rest of the community, how he'd known there were seldom trodden paths to follow. Now I knew.

The shadow vanished as the home came into view, melting back into the natural shadows of the world. Intricately woven vines decorated the small home, and no stone visible told me that much like Trae's home, and many others, it was all of magic. A living thing.

I made my way to the door, up a pathway of dark flowers it took me a moment to recognise.

Hellebore, in a rich dark red that was almost black. Poisonous.

I paused halfway to the door and looked to the rest of the garden. The more I looked, the more poisons I found. I frowned deeply at the implication.

Poisons made from the earth couldn't kill us before, something in our Fae blood fighting against them to reverse their affects, but they could still make us slip into a brief unconsciousness. Or worse, a coma.

Picking my way through the flowers carefully, I continued to the door, knocking on it loudly.

There was no response.

I knocked again. It took a little time but I could hear sound from inside.

The door opened slowly, and Creston's tousled black hair came into view first as he squinted around the door against the daylight, the room behind him black. His eyes widened in surprise as he realised it was me outside the door. He looked around me, frowning. The door creaked open, exposing his bare, tattooed chest to the morning sun.

"Phi," he muttered sleepily as he crossed arms over his chest. "How did you find me?"

I scanned him, checking for any signs that his brother had hurt or upset him. "Kylan led me here."

His face changed for an instant, with emotions I couldn't quite gauge. "Right." He looked down at himself, dressed only in loose pants and nothing else.

"Suddenly self conscious?" I asked dryly. "I have seen you without a shirt before." I had *not* seen him in thin pants that left so little to the imagination I could see the outline of what definitely looked like his cock before. He'd either been in his Guardien leathers or, as of recently, nothing at all, but not much compared to this. He was so alluring, without even trying to be, waking that constant need in me that only seemed to worsen around him lately.

He looked at me for a moment then laughed. "You're right. Uh, come in." He moved to the side to let me step into the darkness of the house. I brushed past him, shivering at the warmth radiating off his body. Now was definitely not the time to look down. As he closed the door, I could hear the vines slithering together.

After a few moments, light started to filter into the room as the vines shifted with Creston's whims, illuminating the house within. I took another step further in, watching as the light reached out and touched the edges of the room.

It was beautiful, every piece of furniture in the room was intricate, carefully formed and even somewhat carved, although carving was unusual for a family of earth users. I took another step, reaching out to touch the carving on the side table that lined the entrance hall.

A hand hastily clasped round my wrist before my fingers reached the surface. "Don't." The single word was a plea.

I looked at him over my shoulder in surprise, finding his eyes were dark and wide. I nodded, trying to pull my hand back, but his hold remained. I turned more towards him, letting him use the grip to pull me in closer.

"I'm sorry." He stroked my wrist, looking down at me. "But I can't risk it getting damaged." He glanced around the room and I followed his gaze.

Upon closer inspection, I saw what I had missed initially. Dust. There was a film of dust over everything. Nothing in the room was used or possibly even touched. I met his gaze again, confusion clear in my expression, hoping the horror I felt was hidden from him. I'd been wrong. There wasn't just one room here that was a shrine. The entire home was one. A shrine to a family lost.

My heart ached for Creston as he tugged me towards the hall hastily, but I didn't say a word. How he chose to deal with his grief wasn't my business, even if it broke my heart.

"Come. My room is fine." He slid his fingers through mine as he led me through his home to his room. Books lined shelves along his walls, his bed covered in tousled dark blankets. Very little else occupied the space but his clothes, although I'd bet weapons hidden were somewhere close by. The room smelt of him, or maybe that was his proximity. Like oak and vanilla, like earth.

CHAPTER 49

Creston let go of my hand as he closed the door behind us, moving past me to sit on the bed. He yawned and ran his fingers through his hair, looking over at me as I stood taking stock of his bedroom. It was really what I had expected, except perhaps the books.

I looked over and met his gaze reluctantly, suddenly feeling awkward. "So..."

He cocked an eyebrow at me. "Seraphine, just come out with it," he said tiredly. "You're here, which is not where I really wanted you to be, but I'm somehow surprised you didn't find my home sooner."

His words stung a little, but I refused to let him see that. "I was worried about you. It's been two days."

"Worried my brother had murdered me in my sleep?" he scoffed. "I get it, he wasn't who he said he was, there is still a lot we don't know, but he's my brother, Phi. You of all people should understand that I've hoped for my brother's return home for longer than I've had a brother."

I sighed and moved over to sit on the corner of the bed, leaving him his space. "I understand, Cres, I promise I do, but this is more than that. He knows where my brother is," I said earnestly, hoping *he* would understand. "He's part of something bigger, it's not as simple as him just coming home. You know that." Looking at him though, I wasn't sure he did know that.

"Do I? Kylan has been gone most of my life. Both my parents died mourning him. I became a Guardien in the hopes of being able to search for him. But he's here. He's home."

But what kind of home is it? I wanted to snap the words at him. He was living in a tomb, not a home. Instead, I kept my mouth shut, knowing that would only lead to a fight. "I...I just, I'm wary okay? *You* were wary of him even more than I was right up until he announced he was your brother, Cres. Please, just take a drop of caution ahead with us?"

He shot me a look of contemplation, his brows furrowed for a moment before he nodded. I could tell he was conflicted by the concept but he knew I was right. It took him a moment longer to speak. "I will." His voice was rougher now, but I couldn't place the emotion so I didn't push any further.

I flopped back against his mattress and stared up at the ceiling, frustrated by the web we were now caught in, and not believing he would be anything close to cautious about the situation. Little lights caught my gaze and I frowned, my thoughts derailed at the sight.

The ceiling was made of woven vines much like the rest of the home was, but the ceiling above his bed seemed to sparkle with tiny lights. Like stars resting above his bed. I felt him shift and turned my head to find him watching me. "Stars?" I asked softly, nodding my head towards the ceiling.

He smiled at me, and it was a genuine smile, one that appeared so rarely, melting away the tension and lighting up his eyes. "Yes, Firefly." The way he said the word sent a shiver up my spine. "Stars. Or as close as I could muster using the gaps in the vines and sap to ensure I don't get rained on in my sleep." He moved, shifting some of the blankets so he could lay beside me. Close enough that I could feel the warmth radiating from his bare skin.

I turned my gaze back to the ceiling. "It's pretty. I like it."

He chuckled softly. "Even though I didn't do it for you, and it wasn't my idea, that makes me very glad I did it."

I turned to him at that. He was breaths from me. If I stretched out my fingers by a few inches I would brush against his side. I resisted the urge to trace my fingers over the tattooed vines that mapped up his left arm and over his chest, as well as the two runes on his right. One for Earth on his shoulder and the Guardien rune on his bicep.

Sensing my gaze he too seemed to refocus on me. He rolled on his side and reached out to touch the pendant where it had settled between my breasts. "What's this?"

I looked down to where his fingers stroked over the stone in the centre of the pendant, chewing on the inside of my lip before speaking, carefully gauging my words. "It was a gift. Given to me through your brother, before he showed me where to find you."

Creston shot me a questioning look, brows once again furrowed over his rich blue eyes. "A gift?" He spoke the words slowly, as if they tasted odd on his tongue. "From... Ky?"

I shook my head. "Uh...no. From Samil."

His eyebrows shot up, and a touch of horror bled into his gaze. "As in Samil? *The* Samil?" He sat up in surprise. "How?"

I realised in that moment how little of my nightmares I had actually shared with him, how they had changed. How they weren't so much nightmares anymore. *But he hadn't been around the past few days, had he?* I looked away from him, considering how much I should be willing to tell him.

"Seraphine?" There was both a question and a demand in the way he said my name. Not Phi, not Firefly, but Seraphine.

It sobered me. "The nightmares. They're more than that." I sat up and turned to face him.

His fingers glided across my chest, and he moved to mirror me, not letting me escape the conversation.

"I've met him, more than once." He frowned at me, opening his mouth to speak before I shook my head to stop him. "I don't quite know how, but he's the cause of them. Or more him searching for me is the cause."

"Samil? The beginning of the Elliphir has been creating your nightmares?" He clasped his hands in his lap, staring at me, and I could tell it took a lot within him not to shout. There was an edge to his voice, somewhere between anger and fear.

I nodded wearily. "Yes. So much has been happening in all other aspects, the first night I saw him I didn't know who he was. But I know now. My nightmares have always been born from him searching for me. For the type of magic I possess."

He stared at me, assessing. His eyes seemed to have darkened, almost black in the dim light of his room. "He is the reason you wake screaming and with everything you touch on fire?" There was a coolness to his tone that made me shiver ever so slightly. It was not a tone I had expected from him, one rife with rage so hot it was ice.

"I—" I hesitated, rubbing at my face in frustration. "No, I mean, technically yes, but it is the shadows that cause that, I had never made it through them until...." I struggled as the words seemed to catch in my throat. "Until the morning Niko was taken," I choked out, my voice rough around the words. "That was the first time I saw him."

Creston watched me with a cool expression. I knew why. He was replaying that morning in his head, the way he'd woken to me after sitting on the floor by the fire, my only concern then that I'd had enough control not to set him on fire the way my nightmares normally ended.

I hadn't told him then, but I hadn't known then what was happening.

"The dream was short that night," I continued, dropping my gaze to my hands. "I didn't know who he was, I just knew running from the shadows led me to him. I woke too quickly to learn anything about him. He seemed both relieved and annoyed in that first time, but in the others he was calmer."

"How many times has he entered your dreams?"

I didn't look up as he spoke, instead toying with the threading of my pants. "Three times. I think, although it is not always him. Sometimes it's me, I seem drawn towards him. Or at least that is what he said, or perhaps to the magic around him." I sighed, rubbing my arms, looking to Creston again.

Everything about his expression was guarded, there was none of the warm openness I was used to. He was calculating every word I spoke. "How?" He leaned towards me.

"He claims I am some kind of Dreamwalker, that I can walk to Faerie, because that's where he resides. I spoke with him in a form that was both here and there, and I could feel the magic around me. I don't understand it but I felt the truth in what he was telling me."

"What about the morning where you woke with the bruises? The blood? What of that time? Was he the reason for your pain and fear then?" He kept his voice level but I knew it wasn't without great restraint.

I opened my mouth, then paused, not having considered it before. "I—uh...I never asked. I didn't think to. I don't know if he was the cause, or whether it was just the shadows that chased me sinking deep."

Creston stared at me for a long moment, eyes narrowed to study me. "The morning of Niko's loss. What do you remember about chasing that shadow from his room?"

I recoiled, the question taking me by surprise. I shook my head, not wanting to have this conversation anymore. "I....I just remember I couldn't lose it. I knew it would lead me where I needed to be." Although had it? I had been led to free the others but Niko hadn't been with them. "Or something like that," I added thoughtfully after a moment.

He nodded. "Do you remember getting outside?" He asked the question gently, but I could sense the weight behind it.

I shook my head again as I thought back. I didn't remember getting outside, I just remembered being there. And then running after the slippery piece of darkness. "No, I don't remember it."

He watched me for a moment in silence, until my own frustration won out.

"Oh, for fuck's sake, tell me what you're getting at. What are you talking about?" I lifted my hands and dropped them back to my lap in a frustrated motion.

"You didn't get outside, Firefly, you *vanished*. Disappeared from inside that room and reappeared outside it, taking off across the grass. I could hardly believe I wasn't imagining things, but you were running and I had no time to stop and process it."

CHAPTER 50

I blinked at him, eyebrows raised in shock. "Vanished?" My mind whirled back to that morning. I couldn't remember climbing out of the window, that much was true. But vanishing and reappearing? That seemed too much. Much more than a gap in my memory caused by the horror that morning was, in both my heart and mind. "Are you sure?"

He nodded, reaching for me then, pulling me to sit closer to him, fingers stroking over my hand. "I didn't know what to do, and then so much else has happened. I didn't know how to bring it up. But you were gone, for barely a breath, then you were outside. You did it before standing on the bed, but I wasn't sure then, until you did it again and showed up outside."

I looked down as his fingers traced over mine, trying to suppress the shiver at the soft touch.

His skin was rougher than mine, worn from years of training harder than anything he gave me. He didn't push me as I absorbed what he was saying, the weight of Samil's words resting heavier on me.

I tore my gaze from our hands to meet his eyes. "What the hell is wrong with me?"

He smiled at me. "Absolutely nothing." He lifted a hand, tucking stray strands of curls over my ear. They wouldn't stay there long but the gesture made my heart stutter in my chest. He slid a finger under my jaw and stroked the edge of my lower lip with his thumb. "There are simply too many things we haven't been told. None of that is your fault, Firefly." His gaze slipped down to my lips as he ran his finger across my lip again slowly.

I had to resist the urge to bite his finger as it glided over my skin. "It feels like my fault," I muttered.

Creston shook his head as he looked down at me. "You're wrong," he said firmly. "But we'll get there, we'll find out what you need to know. Both to understand yourself, and your magic." He looked at me seriously then. "I am sorry I haven't been around the past few days."

"You don't owe me anything. I'm not your keeper, I have no reason to expect you to be constantly around." I half shrugged, knowing the words were almost a lie. I did expect him to be there, because I wanted him to be there.

"Even if that were true, which it isn't, you still deserve better than that. Especially from me." His thumb brushed over my cheek then circled back to my lip.

The gentle action reminded me that the last time we had been alone together, we had been interrupted, on the precipice of something more.

I shifted towards his touch and something coiled low in my body as his whole mood seemed to change with the action. His dark eyes met mine as his free hand slid slowly along my thigh, watching for my response. I moved towards him a little more and that was all the invitation he needed.

He curled his fingers under my thigh, lifting me and twisting so my leg slid across his, leaving me in his lap. His hand slid to my back as his other hand dropped from my face, and gripping at my neck, he pulled me forward. There was no gentleness in the way he kissed me. But I wanted none.

I wrapped my arms around him and ground forward in his lap, pressing my chest to his warm and bare one. I groaned softly against his mouth as he bit my lower lip, his tongue darting over the tender flesh as I parted my lips. I ran my fingers through his hair as his tongue slid against my own.

We kissed each other as if we knew nothing else, as if nothing else was more important than the next touch or sound we could draw from the other. I ground my hips down against him again, and a rumble of approval vibrated through his chest as he pulled back.

"Careful," he growled, only parting us for the warning as his grip on my throat tightened, once again crushing his lips against mine. His other hand slid to the centre of my back as he used the hold on my throat to push me, forcing my back to arch as his lips grazed over my jaw and down my neck.

He explored, kissing and biting his way down my throat until he found the spot that made me shiver in his grasp. He focused on that spot, working at the bundle of nerves that seem to ignite beneath the flesh of my throat.

I was barely aware of the soft moans that slipped from my lips, or my nails digging in against his scalp, torn between pulling him closer and pushing him away. His mouth slipped from my throat, down over my chest, hands moving to slide my shirt up and off swiftly, leaving me in the thin brassiere I wore beneath it.

He reached up to brush aside the pendant as his lips traveled down my chest, eliciting shivers from me, heat pooling low in my body.

The instant his fingers touched the pendant he froze, jerking back. "What the fuck?" he shouted as he shoved me backwards, leaving me suddenly sprawled on the floor.

"Ow," I muttered as I looked up at him, rubbing my hip from the impact.

He stared at me with wide eyes. "Shit. Phi, I'm sorry." He moved forward to help me up, but hesitated at the last moment, eyes trained on the pendant. "Uh...can you take that off?"

I looked down at the necklace.

The pendant seemed be alive, touches of gold mixing through the crimson stone. It looked like a storm building over a sunset.

I reached back for the clasp, only to find it no longer existed. I ran my fingers along the chain to be sure, but there was no clasp to be found anywhere on the length of metal. I pulled the pendant up, trying to work the chain over my head. I could get it past my mouth, but that was as far as it would go. I tried one last thing, drawing on my magic I held it in my hand, bringing the heat higher and higher. Nothing happened. I let it drop back against my skin. "I can't. It's fastened and the clasp is gone. It won't melt either."

He stared at me, his face twisted with mild disgust, as if the thought of it staying sickened him. "Great."

I pulled myself up from the floor. "What happened? It was fine when you touched it before."

He rubbed his hands together. "This time it shocked me, a jolt that went through my entire body. And it was like someone yelled at me."

I blinked at him, confused. "Yelled at you?"

He nodded, his expression clouded with fear and confusion. "Like a warning. Against touching you. But...I don't know. It was more than just the words, it was the overwhelming sensation that touching you was somehow dangerous." He looked away from the necklace to finally meet my eyes again. "I'm sorry, did I hurt you?"

I rubbed my ass. "I've had worse, especially during trainings. I'll be okay."

He reached out for me. "Come here."

I could see the fear in him even as he opened his arms for me. I touched my fingers gently to his, waiting for him to snatch his hand away.

He sighed softly as the touch seemed to reassure him that the sensation wasn't constant, relaxing as he pulled me back into his lap. "It's okay," he assured me as he leaned me against his chest. "Just keep that thing from touching me and I think we'll be okay."

I clutched the pendant in my hand. "I'm sorry. I didn't realise it would hurt you. Kylan didn't say anything about it, just that I had to wear it."

"Had to?" The confusion in his voice was clear, as well as an undercurrent of something I couldn't decipher.

"He threatened, mildly of course, that I'd leave his company wearing it, one way or another."

Creston grew quiet as he stroked my hair. I knew he was deep in thought, so I left him there, enjoying the calming warmth of his embrace, of the sense of safety and peace it seemed to spread through every inch of my being.

I let myself breathe in those moments, closing my eyes and just being. It had only been a few days since I last saw him, but somehow it felt longer, I'd grown so used to him being part of my every day, the days without him had felt emptier. The worrying over what was happening with him and Kylan had not helped ease the distance at all.

After a time he kissed the top of my head. My limbs were stiff as he shifted beneath me. "Come on, Firefly. I think we should go find my brother, see if he knows more that he conveniently forgot to mention, before I'm required for duty."

I reluctantly moved out of his embrace, picking up my shirt and slipping it back on, watching as Creston wandered over to his wardrobe and started to get dressed, pulling on a dark tunic and a pair of equally dark pants.

The uniform of the Guardiens. He strapped a leather sheath around his waist and I soon found where the weapons were. A wooden chest lay at the bottom of his wardrobe. He fitted himself with a short sword and strapped a set of knives to his chest. A smirk lifted the corner of his lips as he caught me watching. "Enjoying the show?" he asked as he closed and sat on the chest to pull on a pair of heavy leather boots.

I flushed and laughed, looking away. "Sorry, I've just never seen you gear up."

He chuckled. "But you have seen me dressed in uniform before, so it's nothing new."

I shrugged. He was right, I must have seen him dressed like this a million times before. Truthfully, I'd probably seen him in the uniform on his very first day.

But this was different, perhaps the result of more unquenched need between us. My fingers found the pendant where it sat on my chest, the stone felt warm, but nothing else. No pain and no messages stirred me.

Creston stood, grabbing a jacket from his closet and pulling it on. The jacket covered the knives on his chest but the short sword stayed in view. He came to me then, tilting my head back and kissing me softly. "You're cute when you blush. Did you know that?" He grinned down at me as he pulled back quickly, dodging the fist I swung at him. He chuckled again, though this time it was deeper, a sound that made me feel warm all over. "Missed," he taunted as he opened the door, waving for me to go through it.

I sent a little tiny ball of fire towards his head as I passed. "Smartass," I muttered over my shoulder as I headed for the front door.

He yelped as he dodged it. "Hey! No fireballs in the house," he chastised as he followed me, but it lacked the weight it should have, an air of fear taking the strength out of it.

"Don't tease me and I won't be required to defend myself with fireballs." I pulled open the front door and stepped outside, only to freeze.

It was dark. Too dark.

I looked up and my eyes widened as Creston ran into my back, clearly not paying enough attention as he came through the door.

"What the..." he trailed off as he saw what I did.

The sky was on fire.

CHAPTER 51

The entire sky was glowing red.

It was barely afternoon, the sun should have been high in the sky. Clouds shrouding the sun I could believe, but not the mottled red darkness that surrounded us. I'd never seen anything like it. Smoke seemed to roll towards us through the trees.

"Cres...." I stepped out of the shelter of his home and he was beside me in an instant.

"I know," he said, scanning our surroundings for any imminent threat. "Something's wrong. Let's go, the smoke looks like it's rising from the Divide." He grabbed my hand and we headed forward together, following the paths back towards The Square, Creston explaining as we moved that he wanted to see if everyone was gathered first, rather than running straight for the blaze.

The closer we got the more I could feel it. Not just the increase in the heat, but the magic. Like a thrumming in the air I knew the flames would be drawn from the hands of Fire-Blessed Elliphae. There was no doubt.

The Square was full of people, more arriving from every side as ash began to rain down over us. Guardiens and Elders were shouting various orders, trying to get everyone inside the larger buildings and out of the ashen air.

We stopped and Creston dropped my hand. "Wait here," he told me quickly, heading off in the direction of a group of Guardiens near the Elders Hall.

I stared after him, then looked around searching for faces in the crowd. I was surprised when I met my father's gaze, his hazel eyes hued by the red in the sky as he hurried towards me. I looked beyond him, seeing my mother and Zavier heading into the Elder's Hall, my older brother shielding our mother from the heat with his own body, an arm wrapped tightly around her shoulders.

My father stopped in front of me and quickly pulled me into his arms, crushing me to his chest as his whole body shuddered. Pulling back he took my face in his hands. "We were worried, Seraphine, we couldn't find you. No one knew where you were. Not even Trae." His tone was quiet but fraught with newly subsiding panic.

My heart threatened to crack in my chest as I looked in his eyes. "I'm sorry, Dad, I side tracked after I left to see him. I was feeling restless. I didn't know anything would happen to cause worry." I felt a pit of guilt open in my stomach. I had caused my parents more fear, the very last thing they needed.

He stroked my cheek. "It's okay, you're okay," he said, almost more to himself than to me. "Come inside with us where it is safer. Trae and Cleo are already there, I made sure of it myself." He stepped back and moved towards the hall, turning with a frown when I didn't immediately follow. "Seraphine?"

I shook my head, my stomach churning at the thought of following him.

Creston reappeared and saved me from having to explain. "It's okay, I have her. Inside is safest for all of us, except her." Creston glanced at me as he addressed my father. "We need her to do more than cower inside a building. Like all of Fire. You'll find none of them in that building." He put his hand on my lower back as he moved beside me.

My father's expression had hardened, and he stared at us for a long moment before nodding. "If she isn't returned to us safely, you will pay for it." He watched Creston with a sharpness to his stare that I was sure only a father could master.

Creston didn't waver under the weight of my father's stare, although a muscle in his jaw ticked at the threat. "If she isn't safe, it's because I'm already dead." I jerked to look up at him but he kept his attention on my father.

"Come back safely, Seraphine. Your mother and I won't lose another child in this," he whispered, voice breaking. Agony crossed his face before he turned from us, hurrying inside as the ash began to fall harder. I knew walking away from a fight, while his second youngest child was running towards it, was all but ruining him, but my father was a smart man. Earth-Blessed wouldn't be of any use to us in this battle. Anything they conjured could be turned against us, more fuel in the fire already raging out of control.

My heart lurched for my family, but Creston was right. I was no value cowering inside a building, not when it was flames that we faced.

Creston pushed at my back gently, guiding me away from the hall. Neither of us said a word as we rushed against the flow of Elliphae heading to safety. We were halfway to the Divide when the flames became visible though the smoke and ash above us.

I slowed and looked to him. "How many are holding this back?"

He reached back and grabbed my hand, urging me into a brisk pace. "All of them."

I could truly feel the flames then and without even seeing them I knew what our Elliphae were doing. I could feel it.

The fire was all magic, two competing sides of it.

We cleared the last of the trees and stepped into the open beneath the inferno.

The flames lashed at the sky, every inch of the lush green Divide covered with their fury, rising far beyond any flames nature would create.

I looked around, trying to get my bearings. Fire gifted lined the Divide at what they deemed was a safe distance, but I could feel and see what they were doing.

They couldn't control the flames of others, they could only layer on their own fire and hope to push the blaze the other way. Fighting fire with fire.

I shook my head. "They can't hold it. None of them can. They're just making it worse," I told him, eyes never leaving the flames.

"Those of Water tried first. The flames will not be quenched." He looked around us, as if searching for someone. Guardiens also lined the flames, offering what they could, pulling fallen Elliphae out of the way as the volume of magic exhausted them. "They think it was lit."

"No," I said quickly, looking up at him in the reddish hue. "The fire is being stoked by magic, from the other side. The Elliphir are doing this, with Elliphae they've stolen." I turned and watched as more of our own fell to exhaustion. I could feel their magic fade from the inferno each time. It made me shiver. I moved closer, not as close as the others but close enough to connect. I called on my fire but stopped myself as the flames from the Divide to started lick out towards me violently, like they were drawn towards the power I'd started to use. My eyebrows shot up.

"Phi…" There was caution in his tone as he stepped closer to me.

"No, Cres, don't." I glanced down the line of the Divide. As far as I could see, Fire-Blessed stood and fell trying to push back at something they couldn't stop. I focused forward, reaching my arms out and stretching the magic within me, until it touched the magic around me. I gasped at the weight of it.

There was so much, hundreds were feeding this wall. I did not know from which side the majority sat, but if it kept burning we wouldn't be safe enough to find out.

I took a slow breath. "Get rid of them, all of them, I don't care how. Pull them all away, pull everyone away." I sensed his hesitation. "Now, Creston! Do it before I lose the connection." The words were an empty threat. The weight of the magic settled like a stone in my stomach.

There was no way I could lose the link to so much magic. Not without serious intervention.

"Hyatt! Haul them back. Now!" Creston ran from my side, shouting to other members of the Guardiens, swearing and threats following as I started to pull. I didn't have the time to wonder when his friend had been found, the magic calling to me too loudly.

I didn't need to open my eyes to know the tide of flames had turned towards me.

Mine.

The word slipped through like a spell cast. I opened my eyes as the flames rushed not at me, but into me.

I threw my head back and cried out as I was engulfed, the flames stripping my body of all pieces of clothing, anything that wasn't me vanished in the flames. I opened myself up to all the power I'd always kept silenced, all the abilities I was taught I shouldn't have. The flames twisted around me, towering higher and higher.

There was a ringing in my ears, and it wasn't until the flames started to recede that I realised it was me. I was screaming. Not in pain but at the battery of so many others. Each person who had created a flame was part of the onslaught against me now. I could feel them all. They were what tore the screams from my body. For what felt like hours, days, I stood there, trying to reel in the flames, trying to get them under control. It felt like it would never end, that I would stand there, burning, until the end of my days, and I wanted to let it go, release it, but knowing my family, my friends, *Creston* would be at risk if I did stopped me from giving up. I couldn't allow anything to happen to them.

I didn't know how long it lasted, how long I stood, screaming and dragging the magic within me, but suddenly there was no more. I dropped then, landing on my knees into the ashes with a thud. I stared down at my hands.

They were blue with the last of the flames, the fire licking at my fingers, even then.

I stayed there like that, naked and flaming amongst the ashes. I was distantly aware of someone moving towards me, and I flinched as cloth touched my shoulders. I wasn't on fire anymore. That was good. Hands stroked at my hair. Words were spoken but I couldn't quite make them out at first, unable to hear through the actual ringing in my ears.

"...got you. You're safe. You did so well. I've got you. You're safe."

I blinked up at an ash marked face and two dark blue eyes. Then a relieved smile. *Creston.* "Hi," I croaked, my voice harsh and worn from the screams.

CHAPTER 52

Creston chuckled, quietly at first, before it deepened into a fit of laughter.

I frowned up at him as he tried to contain himself, not sure what was so funny.

He wiped tears from his eyes, smudging ash over his cheeks. He pulled his jacket tighter around me. "I'm sorry, but you just devoured a wall of flames, turning yourself into a vortex of fire none of us could see through, and your first word is *hi*." He laughed again, seemingly unable to help himself.

I frowned again, then let out a soft, shocked laugh of my own. He had a point.

He pulled me in then, kissing me roughly. "You amaze me," he muttered against my lips before pulling back and looking around. I looked around with him.

The flames were all gone, leaving behind smouldering ashes. I didn't know at what point the Divide's ashes had crumbled to the ground without the fire holding them in place, but the ground was thick with blackness, like ink knocked across a blank page. Beyond the ashes stood figures, watching in silence.

I started to stand but Creston quickly pressed on my shoulder.

"You're naked, Phi, and as much as I enjoy the view, I don't much enjoy sharing with half of our people. Just wait." He shifted onto his knees, shucking off the leather that held knives to his chest and tugging his dark tunic over his head, pulling it over mine as he slid his jacket out of the way.

The fabric was large and flowed over the soft, wider curves of my body, hiding the most intimate parts of me away, while leaving my legs largely exposed. I stood as Creston refitted the knives over his bare chest and pulled his jacket on over them. I stared ahead, trying to see how many faces stared back at us through the clearing smoke.

Dozens, at the least.

A figure stepped forward, illuminated in the still red hue of the day. His hair was an odd shade of red. I realised after a moment he was blond and the red was just from the smoke blocked sunlight.

He glared towards us before he spoke. "The First Blood calls us all. Take this as your warning. Walls no longer divide our shared blood. Tell your Elders that either their lies die, or their blood will write the true histories for us all." His voice echoed far beyond us, sending a chill down my spin.

I knew who they were speaking for.

Samil.

Whether this was his order or not, I knew he was influencing them. After all, he himself had told me he wanted our race reunited as one creation, as we were born to be.

I stepped forward. "Blood is not how our histories need to be rewritten!" I called back to him.

They laughed, looking at each other. Dozens were chuckling in the darkness, faces layered in the shadows of the thick, ashen, but otherwise untouched, forest.

"If you think it is not already dripping with blood then you haven't been paying enough attention, *Phoenix*. For, after all, it is the blood of your kind that soaks it the deepest."

I flinched, frowning. The fact that those who we had feared and sent to the shadows, for longer than I could comprehend, seemed to know more of true histories than I did, filled me with unease. I glanced at Creston over my shoulder.

"You always do seem to look to him, don't you?" The voice came from my other side.

Creston's head snapped around before I turned mine. I knew the voice.

Kylan stood not far from me, seemingly having wandered towards us in the midst of all else. The two males he had arrived with all those weeks ago lingered behind him.

I hadn't thought to see if they were also spies, but their presence now said everything. "You did this, didn't you?"

Kylan only grinned at my accusation, holding a hand over his heart. "Oh, Seraphine, how you wound me." He chuckled, glancing towards the male who had spoken, who had called me a Phoenix. "Ennias, come through. I think you've been dramatic enough for now. There are homes waiting for all of you, by the coastline. Keep to yourselves for now." He gestured behind him, where Veneficus now stood at the edge of the pathway. "V will take you where you need to go." Creston stepped towards his brother, Kylan held up a hand to him. "No, Brother. We agreed."

"That I would make homes, not that you would risk us all to fill them!" Creston snapped.

Kylan gave his brother a tired look. "Oh please, no one got hurt. Isn't that right, bitch?" He leaned to the side to address me.

"*Do not* call her that," Creston growled, tone darkening from shock and frustration to something else.

"Oh, it's fine, he just has a complex because you like me more." I smirked at Kylan as Creston threw me a look of surprise. "I've heard of daddy issues, but little brother issues is new."

"Watch your mouth, I'd hate to watch you vomit blood again," Kylan snarled before he turned from us and headed towards the worst of the ashen remains of the Divide.

A coldness settled in me as I watched him. Creston looked at me, then at the ground as he absorbed the same thing I did. My bruises had come from his brother's hand, the hand that had been left imprinted in my skin when Trae's magic failed to fully heal me.

"Don't," I whispered as I turned towards him. "Don't." I reached out to touch his hand where it gripped the top of his short sword, his knuckles white. "Just leave it." I let go of his hand and stepped in front of him as people wandered past us.

Elliphir crossed the lines that had divided us for centuries, and there was nothing I could do to stop them. Not that I wanted to. If they were here, perhaps my brother would follow. Perhaps everyone we'd lost would.

I tried not to react when I watched Elonis step across the line and head towards Veneficus.

A chill ran up my spine as the male smiled wolfishly at me.

Looking away from him, I searched for the male who'd caused all the destruction and panic. "What do you want Kylan?" I called in his direction as he headed towards the woods.

"That list is far too long for now," he called back. "But you will follow me, you can't help yourself. I'm counting on it." He never stopped, just kept walking until he disappeared into the darkness and ash of the woods beyond.

I paused for a moment, watching as he vanished from sight, hating that he was right.

Creston grabbed my arm as I went to take a step after his brother. "Firefly..." There was warning in his tone despite how softly he spoke the word.

I looked at him over my shoulder. "I have to."

He sighed softly and nodded, letting go of my arm and looking to the other Guardiens who still stood in idle shock. "Pass the message to the Elders. The Elliphir are here and call for true history."

I stepped forward as he spoke, following the path Kylan had taken across the Divide, feeling Creston quickly following behind me.

I found myself in one of the last places I expected to be.

The clearing where Creston had spent hours training me to defend myself, from the very thing that had led me here. An Elliphir.

So much had changed in the weeks since we had first come here. The whole centre of my reality seemed to have shifted, and I could barely remember what it felt like to be that version of myself. My brother was missing, Creston's had returned, the Divide had been torn down and I hadn't had a truly happy moment since.

Kylan stood in the centre by two trees that had never been there before, but that I recognised nonetheless. Because I had seen them in my dreams. I didn't have to guess what was about to happen as the air around us seemed to vibrate.

Shadows slipped to cover the space between the curved trees. Filling the space with a rippling pool of darkness. I knew what waited on the other side.

Faerie.

I tensed at the thought as Kylan turned towards us. "You, brother, weren't invited on this trip, but I doubt it will be an option to leave without you."

"What are you talking about?" Creston frowned, watching the swirling shadows warily.

"It's a doorway," I explained, not taking my eyes off his brother. "He's talking about taking us to Faerie."

Creston blinked at me like I'd slapped him. "Faerie?"

"Yes brother, Faerie," Kylan sighed, looking annoyed at the delay. "Our ancestral home. The place where we all belong. And the place we will all be returned to, as soon as there is enough magic to get us there. But for now, there is enough to take the two of you there."

"Oh, so your chaperoning ends here?" I crossed my arms.

"Unfortunately, there is only enough magic for two, and someone has to make sure my brother comes back safely. Your safety is optional." He grinned, showing his teeth. "Oh, how's the necklace?"

"You knew what it would do?" I asked.

He just shrugged as Creston stiffened beside me. "I had my suspicions about its purpose. It's protective, right?" When I flushed he laughed, "Ah, I see. Sorry, Brother." He shot Creston a look that was anything but sorry.

Creston groaned. "Shut the fuck up, Ky."

I raised my eyebrows at the words, surprised that Creston didn't appear to be as angry as he had been about the necklace earlier now that his brother was standing in front of him.

He just waved his hand. "Whatever, just hurry. Wouldn't want to keep Samil waiting too long. Or else he might step through himself."

Somehow, I knew that was a bad idea. I looked to Creston, turning towards him. "You don't have to come."

He shot me a withering look. "You're smarter than that, Seraphine, don't even try it. If you're going through, I'm coming too. I'm not waiting here with no idea what's happening to you. You can take out one of my knives and cut me off at the knees if you want me to stay here, and even then I don't like your chances. I'm coming."

Kylan clapped his hands once, making me jump. "Perfect, so let's go. I have things that need to be done. Like settling in the first party, and I can't do anything until after you get back here. Can't have you getting trapped over there, now can we?" The way he said it made me feel like he wouldn't mind that reality.

I ignored him as I stepped away from Creston, walking past Kylan to the doorway. The shadows writhed as I drew closer. I shuddered thinking of all the times I had run from them in my nightmares. Now I stepped towards them, sought them out even. Maybe because I knew what they were now, or maybe because I no longer cared if they touched me. I didn't wait for Creston or for more commentary from his brother. I knew what waited.

Faerie waited.

I stepped into the darkness, letting it engulf me.

It was the strangest of sensations, like falling when the ground seems to be further away than expected, the entire body tensed for an impact that hasn't come. It felt as though rain washed over my skin in the darkness, then all of a sudden it was bright.

I caught myself as the ground rushed towards me, pushing my hands into the deep discarded foliage of the forest floor. Air rushed to my lungs as I gasped for the breath I hadn't realised I was missing. My ears rang with a violent ferocity as my whole body seemed to vibrate.

Magic. There was so much magic.

Feeling like I was drowning in it, dropping to my side, I clamped my hands over my ears and cried out against the sensation. The pressure only increased.

Waves of power washed over me, assaulting my senses until I couldn't take anymore. I lurched forward and vomited before collapsing against the colourful mess of fallen leaves.

The last thing I saw before before blackness took me was Creston's form falling to the ground beside me.

CHAPTER 53

Consciousness came slowly, and with a pounding in my skull. I rolled to my side, eyes snapping open as I realised I was no longer laying on the damned forest floor. Instead, I was in a small cot, at the side of a dark room. Movement behind me made me sit up quickly, despite the way my head spun at the action.

"Careful, Nixling. You're still adjusting."

I focused then on the source of the movement.

Golden eyes stared down at me as he held out a cup.

I blinked at him for a moment, trying to reconcile the fact that I was actually in Faerie.

He was exactly how he had been in my dreams, dark curls framed his angular features and warm brown complexion. It took me a moment to absorb it.

Raising my hand slowly, hesitantly, I took the cup from him, sniffing at it. I couldn't smell poison, but that meant very little.

"It's just water," he assured me as he sat on the edge of the cot. "Your first travel here will be the hardest. The magic is an assault in the beginning as it tries to correct the weakness the mortal world inflicts on us."

I took a careful sip of the liquid in the cup. It was cool and plain, water as he'd promised. I looked at him for a moment, taking him in.

He was dressed in a tunic the colour of my eyes, a deep emerald green that slipped into the edge of a pair of dark pants. He wore an equally dark pair of boots that seemed to be laced with silver. His sleeves were rolled and I could see the various runes that marked his skin, many that I still didn't understand.

I cleared my throat before speaking. "Creston? Where is he?" Samil's face darkened a touch as he pointed beyond me, but I didn't care as I twisted to find Creston's form on the floor of the room. The world swam when I went to stand, forcing me to grip the edge of the cot and grit my teeth until it ceased. "You could've left him somewhere better than the floor."

"True. There is another cot, but I didn't much care for it. You were the priority." I felt the cot move with what I assumed was him shrugging but I didn't turn away from Creston.

He was quiet and still on the floor but his bared chest rose and fell.

I frowned. "Where are his weapons?" I took note of each empty sheath on his body before looking at Samil again.

"Away," he said simply. "Couldn't have him getting irrational when he woke." He smirked. "You look spectacular with my gift I must say, it matches the magnificent autumn red of your hair perfectly."

I reached up and touched the stone. "Why can't I take it off?" His smirk faltered for just a moment. Whether it was the challenge, or the fact I already knew I couldn't get it off, that made him hesitate I didn't know.

He plastered it back in place quickly. "It can hardly help protect you if you take it off, now can it?"

"Protect me from what exactly?" I asked, annoyed at his half truths. "Because all it's done so far is cause what I imagine will be a bruised ass." I crossed my arms and settled back on the cot slightly to watch him.

His smirk grew, his gaze flickering to Creston then back to me. "I see."

"No, you don't. I don't need any magic amulet protecting me from who I choose to have close to me." He was pissing me off now. My nails dug into my arms as I tried to pull back my annoyance, trying to stamp out the rising heat I could feel at the edge of my mind.

"You don't?" He stretched out lazily, acting as if he didn't have a care in the world.

"No. I don't," I snapped. "So either tell me how to get it off, or change the course of the magic. Because I would rather not have to fear hurting those around me with it, just because you think you should control who I am touched by."

He chuckled then. "I am so transparent to you then?"

The implications behind the amulet, the way he though he had a right to my body, made me feel wild with rage. "Yes. It is transparent. I care little for what you think you are owed by my existence, it is not my choice to be controlled. So I won't be. If I want to be touched, in any way, it will be by whoever I choose, not whoever you would prefer."

He studied me for a moment, like he was trying to figure out how my mind worked, then nodded slowly. "My apologies. I will have the enchantment... adjusted. For just true threats."

"I would thank you, but it shouldn't have happened from the beginning." I turned my gaze away from him, breathing deeply through my nose in an effort to calm down. The magic felt closer here in Faerie, like a fire was lit constantly in the back of my mind just waiting to be stoked.

A sound from the floor drew my attention, Creston clutched his head as he came to.

I moved slowly, waiting to make sure the world didn't spin before

I went to him, kneeling on the floor beside him and reaching down to touch his hand. "Hey," I said softly.

He moved his hands to look up at me. "What the fuck just happened?" he groaned.

"Magical overload. Takes the weaker ones longer to recover," Samil answered far too cheerfully from the cot.

I shot him a glare as Creston's head snapped to the side, his face paling at the sudden movement, pressing a hand to his mouth. He tried to push himself up then wavered as I assumed his world spun the same way mine had. I put my hand on his chest. "Ignore him and lay down. It's okay, it'll just take a minute until you stop wanting to vomit." I gave him what I hoped was a reassuring smile as he laid back down.

He closed his eyes and groaned again. "Where are we?" he murmured.

I opened my mouth to answer then frowned, looking up at Samil expectantly.

He cocked a dark eyebrow. "Oh, I'm not to be ignored now, huh? We are in an old cottage, in the Autumn Wood. I hadn't expected him to come with you so I was short on choices." He stood then, taking the cup I had left behind to a small table. "I figured leaving you collapsed in the open wasn't the best choice." He sat on the edge of the same table, crossing his arms over his chest. "Like I said, I wasn't expecting him. Ky, however, has travelled here more than once and wouldn't have collapsed, meaning you would have been brought to my actual home."

Creston grunted. "Sorry I ruined your plans, but I'm not really prone to sitting by and watching while people I care about disappear through strange magic doorways."

Flushing at his words, I glanced down at him.

His eyes were open now and he seemed less uneasy. He sat up, propping himself up with his arms bent behind himself, and he hesitated a moment before sitting all the way up, his jacket slipping open to bare his chest.

I moved over to give him space, sitting on the ground beside him, content to go back to ignoring Samil while reassuring myself that Creston was alright.

He turned to me first. "Are you okay?"

I nodded. "I'm fine."

He eyed me carefully for a moment, looking for any hint of a lie, before he turned to assess Samil properly. "So you're the infamous Samil, huh?" He cocked his head as he looked the other male over. "Not quite what I expected."

Something flared in Samil's gaze, but his voice came out smooth and level. "I could say the same," he said silkily. "She dreams of you, before she dreams with me, of course. Seems her dreams exaggerate."

I made a choking sound but neither of them turned from the other.

"At least my part in her dreams is by her choice," Creston hissed at the other male. "Rather than a manipulation."

Samil opened his mouth but I held up a hand, feeling my face starting to flush. "Alright, no thanks. I would like to exit this topic immediately."

Creston looked at me sideways, the hint of a smile there. "You're no fun at all. I want to hear about those dreams," he murmured softly.

I glared at him. Now was not the time. No way had I ever anticipated telling Creston the types of dreams I had about him, though I would need to address Samil on how exactly he had seen them. But later, much later.

"Why are we here?"

Samil watched me for a moment before he answered. "Because your appearances here are far too unpredictable for full discussions. Your home, that island you cower on, is no place for you. Any of you. And never before have I seen division of our race so rife with hatred than in that vile place."

"Did you choose to burn the Divide down?"

"I gave the order, yes. Do you know what is happening to those you call Elliphir beyond that separation? No, I'd wager you don't," he said when I didn't answer. "They starved for generations, then started stealing. It took me far too long to track down every last member of the Midithrias bloods, that island being the final drops left in the mortal realm."

"Isn't Midithrias what the shadows are?" I frowned at him.

He smiled and it felt somewhat sympathetic as he shook his head. "No, Nixling, it's what we all are. Our true name. We are the Blood of Midithrias, a now extinct faction of Faerie. Your histories calls them The Seventeen, to keep the reality of one race from being acknowledged by you."

"Oh," I said, a little defeated, the weight of the lies in our history bearing down on me more with each day. How much was even the truth?

Creston too seemed to deflate beside me. He was a Guardien. Fighting for lies had to cut even deeper for him. I reached out and took his hand, squeezing it gently. He squeezed back just as gently.

"You will all be able to learn true histories when you arrive here. Permanently, not on this little jaunt," Samil assured us when we made to protest. "But your Elders will have to be dealt with, in various ways."

I frowned up at him but Creston beat me to it. "What the fuck does that mean?" Clearly tired of having Samil stand over him, Creston launched to his feet, demanding answers. "Just because they iterate the histories wrong to this generation doesn't make them responsible for all of it," he growled as he stepped forward towards Samil.

I scrambled to my feet and moved to put a hand on his chest, knowing what had caused the reaction in him. His great grandfather was among the Elders and had been the only one left to help raise him through the years before his Settling. "Stop," I warned as I looked at Samil. "Explain, properly. Now."

"Have to keep that leash tight don't you?" Samil strolled away from us to sit on the cot as he chuckled. "What I mean is that they won't hold the power here that they do there. That is all." There was a tone underneath, that said that was not going to be all there was.

"And what of those who took part in what happened to your brother?"

The fury in Samil's gaze as he turned to me made me step back, taking me completely by surprise. Creston grabbed my elbow to steady me as I bumped into him. "They are an entirely *other* story."

The whole cabin dropped a few degrees as rage and agony radiated from Samil, and for the first time I could feel it. The pure power that pulsed in the air was a reminder that the male before us was far, far older than he seemed.

I nodded and that was all I could do.

"Do you know where Seraphine's brother is?" Creston's question surprised me, largely because I hadn't thought to ask it first.

Samil's mood seemed to shift like a leaf on the wind, his expression swiftly changing and hiding the former rawness that had been there. "I know that Nikolias is safe," he told us plainly. "And that is all."

"So you control the Elliphir, yet her brother is still lost to them?" Creston pressed.

Samil only glared at him, his jaw flexing.

"Can you get my brother back home?" I asked, directing his attention back to me.

Some of that rage seemed to fade as he shook his head. "I may be trying to unite our race, but their actions are not under my orders. They are doing what they have done for generations, and that has naught to do with me. While I am trying to unite and return our races to Faerie, they are not mine to command or rule from here. At least not yet. All I have done is started their healing, and all that I can hope is that they will return your brother when things are proven to be peaceful." He glanced at Creston then looked back to me. "This is all far too inflammatory. This is not why we are here."

My heart sank with the small piece of hope I hadn't known I held, falling away from me. I sighed softly. "Just get to the point, Samil, the magical overload has made me tired." My broken heart had much more to do with it, but that was irrelevant to him.

CHAPTER 54

Samil stared at me for a long time, almost as though he could sense the way my heart had cracked, before he walked over to the door, picking up a leather satchel that I hadn't noticed before. "You are here because I wanted to see you in person, meet the person I have waited centuries for. And so that I could give you what you will need. To teach and learn of faerie while I gather what is needed to open a door for long enough to pull all of your home." He brought the satchel back and held it out towards me.

Creston reached out and took it before I could, slinging it over his shoulder. "All of this for some books?" he snarked.

Samil smirked at him. "Well, hardly, those could have been passed to your brother while I convinced her to stay. But you got in the way of that plan." He looked to me again, golden eyes warm again as he did. "I will show you around Faerie soon enough, Nixling. That, I promise."

I made no comment on the weight that promise seemed to hold. "Will we be debilitated again when we return home?"

The twist at the corner of his lips told me that me brushing over the promise did not go unnoticed by him. "No, you will not, if anything you will just feel dulled, nothing more. And the next time you return here it will be easier."

"Spectacular," Creston muttered under his breath before he started to look around. "I'll take my weapons and an escort back to that doorway." He twisted to look at Samil. "I'd say thank you, but I wouldn't mean it."

Samil laughed then, shaking his head. "If not for you presenting yourself as a problem, I might enjoy your company."

"Well, maybe if you weren't invading her dreams and making poorly veiled threats, I might think the same. But I very much doubt it."

"Pity," he said, looking bored. "Your weapons are outside. I will take you both to the doorway, and I'd prefer if those weapons remain away until you're back on your... island." He opened the door, letting in a fresh stream of sunlight that made me squint, reminding me just how dull the light within these walls was. He swept a hand at the open space. "After you."

I hesitated for a moment, looking at Creston over my shoulder before shaking off the unease that had made me pause. I headed out the door, blinking against the brightness until the colours around me settled.

It was all reds, yellows and oranges. We were sunk into the depths of autumn. I could hear the two males behind me, and the sound of Creston rearming himself told me Samil hadn't lied about their whereabouts. I turned my head to the sky.

Despite the heavy fall of leaves upon the ground the canopy above was full, as if it had never seen the loss of a single leaf.

Unable to stop the question that bubbled in me, I directed it to Samil. "Is it always like this?" I couldn't take the fleeting amount of awe from my tone.

"Yes, at least here," he said, sounding almost at peace. "I have called this court my home for some time now. It is a beautiful place to be."

"I don't doubt it." I turned away to look around again. In the distance of the woods I could see a dark spot I only assumed was the doorway.

Creston moved to my side when he was done with the weapons. "Ready?" he asked me softly, seemingly respecting my awe.

"Yes. There's too much turmoil at home for us to hide here for too long." As much as I suddenly, and unexpectedly, yearned to stay, I knew we were both needed at home.

Samil brushed past me, walking ahead of us at a quick pace. "Follow then."

Creston waited until I was moving before he followed. "He's a ray of sunshine," he breathed, keeping his voice low as so not to be heard.

I smiled. He wasn't wrong, but Samil was old and had seen far more than we knew, so I was willing to forgive the lack of warmth in his interactions for that alone, but not for others. The knowledge that even he had no idea where my baby brother was ached like a fresh wound.

Creston caught my hand, as if sensing where my mind had gone. "We'll get him back. I swear."

I looked up at him. "Cres, the only person who seems to know where he is—"

"Is my brother," he finished for me, a resignation in his voice. "I will press him for it. Whatever game he's playing goes beyond this." He squeezed my hand gently. "And beyond anything I can leverage from him. I did ask, in those days, but he wouldn't speak of it. I will keep trying."

The promise was there, but I didn't know how much weight it truly held, so I didn't respond, not wanting to end up in a disagreement in front of Samil. Choosing not to answer, I let my mind drift, taking in the colours that were so much more vibrant here than in Keinteris, enjoying the way my mind fell silent for once. Creston fell silent as well, rubbing his thumb over my knuckles as we followed Samil.

It didn't take us long to reach the doorway. The shadows within it still rippled and curled, as if trying to escape the confines of the branches that surrounded it. We stopped a few feet from it.

Samil leaned against the edge of the curved arch that created the doorway, as if nothing about it bothered him. His comfort on the edge of it made me nervous. "Our time is up for us this adventure, Nixling." He smiled at me, and there was much more to that smile than I could hope to decipher. "But I will see you soon, be sure of that."

Creston made an unhappy noise from beside me at the sentiment. I ignored him for the moment, knowing neither of them required my input to incite each other.

I let go of Creston's hand and strode forward, not letting myself hesitate as I slipped into the shadows of the portal. The sensation was the same but as I landed on my knees on the other side, the agony of being overwhelmed was absent.

The kick that landed against my stomach, however, was a different kind of agony altogether. I landed on my side as my breath wheezed from my lungs in a cry of pain. The second kick hit just as painfully, and it took me a moment to look up.

Kylan smirked down at me. "Hi there, bitch, I was really hoping you'd come through first. Welcome home." He swung his leg to kick again, but I rolled out of reach, managing to remember some of the training Creston had given me, albeit a few moments too late to stop it all.

I pushed myself up on one knee, arm around my waist. "What are you doing?" I spat as he recovered from his missed kick. Looking around, I realised we were alone. Creston hadn't yet appeared through the still present doorway. *Where was he?*

"Let's call it therapy," he snarled as he came towards me again.

I centred myself and this time I lashed out at him, spinning to land a kick against his other leg as his boot made contact with my side. Pain flared through me but he fell as I'd hoped. I hissed a breath and stood. "What have I ever done to you to make you hate me so much?" The words sounded far more of a cry than I had hoped, but all they got me was a glare from stormy eyes as he picked himself up off the ground.

"You took what was mine. That is what you have done to make me hate you," he growled at me as he stepped forward again.

Flames lashed out from me across the ground, my magic reacting to the threat he posed.

He laughed dryly. "And there you are. Cheating."

"My magic is no more a cheat than you kicking me in the stomach while I'm adjusting between realities." I left the flames as they were, a warning and nothing more.

"I saw my chance and I took it." He shrugged.

"Because you are still a child." A deep voice drew my attention behind me. It was not Creston who stalked towards us in the clearing, but Veneficus. He passed me and smacked Kylan up the side of his head as he reached him. "Get ahold of yourself."

Kylan glared at the other male with a gaze full of hatred. "Or what, *Father?*" The word was full of scorn and I recoiled a little as I looked between the two of them.

"Father?" When both heads turned to me, I realised I hadn't just thought the word. I'd said it out loud too.

Kylan laughed then. "On second thought, this might be more fun than kicking you." Veneficus shot him a dangerous look that he ignored. "Ever wonder how exactly you got your precious, special magic, Seraphine? How you, born of earth, suddenly wielded flames more powerful than any you'd ever heard of?"

"Raphael Kylan Vaelle, shut your mouth now or I will seal it for you," Veneficus snapped, taking a threatening step towards Kylan, who just shook his head.

The menace radiating from the older male had no effect on him. "No. I've had enough. Why should I carry the burden and not she? Just because she's more than I am?" Kylan glanced towards the Doorway, as if it suddenly bothered him. Or maybe it was that Creston still had not arrived.

"What are you talking about? What do I have to do with either one of you? Except you hiding my brother from me and you threatening me." I looked at each one of them pointedly.

"Everything, absolutely everything. You see, we are one and the same."

"Last I checked I wasn't a sociopath with anger issues." I crossed my arms as he barked a harsh laugh.

He took a step forward, but two things happened at once before he had a chance to speak. The flames around me flared to try to keep him from coming closer to me, and Creston fell to his knees on this side of the doorway, finally returned as Kylan smirked at me. His next words turned every part of me cold. "Give it time. *Sister.*"

CHAPTER 55

The word rattled around in my head.

Sister.

I looked to Creston, hoping that he somehow knew what was going on.

Confusion marred his features as he took in the scene before him.

Veneficus swore, clearly accepting he had no ability to stop Kylan, as Creston pushed himself up to his feet.

Sister.

Kylan just watched me. "Oh, so now you're silent." He looked over towards his brother and apprehension seemed to flicker through his features for just a moment before he looked back to me.

I frowned at him. "I...I don't—"

Sister.

"Understand? Yes that's because you have been the protected one. The nurtured one. The *loved* one." His tone was soaked in emotion, a cocktail of anger and pain. "Because with you the blood took. Shadow and Earth commingled, causing your Rising, starting your magic, whereas Shadows consumed mine."

My frown deepened. *Born of Shadows and Earth only.* The Phoenix journal. It had said almost the same thing. I turned to Veneficus, eyes wide, looking for an explanation, for understanding.

Creston was striding towards us, but Kylan held up his hand. "This doesn't require your interference, especially when it looks like she's finally catching on."

Creston paused, confusion and frustration twisting his expression.

Always between a rock and a hard place, part of me sneered as I looked away from him and back to Veneficus, wishing that just once he'd unleash that feral rage inside him in a circumstance where it was helpful.

"I really did think you would be smarter," Kylan taunted, resting his hands on his hips as he smirked at me.

Sister.

The word haunted me. I didn't look away from Veneficus again, to see what more there was in Creston's reaction to his brother's commentary.

Veneficus' gaze held mine. His grey flecked emerald gaze. *My own gaze.* I'd never paid any attention to it before, it hadn't meant anything. Until now. I shared his eyes.

I wondered suddenly why he was bald. As part Faerie, our kind didn't lose their hair. Only by choice were they bald. "What colour is your hair?" I found myself asking, barely aware of the words as I spoke them. They sounded far away, like someone else had spoken them.

His expression twisted in a pained way. "Red." Though I had already known, the answer still struck me.

Like a physical blow, I stepped back. "So my mother lied. All this time, she swore I could only be my father's...be Varis Nantir's child." I felt sick, for once glad for an empty stomach.

He shook his head and stepped forward, hands out in an almost pleading movement. "No, Seraphine, she did not, she does not know. And he is your father, he raised you."

My deep frown returned. "What do you mean? How can she not know?"

Kylan laughed, a rough empty sound scrapping over my senses. "That's the real kicker. Tell her, *Dad*." The word practically dripped with scorn. "Tell her how you brought us into being."

Veneficus had the sense to look ashamed, dropping his gaze towards the ground. "Nightmares," he murmured.

"I'm sorry, did you just say nightmares?" Just like that, Creston's silence was broken. He seemed to have caught up with what was happening. Maybe not with all that he'd missed but the dots were obvious connections now. I knew why he had piqued at that specific term.

"Yes. Nightmares, or Dreams, but I call them Nightmares. I regret what was done." He looked over at Creston, then back to me. "But I cannot take them back."

"You raped our mothers? In their dreams?" Creston snarled, and I felt numb as I stared at the male who was apparently my blooded father, because of magically created dreams.

Veneficus recoiled, looking horrified at the accusation. "No! No I...I created dreams, over the course of months. Dreams where I became nothing more than a nighttime fantasy of the subconscious. I call them nightmares because of my regrets, not because they were filled with any brutality. I swear that."

"The result remains the same. Our mothers bore your children with no knowledge of it," I said finally, feeling ill. My parents had always had reason to question why I was so distinctly different, but instead of allowing it to destroy the family I had, they had fought every external force and trusted each other, loving me as though there was no reason to question anything about me or my magic. They had been right to trust each other, but it didn't fix this, it didn't erase the fact that Veneficus had fathered me in secret, in this manipulation of magic and wills that I was caught in.

Creston's expression was twisted with revulsion, but as his eyes met mine it morphed, protectiveness overruling the rest as he came to me. The flames around me disappeared as soon as he was within reach.

I looked up at him, beyond done with all of this. This was another revelation I had no space for in my mind, and it took a lot of effort to keep from becoming overwhelmed. "Home?" I pleaded softly.

He nodded immediately, and wrapping his arm around my waist, he started to lead me away.

Kylan made no moves to stop us, just watched as we turned away, although his smugness dulled as Creston and I turned our backs to him.

"Seraphine," Veneficus called, making us pause. I didn't turn. "It was asked of me. I am sorry, but telling them won't help. They are pained enough. Do not take yourself from your father."

I leaned my face into Creston's chest, taking comfort in his warmth as we started walking again, leaving Veneficus and Kylan standing in what had been our clearing, but was now irrevocably tainted with memories and truths I didn't want.

CHAPTER 56

I was surprised when we reached my home and Zavier waited outside my room. He frowned as he realised I was leaning heavily on Creston.

In truth it wasn't just the exhaustion of the day. My stomach hurt from the kicks I'd endured, but I couldn't tell that to the male who held me up.

"I wanted to make sure you came home safely. To tell Mother and Father." He looked between the two of us as we stopped before him. "Is it true?"

My head snapped up in surprise. "Is what true?" Could he already know? How? I opened my mouth to reject whatever he thought, when he smiled at me.

"Did you really turn yourself into a ball of flames?"

I blinked at him in shock. I'd almost forgotten. The Divide coming down was the last thing on my mind. Being forced to Faerie to meet Samil in person and then outed as the result of a nightmare had pushed the rest of the day's events far from my thoughts.

Creston recovered first and chuckled, even though it was hollow. "She did. It was pretty incredible, once you got over the agonising fear she was dead inside all that fire."

Zavier's grin spread as he looked down at me. "You're such a freak."

I moved away from Creston as my brother stepped forward and pulled me against his chest. "Thank you," he murmured in my ear. "I'm proud of you."

I rested my head against his shoulder, pleasantly surprised. Being held by my brother wasn't something that happened often. It made my chest tighten as he pulled back.

He squeezed my shoulders. "Trae and Cleo are waiting inside your room. They wouldn't leave." He stepped back. "I got some of the questions I had answered. Does Trae always give reading assignments?"

I laughed then, a real laugh that seemed to relax my whole body.

"You're just lucky you've never gotten caught carting thirty of them around," Creston muttered as he opened my door and looked in.

Zavier laughed. "Noted. Let me know if you need me, I'll be inside." With that he headed off to the main house to let our parents know I'd returned safely.

Once again, I knew I should follow him. A good daughter would go inside, would comfort her parents and assure them she was fine. But instead I slipped inside my room, letting Creston close the door behind me, choosing the easier option.

Trae and Cleo sat on the rug in the middle of my floor, a small stack of books with them. They looked up as we came in, falling silent.

I went straight to my bed, curling up on my side so I was looking at them but said nothing.

Creston watched me, then slipped the satchel off his shoulder and handed it to Trae. "Here, presents from Faerie." He let a shocked Trae take the satchel and moved over to sit beside me, resting his hand on my thigh.

Trae stared at the satchel in awe for a full minute before he seemed to find the words. "Faerie?" His voice was almost a squeak as he opened up the leather, pulling out the books inside with reverent care. "As in *the* Faerie?"

"No, the other one. Yes, of course." Creston snorted and shook his head, his thumb stroking over the bare flesh of my thigh where his shirt left it exposed.

I laid my hand across my stomach as subtly as I could as I watched Trae.

The books were beautiful, all darkly bound with aged leather. He read the titles but I was beyond paying attention to them.

Cleo laughed at his excitement, teasing him as he argued with her about something he'd said.

Their voices were a blur, just an indistinguishable sound that I tuned out like white noise. It was all beyond me, my mind in too many other places to be in the room with them.

The bed shook with Creston's laughter and I knew he was making fun of Trae too, without really processing what they were saying.

I wasn't my father's daughter. Not by any blood. It cured me of the questions of my magic's origin, but tore a new hole in my heart.

Sister.

The way Kylan had said it haunted me. It was why he hated me so much. He had lost everything in his life because of his magic, unfairly so, as we were learning, and here I was with a home and a family. *And his brother.*

The thought sat like a stone in my stomach.

We shared a brother. *A half brother*, I corrected myself. We shared no blood but we did share that, an awful link built out of hatred on one side and pained love on the other.

I didn't look at Creston, but his thumb never stopped on its path as he left me to my thoughts. He knew I wasn't here, and he let me be where I needed. I think he even stopped the others drawing me in. I loved him for that I realised, and I did look at him then.

He was talking to Cleo, smiling. His jaw was darker than usual with the stubble that had grown over the past few days, all the distractions getting in the way of his care for himself. His hair was pushed back as if he'd just run his fingers though it. Maybe he had, I didn't know. What I did know was that the curls would fall to the sides again, over his brow. They always did. The same way my curls always found a way to escape and wind up in my face. His dark blue gaze met mine for a moment, and he half smiled and squeezed my thigh, breaking the rhythm his thumb had been making.

But it was enough. Enough to make me give him a mirror smile, enough for me to want to hear what the others were saying.

"I just can't believe it," Trae murmured in awe, for what I assumed wasn't the first time. I looked over at him as he stroked his hands over the cover of one of the books. "These make all the books I have look like like trash. They're so well preserved."

"It's probably the magic." It was the first I'd spoken since we'd arrived and it drew everyone's attention.

Cleo gave me a small smile, and I knew she'd taken full note of my silence, and perhaps sensed the spiral of my thoughts, but Trae grinned in full. "You're probably right. Is it really in the air over there?" There was wonder in his tone. For creatures made with magic in our blood, it was almost funny how exciting we found the prospect of the true realm of Faerie.

"The whole world seems to vibrate with it. After you stop feeling like it's ripping apart every fibre of your being." I half shrugged.

Cleo made a face of disgust. "I will be the first to say it, that is not a part that I am looking forward to whatsoever."

"I'll agree with that. But if this is only a taste of their libraries, I want more." Trae grinned over the book he opened up.

Creston laughed. "Ah yes, the rest of us are worried about wars and pain, but Trae here is just worried about libraries."

I smiled at my friend. "Let him have his moment, Cres. After all, he gets to read all of that first and help us understand the rest of what we're in for, the least we can do is humour him for a few moments now." Creston just rolled his eyes, but his small, warm smile remained.

"And we will humour him again for the first few days after he finds a great Faerie library to lose himself in," Cleo added, smiling across at Trae as he started to leaf through the book in his hands.

He held it with reverence, gentle with each move he made.

I wanted to tell him that surely there was enough magic to keep the pages together but I held my tongue, looking back to Cleo. "What happened after the fire was done? With the Elders and the message about the Elliphir here?" I asked her.

She tore her gaze away from Trae. "There was some confusion. The Elders told us to return to our homes, that things would become clear later and that no one should approach the new houses on the coastline. That the Elliphir should not be incited or approached away from there either. With the Divide gone we're left fully exposed," she said. "Overall, they did as the Elders do, hide. The only reason we all heard the warning is because it was announced in front of us by V."

My already fragile mood darkened again. "Veneficus brought the message?"

She nodded. "Yes, why?"

I glanced at Creston then looked back at her. "He's Elliphir."

Her eyes widened and she shook her head. "No, no, he can't be, I've seen him manipulate air."

"I swear to you, Cleo, he is Elliphir," I said tiredly. "I'm absolutely sure of it. I don't know how he manipulated air to teach you, but I've seen the reality." I left out the rest of what he was, unsure I could have spoken the words even if I had wanted to.

"Perhaps these are topics we should leave for now?" Creston asked gently, squeezing my thigh again, offering me support how he could without giving too much in front of the others.

"I have topic suggestions," Trae offered, finally looking up from the book in his hands. "Who wants to hear about the types of beings waiting for us in Faerie?" He practically vibrated with excitement and we couldn't help but agree.

So, that is what we did.

Creston provided us all with fruit and Cleo got us water to drink as we got comfortable for Trae to read to us, teaching us about those we would live amongst when we arrived in Faerie. He would make an excited noise whenever he came across one he had heard of before, hypothesising about what they'd look and sound like, what their magic would be like.

Creston and Cleo asked more questions than I did, at least for now. But we ate, we drank and we listened, until hours had passed and we were all too tired to hear any more. Even Trae was exhausted as he put down the book.

I didn't know whose idea it was for them to stay, but it didn't bother me as my eyelids grew heavy with weariness.

Trae made a bed for himself and Cleo, and they curled up beneath spare blankets as Creston dimmed the lanterns in the room. I could have done it if asked, but he hadn't.

I yawned as he crawled into the bed beside me, kissing my shoulder gently as he curved his body around mine. "Sleep, Firefly," he murmured against my skin, and truly I couldn't think of a better idea.

CHAPTER 57

The dream was the last thing I wanted as I opened my eyes, once again beneath the canopy of the Autumn Woods. I groaned.

Though I was laying on the ground and hadn't had to fight through the shadows, being here frustrated me. I shifted and knew I was wearing the dress again without looking. I could feel the way it spilled around me. "You couldn't have given me one night? Just one night of rest?" I turned my head and found Samil exactly where I expected he would be, sitting on the ground beside me.

He just shrugged. "I was bored and felt it when you slipped into another dream. So I redirected you here."

I turned my head away from him and closed my eyes. "The fact that you know what I dream of outside this creeps me out. I hope you know that." I just wanted to sleep, I wanted the blackness. The peace away from my existence, yet again, I was denied it.

"I hadn't told you about that for a reason. Blame your friend for that."

I barked out a laugh at that, looking at him again. "You really expect me to blame Creston because you watch my dreams? Does that actually work for you normally? Blaming others?"

He looked down at me with those golden eyes. "Well, I am one of the few able to lie here. So often it does work for me." He grinned, a dimple appearing on his left side. I just shook my head again and he sighed. "Honestly, I think I was sharing your dreams long before I realised it was you creating them in me."

I scrunched up my nose in disgust. "Yeah, no, I have enough to deal with. I don't need to know." I stared back at the slowly shifting canopy above. "Did you know who my father was?" I asked after a beat of silence.

He cleared his throat and shifted awkwardly beside me. "I more than knew. I tasked him with the role."

I went very still as I processed what he had said, rage tearing the exhaustion from my body as it clicked. I sat up and I turned towards him. "Excuse you?" I asked, pinning him with a glare of disbelief.

He had the decency to at least look ashamed. "I can explain it. The division of our kind, it has caused the decay of the Phoenix bloodlines. More are needed, more will be born now that I am bringing us all together, but I cannot wait for a new generation to grow to guess that one may be enough. Not when your birth was already conscripted."

I stared at him, disbelief halting all mental processes. I couldn't even find the words to express what I felt. So I didn't. I reached for the fragments in my mind, the piece of me that could feel the warmth of my reality. I grasped at it, ripping myself from the dream.

I sat upright with a gasp, a sheen of sweat on my flushed skin.

Creston was alert in the same instant, body tensed as he sat up and looked around, a blade in his fist, teeth bared.

"It's okay," I whispered as I forced myself to lay back down.

He stared around the room for a moment longer to reassure himself before he laid back down beside me, resting his head on his hand. "What happened?" he asked, his voice barely a whisper.

I laid my hand on his chest, trying to tether myself back to this reality. His heart was pounding from being woken out of a dead sleep, but it helped. I counted the beats as they slowed, gathering my thoughts. "He pulled me in, offered some more difficult pieces of information. I decided I wasn't in the mood to listen." I closed my eyes and tugged the blanket up my shoulders more, leaving my hand where it was.

Creston tucked the blade under the pillow he laid on. "I'm sorry, Firefly." He kissed the top of my head, tucking me back into his chest.

I huffed out a sigh. "No one seems to leave me alone anymore," I murmured.

His chest vibrated with a silent laugh. "Seraphine, I don't think you've ever been left alone about who you are, but you're about to reach the Settling, and things always change then. Your powers will grow. To me, it seems expected that extraordinary things are connected to you," he said softly, almost reverently. "You were always so extraordinary to me, even as a child." There was a warmth in his tone that settled over me, relaxing me.

I smiled against his chest. "Was that while I was being beat up by other kids or after?"

He choked on a laugh. "Even then, I could see it in you. I knew you could have handled them yourself, but you didn't know how to fight without magic and didn't want to hurt them."

"You certainly had no issues hurting them," I teased as I poked a finger into his side.

His laugh was audible this time, and he shifted so my head slipped back onto the pillow. I could see his grin as he leaned over me in the dim light. "No, no I didn't, and they got what they deserved for hurting you." His hand slid across my thigh, tugging me closer as he looked down at me.

I pulled him closer, sliding my hand to the back of his neck and kissing him deeply. He sank down into me as we kissed. It was slow and relaxed, as if we were in no rush, as if my whole body didn't burn from his touch.

His hand climbed my thigh slowly, but it wasn't until his hand squeezed my hip that I groaned. His fingers dug into, the freshly bruised flesh, from the worst of Kylan's kicks.

Creston pulled back at the reaction, noticing the sound I let out was not one I usually made for him, eyes narrowed as he pushed away the blanket and exposed my bare hip. I turned to look as well.

Even in the dim firelight I could see the mottling of my flesh, a dark shape over my hip.

He moved his fingers over my bruised skin carefully as he looked up at me. "Care to explain when this happened?" he asked quietly, raising an eyebrow. "Seeing as we were already on the topic of me hurting people who cause you pain."

I pulled at the blanket and he moved his hand to let it slip over my body, though he still watched me expectantly, waiting. I shook my head. "You took your time coming back from Faerie. Your brother has some unresolved anger issues."

His expression dropped and I immediately regretted the comment.

I clamped a hand over his mouth as he started to say something. "Do not apologise to me. Not for that. He'd have done it anyway. He hates me. It has little to do with you." I stared at him, keeping my hand over his mouth until he nodded once. Then I pulled it away.

"I stopped when you went through," he explained. "Samil asked me who I was to you. I didn't know that he was delaying me, I thought he was just taking advantage of me being without you." He stayed half propped above me as he spoke, and glancing towards the now covered bruises he sighed, meeting my gaze again. "Where else?" The words were even quieter. He didn't ask how. Maybe he could guess, or maybe it didn't matter.

"My stomach," I whispered to him.

He nodded, twisting over me. He never moved the blankets but kissed where he guessed the bruises were.

The gentle sensations sent a flutter through something low in me.

He kissed my hip too, and then laid beside me, pulling me back into his arms. I knew the kisses were his version of a sorry, and though I had only asked him not to say the words, I was grateful for the gesture.

We stayed like that, him stroking my hair as I listened to his heartbeat, until my eyes grew heavy again and I was slowly lulled back into a blissfully dreamless sleep.

When I woke I was alone. Well, alone in the bed. I turned on my side and found Cleo still asleep in the cot across from me. I stretched and yawned.

Neither Trae nor Creston were anywhere to be seen, but the stack of books still sat in the corner, telling me that at the very least Trae was still somewhere close by. I doubted we'd be able to part him from those pages very often for the near future.

I slipped out of bed, my bladder driving me to find the bathroom quickly before trying to find the boys. I stared at the shower, suddenly filled with longing for the simplest of things. I stripped off Creston's shirt, noting the little stripes of ash that marked my skin, as did the still fresh angry bruises.

Trying to ignore the new marks, I heated the water, stepping beneath the never ending flow. I took my time, washing the ash from my body as well as the tension from my muscles. My curls came last, and the biggest task I had to wrangle was getting the unforgiving knots from my hair, but I eventually managed, watching the ashes from my hair disappear down the drain. I slipped back to my room wrapped in a towel, feeling more myself than I had in days.

It was odd how the simplest action, even if it was just a shower, could affect so much about how you feel.

Cleo was awake when I returned, smiling at me sleepily. "I thought I'd been abandoned until I heard you in there. Where are the other two?" She sat up, raising her arms above her head and stretching, groaning loudly.

I shrugged in answer, rifling through my closet and fishing out the pieces I needed, pulling on my brazier and underwear before a pair of dark pants. I tugged on a long sleeved tunic as I looked over at her. "Should we go find them?" I asked, wandering back to my bed, sitting on its edge and running a brush through my hair while it was still wet. It was the only way to make sure I didn't look like a dandelion when it dried.

"I think they can manage to get back when they're ready. Plus, I've hardly seen you lately." She sat up and pulled her knees to her chest. "How are you, Phi? How are you really?" she asked firmly, knowing I was about to brush her aside.

I looked at her for a long moment, weighing the words in my mind before I spoke them. "I'm tired," I told her honestly. "I'm just so very tired. And it all feels like I should never have pushed, should never have asked the questions I did. Things would be calmer if I hadn't."

She shook her head. "You can't know that, Phi. From what I can see, everything that is happening, is happening for a reason. It's built up for hundreds of years before we were even thought of, let alone born. We have just had the misfortune of living through great change, and while it is a burden, I know in my heart it's necessary. For more.

For us to move beyond what we've been taught to follow blindly, into something better. Into Faerie." The ghost of a smile played on her lips at the word. "I can hardly believe we get to be apart of it."

I watched her, absorbing what she was saying. Spending so much time with Trae was rubbing off on her. She'd always been smart, had seen things in a different way to me, but she'd become almost philosophical. "Maybe you're right," I muttered. But then again, it was only parts of her reality that were being pulled apart, and all her new realities were full of brighter futures. Mine exposed lies, pain and more manipulation than I could stomach. I tried to smile at her, searching for any other topic to talk about.

She brightened, reading my need to change the subject. "Was it really full of magic?"

I nodded, setting down my brush. "It really is. You'll love it there, Cleo." I paused, considering the chance we were being given, what it actually meant to go to Faerie. "Actually, I think we all might." I just couldn't shake the feeling there was a cost we were not yet aware of.

Or perhaps I was just growing to fear that nothing in my reality was without cost.

CHAPTER 58

We both jumped as the door swung open without warning.

Trae entered, followed by Creston, and to my surprise Zavier. Each carried food and my treacherous stomach growled at the sight.

I notoriously forgot to eat lately, not out of any desire to change my body, but simply because the need got lost somewhere in my mind, until something reminded me and I realised I was starved.

Given the way Creston looked at me as he handed me an overflowing plate, I knew forgetting would not be an option this morning, and part of me was thankful for it. He sat beside me while Trae and Zavier sat on stools that slithered from the floor as they were summoned.

I bit into a fresh piece of buttered bread and had to stifle a groan. Creston grinned and winked at me. "Nice of you two to finally wake," he teased, and I realised he'd gotten changed. Had he gone home while I'd slept?

Instead of asking, I stuck my tongue out at him before taking another bite of the bread.

Cleo laughed softly. "We do need some beauty rest occasionally. Although, I was a little afraid I'd wake up to Phi in a mini blaze." She shot me a warm, somewhat apologetic smile as I looked to her.

I rolled my eyes. "The nightmares are getting easier to come out of,"

I assured her around another bite of the bread.

"Probably because things here are a nightmare." Zavier never looked up from his plate as he spoke and my heart sunk. He was right in some ways, but he didn't know that the dreams were no longer nightmares in the way they had been.

"It will all settle, in the end, maybe even for the better," Creston said, trying to sound reassuring. "Too many of us know the pain of losing someone to the Elliphir. If they are no longer separated from us, we can no longer lose people to them. Even if Elliphir magic still blooms in children, they wouldn't have to go anywhere to learn it." All eyes turned to him and he shifted uncomfortably under the scrutiny. "I spent time talking to my brother, after his show of force that dawn," he said quietly, looking down at his hands. "I wanted to understand how he had magic. The Elders have used fear to push away what we're now learning is just another side of our own magic." He glanced at me. "Even Samil made sense when he wasn't being a dick. He wants us as one, the way we were before fear got between us all."

My friends nodded at the mention of Samil's name, making me assume an explanation of his presence had been part of what I hadn't been paying attention to when they spoke last night. Part of me was relieved I didn't have to explain it.

"But if that's the case, if all they want is peace and to be returned here, then where is our brother? He's a child, he never did anything to them and he certainly isn't of their magic. Why is he still missing?" The words out of Zavier's mouth were conversational, but the tone wasn't. He was furious Niko was still gone.

"Samil can't free him. Kylan hates me, and I think that is why none of the children have been brought back." My brother's eyes shot to me at my answer, lips thin at the mention of Kylan, but I just shook my head.

"Or," Trae piped in, "Because the children are the only card they hold right now. Really, think about it," he said when it looked like Zavier was about to interrupt him. "There are a comparatively small number of them here, in their own little settlement of houses. But that is tenuous, people are filled with fear. Fear that comes with this kind of shock. No one has truly been exposed to the newer realities more than we have, it's going to take time for things to change. But if they brought the children back first, who's to say they wouldn't be slaughtered after all children were safe? They're playing it smart. They're keeping leverage. Maybe Niko is additional leverage, sure, but all the other missing children are leverage against the Elders. They can't now justify risking them, not without the Elliphae turning against them."

I continued to eat, finishing the piece of bread. The others grew quiet for a moment, weighing Trae's words. He was right, though he usually was. This all wasn't as simple as stolen children.

"They're starving," Creston said quietly, almost hesitantly, after a few minutes of silence.

"What do you mean?" Cleo asked, frowning at him.

Creston looked around at us guiltily. "Ky told me. Their magic... it drains. It's dark. They used to hunt, but meat made them as sick as it makes us, so they started to starve. They couldn't grow food without earth magic, anything they tried to farm would die before a harvest was possible. So at some point, when they came to take Elliphir, someone took Elliphae, too. To help them survive. Throughout the past, it was only ever one or two a year. But their people have grown and it was no longer enough."

"So they started taking more," Trae supplied thoughtfully, picking at his food as he mulled it over in his head.

"It makes sense. It doesn't make it okay, not for those children, but it makes sense." I popped some grapes into my mouth to keep my real response from being aired, and once again we all hung in silence, eating and thinking.

Creston knew of this, had learned all of this in the past few days while he hid away with his brother, and hadn't bothered to say anything until now. It made me uneasy. *What else had been shared in that house that he hadn't shared?*

"This feels like a conversation for a room full of Elders, not us," Zavier sighed and set down his plate.

"I think the problem with that, is in reality the Elders have grown too arrogant in their place to have these conversations." Trae got up and stretched. "They stopped learning and started hiding, both from history and from themselves, then they passed it to us. Slowly at first I'd guess, then it would have become easier and easier with each new generation."

"What of the rest who knew? Where are they in this? Some Elliphae here are older than the Elders," Cleo added.

"True," he said thoughtfully. "But maybe that, in itself, is the answer. Why would they reject being Elders if they didn't have something against it? There's always unrest whenever the Elders present themselves, when they parade in front of us all. There are those who refuse to be anywhere near them." Trae moved across the room and sat with Cleo.

"And yet they allowed us all to be taught false histories?" I asked.

"Isn't that what you four have been doing?" Zavier said pointedly, raising his brows. "Well? You've had Trae tearing through our histories for truths, and yet you've kept it largely to yourselves," he pushed.

"Because we weren't sure what we were actually doing, nor what to do with what we knew. I couldn't exactly scream it from The Square, not without risking my well-being." My eyebrows drew in tightly, frustrated by his interpretation.

"Exactly. We can't sit here and point blame at those who are protecting themselves by keeping their mouths shut." Zavier shrugged.

I took some more food from my plate, chewing it slowly as I thought about everything. Part of me wanted to go back to sleep, to keep avoiding the oncoming storm I knew was coming, but even there I didn't quite feel safe. I didn't have total control over what happened. I kept eating as the others kept talking, getting lost in my own thoughts rather than theirs.

It wasn't until Cleo, Trae and Zavier all stood that I turned my attention back to them, realising I had zoned out again and missed an entire conversation.

"If I find anything new I'll come straight to find you," Trae said and packed up the books into the satchel and all the excess furniture disappeared.

I looked at Creston for an explanation.

As he leaned back on my bed beside me, he smiled. "They're going home for a while. And we're going for a walk." He looked me over slowly as the others headed out. "I think I prefer you in my shirts," he murmured before standing up, offering me his hand. "But you and I have some things to sort out."

CHAPTER 59

The 'things' we needed to sort out left me standing at the edge of the poison flower bed that led to the door of Creston's family home. I waited there as he slipped inside, realising that when he had come earlier he had left behind his blades.

I'd opted to wait outside rather than following him in, not much feeling like walking through the shrine today. I looked over the garden instead.

There was so much beauty in deadly things, especially in the ones nature created. Why their home was surrounded by poison, I wasn't sure. Maybe it was just an extension of grief made magic. I made a mental note to ask my mother about it another time.

I leaned down, running my fingers over the petals of one of the Hellebore flowers. Being of the magic I was, I knew I would never be able to feel the life in these things the way that Trae or Creston would, but I could feel the hum, the presence of magic underneath everything else. I stood up as the door to the house opened.

Creston was once again armed, leather sheaths over his chest and short sword at his side. He came straight towards me. "Ready?"

"What's with the flowers?" I asked on impulse.

Creston glanced at the garden as if just noticing it. "My mother grew them, a long time ago. She was a healer, and she worked with the poisons towards the end. Making different medicines, she said." His expression grew dark, suddenly far from that garden. "I suspect there was more to it than that. But I keep them anyway."

I regretted asking as I watched the way it affected him. I stepped up and took his hand. "So where are we going?" I prompted, trying to draw him back to me.

His expression didn't lighten as he looked at me. "To see our brother."

I dropped his hand immediately and made a face. "Please do not call him that."

"That is what he is, Firefly, we both share blood with him. Separate blood, but he is brother to us both." He tried to keep his tone light, like it was a joke, but I could see the tension in his face.

"No, Cres, he's not," I snapped. "He's your brother, but to me? To me, he's just another person who wasn't like me." I looked away from him. "The dream I woke from last night, with Samil? He told me he is the reason I was born. That he instructed Veneficus." I shuddered. "Do not call him my brother." I shot him a hard look. "Especially not if you want to touch me, ever again. Understood?"

He watched me for a long moment then nodded.

"Great. Now lead the way." I waved my hand for him to step past me.

He rolled his eyes but did so anyway. "You know, if not touching you again wasn't such a weighty threat you might not have won that," he quipped on his way past, trying to lessen the tension.

I scoffed and started to follow him, not wanting to say anything else when things between us already felt strange.

The new houses made for the Elliphir were placed by the coast. They were small but they'd been pulled up suddenly. As we approached them, I could tell something was wrong.

Homes made by magic didn't wilt, but these ones had. The vines were dark and dry, and the smell of rotting foliage reached my nose, making me gag.

Was this what they meant by the sheer presence of them drawing the life from everything around them? I knew their magic was a reverse, ours gave for the most part, but to actually see for myself how theirs took... I could understand how they could become desperate.

They had barely been in these homes for a day and they were clearly dying already. It wasn't sustainable at all.

"I don't think I actually believed him," Creston muttered under his breath. I kept my comments to myself, not wanting to upset the tentative peace.

We headed down closer, but before we got too close to the houses, Kylan appeared, walking towards us out from the centre of the little settlement.

He held himself with a smug self assurance, smirking at me as he approached. He seemed too focused on his own arrogance to pay any attention to the way Creston's mood had changed entirely.

Maybe it was all the time we had spent together, but I could certainly feel the way his anger radiated out from his rigid stance.

Kylan stopped in front of us, and whatever smart comment he was about to make became irrelevant as Creston launched himself forward, punching his brother in the face. Hard.

Kylan groaned as he found himself on the ground, staring up at his brother in shock, his lip cracked and blood pooling against it. "What the fuck?" he exclaimed as he got back to his feet.

"If you were anyone else I'd have done more. Take it as a warning. I don't care how bad your life has been, *she*," Creston pointed towards me as he growled at his brother, "Was not the cause. And if you hurt her again like you did, then next time I'll carve a reminder in your fucking chest. Got it?"

I stood very still as Kylan's gaze flashed towards me, storm eyes full of rage before he looked back to his brother, licking the blood from his lip. "Got it," he replied roughly, stepping back out of his brother's reach.

"Good." Creston shook himself, rolling out his shoulders and calming himself. "I'll fix all the houses and give you more food."

His offer to help his brother shouldn't have come as a surprise to be, but I had to tense every muscle in my body to avoid rocking back on my heels. How did Creston go from making Kylan bleed to defend me straight to helping him, just like that?

Kylan nodded. "Thank you. The others will appreciate it. Is that all you came here for?" He crossed his arms over his chest as he watched us. His ego was bruised, as well as his face probably, but I knew there would be more to deal with later.

Creston shrugged. "And to see if the Elders have spoken with you yet."

Kylan laughed and shook his head. "No, no one has come near us except you. We are still waiting, as are many others." He looked pointedly at me. "Little brothers included."

I bit my tongue. He was dropping bait that I would not bite.

He cocked an eyebrow at me when I remained silent. "Huh. You're telling me she can actually keep her mouth shut? That's a surprise."

Creston rolled his eyes, also refusing to be baited. "I'm going to fix the homes. Hopefully it will help when the Elders do come to start reversing their mistakes." He looked at me over his shoulder. "Wait for me?"

I nodded once, still keeping my mouth shut.

Creston turned back to Kylan and waved him forward. "Come on.

Let's go."

Kylan put a hand over his chest in mock offence and let out a soft gasp. "You mean you don't trust me to stay here with her?"

"Oh, shut up and go be useful for once," I snapped, the silence proving to be too much.

Kylan winked at me as Creston shoved him in the direction of the houses. "Go."

He just chuckled and headed down the hill. Creston shook his head and followed him down without another word.

I watched them go with a sigh. I didn't really want to be close to Kylan, but the other Elliphir made me curious. I knew if things progressed I would have more than enough chances to meet more Elliphir. Other than the ones I had almost killed.

CHAPTER 60

I found myself wandering away from the hill, back towards a tree that grew at the edge of the forest before the coast. I sat down against the trunk and turned my face towards the sun as it filtered through the wall of clouds that surrounded our home. That kept us safe here. *Safe from what?* For the first time I wondered.

Samil had claimed to have struggled to find us, was that part of why? So much magic surrounded us, but it was nothing compared to what waited for us in Faerie. And yet he couldn't find us, and the way he said it had made it seem like centuries of searching.

It made little sense for the Elders to hide us from our own, unless there was more they had to gain from us being kept away.

I sighed and gently hit my head against the trunk of the tree. Very little made sense anymore.

My own existence was manipulated by at least two other people, all to make sure there was a Phoenix. For what? Other than absorbing the inferno that had threatened us, I had done almost nothing of value with the magic I had.

I needed to delve deeper into the journal, gather answers from another Phoenix. If we were so important surely she had to have known too, and with any luck maybe she had shared something more in those pages.

I was too deeply lost within my thoughts to realise I was no longer alone.

Creston cleared his throat and made me jump, my eyes snapping open. He grinned at me as I flushed with embarrassment. "All done." He held a hand out to me. I took it and pulled myself up.

"So were you planning to punch him in the face the whole time or was that an accident?" I asked, brushing the dirt off my pants, looking at him from the corner of my eye.

He tapped under my chin gently. "It doesn't matter. He got the message." He jerked his head to the side. "Let's go."

"To punch more people?"

He shot me a withering look as I laughed softly. "No, Firefly, just trust me, okay?" He ran his fingers through his dark curls and grinned at me in that earnest way that made my heart stutter.

"I do trust you, but I still want to know what you're planning." I shoved at his chest playfully.

The shove only succeeded in making him laugh as he wrapped his arm around my waist. "Come on, save the violence for when we're back to actual training." He squeezed me gently as he led us away from the coast.

I glanced behind me idly, meeting the stare of grey blue eyes. I knew Kylan watched us leave as I turned away again.

Trusting him ended with him leading me through a strangely thick section of shrubbery on the east side of the island, not too far from my home. I wondered why he didn't use his magic, instead holding the branches out of my face as we moved through the trees, but the question died on my lips when I stepped around him on the other side.

Beyond the trees was a small cleared stretch of land, several feet in either direction, but it wasn't the grassy ground that had my attention, it was the ocean view that the spot revealed. This part of the island was a little higher than most parts, just high enough to keep out of the spray of water from the waves that crashed into the rocks below. I stepped to the edge, looking down at the frothing sea.

"What is this?"

"It's a spot I made as a teen, only Hyatt knows about it." He moved up behind me, looping his arm around my waist as if scared I would fall. "As far as I'm aware at least. It was his idea."

I looked up at him. "His idea?"

He smiled, but there was something in his eyes, something swirling in that blue that I didn't quite understand. "We needed somewhere to be delinquents I guess, especially after we became Guardiens and were on everyone's radar."

"Where is he now?"

"Safe at home, as far as I know. One of the Rangers found him a few hours before the fire started. He was with two others, they got lost, said that the forest around them changed." He pulled me in closer to the warmth of his body against the cooler ocean air, even though he knew the cold didn't bother me. "He was lucky."

"You said he'd be fine, and he was." I leaned into his hold, letting the warmth of his touch seep into me. It seemed to drag everything away. Stress, pain and worry didn't touch me for just these moments, though I knew it would return.

"Thank you," I told him as I looked out over the water again. "For bringing me here, and for the distraction"

"I have no idea what you're talking about, you showed me your secret hiding place, the least I can do it show you mine."

"I'm pretty sure you stalked me out to my hiding place." I laughed softly.

"Stalk seems excessive, I simply take your safety very seriously." He turned me so my chest was pressed to his, tilting my chin and leaning down to kiss me softly. "But you're welcome."

My heart thudded in my chest as I kissed him back, that tingle of awareness tearing through my body, making me all too conscious of everywhere he touched me, with his hand pressing into my lower back while he drew the kiss out at a languid pace, like he had all the time in the world to explore the sensation. Gentle kisses and touches seemed to so easily have become our normal, but this was something else, something that sent a bolt of need through me, and I pressed myself closer, wanting more, ignoring the ache of my bruises.

He pulled back, hand resting on my jaw, thumb brushing at my lower lip, his eyes dark. "Not here."

I was a little breathless, and disappointed, but I managed to nod slowly.

"When I fuck you, Seraphine, it won't be in the dirt." He dropped his forehead against mine. "When I can touch you, all of you, without you jerking away from the pain someone else inflicted on your body."

"They're just bruises." I took a slow breath, trying to centre myself.

He went quiet for a moment that seemed to stretch, before sighing and pulling away. "We should go, no one will know to look for us here." He stepped away, boxing away all that warmth and closeness, gesturing back the way we'd come.

He wasn't wrong, the sun was growing low in the sky and I could hardly believe another day was over. Without a word I started to push my way through the trees that kept this place hidden.

Another day without Niko, a voice whispered in the back of my mind. I shut it off. I couldn't think like that or I'd never make it to the day we got him home.

Creston wrapped his arm around my waist again when we were clear of the trees, leaving our new hiding spot to walk towards my home. We didn't talk much on the way, but we didn't need to.

Both of us were weighed down by everything that had happened. The silence was nice in contrast. It was calming.

Creston kissed me goodbye once he had me safely outside my home, and promising to be back in the morning, he slipped away into the growing night.

I went inside, going in search of my family. I found them in the main living area.

My father kissed my forehead as he passed me on the way out of the kitchen, a glass of something pungent in his hand. "Are you okay?" he asked, looking me over quickly, like he now needed constant reassurance his remaining children were whole.

"I'm okay," I lied, knowing that if I told him half of how I was feeling and what was going on he'd never let me out of his sight again.

"Come here," my mother called from the living room, where she and Zavier lounged in chairs. "Join us."

I did, taking a seat by my mother and letting her play with my hair as my brother and father toyed with their magic, making new clothes and touching up some of the pieces in the house. I let the hours slip away, taking some solace out of the time with my family, offering what I could to them by being present, rather than another shadow their hearts carried.

When I finally crawled into bed my entire body ached, but my belly was full, my heart hurt a little less and sleep took me, with a dream quickly following.

It was dark.

And it wasn't the Autumn Woods.

I was inside, I could feel the stone under my feet. Looking around, there was little light, but a crack shone through across from me. I took a step forward and drew back a heavy curtain. I stood on the edge of a balcony, looking out over grey skies and mist covered mountains. I frowned.

Where was I? I'd never seen these mountains before. I turned as the sound of fabric moving drew my attention to the room behind me. A bedroom, all furnishings rich dark colours. The movement continued, and my eyes were drawn to the bed in the centre of the room. A mane of dark hair was all I could see at first. I took a step closer and the form shot upright.

Grey eyes so pale they were almost white met mine as the dark curls fell around piercing, angular features, so perfect they could have been carved by an artist into stone. "Who are you?" he grumbled, voice deep with sleep as he pushed his hair back. It shimmered with a purple hue as the light from the window washed over it.

I noticed then the familiar sensation of magic that wasn't quite reachable. Faerie. I stumbled back quickly with a groan. "This isn't a dream, is it?"

His eyebrows shot up, suddenly more alert. He moved from the bed, and as he did I noticed his veins seemed to stick out, black beneath an oddly coloured skin. Purple? I couldn't tell in the light. He prowled towards me and I scrambled back onto the balcony, searching for the warmth, the link within me that would pull me out.

"Who are you?" he asked again as he stalked towards me.

"Sorry!" I called as the world shuddered and I sank back into dark-

ness.

I woke with a start, sweaty and confused. I had never Dreamwalked to anywhere but the Autumn Wood before. I had no idea where I had been, or who the male with the purplish skin had been. I shuddered as I laid down again, afraid to fall back asleep for a long while, only returning to it when exhaustion gave me no other choice.

CHAPTER 61

For five days nothing happened.

The Elders made no move, the Elliphir remained waiting and the Elliphae grew restless.

I spent most of my time with the others at Trae's where he was studying every last book with the utmost care.

Zavier came with me most days, Creston as well when he wasn't called to duties.

I'd had no new dreams with Samil, nor did I revisit the stranger in the dark room. Actually, I wasn't dreaming at all. Perhaps because each day I would train, if not with Creston then with Zavier or Trae. Neither of the two were as well trained as a Guardien but they were taller and stronger than me, and given that was likely the demographic I would face, it was more than enough.

On the sixth day, I was stretched out on the floor of Trae's living room, the Phoenix journal laying open in front of me. So far I hadn't learned much more about the importance of our births, but there had been a listing of magical instructions, ways in which I could use my magic as a physical force. I hadn't yet tried them but they had piqued my curiosity. I looked up from the pages to find that Cleo was asleep in an armchair by the window and Trae was buried in a pile of books so high I could barely see him from this angle without craning my neck.

Somewhere within that pile was his version of the journal. It was just the three of us today. I sighed and sat up.

Trae looked up at me over the pages he held. "You okay?" he asked as he set the book down carefully.

I nodded. "Yeah, just feeling a little restless. Find anything worth sharing in there?"

He smiled. "Uh, well, this book is on how the Faerie Courts and monarchies function."

"Sounds fascinating." I chuckled as I stood and stretched my tight muscles.

"I mean to me, yes." His eyes were alight now and I knew I'd flicked the switch in him. He needed no more invitation than my attention to keep going. "It both works on bloodlines and on marriages. But here's the clincher, they're matriarch reliant."

I cocked an eyebrow at him. "Should I know what that means?"

More than happy to elaborate, he continued, "Kings don't hold their thrones. I mean, they can be given crowns and called king, but they're reliant on a queen."

"Like bees?"

He shot me a horrified look. "Technically, yes, but it's so much more than that. Any worthy female can reign alone but a male only has thirteen days to remain king without a new queen ascending. So there are princes who truly never become kings. I find it a fascinating contrast to humanity." He grinned at me. "I know, boring, but there's a lot to learn. It's literally an entirely other world."

I grinned at him. "I get it, Trae, I really do. What else have you found?"

He brightened even more. "They have twelve courts. There used to be a thirteenth, but it was absorbed after a war it started. This book doesn't explain the war, and I haven't gotten to all twelve courts yet but I'm getting there."

"I am so very glad we have you, Trae, we're all going to need you when we arrive. Even before that. We have so much we have never been taught." I sighed in frustration. We were blind babes in the woods. Everything that had been kept from us was a weakness we didn't know how to defend.

He grunted in acknowledgement, sipping from a chalice and yawning. "We also have so much more to learn."

Snorting, I agreed. "They did make us believe that Faerie was a place we would never be. So why would they teach us about it?" I rubbed my eyes, considering whether I should copy Cleo and have a nap. Our understanding of Faerie had always been about us being left behind by it, never about what lies within it.

"Because why would they teach us about a place where they lose all power?" He half shrugged and picked the book up again.

He did have a point. The more things pushed towards Faerie, the more it felt the Elders were just holding on to whatever power they had gained by bringing us all here.

I ran both my hands through my hair as I thought about it. Both my uncle and great grandfather sat as Elders, but I didn't know either of them well enough to speak to their character or integrity. They were more phantoms in my life than they were family members. Cleo too had a great uncle on the Elders list.

The front door opened with a crack, jolting Cleo awake and pulling Trae to his feet.

Creston burst around the corner, his breathing heaving and eyes wide. He was in full Guardien gear. "We have a problem," he huffed, looking us over. "Move."

We didn't need much more than that. We had been waiting days for things to change. We were out the door behind him in under a minute, in a dead run towards The Square.

There was a crowd slowly gathering, and as we broke to the front of it, we stopped dead.

Three pikes had been erected in the middle of the large space, woven with vines made by earth magic. And from each one hung the body of an Elliphir. Two I recognised from the Reaper, the males Kylan had arrived with were both dead.

"The Elders made a choice," Trae whispered in horror as we all stared in shock.

"They made the wrong one," I said with surety. They had just condemned us all to a war, I could feel it. Though the words had never been spoken, war was what we had been waiting to avoid. I turned to Creston. "Where are the others?"

"I'm hoping at the settlement," he replied, scanning the crowd, looking for threats. He stood close behind me, so close I could practically feel him pressed against me, one hand between my shoulder blades, ready for anything. "Let's get out of here before the word spreads. Things are going to get ugly, fast. This is a declaration. They're not making peace, and they're not revoking their false histories."

I looked to Trae and Cleo.

He took her hand. "We'll watch, and come to you if things get worse." He glanced at the bodies. "If that's even possible."

Creston nodded. "There are Guardiens stationed around, but they're the Elders' appointments, not the regular crew. They're the ones who strung them up. This won't be all they do." He looked around swiftly, examining the growing crowd. His gaze lingered on the uniformed members of the Elders' Guardiens.

This was far from the first time an execution of an Elliphir had been displayed in this square, but I hadn't seen one since I was younger than

Niko. They were a barbaric reminder of the hate we had been taught to harbour. But this was worse, this was a rejection of a lifeline.

Creston looked down at me. "Are you coming?"

Trae grabbed my hand before I could move, and I caught both his and Cleo's almost panicked stares. "Be careful, Seraphine," he pleaded softly.

"I will." I looked between the two of them, squeezing his hand quickly. "Keep each other safe until we get back."

They nodded, and Cleo stepped into Trae's side, her own hands trembling. "Don't do anything reckless, Phi, please."

I flashed her a grin that was anything but comforting. "I'll do my best." I looked to Creston and nodded. "Let's go." We headed off together, rushing out of the crowd towards the coastline. "Where is Kylan?" I asked as we sped up our pace.

"He was safe. At home." Creston's tone was guarded and I almost stumbled at the admission.

I slowed to a stop, no longer feeling rushed as a weight formed in my stomach.

Creston noticed quickly and stopped as well. "We are in a hurry, Seraphine." He was anxious, shifting from foot to foot, but unwilling to leave me behind. After punching him in the face and threatening him, he still let Kylan return to the home?

"For how long?" I asked, staring at him. Creston hadn't mentioned the fact, but had returned to his home every night over the past few days. I hadn't questioned the fact, not seeing it as odd until now.

His lips pressed together in a flat line as he seemed to weigh up his reply. "He never left. When the houses were built, they were never for him. They are not his home."

"Neither is the house in which you live, Creston. That is no one's home. It is a shrine, a tomb." The words were out before I could stop them. I regretted them when he recoiled.

"Not all of us have been blessed with a whole family, Seraphine. I get a glimpse at a piece of mine, and you take it as a personal offence." His hands clenched into fists.

I could see the anger rising in him, but I was beyond keeping my mouth shut now. "He's a sociopath!" I yelled. "He has my brother somewhere, doing who knows what, and yet you're sitting in your home with him each night doing what? Playing 'what could be'? It's ridiculous!" My chest heaved, but the words, the thoughts, were finally out in the open.

"Stop," he snarled, stepping towards me. "You don't get a say here. He's *my* brother. He's *my* family, the only chance I have to have one."

I shook my head at him, stepping forward and poking at his chest. "No. He's the only *blood* choice you have. Family goes far beyond that. I've never known you to be naive, Creston, but with him? You're a straight up idiot."

He knocked my hand away from his chest. "Leave it alone, Seraphine. It is my choice."

"Will it still be your choice when he kills us all?" I bit back.

His expression darkened into something I barely recognised and he turned away from me, clenching and unclenching his fists. "We don't have time for this. We have to check on the Elliphir." He was closing himself off, shutting down as he looked at me over his shoulder after a long moment, his expression carefully neutral. "Are you coming?"

I took a heavy breath as I watched him. There was so much more I wanted to say, but now wasn't the time. He was right about that. But my stomach churned, knowing each night he left me alone, he'd been going home because his brother was there. I pushed past him, swallowing what I could of my excess anger. It would be dealt with later. We began running once more, racing to reach the settlement.

As if summoned by our mere proximity, Kylan stepped out of the trees as we finally approached the coast, both barely breathless with the adrenaline that had pushed us forward, though I could feel the way my heart pounded. Anger and exertion drove it wild, like a caged animal in my chest.

"Of course you brought *her*," Kylan sneered, tone dripping with disgust.

"She can help." Creston nodded towards the smoke that was starting to rise from behind his brother.

I couldn't be sure if he'd felt the fire destroying his magic already, knowing before the smoke became visible, but as I reached out I could feel it too.

Kylan's head snapped around, and he took a moment to watch the smoke as shouts rang out. He turned to glare at me quickly before returning his attention to his brother.

"I knew they'd send others here," Creston explained softly, carefully. As though he could be blamed for the flames instead.

Kylan's eyes narrowed as his gaze flicked back to me briefly. "I told you, brother. Love or blood, you don't get to keep both." He glanced at me again, and tilted his head. "Unless you're offering it from your veins."

I flinched and stepped back, glancing at Creston, only to find he wouldn't look at me. Anger welled within me, forcing me to bite back the snarl that rose in me alongside it. "I have a counter offer. I'll keep both and you can have nothing."

Kylan laughed, dark and icy. "Strong words, Fire bitch. But I think you're forgetting, you don't know where your blood is."

I felt the flames flare in my hands before I was aware I'd reached for my magic. "Yeah, why don't you tell me more about that?" Screams rang out from the houses below. "While your people are left to burn."

He grimaced, the smug expression slipping. "Fine. Help them," he snapped, then paused. "Or don't. Your Elders have already ensured that your brother is staying exactly where he is. So it's really your call. What will it be? I'm sure my honourable brother will love you more for hearing their screams as they die."

I watched him for a moment, then started forward. I wouldn't let people die for no reason. I chose to ignore his words, those dangerous words, knowing the thing that stretched between Creston and I was growing taut, thin, easily breakable.

He stepped into my path, holding up a hand but not touching me. He'd learnt the hard way not to touch me while I was an open flame. I could see in his expression he had too much to say for this moment, and maybe some part of me truly didn't want to hear what he had to say.

"Don't," I warned before he could speak, anger still pulsing through me. "He's right. You need to choose. You're either on my side, by my side, or in my fucking way." The ground beneath me began to burn as I reached out to feel the flames consuming the houses, trying to find where they started.

Creston flinched, looking at me with a rawness I couldn't decipher. He nodded once.

More rage rose within me. His silence was deafening.

He got out of my way.

I stalked past him, heading down the hill towards the houses. The flames may have been started by magic but they weren't controlled by it. I couldn't sense anyone feeding the magic now, but these fires hadn't been started without an Elliphae.

I moved to the first two houses, pushing the flames into themselves, fighting against the magic in them until I my power won, and they vanished, leaving a kind of thrumming energy pulsing over my skin, like the excess magic was looking for somewhere to land. A smile tugged at my lips, the rush of power felt so *right* inside me, and I needed more.

Two Elliphir rushed through the door as I stood there, a girl around my age with dark hair and a guy with vivid eyes holding her hand. They nodded once before they ran, shadows rippling around them as they tried to hide within them.

I moved from house to house, repeating the process, that burn and thrum of power inside me increasing with every one, waiting to be repurposed, to be unleashed.

As the flames vanished in the last home, I was surprised to see a familiar face step out.

The blond Elliphir who had called the demands after burning through the Divide.

"You," I said in surprise before I could help myself.

"Seems you've taken two infernos from me this week. Such a giver you are," he crooned. "In return, I'll give you my name. Ennias Zade, but you may call me Zade." He bent in a mock bow and grinned up at me, straightening. My lip curled at the way he used a Fae custom in such a setting, offering me his name like I could trust him. "I believe you also know my companion." He gestured behind him.

Elonis stepped into sight, a slight smirk twisting at his lips as he spotted me. "I truly hope your brother shares the proclivity for help-fulness," he drawled as Zade started to step out of the door, but I was faster.

Flames erupted in his path. "My brother?" I cocked an eyebrow as they both stepped back, their grins fading.

"Did Ky not mention it?" Zade tutted as he moved back from the heat a little more. "Always one to steal glory from others. See, I was the one who took Niko from you, who lured him from his bed."

"And I closed the cage that held him. Barely a breath from the cage you managed to open." Elonis taunted from behind the other male. "Ironic, isn't it? That you were so close, but didn't look hard enough. If you and that Guardien had done even the slightest sweep, he would have been returned."

CHAPTER 62

I flinched, clenching my jaw. "You're lying." Red crept into the edges of my vision and my heart pounded.

Zade chuckled softly. "You know the best part of it all?" He leaned dangerously close to the flames as he spoke. "He thought it was you. That's what he saw. His big sister asking for his help. He didn't even question it, just rushed away from home behind you. Sad really, he never even saw through the glamour before I put him into the cage. He cried and asked you why you were doing this to him."

Fresh pain ripped through me, the flames growing as it bled into them. "No."

The grin turned vicious as he shared a look with Elonis, who was clearly just as amused by the story and my reaction to it. He leaned closer to the flames again, seeming to forget them for the moment. "He still doesn't understand why you abandoned him. But don't worry, the other children are comforting him. Telling him just what he needs to hear."

"Why?" I hissed. "Why torment him like that? Why add to his fear?"

His eyes glinted dangerously in the light of the flames. "Because I could," he said simply. "Elliphae have tormented us for generations. I have returned the favour for almost as many. And because it's fun to watch them break, to watch the hate for their own blossom in their hearts and minds."

Something snapped within me, all the rage and tension rushing from my body, all at once. Fire erupted, all around me. I gave in to the rage Creston had stopped in me once before. He was not there to stop me now as I let go, the flames feeding on my sudden thirst for vengeance.

They rushed around both males, and dully I heard the moment the fire reached them, as they began to scream in unison.

My ears rang too loudly to process the sound. I watched as they each vanished in the heat, their lives flickering against my senses as they died.

I saw no flames. All I could see was my brother's wide, tearful eyes. I had to fix it, I had to. This would help. If the people who had hurt him no longer existed, maybe it would take away whatever pain he was in, or help him when I got him home.

Maybe that was it. I was helping take away the source of his nightmares before he came home. I was making him safe.

Flames crept up along my legs like vibrant orange and blue fingers of a suddenly tamed beast, scorching away the hem of my dress until it hung in tatters over my thighs.

I glanced around to the buildings that surrounded me, my gaze tainted by the ravenous fire that consumed it all, the roar of it filling my consciousness. I closed my eyes and listened, to the way the walls groaned and creaked in protest as the flames erupted to further destroy the homes I had tried to save just moments ago. I felt the sea of red and blue that moved through them with a lifelike hunger, tearing it all away.

Until it was as if they had never existed at all.

I opened my eyes again to watch the flames, no longer under my control as they spread, but still on the edge, an edge I could take them back from again if I wished. I could stop it all, with a movement and a thought, but I didn't.

Extending my hands out as the fire climbed higher, a soft laugh escaped my lips as they automatically reached for my flesh, not burning by caressing the body that gave them life. I walked through them without fear of them. I was their centre, they started and ended within me. Hurting me would only result in their own destruction.

I watched the settlement burn. I knew I had been alone here now, with the exception of Zade and Elonis, knowing now that I'd have felt if any magic of mine had killed any others.

A peace settled in me with that knowledge, blocking out the piece of me that screamed in horror at what I had just done. But that voice was part of a different person.

A person I had locked down deep for this.

I was a Phoenix. Rising from my own ashes was my very nature. And so I would. My whole body vibrated with the realisation, my face flushing for a moment as I shuddered under the weight of the sensation.

I tucked my magic away, back into the depths of myself, heading back up the hill. Creston and Kylan were gone, probably to escort away the other Elliphir. I wondered idly at what point they had left.

Had they seen them die? Heard their screams? Or had they left expecting them to follow behind?

I wasn't sure I cared.

They had caused my brother pain that went beyond the physical, who knows how many others they had each damaged, let alone what else they had done to them. They were safer with them gone, even if only slightly.

I turned and headed back towards The Square, walking at first as my magic calmed and so did my mind.

I fell into a run once I was sure I was calm enough. I let the houses keep burning.

They were far enough from everything else that I didn't fear the fire spreading before it died out. If the Elders came to see their handiwork, perhaps they would only assume they had succeeded with their initial fires. They would have no reason to believe otherwise.

People still lingered in The Square when I arrived.

I paid them little attention and kept my gaze away from the dead that hung in the air, spotting Trae and Cleo on the far side. Zavier had joined them at some point.

I wondered idly if I should tell him that I had killed our brother's kidnappers, but by the time I reached them I had convinced myself it wasn't necessary. It was my burden to bear, not his.

Cleo spotted me first, her gaze gliding over me. "Phi!" She stepped away from Trae, drawing both his and my brother's attention to me. All three of them looked at me in shock.

I frowned at them. "What?" Cleo grabbed my arm and started to drag me from The Square. My confusion deepened, and I pulled my arm from hers and looked between the three of them. "What the fuck is wrong?" *Did they know? Had someone seen me that I didn't know about? Did they know so soon, that I was a murderer?* My mind spun, until my brother spoke.

"Your face," Zavier said softly from my side. I looked at him quickly then back to Cleo.

"What's wrong with my face?" I demanded, fear edging my voice.

Cleo dug into the bag she had slung over her shoulder, and I noticed idly that Trae had a satchel on his back too. Whatever they could grab before we ran here with Creston.

I blinked at her as she held something out to me, looking down at the circular piece of metal she held, realising what it was. A mirror. I flipped it to its reflective side, holding it up. The same rune I had stared at my whole life stared back at me.

A Phoenix rune was set in my flesh. Burned into the skin of my left cheek below my eye, in a red as vivid as my blood. I reached up with my free hand to run my fingers over the symbol.

It was barely larger than my eye and sat just below the gentle jut of my cheekbone. While tender, the skin was fully healed, as though the mark had existed there for years. I looked up at Cleo over the mirror.

"What did you do?" she whispered, her crystalline eyes a little wider than usual as she stared at me.

I just shook my head. "I don't know," I whispered back.

While she looked at me, I felt the familiar brush of magic. Panicked, I slammed my mind closed to her. Her eyes narrowed and I shook my head. She could not look into my mind. Not now.

Trae took the mirror and shoved it back in Cleo's bag. "It doesn't matter. Things here are about to get ugly." He gestured to where more of the Elder appointed Guardiens flowed into The Square.

They were always dressed in red, to make it clear who they were bound to.

I had never found it odd, until this moment. Trae grabbed my arm. "Focus. We need to go."

I nodded.

Cleo grasped Trae's hand tightly as we headed off, my brother staying close by my side.

I half turned to him as we walked. "Creston?"

He shook his head. "I saw him leave with you, we haven't seen him since. We thought he would come back with you."

A pit formed in my stomach. "No, he wasn't with me. He left with the others."

CHAPTER 63

As the door closed and sealed behind us I understood then that Trae's home had become a haven.

We were safer here than anywhere else, and that was what we all needed now.

Cleo set down her bag and came to me, looking at me carefully. "Will you tell me?" she breathed, keeping her voice low.

I glanced at the others. Her voice was soft enough that neither Trae nor Zavier looked towards us. They were busy putting their own things down. I looked back to my best friend. "Later," I told her just as quietly, though I knew it was a lie.

She watched me a moment longer. Whatever she saw in my face was enough. She squeezed my arm and moved away, going over to sit beside Trae on his couch.

I stood there, in the opening to the room, watching them all absently.

"What do we do now?" Zavier asked as he sat on the floor.

"We wait." Trae shrugged. "The Elders all but declared war, and it will come. For today, we let the rest of our people panic. And we prepare." Vines lifted books, slithering over the floor and through the air.

Each of us was presented with a separate task. A heavy journal landed in my hands as I opened them, looking up at Trae in question.

"We learn everything we can about what the Elliphir really are. And maybe that will keep more of us alive," he said.

Finding no other option, I sat, delving into the journal that was supposed to offer more insight. It seemed to just overlay more of what we already knew. Vague hints at truths deeply buried by the Elders over time. *We need better sources.* I thought in frustration, then paused as another thought occurred to me. "What if there is another way?"

Three sets of eyes turned to me. "How?" Cleo asked beating the others to it.

"I could ask one. Actually I could ask the original one. Samil." I set the heavy journal on the ground.

Trae's eyebrows shot up. "I thought you said he hadn't come to you in your dreams again?"

I had been more open with them about all things in my dream-scapes in the days after Creston and I visited Faerie, and this moment made me glad for it. "He hasn't, but somehow I suspect that's more about me. I think I've figured out how to block him out, but I can go to him too." I got up again, moving over to the empty chair in the corner.

The one Creston had taken to, but that sat empty now.

"I don't really know how to do it," I muttered, embarrassed, sinking down onto the chair. No one said anything and I knew they were watching me. I tried to ignore that fact. "And I've never tried while awake," I murmured.

Cleo, realising I couldn't do it with an audience, turned to my brother, pulling him into a conversation I drowned out, discussing the best season to grow his favourite fruits.

Closing my eyes, I tried to open myself, stretch my being, needing to find that thing inside me that let me Dreamwalk, hoping it would work like this.

I thought of the Autumn Wood and of the red dress. Reaching up to my chest, I grasped the pendant I had almost forgotten hung there. I gasped, suddenly feeling like I was falling.

I opened my eyes and was no longer seated. Instead, I stood where I'd imagined myself, deep in Autumn. Looking around, I saw the doorway wasn't here, which left me lost. I had no clue where to start looking for Samil, nor where I was within Faerie beyond the Court of Autumn somewhere. My fingers stroked over the pendant again, and deciding it was worth the chance, squeezed it roughly, until the metal and stone dug deep into my skin, picturing molten eyes, warm tattooed skin and dark hair.

"Looking for me?"

I jumped and turned as Samil spoke from behind me.

He watched me warily, standing a few feet away. Much further than he usually would.

"Yes. I need your help." I let go of the pendant. His eyes followed its fall before he looked back to me. "And given everything I have to swallow just to talk to you right now, you owe me."

He seemed to evaluate then, before nodding. "Perhaps you are right. What is it that you need, Seraphine?"

A rush of tension slid from me. "A war is coming. The Elders won't step down and expose the truths they've hidden. I need to know how to stop it, how to hold back what the Elliphir will bring against us. I need to be able to keep my family, my friends, as safe as they can be. I can feel the brutality coming."

"Nixling." He said the word sadly, as if it pained him. "If they have bound their blood to war, not even I could stop that. I told you, the atrocities on that isle have been far more than any I've seen elsewhere."

I shook my head, refusing to believe he was unable to do anything. "There has to be something. Some way to hold them back." I stepped forward towards him without thinking about it, brushing my hair out of my face as I looked up at him. "Please. Please help me in this."

His eyes flared wider as he stepped closer with a speed that shocked me, turning my head. He pushed my hair back further, fully exposing my left cheek. He hissed a breath, then threw his head back and laughed. A deep, hearty sound of joy and exhilaration.

I pulled my chin from his grip, breathing shakily.

He opened his arms to the sky, shouting, "Finally!" He laughed more, and when he looked to me again his golden eyes seemed to glow. "A Phoenix truly worthy." There was reverence in his tone, but it sent a chill through me.

I stepped back from him, fear replacing the need for help.

He waved his hands. "Do not fret, Nixling, I mean you no harm. I have merely waited a very long time to see the blood mark returned."

"It's not why I came," I said, touching my cheek. Though I craved answers about it, I needed to focus on the bigger issues at hand. Nothing else could matter yet.

Samil nodded. "But you see, it is also your answer. You ask me what you need to hold back the Elliphir, but it is quite simple. It is you, you are what is needed. Shadows cannot exist without a flame." He smiled at me, his dimples appearing quickly. "You are a Phoenix, Seraphine. Stand in their way."

I stared at him. It seemed ridiculous, but the words seemed to vibrate within me, echoing my own earlier thoughts. It took me time, but it sank in, took root within me. "Thank you," I told him softly, though he was probably the last person who deserved my thanks.

"I will cherish those words, for I fear they will rarely cross your lips for me." His smile dipped a little, but the glint in his eyes remained.

I said nothing, closing my eyes and starting to reach for myself, my body in my reality, then paused, opening my eyes again. "When Creston lingered here, you asked him what I was to him. What did he say?"

Samil's expression sobered. "I should have known you would ask." *He flashed me a lopsided grin.* "I could lie, but I will not in this instance, because of the confusion and uncertainty he showed me. When I asked him what you were to him, he took a moment to answer."

"And what was his answer?" *My voice was barely above a whisper.*

"He said he was yours, for whatever you decided that means, and that he was fairly sure that is what he was always destined to be. From the first moment he saw you. That's why he doesn't fear my interference." *Samil watched me carefully as he spoke.*

My heart lurched and I closed my eyes, the pain sharp as it tore through me. "Thank you," *I whispered once more as I drew myself back.*

"When we next speak, I will ask who you killed."

The coldness the words spread through me almost stopped me from leaving, making my grip on the warmth slip for a moment. I quickly regained myself and found my reality, tearing myself back to my true body.

I rocked forward in the chair with a gasp. The room was darker now.

Zavier looked up at me. "Guys, she's back!" he called, making Cleo and Trae scramble into the room with half filled plates of food in hand.

"You were gone for hours," Trae explained, setting his plate down on a small table by the entry.

Hours? I had never walked without sleep before, so I suppose it made sense that it didn't fall on the same wave of time.

"Did it work?" Cleo asked as she moved further into the room.

I looked up at them and nodded. "It did. I know what is needed."

I got up from the chair. "But I need to go, there's something I have to do. Someone else who needs to be here before we start with any plans."

None of them moved to stop me, or even said a word, as I headed for the door. They all knew. Trae opened the way for me and I hurried out into the night.

CHAPTER 64

I didn't know at what point I started running, all I knew is that I was. My feet were bare and I felt each cut that measured against my tender flesh, but I paid them no mind. I had to find him. Knowing what he had told Samil opened a rift in my heart, answered questions in me that I had never given voice to.

Creston had staked himself on being mine, to the very male responsible for my existence. What he didn't yet know, was that if he were mine, then I was his. As surely as I breathed, I knew that. No one I had ever known, ever been touched or kissed by, set in motion the heat he did. Heat that for once had nothing to do with the magic within me. It was something else entirely.

His home came into view as I ran, the poison flowers shimmering in the bright moonlight. No light shone from any window as I got closer but that was no deterrent. I had seen the way in which he was so prone to sealing his home. It meant nothing that the house didn't glow in the night.

My hands pounded against the door as I landed against it, black marks forming where I touched the living woods, my emotions extending into my magic. I tried to pull it back as I continued to knock on the door. "Creston? It's me," I called as I knocked.

Panic bloomed in my chest as no response came.

I kept knocking, slamming my fists against the door. "Please don't let me be too late," I whispered. "Let me in. Creston! Please. Please, be here." I pounded harder, tears blurring my vision as I begged for him to open the door. "Please, please, Cres. Open the door. Open the DOOR!" I screamed.

The door starting to crack as the heat from my flesh tore away at it.

I slipped to my knees. "Open the door," I whimpered, dropping my head against the rough wood of the door. *I was too late.*

He had chosen, and it hadn't been me.

My hands splayed beside my head as I sobbed, the events of the day suddenly crashing over me.

I was a murderer. I'd stood by and watched two people burn. I could hear their screams clearer now, echoing through my mind, and knew that they would haunt me. I had pushed away the only person who ever truly seemed able to soothe me. "You're supposed to be here. You aren't supposed to leave me." The words ripped another sob from me.

"I'm here," a voice called quietly from behind me.

I turned quickly. Just as suddenly as the pain had overtaken me, it was washed away by the joy that rose in me.

Though my tear blurred vision, there he stood, dark hair pushed back. Clothed in his Guardien gear, he watched me from the end of the pathway to his door. So close.

A strangled sound came from my throat as I scrambled to my feet and ran to him, colliding with his body in my haste.

He caught me, hands stiff as I pressed myself into him.

"I thought you'd left," I murmured against his chest before I pulled back. My relief in seeing him had overwhelmed everything else I felt. My tears blurred my vision and I wiped my eyes to see better as I looked up at him.

Something didn't seem right. The blur didn't quite shift. The light didn't hit his eyes right, and he wasn't as tall as he should have been.

Fear swelled in me in the same moment the realisation must have dawned in my face.

A smile crept across his face, but it was all wrong. It couldn't be his smile.

That's not him, my mind hissed.

I took a step back, but he was standing too close, and I was too slow.

A hand quickly gripped the hair at the base of my head, pinning me in place. He held his hand out, a dagger appearing in his grasp as he held me tightly.

The blade was made of the same shadows that had grabbed for me in my nightmares, that I had chased and destroyed in the woods to rescue children. It materialised out of nothing, but it was solid and like ice as he buried it through my stomach. His strange smile grew to a laugh as the blade vanished within me.

I half collapsed to my knees with a cry of pain, his grip on my hair all that kept me upright. I clutched at my stomach, fingers slick and sticky with something hot, while ice spread within me, tearing at my insides.

Pain blinded me and I blinked heavily, fighting for my sight, fighting to understand. I tried to warm myself, to push the ice away, but it only seemed to bury itself deeper.

Storm eyes watched me with glee. "The sound of you dying, that is a sound I will cherish. Know that," he whispered in my ear before he threw me to the ground.

I cried out, the movement causing ice to rip apart my organs.

"I warned you both, he can only have both if it is this way."

My world slipped to blackness and pain.

His mocking followed me down into the nothingness. *"Bye bye, little Firefly."*

Epilogue

I had never known true cold in my life, not even for a moment, but I knew it now. It lived inside me, tearing through every part of me it could reach.

It begged me to let go, to surrender the last piece of warmth inside myself that held it back.

The light inside me guttered, flickering briefly, as though it considered going out all on it's own.

Phi. I could hear the word, and the voice that carried it came with bright jade eyes. *Phi, where are you?*

I was needed. Someone needed me.

Others did too, but I couldn't remember them now, I could only see him, my vibrant little brother.

Niko needed me. He needed me not to let the cold win.

The thought seemed to be enough, forcing that light inside me not only to shine, but to stretch out, cutting through the cold, until I felt as though I were burning.

The burning I could survive, so long as the ice was gone I could live with the burn.

The cold slithered through my veins, treating as the light dimmed slowly, settling back at the centre of my being with it's usual glow.

I sank against the hard earth, but only for a moment, only until hands found me. They were warm hands, and where they met my skin, searching my body for wounds frantically, a tingle, like a current, followed.

They could save me, I knew they could save me, and I had done all I could.

My body shook against the grip, and I let myself go, letting new, angry words follow me down into the dark again.

"Don't you dare die on me, Seraphine."

The Blood of Midithrias Story will continue in
BURNING

Acknowledgements

There are so many people to thank for the existence of this work, and my continued ability to write, to list them all would take too long, but you know who you are.

I am forever grateful to have had the chance to tell this story, and to be able to continue to do so in the books that are still to come.

This story would not be what it is without the hard work of my editor, thank you for all the madness you embrace to help smooth out the sharp edges of this story.

About the
Author

To find out more about the Author, receive updates on upcoming
projects, or for extra content visit:
amberyvewriting.com
or find her on social media
@amberyvewriting

Dedicated to my Mama, who taught me what a gift reading is.